A Night in His Arms

ANNIE WEST
CAT SCHIELD
KATE CARLISLE

First Published in Great Britain 2017
By Mills & Boon, an imprint of HarperCollins*Publishers*
1 London Bridge Street, London, SE1 9GF

A NIGHT IN HIS ARMS © 2017 Harlequin Books S. A.

Captive In The Spotlight, Meddling With A Millionaire and *How to Seduce a Billionaire* were first published in Great Britain by Harlequin (UK) Limited.

Captive In The Spotlight © 2013 Annie West
Meddling With A Millionaire © 2011 Catherine Schield
How to Seduce a Billionaire © 2011 Kathleen Beaver

ISBN: 978-0-263-92971-3

05-0717

Our policy is to use papers that are natural, renewable and recyclable products and made from wood grown in sustainable forests.The logging and manufacturing processes conform to the legal environmental regulations of the country of origin.

Printed and bound in Spain
by CPI, Barcelona

CAPTIVE IN THE SPOTLIGHT

BY
ANNIE WEST

Annie West has devoted her life to an intensive study of tall, dark, charismatic heroes who cause the best kind of trouble in the lives of their heroines. As a sideline she's also researched dream-worthy locations for romance—from bustling, vibrant cities to desert encampments and fairytale castles. It's hard work, but she loves a challenge. Annie lives with her family at beautiful Lake Macquarie, on Australia's east coast. She loves to hear from readers and you can contact her at www.annie-west.com or at PO Box 1041, Warners Bay, NSW 2282, Australia.

In memory of our special Daisy,
canine member of the family for almost sixteen years
and ever-supportive writer's companion.

And with heartfelt thanks to Josie, Serena and Antony
for your advice on Italian language, law and locations.

CHAPTER ONE

FOR FIVE GRIM years Lucy had imagined her first day of freedom. A sky the pure blue of Italian summer. The scent of citrus in the warm air and the sound of birds.

Instead she inhaled a familiar aroma. Bricks, concrete and cold steel should have no scent. Yet mixed with despair and commercial strength detergent, they created a perfume called 'Institution'. It had filled her nostrils for years.

Lucy repressed a shudder of fear, her stomach cramping.

What if there had been a mistake? What if the huge metal door before her remained firmly shut?

Panic welled at the thought of returning to her cell. To come so close then have freedom denied would finally destroy her.

The guard punched in the release code. Lucy moved close, her bag in one clammy hand, her heart in her mouth. Finally the door opened and she stepped through.

Exhaust fumes instead of citrus. Lowering grey skies instead of blue. The roar of cars rather than birdsong.

She didn't care. *She was free!*

She closed her eyes, savouring this moment she'd dreamed of since the terror engulfed her.

She was free to do as she chose. Free to try taking up the threads of her life. She'd take a cheap flight to London and a night to regroup before finishing the trip to Devon. A night somewhere quiet, with a comfortable bed and unlimited hot water.

The door clanged shut and her eyes snapped open.

A noise made her turn. Further along, by the main entrance, a crowd stirred. A crowd with cameras and microphones that blared 'Press'.

Ice scudded down Lucy's spine as she stepped briskly in the opposite direction.

She'd barely begun walking when the hubbub erupted: running feet, shouts, the roar of a motorbike.

'Lucy! Lucy Knight!' Even through the blood pounding in her ears and the confusion of so many people yelling at once, there was no mistaking the hunger in those voices. It was as if the horde had been starved and the scent of fresh blood sent them into a frenzy.

Lucy quickened her pace but a motorbike cut off her escape. The passenger snapped off shot after shot of her stunned face before she could gather herself.

By that time the leaders of the pack had surrounded her, clamouring close and thrusting microphones in her face. It was all she could do not to give in to panic and run. After the isolation she'd known the eager crush was terrifying.

'How does it feel, Lucy?'

'What are your plans?'

'Have you anything to say to our viewers, Lucy? Or to the Volpe family?'

The bedlam of shouted questions eased a fraction at mention of the Volpe family. Lucy sucked in a shocked breath as cameras clicked and whirred in her face, disorienting her.

She should have expected this. Why hadn't she?

Because it was five years ago. Old news.

Because she'd expected the furore to die down.

What more did they want? They'd already taken so much.

If only she'd accepted the embassy's offer to spirit her to the airport. Foolishly she'd been determined to rely on no one. Five years ago British officials hadn't been able to save her from the grinding wheels of Italian justice. She'd stopped expecting help from there, or anywhere.

Look where her pride had got her!

Lips set in a firm line, she strode forward, cleaving a path through the persistent throng. She didn't shove or threaten, just kept moving with a strength and determination she'd acquired the hard way.

She was no longer the innocent eighteen-year-old who'd been incarcerated. She'd given up waiting for justice, much less a champion.

She'd had to be her own champion.

Lucy made no apology when her stride took her between a news camera and journalist wearing too much make-up and barely any skirt. The woman's attempt to coax a comment ended when her microphone fell beneath Lucy's feet.

Lucy looked neither right nor left, knowing if she stopped she'd be lost. The swelling noise and press of so many bodies sent her hurtling towards claustrophobic panic. She shook inside, her breathing grew choppy, her stomach diving as she fought the urge to flee.

The press would love that!

There was a gap ahead. Lucy made for it, to discover herself surrounded by big men in dark suits and sunglasses. Men who kept the straining crowd at bay.

Despite the flash of cameras and volleys of shouts, here in these few metres of space it was like being in the eye of a cyclone.

Instincts hyper-alert, Lucy surveyed the car the security men encircled. It was expensive, black with tinted windows.

Curious, she stepped forward, racking her brain. Her friends had melted away in these last years. As for her family—if only they could afford transport like this!

One of the bodyguards opened the back door and Lucy stepped close enough to look inside.

Grey eyes snared her. Eyes the colour of ice under a stormy sky. Sleek black eyebrows rayed up towards thick, dark hair cropped against a well-shaped head.

The clamour faded and Lucy's breath snagged as her eyes

followed a long, arrogant nose, pinched as if in rejection of the institutional aroma she carried in her pores. High, angled cheekbones scored a patrician face. A solid jaw and a firm-set mouth, thinned beyond disapproving and into the realm of pained, completed a compelling face that might have stared out from a Renaissance portrait.

Despite the condemnation she read there, another emotion blasted between them, an unseen ripple of heat in the charged air. A ripple that drew her flesh tight and made the hairs on her arms rise.

'Domenico Volpe!'

Air hissed from Lucy's lungs as if from a puncture wound. Her hand tightened on her case and for a moment she rocked on her feet.

Not him! This was too much.

'You recognise me?' He spoke English with the clear, rounded vowels and perfect diction of a man with impeccable lineage, wealth, power and education at his disposal.

Which meant his disapproving tone, as if she had no right even to recognise a man so far beyond her league, was deliberate.

Lucy refused to let him see how that stung. Blank-faced withdrawal was a tactic she'd perfected as a defence in the face of aggression.

How could his words harm her after what she'd been through?

'I remember you.' *As if she could forget.* Once she'd almost believed… No. She excised the thought. She was no longer so foolishly naïve.

The sight of him evoked a volley of memories. She made herself concentrate on the later ones. 'You never missed a moment of the trial.'

The shouts of the crowd were a reminder of that time, twisting her insides with pain.

He didn't incline his head, didn't move, yet something flickered in his eyes. Something that made her wonder if he, like she, held onto control by a slim thread.

'Would you have? In my shoes?' His voice was silky but lethal. Lucy remembered reading that the royal assassins of the Ottoman sultan had used garrottes of silk to strangle their victims.

He wouldn't lower himself to assault but he wouldn't lift a finger to save her. Yet once long ago, for a fleeting moment, they'd shared something fragile and full of breathless promise.

Her throat tightened as memories swarmed.

What was she doing here, bandying words with a man who wished her only ill? Silently she turned but found her way blocked by a giant in a dark suit.

'Please, *signorina*.' He gestured to the open car door behind her. 'Take a seat.'

With Domenico Volpe? He personified everything that had gone wrong in her life.

A bubble of hysterical laughter rose and she shook her head.

She stepped to one side but the bodyguard moved fast. He grasped her arm, propelling her towards the car.

'Don't *touch* me!' All the shock and grief and dismay she battled rose within her, a roiling well of emotions she'd kept pent up too long.

No one had the right to coerce her.

Not any more.

Not after what she'd endured.

Lucy opened her mouth to demand her release. But the crisp, clear order she'd formulated didn't emerge. Instead a burst of Italian vitriol spilled out. Words she'd never known, even in English, till her time in jail. The sort of gutter Italian Domenico Volpe and his precious family wouldn't recognise. The sort of coarse, colloquial Italian favoured by criminals and lunatics. She should know, she'd met enough in her time.

The bodyguard's eyes widened, his hand dropping as he stepped back. As if he was afraid her lashing tongue might injure him.

Abruptly the flow of words stopped. Lucy vibrated with fury but also with something akin to shame.

So much for her pride in rising above the worst degradations of imprisonment. As for her pleasure, just minutes ago, that she'd left prison behind her… Her heart fell. How long would she bear its taint? How irrevocably had it changed her?

Despair threatened but she forced it down.

Fingers curling tight around the handle of her bag, she stepped forward and the bodyguard made way. She kept going, beyond the cordon that kept Domenico Volpe from the straining paparazzi.

Lucy straightened her spine. She'd rather walk into the arms of the waiting press than stay here.

'I'm sorry, boss. I should have stopped her. But with the media watching…'

'It's okay, Rocco. The last thing I want is a press report about us kidnapping Lucy Knight.' That would really send Pia into a spin. His sister-in-law was already strung out at the news of her release.

He watched the crowd close round the slim form of the Englishwoman and something that felt incredibly like remorse stirred.

As if he'd failed her.

Because she'd looked at him with unveiled horror and chosen the slavering mob rather than share a car with him? That niggling sense of guilt resurfaced. Nonsense, of course. In the light of day logic assured him she'd brought on her own destruction. Yet sometimes, in the dead of night, it didn't seem so cut and dried.

But he wasn't Lucy Knight's keeper. He never had been.

Five years ago he'd briefly responded to her air of fresh enthusiasm, so different from the sophisticated, savvy women in his life. Until he'd discovered she was a sham, trying to ensnare and use him as she had his brother.

Domenico's lips firmed. She'd looked at him just now with those huge eyes the colour of forget-me-nots. A gullible man might have read fear in that look.

Domenico wasn't a gullible man.

Though to his shame he'd felt a tug of unwanted attraction to the woman who'd stood day after day in the dock, projecting an air of bewildered innocence.

Her face had been a smooth oval, rounded with youth. Her hair, straight, long and the colour of wheat in the sun, had made him want to reach out and touch.

He'd hated himself for that.

'She's some wildcat, eh, boss? The way she let fly—'

'Close the door, Rocco.'

'Yes, sir.' The guard stiffened and shut the door.

Domenico sat back, watching the melee move down the street. A few stragglers remained, their cameras trained on the limousine, but the tinted windows gave privacy.

Just as well. He didn't want their lenses on him. Not when he felt…unsettled.

He swiped a hand over his jaw, wishing to hell Pia hadn't put him in this situation. What did the media frenzy matter? They could rise above it as always. Only the insecure let the press get to them. But Pia was emotionally vulnerable, beset by mood swings and insecurities.

It wasn't the media that disturbed him. He ignored the paparazzi. It was *her*, Lucy Knight. The way she looked at him.

She'd changed. Her cropped hair made her look like a raunchy pixie instead of a soulful innocent. Her face had fined down, sculpted into bone-deep beauty that had been a mere promise at eighteen. And attitude! She had that in spades.

What courage had it taken to walk back into that hungry throng? Especially when he'd seen and heard, just for a moment, the pain in her hoarse curses.

For all the weeks of the trial she'd looked as if butter wouldn't melt in her mouth. How had she hidden such violent passion, such hatred so completely?

Or—the thought struck out of nowhere—maybe that dangerous undercurrent was something new, acquired in the intervening years.

Domenico sagged in his seat. He should ignore Pia's pleas and his own ambivalent reactions and walk away. This woman had been nothing but trouble since the day she'd crossed his family's threshold.

He pressed the intercom to speak to the driver. 'Drive on.'

Twenty minutes till the bus came.

Could she last? The crowd grew thicker. It took all Lucy's stamina to pretend they didn't bother her. To ignore the cameras and catcalls, the increasingly rough jostling.

Lucy's knees shook and her arm ached but she didn't dare put her case down. It held everything she owned and she wouldn't put it past one of the paparazzi to swipe it and do an exposé on the state of her underwear or a psychological profile based on the few battered books she possessed.

The tone of the gathering had darkened as the press found, instead of the easy prey they'd expected, a woman determined not to cooperate. Didn't they realise the last thing she wanted was more publicity?

They'd attracted onlookers. She heard their mutterings and cries of outrage.

She widened her stance, bracing against the pushing crowd, alert to the growing tension. She knew how quickly violence could erupt.

She was just about to give up on the bus and move on when the crowd stirred. A flutter, like a sigh, rippled through it, leaving in its wake something that could almost pass for silence.

The camera crews parted. There, striding towards her was the man she'd expected never to see again: Domenico Volpe, shouldering through the rabble, eyes locked on her. He seemed oblivious to the snapping shutters as the cameras went into overdrive and newsmen gabbled into microphones.

He wore a grey suit with the slightest sheen, as if it were woven from black pearls. His shirt was pure white, his tie perfection in dark silk.

He looked the epitome of Italian wealth and breeding. Not

a wrinkle marred his clothes or the elegant lines of his face. Only his eyes, boring into hers, spoke of something less than cool control.

A spike of heat plunged right through her belly as she held his eyes.

He stopped before her and Lucy had to force herself not to crane her head to look up at him. Instead she focused on the hand he held out to her.

The paper crackled as she took it.

Come with me. The words were in slashing black ink on a page from a pocketbook. *I can get you away from this. You'll be safe.*

Her head jerked up.

'Safe?' *With him?*

He nodded. 'Yes.'

Around them journalists craned to hear. One tried to snatch the note from Lucy's hand. She crumpled it in her fist.

It was mad. Bizarre. He couldn't want to help her. Yet she wasn't fool enough to think she could stay here. Trouble was brewing and she'd be at the centre of it.

Still she hesitated. This close, Lucy was aware of the strength in those broad shoulders, in that tall frame and his square olive-skinned hands. Once that blatant male power had left her breathless. Now it threatened.

But if he'd wanted to harm her physically he'd have found a way long before this.

He leaned forward. She stiffened as his whispered words caressed her cheek. 'Word of a Volpe.'

He withdrew, but only far enough to look her in the eye. He stood in her personal space, his lean body warming her and sending ripples of tension through her.

She knew he was proud. Haughty. Loyal. A powerful man. A dangerously clever one. But everything she'd read, and she'd read plenty, indicated he was a man of his word. He wouldn't sully his ancient family name or his pride by lying.

She hoped.

Jerkily she nodded.

'Va bene.' He eased the case from her white-knuckled grip and turned, propelling her through the crowd with his palm at her back, its heat searing through her clothes.

Questions rang out but Domenico Volpe ignored them. With his support Lucy rallied and managed not to stumble. Then suddenly there was blissful space, a cordon of security men, the open limousine door.

This time Lucy needed no urging. She scrambled in and settled herself on the far side of the wide rear seat.

The door shut behind him and the car accelerated away before she'd gathered herself.

'My bag!'

'It's in the boot. Quite safe.'

Safe. There it was again. The word she'd never associated with Domenico Volpe.

Slowly Lucy turned. She was exhausted, weary beyond imagining after less than an hour at the mercy of the paparazzi, but she couldn't relax, even in this decadently luxurious vehicle.

Deep-set grey eyes met hers. This time they looked stormy rather than glacial. Lucy was under no illusions that he wanted her here, with him. Despite the nonchalant stretch of his long legs, crossed at the ankles, there was tightness in his shoulders and jaw.

'What do you want?'

'To rescue you from the press.'

Lucy shook her head. 'No.'

'No?' One dark eyebrow shot up towards his hairline. 'You call me a liar?'

'If you'd been interested in rescuing me you'd have done it years ago when it mattered. But you dropped me like a hot potato.'

Her words sucked the oxygen from the limousine, leaving a heavy, clogging atmosphere of raw emotion. Lucy drew a deep breath, uncaring that he noted the agitated rise and fall of her breasts as she struggled for air.

'You're talking about two different things.' His tone was cool.

'You think?' She paused. 'You're playing semantics. The last thing you want is to *rescue* me.'

'Then let us say merely that your interests and mine coincide this time.'

'How?' She leaned forward, as if a closer view would reveal the secrets he kept behind that patrician façade of calm. 'I can't see what we have in common.'

He shook his head, turning more fully. Lucy became intensely aware of the strength hidden behind that tailored suit as his shoulders blocked her view of the street.

A jitter of curious sensation sped down her backbone and curled deep within. It disturbed her.

'Then you have an enviably short memory, Ms Knight. Even you can't deny we're linked by a tie that binds us forever, however much I wish it otherwise.'

'But that's—'

'In the past?' His lip curled in a travesty of a smile. 'Yet it's a truth I live with every day.' His eyes glowed, luminous with emotions she'd once thought him too cold to feel. His voice deepened to a low, bone-melting hum. 'Nothing will ever take away the fact that you killed my brother.'

CHAPTER TWO

LUCY KNIGHT SHOOK her head emphatically and for one crazy moment Domenico found himself mourning the fact that her blonde tresses no longer swirled round her shoulders. Why had she cut her hair so brutally short?

After *five years* he remembered how that curtain of silk had enticed him!

Impossible. It *wasn't* disappointment he felt.

He'd spent long days in court focused on the woman who'd stolen Sandro's life. He'd smothered grief, the urgent need for revenge and bone-deep disappointment that he'd got her so wrong. Domenico had forced himself to observe her every fleeting expression, every nuance. He'd imprinted her image in his mind.

Learning his enemy.

It wasn't attraction he'd felt then for the gold-digger who'd sought to play both the Volpe brothers. It had been clear-headed acknowledgement of her beauty and calculation of whether her little girl lost impression might prejudice the prosecution case.

'No. I was *convicted* of killing him. There's a difference.'

Domenico stared into her blazing eyes, alight with a passion that arrested logic. Then her words sank in, exploding into his consciousness like a grenade. His belly tightened as outrage flared.

He should have expected it. Yet to hear her voice the lie strained even his steely control.

'You're still asserting your innocence?'

Her eyes narrowed and her mouth tightened. Was she going to blast him with a volley of abuse as she had Rocco?

'Why wouldn't I? It's the truth.'

She held his gaze with a blatant challenge that made his hackles rise.

How dare she sit in the comfort of *his* car, talking about *his* brother's death, and deny all the evidence against her? Deny the testimony of Sandro's family and staff and the fair judgement of the court?

Bile surged in Domenico's throat. The gall of this woman!

'So you keep up the pretence. Why bother lying now?' His words rang with the condemnation he could no longer hide.

Meeting her outraged his sense of justice and sliced across his own inclinations. Only family duty compelled him to be here, conversing with his brother's killer. It revolted every one of his senses.

'This is no pretence, Signor Volpe. It's the truth.'

She leaned closer and he caught the scent of soap and warm female skin. His nostrils quivered, cataloguing a perfume that was more viscerally seductive than the lush designer scents of the women in his world.

'I did not kill your brother.'

She was some actress. Not even by a flicker did she betray her show of innocence.

That, above all, ignited his wrath. That she should continue this charade even now. Her dishonesty must run bone deep.

Or was she scared if she confessed he'd take justice into his own hands?

Domenico imagined his hands closing around that slim, pale throat, forcing her proud head back…but no. Rough justice held no appeal.

He wouldn't break the Volpe code of honour, even when provoked by this shameless liar.

'Now who's playing semantics? Sandro was off balance when you shoved him against the fireplace.' The words bit out from between clamped teeth. 'The knock to his head as he fell killed him.' Domenico drew in a slow breath, clawing back control. The men of his family did not give in to emotion. It was unthinkable he'd reveal to this woman the grief still haunting him.

'You were responsible. If he'd never met you he'd be alive today.'

Her face tightened and she swallowed. Remarkably he saw a flicker of something that might have been pain in her eyes.

Guilt? Regret for what she'd done?

An instant later that hint of vulnerability vanished.

Had he imagined it? Had his imagination supplied what he'd waited so long to see? Remorse over Sandro's death?

He catalogued the woman beside him. Rigid back, angled chin, hands folded neatly yet gripping too hard. Her eyes were different, he realised. After that first shocked expression of horror, now they were guarded.

The difference from the supposed innocent he'd met all those years ago was astounding. She'd certainly given up playing the ingénue.

She looked brittle. He sensed she directed all her energy into projecting that façade of calm.

Domenico knew it was a façade. Years of experience in the cutthroat world of business had made him an expert in body language. There was no mistaking the tension drawing her muscles tight or the short, choppy breaths she couldn't quite hide.

How much would it take to smash through to the real Lucy Knight? What would it take to make her crack?

'If you admitted the truth you'd find the future easier.'

'Why?' She tilted her head like a bright-eyed bird. 'Because confession is good for the soul?'

'So the experts say.'

He shifted into a more comfortable position as he awaited her response. Not by a flicker did he reveal how important this was to him.

Why, he didn't know. She'd already been proven guilty in a fair trial. Her guilt had been proclaimed to the world. But seeing her so defiant, Domenico faced an unpalatable truth. He realised with a certainty that ran deep as the blood he'd shared with his brother that this would never be over till Lucy Knight confessed.

Closure, truth, satisfaction, call it what you would. Only she could lay this to rest.

He hated her for the power that gave her.

'You think I'll be swayed by your attempts at psychology?' Her mouth curled in a hard little smile he'd never seen in all those weeks of the trial. 'You'll have to do better than that, Signor Volpe. If the experts couldn't extract a confession, you really think you will?'

'Experts?'

'Of course. You didn't think I was living in splendid isolation all this time, did you?' Her words sounded bitter but her expression remained unchanged. 'There's a whole industry around rehabilitating offenders. Didn't you know? Social workers, psychologists, psychiatrists.' She turned and looked out of the window, her profile serene.

Domenico fought the impulse to shake the truth from her.

'Did you know they assessed me to find out if I was insane?' She swung her head back around. Her face was blank but for the searing fire in her eyes. 'In case I wasn't fit to stand trial.' She paused. 'I suppose I was lucky. I can't recommend jail as a positive experience but I suspect an asylum for the criminally insane is worse. Just.'

Something passed between them. Some awareness, some connection, like a vibration in the taut air. Something that for a moment drew them together. It left Domenico unsettled.

Any connection with Lucy Knight was a betrayal of Sandro.

Anger snarled in his veins. 'You're alive to complain about your treatment. You didn't give my brother that option, did you? What you did was irrevocable.'

'And unpardonable. Is that why you spirited me away from the press? So you can berate me in private?'

She lounged back in her corner and made a production of crossing her legs as if to reinforce her total lack of concern. Even in her drab navy skirt and jacket there was no hiding the fact she had stunning legs. He was honest enough to admit it was one of the things that had drawn him the day they met. That and her shy smile. No wonder she'd always worn a skirt in court, trying to attract the male sympathy vote.

It hadn't worked then and it didn't work now.

'What a ripe imagination you have.' He let his teeth show in his slow smile and had the satisfaction of seeing her stiffen. 'I have better things to do with my time than talk with you.'

'In that case, you won't mind if I enjoy the view.' She turned to survey the street with an intense concentration he knew must be feigned.

Until he realised she hadn't seen anything like it for five years.

It was even harder than she'd expected being near Domenico Volpe. Sharing the same space. Talking with him.

A lifetime ago they'd shared a magical day, perfect in every way. By the time they'd parted with a promise to meet again she'd drifted on a cloud of delicious anticipation. He'd made her feel alive for the first time.

In a mere ten hours she'd fallen a little in love with her debonair stranger.

How *young* she'd been. Not just in years but experience. Looking back it was almost inconceivable she'd ever been that naïve.

When she'd seen him again it had been at her trial. Her heart had leapt, knowing he was there for her as she stood alone, battered by a world turned into nightmare. She'd waited day after day for him to break his silence, approach and offer a crumb of comfort. To look at her with warmth in his eyes again.

Instead he'd been a frowning dark angel come to exact retribution. He'd looked at her with eyes like winter, chilling her to the bone and shrivelling her dreams.

A shudder snaked through her but she repressed it. She was wrung out after facing the paparazzi and *him*, but refused to betray the fact that he got to her.

She should demand to know where they were headed, but facing him took all her energy.

Even his voice, low and liquid like rich dark chocolate laced with honey, affected her in ways she'd tried to suppress. It made her aware she was a healthy young woman programmed to respond to an attractive man. Despite his cold fury he made her aware of his masculinity.

Was it the vibration of his deep voice along her bones? His powerful male body? Or the supremely confident way he'd faced down the press as if he didn't give a damn what they printed? As if challenging them to take him on? All were too sexy for her peace of mind.

The way he looked at her disturbed, his scrutiny so intense it seemed he searched to find the real Lucy Knight. The one she'd finally learned to hide.

Lucy stifled a laugh. She'd been in prison too long. Maybe what she needed wasn't peace and quiet but a quick affair with an attractive stranger to get her rioting hormones under control.

The stranger filling her mind was Domenico Volpe.

No! That was wrong on so many levels her brain atrophied before she could go further.

She made herself concentrate on the street. No matter what pride said, it was a relief to be in the limo, whisked from the press in comfort.

Yet there'd be a reckoning. She'd given up believing in the milk of human kindness. There was a reason Domenico Volpe had taken her side. Something he wanted.

A confession?

Lucy pressed her lips together. He'd have a long wait. She'd never been a liar.

She was so wrapped in memories it took a while to realise

the streets looked familiar. They drove through a part of Rome she knew.

Lucy straightened, tension trickling in a rivulet of ice water down her spine as she recognised landmarks. The shop where she'd found trinkets to send home to her dad and Sylvia, and especially the kids. The café that sold mouth-watering pastries to go with rich, aromatic coffee. The park where she'd taken little Taddeo under Bruno's watchful eye.

The trickle became a tide of foreboding as the limousine turned into an all too familiar street.

She swung around. Domenico Volpe watched her beneath lowered lids, his expression speculative.

'You can't be serious!' Her voice was a harsh scrape of sound.

'You wanted somewhere free from the press. They won't bother you here.'

'What do you call that?' The pavement before the Palazzo Volpe teemed with reporters. Beyond them the building rose, splendid and imposing, a monument to extreme wealth and powerful bloodlines. A reminder of the disastrous past.

Lucy's heart plunged. She never wanted to see the place again.

Was that his game? Retribution? Or did he think returning her to the scene of the crime would force a confession?

Nausea swirled as she watched the massive palazzo grow closer. Horror drenched her, leaving her skin clammy as perspiration broke out beneath the cloth of her suit.

'Stop the car!'

'Why? I wouldn't have thought you squeamish.' His eyes were glacial again.

She opened her mouth to argue, then realised there was no point. She'd been weak to go with him and she had to face the consequences. Hadn't she known he'd demand payment for his help?

Lucy lifted one shoulder in a shrug that cost her every ounce of energy. 'I thought you wouldn't like the press to know we were together. But on your head be it. I've got nothing more to lose.'

'Haven't you?' His tone told her he'd make it his business to find her soft spot and exploit it.

Let him try. He had no notion how a few years in jail toughened a girl.

He fixed his gaze on her, not turning away as the vehicle slowed to enter a well-guarded entrance. The crowd was held back by stony-faced security men. Anxiously Lucy scanned them but couldn't recognise any familiar faces.

Surreptitiously she let out a breath of relief.

Then the car slipped down a ramp. They entered a vast underground car park. A fleet of vehicles, polished to perfection, filled it. She saw limousines, a four wheel drive, a sleek motorbike and a couple of sports cars including a vintage one her dad would have given his eye teeth to drive.

Out of nowhere grief slammed into her. She'd missed him so long she'd finally learned to repress the waves of loss. But she hadn't been prepared for this.

Not now. Not here. Not in front of the man who saw himself as her enemy.

Maybe grief hit harder because it was her first day of freedom. The day, by rights, when she should be in her dad's reassuring embrace. But all that was gone. Lucy swallowed the knot of emotion clogging her throat, forcing herself to stare, dry-eyed, around the cavernous space.

'How did you get permission to excavate?' She was relieved her voice worked. 'I thought this part of the city was built on the ancient capital.'

'You didn't know about the basement car park?' His voice was sceptical.

Finally, when she knew her face was blank of emotion, Lucy met his stare. 'I was just the au pair, remember? Not the full-time nanny. I didn't go out with the family. Besides, Taddeo was so little and your sister-in-law—' she paused, seeing Domenico's gaze sharpen '—she didn't want him out and about. It was a struggle to get permission to take him to the park for air.'

Gun-metal grey eyes met hers and again she felt that curious beat of awareness between them. As if he knew and understood. But that was impossible. Domenico Volpe hated her, believed she'd killed his brother. Nothing would change his mind.

'The car park was necessary for our privacy.' His shoulders lifted in a shrug that indicated whatever the Volpe family needed the world would provide. *Naturally.* 'There was an archaeological survey but fortunately it didn't find anything precious.'

Lucy bit back a retort. It wouldn't matter how precious the remains. The Volpes would have got what they wanted. They always did. They'd wanted her convicted and they'd got their way.

The car slid to a halt and her door opened.

Lucy surveyed the big man holding it. Her heart gave a flip of relief as she saw it was the guy who'd tried to strong-arm her into the car earlier. Not a spectre from the past. But embarrassment warred with relief as she recalled how she'd abused him.

'Thank you.' She slid awkwardly from the seat, not used to a skirt after years in regulation issue trousers.

Silently he inclined his head.

Damp palms swiping down her skirt, Lucy located the rest of the security staff. Her heart clenched as she thought she saw a familiar figure in the dim light but when he moved Lucy realised it was another stranger. Her breathing eased.

'This way, *signorina*.' The bodyguard ushered her towards a lift.

Minutes later she found herself in a part of the palazzo she'd never visited. But its grand dimensions, its exquisitely intricate marble flooring and air of otherworld luxury were instantly familiar.

Her skin prickled as she inhaled that almost forgotten scent. Of furniture polish, hothouse flowers and, she'd once joked, money. Memories washed over her, of those first exciting days in a new country, of her awe at her surroundings, of that last night—

'Ms Knight?' *Lucy*, he'd called her once. For a few bright, brief hours. Instantly Domenico slammed the memory of that folly into an iron vault of memory.

She spun around and he saw huge, haunted eyes. Her face had paled and her fine features were pinched.

The mask slipped at last.

He should feel satisfaction at her unease in his family home. But it wasn't pleasure he experienced. He had no name for this hyper-awareness, this knife-edge between antipathy and absorption.

Sensation feathered through him, like the tickle of his conscience, teasing him for bringing her here.

Lucy Knight had fascinated him all those years ago. To his chagrin he realised she still did. More than was desirable. It was one thing to know your enemy. Another to respond to her fear with what felt too much like sympathy.

As he watched the moment of vulnerability was gone. Her face smoothed out and her pale eyebrows arched high as if waiting for him to continue.

'This way.' He gestured for her to accompany him, conscious of her beside him as they headed to his side of the palazzo. She was a head shorter but kept pace easily, not hesitating for a moment.

He had to hand it to her; she projected an air of assurance many of his business associates would envy. Twice now he'd seen behind the façade of calm but both times it had been a quick glimpse and the circumstances had been enough to discomfit anyone.

In his study he gestured for her to take a seat. Instead she prowled the room, inspecting the bookcases, the view from the window and, he was sure, scoping out a possible escape route. There was none.

Instead of taking one of the sofas near the fireplace as he'd intended, Domenico settled behind his desk.

'Why have you brought me here?'

She stood directly before the desk, feet planted as if to ground herself ready for attack.

'To talk.'

'Talk?' The word shot out. 'You had your chance to talk five years ago. As I recall, you weren't interested in renewing our acquaintance.' Her tone was bitter and her eyes glittered with fury.

The difference between this Amazon and the girl he'd briefly known struck him anew.

'And to separate you and the press.'

'No altruistic rescue then.' She gave no indication of disappointment, merely met his gaze in frank appraisal.

'Did you expect one?'

'No.' She answered before he'd finished speaking.

Why did her readiness to distrust rankle? He hadn't expected doe-eyed innocence. The scales had been ripped from his eyes long ago.

'Feel free to sit.'

'No.' She paused. 'Thank you. I prefer to stand.' She swallowed hard.

Thanking him must almost have choked her.

As having her in his home revolted every sensibility. Was Sandro turning in his grave? No. Sandro would have approved of his actions.

'For how long?' She watched him closely.

'As long as it takes.'

She frowned. 'As long as what takes?'

Domenico leaned back in his chair. He sensed it was too early to reveal his full intent. Better proceed slowly than rush and have her refuse out of hand.

'For the press to lose interest in this story.'

'There *is* no story. It happened so long ago.'

Domenico's belly clenched. 'You think what happened means nothing now? That it's all over?'

Her head shot up. 'It *is* over. I've served the sentence for manslaughter and now I'm free. If there was anything I could do to bring your brother back I would.' She heaved a deep breath that strained her breasts against the dark fabric. 'But there's not.'

'You cut off my brother's life in his prime.' Anger vibrated in his words and he strove to modulate his voice. 'You made my sister-in-law a widow before her time. She was barely a wife, still struggling to adapt to motherhood, and suddenly she was alone.'

Sky blue eyes met his unflinchingly.

Did none of it matter to her?

'Because of you my nephew will never know his father.' The words grated from a throat scraped raw with anger. 'You denied them both that. You left a gaping hole in his life.'

As she'd ripped a hole in Domenico's life. Even now he found it hard to believe Sandro was gone. The older brother who'd been his friend, his pillar of strength when their parents had died and Domenico was still a kid. His mentor, who'd applauded his tenacity when he'd branched out as an entrepreneur, building rather than relying on the family fortune and traditions.

He wanted her to know the pain she'd caused. To *feel* it. The civilised man he was knew she'd paid the price society saw fit for her crime. The wounded, grief-stricken one wanted more. Remorse. Guilt. A confession. *Something.*

'You can't control the press.' She spoke as if nothing he'd said mattered, brushing aside so much pain.

For a full thirty seconds Domenico stared at the woman who'd destroyed so much, yet felt so little. He couldn't understand how anyone could be so devoid of compassion. He wished he'd never sullied himself by helping her, even if it wasn't for her benefit.

But he refused to let Sandro's family suffer any more because of Lucy Knight.

'I can starve them of fresh news.'

'But there *is* no news.'

'You're out of jail. The murderess set free.'

Her chin jutted. 'The charge was manslaughter.'

Domenico bit down the need to tell her legalistic quibbling didn't change the fact of Sandro's death. Instead he reached for the glossy pages on his desk.

'There's still a story. Especially after this.'

'What is it?' She stepped forward, her expression closed, but he read the rigidity of her slim frame, as if she prepared for the worst.

For a second Domenico hesitated. Why, he didn't know. Then he tossed the magazine across the gleaming surface of the desk.

She tilted her head to read it where it lay, as if not wanting to touch it. He couldn't blame her. It was the sort of trash he avoided, but Pia, his sister-in-law, was obviously a fan. She'd brought it to his attention, hysterical that the sordid tragedy was being resurrected.

Eventually Lucy Knight reached out and flipped the page with one finger. The story spread across both pages. Her likeness featured beside the text. Another picture of her and an older man, her father. Then more of a rather hollow-eyed woman and a gaggle of children.

He watched Lucy Knight's eyes widen, heard her breath hitch, then a hiss of shock. She'd turned the colour of ash. Even her lips paled. Rapidly she blinked and he could have sworn tears welled in those remarkable eyes.

Then, with a suddenness that caught him off guard, the woman he'd thought as unfeeling as an automaton swayed off balance and he realised she was going to faint.

CHAPTER THREE

LUCY STARED AS the text blurred and dipped. She blinked, torn between gratitude that she couldn't make out all the snide character assassination and desperation to know the worst.

She thought she'd experienced the worst in prison. With the loss of her father, her friends, freedom, innocence and self-esteem.

She'd been wrong.

This was the final betrayal.

She struggled to draw breath. It was as if a boulder squashed her lungs. She slammed a hand on the satiny wood of the desk, her damp palm slipping as she fought to steady herself.

Darkness rimmed her vision and the world revolved, churning sickeningly like a merry-go-round spinning off kilter.

There was a pounding in her ears and a gaping hole where her heart had been.

Hard fingers closed around her upper arm.

It was enough to drag her back to her surroundings. She yanked her arm but the grip tightened. She felt him beside her, imprisoning her against the desk.

From somewhere deep inside fury welled, a volcanic force that for a glorious moment obliterated the pain shredding her vitals.

Driven by unstoppable instinct Lucy pivoted, raised her hand and chopped down on the inner elbow of the arm that captured her. At the same time she jabbed her knee high in his groin. Her hand connected with a force that almost matched the strength in that muscled arm. But her knee struck only solid thigh as he sensed her attack and shifted.

Yet it worked. She was free. She stood facing him, panting from adrenalin and overflowing emotions.

Gimlet eyes stared down at her. Glittering eyes that bored deep into her soul, as if he could strip away the self-protective layers she'd built so painstakingly around herself and discover the woman no one else knew.

Her chest rose and fell as she struggled for air. Her pulse thundered. Her skin sizzled with the effervescence in her bloodstream.

The muzzy giddiness disappeared as she stared back at the face of the man who'd stripped away her last hope and destroyed what was left of her joy at being free.

Far from fainting, she felt painfully alive. It was as if layers of skin had been scored away, exposing nerve endings that throbbed from contact with the very air in this cloistered mansion.

'Don't touch me!'

Instead of backing off from her snarling tone he merely narrowed his eyes.

'You were going to faint.' The rumble of his voice stirred an echo inside her.

'I've never fainted in my life.' She shoved aside the knowledge that he was right. Until the shock of his touch she'd been about to topple onto his pristine parquet floor.

'You needed support.' His words betrayed no outrage at her attack. It was as if he, like she, was no longer bothered by social niceties. As if he understood the primitive intensity of her feelings.

That disturbed her. She didn't want him understanding anything about her. She didn't like the sense that Domenico Volpe had burrowed under her skin and was privy to her innermost demons.

Something shifted in his gaze. There was a subtle difference in those deep-set eyes that now shone silver. Something in the line of his lips. Her eyes lingered there, tracing the shape of a mouth which now, relaxed, seemed designed solely for sensual pleasure.

A gossamer thread of heat spun from her breasts to her pelvis, drawing tight—a heat she'd felt only once before.

Had his expression changed, grown warm? Or had something inside her shifted?

Lucy bit her lip then regretted the movement as his gaze zeroed in on her mouth. Her lips tingled as if he'd reached out and grazed them with a questing finger.

A shiver of luxurious pleasure ripped through her. Fire ignited deep within, so hot it felt as if she were melting. Her pulse slowed to a ponderous beat then revved out of control.

She'd known Domenico Volpe was dangerous. But she hadn't known the half of it.

She swallowed hard and found her voice, trying to ignore her body's flagrant response.

'You can move back now. I can stand.'

He took his time moving. 'Yet sitting is so much more comfortable, don't you think?'

He said no more but that one raised eyebrow told her he saw what she'd rather not reveal. That her surge of energy was short-lived. Lucy felt a dragging at her limbs. Her knees were jelly and the thought of confronting him here, now, was almost too much to bear.

Had he guessed her visceral response to his flagrant masculinity? That would be the final straw.

She grabbed the magazine, crushing its pages.

'Thank you. I will take that seat now.'

He nodded and gestured to a long sofa. Instead she took the black leather swivel chair that looked like something from an exclusive design catalogue, a far cry from the sparse utilitarian furniture she'd grown used to. It was wickedly comfortable and her bones melted as she sank into it. It was massive, built to order, she guessed, for the man who took a seat across from her. Lucy tried to look unfazed by such luxury.

'You didn't know about the article?'

Lucy refused to look away from his keen gaze. Confrontation was preferable to running. She'd learned that in a hard school. But looking him in the eye was difficult when her body hummed with the aftermath of what she could only describe as an explosion of sexual awareness.

'No.' She glanced down at the trashy gossip mag and repressed a shiver. It was like holding a venomous snake in her palm. 'I had no idea.'

'Would you like something? Brandy? A pot of tea?'

Startled by his concern, she turned to find Domenico Volpe looking almost as surprised as she was, as if the offer had slipped out without volition.

It was no comfort to know she must look as bad as she felt for him to offer sustenance.

'No. Thank you.' Accepting anything from him went against every instinct.

Already he moved towards the desk. Obviously it didn't matter what she wanted. 'I'll order coffee.'

Lucy's gaze dropped to the magazine. How could Sylvia have done this? Did she despise Lucy so much?

Silently her heart keened. Sylvia and the kids had been Lucy's last bright hope of returning to some remnant of her old life. Of having family again. Of belonging.

Quotes from the article floated through her troubled mind. Of her stepmother saying Lucy had 'always been *different*', 'withdrawn and moody' but 'hankering after the bright lights and excitement'. That she put her own needs first rather than those of her family. There was nothing in the article about Sylvia's resentment of her husband's almost grown daughter, or the fact that Lucy had spent years as unpaid nurserymaid for Sylvia's four children by a previous marriage. Or that Sylvia's idea of bright lights was a Saturday night in Torquay and a takeaway meal.

Nothing about the fact that Lucy had left home only when her dad, in his quiet way, had urged her to experience more of the world rather than put her life on hold to look after the younger children.

She'd experienced the world all right, but not in the way he'd had in mind.

As for the article, taken from a recent interview with Sylvia, it was a lurid exposé that painted Lucy as an uncaring, amoral gold-digger. It backed up every smear and innuendo that had been aired in the courtroom. Worse, it proved even her family had turned against her.

What would her stepsiblings think now they were old enough to read such malicious gossip?

Lucy's heart withered and she pressed a hand to her throat, trying to repress rising nausea. Sylvia and she had never been close but Lucy had never thought her stepmother would betray her like this. The article's spitefulness stole her breath.

Until now she'd believed there was someone believing in her. First her father and, after he died, Sylvia.

She felt bereft, grieving all over again for her dad who'd been steadfastly behind her. Never having known her long-dead mother, Lucy's bond with her father had been special. His faith and love had kept her strong through the trial.

Lucy had never been so alone. Not even that first night in custody. Even after the conviction when she knew she had years of imprisonment ahead. Nor facing down the taunts and jeers as she'd learned to handle the threats from prisoners who'd tried to make her life hell.

The magazine was a rag but an upmarket one. Sylvia had sold her out for what must be a hefty fee.

Lucy blinked stinging eyes as she stared at the vile publication in her lap.

She thought she'd known degradation and despair. But it was only now that her life hit rock bottom.

And Domenico Volpe was here to see it.

She shivered, chilled to the marrow. How he must be gloating.

'The coffee will be here soon.'

Lucy looked up to find him standing across from her, watchful. No doubt triumphing at the sight of her down and out. Framed by the massive antique fireplace and a solid wall of books, he looked the epitome of born and bred privilege. From his aristocratically handsome features to his hand stitched shoes he screamed power and perfection.

Once the sight of him had made her heart skip with pleasure. But she'd discovered the real Domenico Volpe when the chips were down. He'd sided with his own class, easily believing the most monstrous lies against her.

Slowly she stood, pride stiffening her weary legs and tilting her chin.

'It's time I left.'

Where she'd go she had no idea, but she had to escape.

She had just enough money to get her home to Devon. But now she had no home. Her breath hitched as she thought of Sylvia's betrayal. She wouldn't be welcome there.

Pain transfixed her.

'You can't leave.'

'I'm now officially a free woman, Signor Volpe, however much you resent it. If you try to keep my here by force it will be kidnap.'

Even so a shiver of apprehension skated down her spine. She wouldn't put anything past him. She'd seen his cadre of security men and she knew first hand what they were capable of.

'You mistake me for one of your recent associates, Ms Knight.' He snapped the words out as if he wanted to take a bite out of her. 'I've no intention of breaking the law.'

Before she could voice her indignation he continued. 'You need somewhere private; somewhere the press can't bother you.'

His words stilled her protest.

'And?'

'I can provide that place.'

And pigs might fly.

'Why would you do that?' She'd read his contempt. 'What do you get out of it?'

For the longest moment he stood silent. Only the hint of a scowl on his autocratic features hinted he wasn't used to being questioned. Tough.

'There are others involved,' he said finally. 'My brother's widow and little Taddeo. They're the ones affected the longer this is dragged through the press.'

Taddeo. Lucy had thought of him often. She'd loved the little baby in her care, enjoying his gurgles of delight at their peekaboo games and his wide-eyed fascination as she'd read him picture books. What was he like now?

One look at Domenico Volpe's closed face told her he'd rather walk barefoot over hot coals than talk about his nephew with her.

'So what's your solution?' She crossed her arms over her chest. 'Walling me up in the basement car park?'

'That could work.' He bared his teeth in a feral smile that drew her skin tight. 'But I prefer to work within the law.' He paused. 'I don't have your penchant for the dramatic. Instead I suggest providing you with a bolthole till this blows over. Your bag is already in your room.'

Her room.

Lucy groped for the back of the chair she'd just vacated, her hand curling like a claw into the plump, soft leather. She tried to speak but her voice had dried up.

Her room.

The memory of it had haunted her for years. Ever since arriving here she'd been cold to the core because she knew that room was upstairs, on the far side of the building.

'You can't expect me to stay there!' Her voice was hoarse with shock. 'Even *you* couldn't…' She shook her head as her larynx froze. 'That's beyond cruel. That's *sick*.'

His eyes widened and she saw understanding dawn. His nostrils flared and he stepped towards her, then pulled up abruptly.

'No.' The word slashed the clogged silence. 'That room hasn't been used since my brother died. There's another guest room at your disposal.'

Relief sucked her breath away and loosened her cramped muscles. Slowly she drew in oxygen, marshalling all her strength to regroup after that scare.

'I can't stay in this house.'

He met her gaze silently, not asking why. He knew. The memories were too overwhelming.

'I'll find my own place.'

'And how will you do that with the press on the doorstep?' He crossed his arms over his chest and leaned a shoulder against the fireplace, projecting an air of insouciance that made her want to slap him. 'Wherever you go they'll follow. You'll get no peace, no privacy.'

He was right, damn him. But to be dependent on him for anything stuck in her craw.

The door opened and a maid entered, bearing a tray of coffee and biscuits. The rich aroma, once her favourite, curdled Lucy's stomach. Instinctively she pressed a hand to her roiling abdomen and moved away. Vaguely she heard him thank the maid, but from her new vantage point near the window Lucy saw only the press pack outside. The blood leached from her cheeks.

Which was worse? Domenico Volpe or the paparazzi who'd hound her for some tawdry story they could sell?

'If you don't mind, I'll take you up on the offer of that room. Just to freshen up.' She needed breathing space, time away from him, to work out what to do.

Lucy swung round to find him watching her. She should be used to it now. His scrutiny was continual. Yet reaction shivered through her. What did he see? How much of what she strove to hide?

She banished the question. She had better things to do than

worry about that. Nothing would change Domenico Volpe's opinion. His reluctant gestures of solicitude were evidence of ingrained social skills, not genuine concern.

'Of course. Take as long as you like. Maria will show you up.'

Lucy assured herself it wasn't satisfaction she saw in that gleaming gaze.

'No! I said I can't talk. I'm busy.' Sylvia's voice rose and Lucy thought she discerned something like anxiety as well as anger in her stepmother's words. She gripped the phone tighter.

'I just wanted—'

'Well, I *don't* want. Just leave me alone! Haven't you done enough damage to this family?'

Lucy opened her mouth but the line went dead.

How long she sat listening to the dialling tone she didn't know. When she finally put the receiver down her fingers were cramped and her shoulders stiff from hunching, one arm wrapped protectively around her stomach.

So that was it. The severing of all ties.

A piercing wail of grief rose inside her but she stifled it. Lucy told herself it was better to face this now than on the rose-covered doorstep of the whitewashed cottage that had been home all her life.

Yet she couldn't quite believe it. She'd rung her stepmother hoping against hope there'd been some dreadful mistake. That perhaps the press had published a story with no basis. That Sylvia hadn't betrayed her with that character assassination interview.

Forlorn hope! Sylvia wanted nothing to do with her.

Which left Lucy with nowhere to go. She had no one and nothing but a past that haunted her and even now wouldn't release its awful grip.

Slowly she lifted her head and stared at the panelled door separating the bedroom from the second-floor corridor.

It was time she laid the ghost of her past to rest.

* * *

She wasn't in the room he'd provided but she hadn't tried to leave. His security staff would have alerted him. There was only one place she could be, yet he hadn't thought she'd have the gall to go back there.

Domenico's stride lengthened as he paced the corridor towards the side of the palazzo that had housed Sandro's apartments. Fury spiked as he thought of Lucy Knight there, in the room where she'd taken Sandro's life. It was an intrusion that proved her contempt for all he and his family had lost. A trespass that made his blood boil and his body yearn for violence.

The door was open and he marched across the threshold, hands clenched in iron fists, muscles taut and fire in his belly.

Then he saw her and stopped dead.

He didn't know what he'd expected but it wasn't this. Lucy Knight was huddled on the floor before the ornate fireplace, palm pressed to the floorboards where Sandro had breathed his last. Domenico remembered it from the police markers on the floor and photos in court.

Her face was the colour of travertine marble, pale beyond belief. Her eyes were dark with pain as she stared fixedly before her. She was looking at something he couldn't see, something that shuttered her gaze and turned it inwards.

The hair prickled at his nape and he stepped further into the room.

She looked up and shock slammed him at the anguish he saw in her face. Gone was the sassy, prickly woman who'd fought him off when he'd dared touch her.

The woman before him bore the scars of bone-deep pain. It was clear in every feature, so raw he almost turned away, as if seeing such emotion was a violation.

A shudder passed through him. Shock that instead of the anger he'd nursed as he strode through the house, it was something like pity that stirred.

'I'm sorry.' Her voice was a rasp of laboured air. 'It shouldn't have happened. I was so young and stupid.' Her voice faded as she looked down at the patina of old wood beneath her hands. 'I should never have let him in.'

Domenico crossed the room in a few quick strides and hunkered beside her, his heart thumping.

She admitted it?

It didn't seem possible after all this time.

'If I hadn't let him in, none of it would have happened.' She drew a breath that shook her frame. 'I've gone over it so often. If only I hadn't listened to him. If only I'd locked the door.'

Domenico frowned. 'You had no need to lock the door against my brother. I refuse to believe he would have forced himself on you.'

The idea went against everything he knew about Sandro. His brother had been a decent man. A little foolish in his choice of wife, but honourable. A loving brother and doting father. A man who'd made one mistake, led astray by a beautiful, scheming seductress, but *not* a man who took advantage of female servants.

That blonde head swung towards him and she blinked. 'I wasn't talking about your brother. I was talking about the bodyguard, Bruno.' Her voice slowed on the name as if her tongue thickened. Domenico heard what sounded like fear in her voice. 'I shouldn't have let Bruno in.'

Domenico shot to his feet. Disappointment was so strong he tasted it, a rusty tang, on his tongue.

'You still stick to that story?'

The bruised look in her eyes faded, replaced by familiar wariness. Her mouth tightened and for an instant Domenico felt a pang almost of loss as she donned her habitual air of challenge.

A moment later she was again that woman ready to defy the world with complete disdain. Even curled up at his feet she radiated a dignity and inner strength he couldn't deny.

How did she do it? And why did he let it get to him? She was a liar and a criminal, yet there was something about her that made him wish things were different.

There always had been. *That was the hell of it.*

His gut dived. Even to think it was a betrayal of Sandro.

'I don't tell stories, Signor Volpe.' She got to her feet in a supple movement that told him she hadn't spent the last years idle. 'Bruno killed your brother but—' she raised her hand when he went to speak '—don't worry, you won't hear it from me again. I'm tired of repeating myself to people who won't listen.'

She made to move past him but his hand shot out to encircle her upper arm. Instantly she tensed. Would she try to fight him off as she had downstairs? He almost wished she would. There'd be a primitive satisfaction in curbing her temper and stamping his control on that fiery, passionate nature she hid behind the untouchable façade.

Heat tingled through his fingers where he held her. He braced himself but she merely looked at him, eyebrows arching.

'You wanted something?' Acid dripped from her words.

Domenico's eyes dropped to her mouth, soft pink again now that colour had returned to her face. The blush pink of rose petals at dawn.

A pulse of something like need thudded through his chest. He told himself it was the urge to wring her pretty neck. Yet his mouth dried when he watched her lips part a fraction, as if she had trouble inhaling enough air. There was a buzzing in his ears.

Her eyes widened and Domenico realised he'd leaned closer. Too close. Abruptly he straightened, dropping her arm as if it burnt him.

'I want to know what you plan to do.'

He didn't have the right to demand it. Her glittering azure gaze told him that. But he didn't care. She wasn't the only one affected by this media frenzy. He had family to protect.

'I want to find somewhere private, away from the news hounds.'

He nodded. 'I can arrange that.'

'Not here!' The words shot out. A frisson shuddered through the air, a reminder of shadows from the past.

'No, not here.' He had estates in Italy as well as in California's Napa Valley and another outside London. Any of them would make a suitable safe house till this blew over.

'In that case, I accept your generous offer, Signor Volpe. I'll stay in your safe haven for a week or so, until this furore dies down.'

She must be more desperate than she appeared. She hadn't even asked where she'd be staying. Or with whom.

CHAPTER FOUR

LUCY WOKE TO silence.

Cocooned in a wide comfortable bed with crisp cotton sheets and the fluffiest of down pillows, she lay, breathing in the sense of peace.

She felt…safe.

The realisation sideswiped her.

Who'd have thought she'd owe Domenico Volpe such a debt? A solid night's sleep, undisturbed till late morning judging by the sunlight rimming the curtains. She couldn't remember the last time she'd slept so long or so soundly.

Lucy flung back the covers, eager to see where she was. Last night she'd left from the helipad on the roof of the palazzo and headed into darkness. Domenico Volpe had said merely she'd go to one of his estates, somewhere she could be safe from press intrusion.

After yesterday's traumas that had been good enough for her. She desperately needed time to lick her wounds and decide what to do. With no friends, no job and very little money the outlook was grim.

Till she pulled back the curtains and gasped. Strong sunlight made her blink as she took in a vista of wide sky, sea and a white sand beach below a manicured garden.

It was paradise. The garden had an emerald lawn, shade trees and sculpted hedges. Pots of pelargoniums and other plants she couldn't identify spilled a profusion of flowers in a riot of colours, vivid against the indigo sea.

Unlatching the sliding glass door, Lucy stepped onto a balcony. Warmth enveloped her and the scent of growing things. Birds sang and she heard, like the soft breath of a sleeping giant, the gentle shush of waves. Dazzled, she stared, trying to absorb it all. But her senses were overloaded. Tranquillity and beauty surrounded her and absurdly she felt the pinprick of hot tears.

She'd dreamed of freedom but had never imagined a place like this. Her hands clenched on the railing. It was almost too much to take in. Too much change from the grey, authoritarian world she'd known.

A moment later she'd scooped up a cotton robe and dragged it on over her shabby nightgown. She cinched the tie at her waist as she pattered down the spiral staircase from her balcony.

Reflected light caught her eye and she spied a huge infinity pool that seemed to merge with the sea beyond. Turf cushioned her bare feet as she made for the balustrade overlooking the sea. Yet she stopped time and again, admiring an arbour draped with scented flowers, a pool that reflected the sprawling villa, unexpected groves and modern sculptures.

'Who are you? I'm Chiara and I'm six.' The girl's Italian had a slight lisp.

Lucy turned to meet inquisitive dark eyes and a sunny smile. Automatically her lips curved in response to the girl's gap-toothed grin, stretching facial muscles Lucy hadn't used in what seemed a lifetime.

'I'm Lucy and I'm twenty-four.'

'That's so old.' The little girl paused, looking up from her hidey-hole behind a couple of palm trees. 'Don't you wish you were six too?'

Unfamiliar warmth spread through Lucy. 'Today I do.' How wonderful to enjoy all this without a care for the future that loomed so empty.

It had been years since she'd seen a child, much less talked with one. Looking into that dimpled face, alight with curiosity, she realised how much she'd missed. If things had been different she'd have spent her life working with children. Once she had the money behind her to study, she'd intended to train as a teacher.

But her criminal record made that impossible.

'Will you play with me?'

Lucy stiffened. Who would want her daughter playing with an ex-con? A woman with her record?

'You'd better talk to your mummy first. You shouldn't play with strangers, you know.'

The little girl's eyes widened. 'But you're not a stranger. You're a friend of Domi's, aren't you?'

'Domi?' Lucy frowned. 'I don't know—'

'This is his house.' Chiara spread her hands wide. 'The house and garden. The whole island.'

'I see. But I still can't play with you unless your mummy says it's all right.'

'Uncle Rocco!' The little girl spoke to someone behind Lucy. 'Can I play with Lucy? She says I can't unless Mummy says so but Mummy's away.'

Lucy spun round to see the stolid face of the big security guard she'd lambasted outside the prison. Did it have to be him of all people? Heat flushed her skin but she held his gaze till he turned to the little girl, his features softening.

'That's for Nonna to decide. But it can't be today. Signorina Knight just arrived. You can't bother her with your chatter.' He took the child by the hand and, with a nod at Lucy, led her to the villa.

Lucy turned towards the sea. Still beautiful, it had lost some of its sparkle.

At least Rocco hadn't betrayed his horror at finding his niece with a violent criminal. But he'd hurried to remove her from Lucy's tainted presence.

Pain jagged her chest, robbing her of air. Predictable as

his reaction was, she couldn't watch them leave. Her chest clamped around her bruised heart and she sagged against the stone balustrade.

Lucy had toughened up years ago. The naïve innocent was gone, replaced by a woman who viewed the world with cynicism and distrust. A woman who didn't let the world or life get to her any more.

Yet the last twenty-four hours had been a revelation.

She'd confronted the paparazzi, then Domenico Volpe, learnt of Sylvia's betrayal and faced the place where her life had changed irrevocably. Now she confronted a man's instinct to protect his niece, from *her*.

All tore at her precious self-possession. It had taken heartache, determination and hard-won strength to build the barriers that protected her. She'd been determined never to experience again those depths of terror and pain of her first years in prison. Until now those barriers had kept her strong and safe.

Who'd have thought she still had the capacity to hurt so much?

She leant on the railing, eyes fixed on the south Italian mainland in the distance.

Domenico took in her slumped shoulders and the curve of her arms around her body, hugging out a hostile world.

It reminded him of the anguish he thought he'd spied yesterday in her old room at the palazzo. She'd hunched like a wounded animal over the spot Sandro had died. The sight had poleaxed him, playing on protective instincts he'd never expected to feel around her.

Almost, he'd been convinced by that look of blind pain in her unfocused eyes. But she'd soon disabused him. It had been an act, shrewd and deliberate, to con him into believing her story of innocence.

Innocent? The woman who'd seduced his brother then killed him?

He'd once fancied he felt a connection with the girl who'd

burst like pure sunshine into his world. But before he could fall completely under her spell tragedy and harsh truth had intervened, revealing her true colours.

A breeze flirted with her wrap, shifting it against the curve of her hip and bottom.

She didn't look innocent.

He remembered her trial. The evidence of Sandro's Head of Security and of Pia, Sandro's widow, that Lucy Knight had deliberately played up to Sandro, flirting and ultimately seducing him.

When it became clear her relationship with Sandro was core to the case against her, Lucy Knight had offered to have a medical test proving her virginity.

You could have heard a pin drop in the courtroom as all eyes fixed on her nubile body and wide, seemingly innocent eyes. Every man in that room had wondered about the possibility of being her first. *Even Domenico.*

The prosecution had successfully argued it was her intentions that mattered, not whether the affair had yet been consummated. In the end a medical test was deemed immaterial but for a while she'd cleverly won sympathy, despite the rest of the evidence.

Having seen her in action, Domenico had no doubt she knew exactly how to seduce even the most cautious man.

He traced the shapely line of her legs down to her bare feet and something thudded in his chest. Was the rest of her bare beneath that wrap?

His body tightened from chest to groin as adrenalin surged. His pulse thudded. Physical awareness saturated him and he cursed under his breath.

Hunger for Lucy Knight was *not* to be contemplated.

Yet the hectic drumming in his blood didn't abate.

As if sensing him, she turned her head. 'You! What are you doing here?' She spun to face him, legs planted wide and hands clenched at her sides, a model of aggressive challenge.

Except for the robe's gaping neckline and the flutter of cotton around bare thighs that highlighted her femininity.

Domenico reminded himself he liked his women accommodating. Soft and pliant. Warrior queens with lofty chins and defiance in every sinew held no appeal.

Till now.

His body's wayward response angered him and guilt pricked. This woman had destroyed Sandro.

'This is my property. Or had you forgotten?'

'You implied I'd be here alone.'

'Did I? Are you sure?' Of course she wasn't. He'd chosen his words carefully. Even to his enemies, Domenico didn't lie. Seeing her skittishness, he'd deliberately neglected to mention he'd arrive here today. 'I fail to see what my travel plans have to do with you.'

He waited for her to splutter her indignation. But she merely surveyed him through slitted eyes. He sensed she drew her defences tight, preparing for battle.

Was she like this with everyone or just him?

'You came to make sure I don't steal the silver.' The sarcastic jibe almost hid her curiously flat tone. Yet he heard that hint of suppressed emotion, as if she was genuinely disappointed.

As if what he thought mattered.

Domenico frowned, instinct and intellect warring. He *knew* what she was, yet when he looked at her he *felt*…

Abruptly she pulled her robe in tight, as if only now realising the loose front revealed the shadow of her cleavage. Methodically she knotted the belt, all the while holding his gaze. Why did it feel as if she were putting on armour, rather than merely covering herself?

Did she know, with the light behind her, the wrap revealed rather than concealed her curves? Was it a deliberate ploy to distract him?

His voice was harsh. 'I leave it to my security staff to watch for thieves.'

Did she flinch? He remembered her rosy flush in court when

evidence had been presented about the jewellery she'd either been given or had stolen from Sandro.

No sign of a blush now.

'What do you want?' Her insolence made his hackles rise.

It was on the tip of his tongue to deny he wanted anything, but pragmatism beat pride. He was here for one reason only and the sooner he fixed it the sooner he could put Lucy Knight firmly in the past.

'I do have some business to discuss with you but—'

'Ha! I knew it!' She folded her arms and Domenico had to force his gaze above the plump swell of her breasts, accentuated by the gesture.

'Knew what?' To his chagrin he'd missed something. He who never missed a nuance of any business negotiation.

'That it was too good to be true.' Her lip curled. 'No one gives anything for nothing. Especially you.' Her gaze flicked him from head to toe as if she read his body's charged response to her. His skin drew tight. Fury spilled and pooled. At her dismissive tone. At himself for the spark of arousal he couldn't douse.

'You're here, aren't you? Safe from the media?'

'But at what price?' She stepped close, eyes flaring wide as if she felt it too, the simmer of charged awareness, palpable as a caress against overheated flesh. 'There are strings attached to this deal, aren't there? A price I have to pay?'

Domenico looked down his nose with all the hauteur six centuries of aristocratic breeding could provide. No one doubted his honour. Ever.

'I'm a man of my word.' He let that sink in. 'I offered you sanctuary and you have it. There are no strings.'

Yet if she hadn't been so stressed yesterday she'd have made sure of that before agreeing to his offer.

Domenico muffled a sliver of guilt that he'd taken advantage of her vulnerability. The stakes were too high, the trouble she could cause too severe for him to have second thoughts.

Her perfectly arched eyebrows rose. 'I'm free to leave?'

Domenico stepped back and gestured to the boats moored in the bay. 'I will even provide the transport.'

He wished she'd take him up on the offer. Yes, he wanted more from her but instinct warned him to be rid of her. He didn't relish the discordant tumble of his reactions to her. There was nothing logical or ordered about them. She made him feel…things he thought long dead.

Her eyes bored into his, as if she sought the very heart of him. 'But you want me out of the limelight.'

'Of course.' He shrugged. 'But I'm not keeping you prisoner. There are laws in this country.'

Her breath hissed and she stiffened, reading his implication. That one of them at least was honest and law-abiding.

Her mouth tightened but otherwise her face was blank. So much for vulnerability. Lucy Knight was as tough as nails.

'If you're staying…' He looked at her expectantly but she said nothing. 'We can discuss business when you're dressed.' He glanced at his watch. Eleven o'clock. 'Shall we say midday?'

'Why delay? I'd rather know what you want now.'

She spoke as if he hid something painful from her. He almost laughed at the idea. Once he made his offer she'd be eager enough.

'You're hardly dressed for business.'

She stuck her hands on her hips, her pose challenging and provocative. 'You'd be more comfortable if I wore a suit? Why can't you tell me now?' Again those delicate eyebrows rose, as if she silently laughed at him.

Something snapped inside.

He stalked across till he stood close enough to inhale the scent of soap and fragrant female flesh. Close enough to hook an arm round her and haul her flush against him if he chose. Instead he kept his hands clenched at his sides.

She refused to shift. Even though she had to tip her head back to look at him, exposing her slim throat. Heat twisted in his belly, part unwilling admiration at her nerve, part implacable fury.

His gaze held hers as his pulse thumped once, twice, three times. The artery at her throat flickered rapidly and she swallowed. Yet she didn't look away.

Charged seconds ticked by. Her pupils dilated. His senses stirred. Did he imagine that hint of musky arousal in his nostrils? The quiver of anticipation in the air?

Her breasts rose with her rapid breathing, almost but not quite brushing against him. The woman staring back defiantly was no modest, unprotected innocent.

The thought pulled him up. He'd almost forgotten this was about her, not him.

She wasn't as unaffected as she pretended. He saw the fine tremor running under her skin. Her tongue flicked out to swipe her lips and he bit back a smile. For it wasn't a consciously slow, seductive movement but sure evidence her mouth had dried. Nerves or arousal?

Domenico leaned close, letting the heat of her body drench him. Her lashes flickered and her trembling pulse accelerated. His quickened too.

Holding her gaze, he reached out and snagged her belt. Instantly she stiffened, but she didn't retreat.

Was that a challenge in her eyes?

Her breath was a warm, sweet sigh against his chin as he tugged the bow undone, loosening the fabric around her.

Domenico bent his head and her pursed lips softened. Her eyes widened and something flickered there. Fear or anticipation?

'My office in an hour. You'll be less easily distracted if you're fully dressed.'

He straightened, spun on his heel and left her.

Lucy's breath came in great gulps. Her heart pumped so hard she thought it might jump out of her ribcage.

Domenico Volpe strolled back to the villa with an easy, loose-limbed grace that made her want to hurl something at his broad back. In dark trousers and an open-necked shirt he was the picture of elegant ease. He looked casual, sexy, utterly unaffected by the charge of erotic energy that hammered through her.

She shivered despite the molten heat inside. Her nipples were tight buds of need and she was wet between the legs. Because of the way he'd *looked* at her. Just looked!

How was that possible?

She shook her head, torn between shock, fury and shame. Her body betrayed her. *And he knew it.*

She'd read triumph in his eyes when he'd undone her belt. Had he sensed the voluptuous shiver she couldn't suppress? The tension in her body that had as much to do with fighting her traitorous desire as standing up to him?

With fumbling hands she pulled the wrap tight, as if it made any difference now. He didn't even look back. He was so confident he'd made his point.

That she was vulnerable to him. That she…desired him.

The realisation blasted Lucy's ragged confidence. She wanted to pretend it wasn't true. But hiding would get her nowhere. She had to face it.

Yet surely the fledgling attraction she'd once felt for him was dead, crushed by his cruel assumption of her guilt. She assured herself this wasn't about Domenico Volpe. It was what he represented—hot animal sex. Despite his shuttered gaze and his insultingly casual contempt, there was no mistaking the virile male beneath the expensive clothes.

Who wouldn't be affected by such a potently masculine man?

Lucy had been celibate so long, so cut off from attractive men. This was her body's way of reminding her she was female, that was all.

She shoved aside the fact that she'd felt nothing like this around Chiara's Uncle Rocco.

Maybe her distrust of Domenico Volpe, the fact that her emotions were engaged because of the past, gave a piquancy to her response.

Whatever it was, she had no intention of succumbing to weakness. As he'd soon learn.

He was seated at an enormous desk when she entered his study. Of course he'd take the position of power. Lucy had dealt with enough officials to recognise the tactic.

He was like the rest. Predictable.

He turned from the computer to survey her, taking in her denim skirt and the blue shirt that matched her eyes. It was the nicest one she owned and had always made her feel confident. Now it was years out of date and a snug fit around the bust but it was the best she could do.

His appraising glance told her he wasn't impressed. Or was he recalling her standing, spellbound, as she let him undo her robe? The idea stiffened her resolve and she crossed the room, leaving the door open.

'You had business to discuss?' She sat in the chair before his desk and crossed her legs in a show of nonchalance.

He seemed riveted to the movement and she suppressed a surge of satisfaction. So, he wasn't as remote as he appeared. The knowledge gave her a sliver of hope.

'Yes.' He cleared his throat. 'I have a proposition for you.'

'Really? I'd have thought I was the last woman you'd ever proposition, Signor Volpe.'

His gaze darted to her face and she read simmering anger there. She could deal with anger. She clung to her own like a lifeline. It was preferable to the other feelings he evoked.

'Do tell,' she purred. 'I'm all ears.'

She had to bite back a smile when a frown furrowed his brow. She liked the fact that she pricked his self-possession. It wasn't fair that even scowling he still looked lethally gorgeous. Not that she cared.

'You want privacy and peace from the press. I want you out of the limelight. Our interests coincide.'

'So?'

'So I'd like to make the situation permanent.'

It was Lucy's turn to frown. 'I don't understand.'

He pushed a typed document towards her. 'Read that and you will. I've had it drawn up in English.'

'How considerate.' Perhaps he thought her Italian, learned behind bars, was inadequate. He had no idea the hours she'd spent poring over Italian legal documents.

She slid the paper towards her. It was a contract. She turned the page, heart racing as she read what he planned. She could barely believe it.

Finally she sat back. 'You really are desperate to keep me quiet.'

His dark eyes gleamed. 'Hardly desperate.'

'No? A lot of people would be fascinated to know how much you're offering to stop me talking.'

His look turned baleful. His voice when it came was a lethal whisper scudding through the silence. 'Is that a threat?'

'No threat, Signor Volpe. An observation.'

His eyes pinioned her and her breathing grew shallow. But she refused to be intimidated.

'I want peace for my family.' Yet his eyes didn't plead, they demanded. 'You can't say the offer isn't generous.'

'Generous?' The money on the table was stupefying. Enough to fund that new start in life she'd longed for. Enough to establish herself immediately, even though what was left of her family rejected her. Looked at that way, it was tempting.

'On condition that I don't talk about your brother, his wife, their son, their household, you or anyone associated with your family or the court case.' She ticked the list off on her fingers. 'Nor could I discuss my time in jail or the legal proceedings.'

Indignation settled like a burning ember, firing her blood. 'I'd be gagged from making any comment, ever.'

'You have to earn the money I'm offering.' He shrugged those powerful shoulders, leaning back behind the massive desk, symbol of the power he wielded.

'Earn!' Lucy was sick of being the one ground down by those in authority. The one forced to carry the blame.

Searing anger sparked from that slow burning ember in her belly. She pushed the document across the desk.

'No.'

'Pardon?'

Lucy loved his perplexed expression. How many people said no to this man? She bet precious few women ever had.

'I'm not interested.'

'You've got to be joking. You need money.'

'How do you know that?' She leaned forward. 'Don't tell me you managed to access my private bank details.' She shook her head. 'That would be a criminal offence.'

His teeth bared in a grimace that told her he fought to retain his temper. Good. Goading him was the closest she'd get to revenge and she was human enough to revel in it.

'If you expect a better offer you'll have a long wait. My price is fair.'

'Fair?' Her voice rose. 'No price is *fair* if I can't tell my side of the story. You really expect me to forget what happened to me?' Disbelief almost choked her. 'If I took your blood money it would be tantamount to admitting guilt.' The thought made her sick to the stomach.

'And so?'

'Damn you, Domenico Volpe!' Lucy shot from her chair and skewered him with a glare that should have shrivelled him to ashes in his precious executive chair. 'I refuse to soothe your conscience or that of your sister-in-law.'

He rose and leaned across so his face was a breath away from hers.

'What are you implying?'

'Don't play the innocent.' She braced her hands on the table, firing the words at him. 'Your family's influence was what convicted me.'

'You have the temerity to hint the trial wasn't fair? Because of us?'

She had to give him credit. He looked so furious he'd have

convinced anyone. Except someone who'd been behind bars for years because of his precious family.

'Come *on*! What chance did I stand with an overworked public defender against your power and influence?'

'The evidence pointed overwhelmingly to you.'

'But it wasn't true.' Her breath came in uneven pants as she faced him across the desk.

'You'd be well advised to sign.' His look sent a tremor of fear racing through her.

But he couldn't hurt her. Not now. She was free. She had no one and almost no money, but she had integrity. He couldn't take that.

'Now who's making threats?' She stared into eyes that glowed like molten steel.

Deliberately she leaned across his desk, her lips almost grazing his cheek, her nostrils filling with the heady spice scent of him. His eyes widened in shock and she wondered if she'd looked like that out in the garden when he'd come close enough to kiss her.

'I don't respond to threats,' she breathed in a whisper that caressed his scrupulously shaved jaw. 'The answer is still no.'

CHAPTER FIVE

DAMN THE WOMAN.

Domenico paced his study, furious he hadn't broken the deadlock. Lucy Knight still rejected his offer.

It stuck in his craw to give her anything but it was the only way to stop her selling her story. Then what privacy would Pia and Taddeo have? The scandal could go on for years, dogging Taddeo as he grew.

Money was the obvious lever to get what he needed. She was desperate for cash. If she'd had funds she'd have spent it on a top-flight defence team.

A splinter of discomfort pierced him, remembering her inexperienced, under-prepared lawyer. Watching his ineffectual efforts had made Domenico actually consider intervening to organise a more capable defender.

To defend the woman who'd killed Sandro!

Perhaps if he hadn't known she was guilty he would have. But how could he doubt the overwhelming evidence against her?

A mere week before Sandro's death Lucy Knight had bumped into Domenico, literally, at an exhibition of baroque jewellery. He was supervising the inclusion of some family pieces but had been distracted, outrageously so, by the charms of the delightful young Englishwoman who'd blushed and stammered so prettily. She'd looked at the gems with unfeigned delight and at him with something like awe.

Yet it was her hesitation to accept his spur of the moment invitation to coffee that had hooked him. How long since a woman had even pretended to resist him?

Coffee had turned into a stroll through the Forum, lunch at a tucked away trattoria and an afternoon sightseeing. He'd enjoyed himself more than he could remember with a woman who was just Lucy to his Domenico. A woman whose eyes sparkled with unconcealed awareness, yet who trembled with innocent hesitation when he merely took her hand. She was smart, fun and refreshingly honest. Enough to make him believe he'd found someone special and rare.

She'd evoked a slew of emotions. Passion, delight and a surprising protectiveness that had kept him from sweeping her off to his bed then and there. For the connection between them had been sizzling, each touch electric.

She'd been different from every other woman, her impact so profound he'd suggested meeting again when he returned to Rome.

In New York he'd counted the hours to his return.

Till he'd seen Lucy in a news report, doused in his brother's blood as she was led away by the police.

His heart stuttered at the memory.

Then piece by piece he'd heard from Pia and Sandro's staff the truth about Lucy. How she'd seduced his brother and flaunted her power over him.

She must have known who Domenico was at the gallery and engineered the meeting. Why stick with Sandro, whose wife was already making a fuss about his affair, when his brother—just as rich and single to boot—was available? *And just as susceptible.*

Domenico thrust a hand through his hair. He'd fallen for her with an ease that shamed and angered him.

No. She'd brought on the result of the trial herself.

Yet he couldn't douse his awareness of her. The delicacy of her features snagged his attention again and again, as did the proud, wilful angle of her jaw that appealed even as it repelled.

All afternoon he'd watched her. She appeared fascinated by the grounds, apparently content with the tranquillity here. Which made him wonder what her life had been like behind bars that she should revel in solitude.

There it was again. This unholy interest in the woman. She should mean nothing to him but a problem to be solved. Instead he found himself…intrigued.

And that tiny dead of night niggle was back, disturbing his rest.

He strode to the window, hands jammed in his pockets.

She gave him no peace. There she was at the end of the garden. The afternoon sun burnished her hair, making it glint like gold as she tipped her head back. Her obvious sensual delight was far too alluring, the way she held her arms open to embrace the heat, her deep breaths that drew his eyes to her delectable breasts.

She stiffened, head turning and arms folding in a classic defensive pose. Her tension was obvious as a figure approached from the villa. Rocco, his Head of Security.

Rocco held out a broad-brimmed hat. For a moment she stood stiff, as if unwilling to accept it. Then Rocco spoke and her defensive posture eased. She took the hat and put it on. Rocco spoke again and she shook her head. Was that laughter he caught in the distance?

Domenico stared, fascinated. Lucy Knight was so wary, stiffening the instant he or his security staff came near. To see her relaxed and laughing… Why? Because Rocco had offered her protection from the sun? It was a simple consideration anyone would offer.

Yet look how she responded. Now they were in conversation. She must be asking about landmarks for he pointed to the mainland and she nodded, leaning close.

Domenico frowned, not liking the swirl of discontent that rose as he watched them together.

The difference in her was remarkable. Domenico recalled the way her face had lit up at lunch when the maid served a delicious tiramisu, saying it was the cook's speciality, prepared to welcome the new guest. Lucy's eyes had widened then softened with appreciation and shock before she realised he was watching and looked away. Later she'd made a point of telling the maid how much she'd enjoyed the dessert.

The tiramisu was a little thing, a familiar courtesy to a guest, yet Lucy Knight had responded with surprised delight.

Was she so unused to consideration or kindness?

Given how she'd lived for the past several years it wasn't surprising.

What had she said when she'd rejected his offer out of hand? That she didn't respond to threats?

Domenico's brain snapped into gear. He'd seen her proud defiance, her cool calm and her haughty, almost self-destructive need to assert her independence. Look at the way she'd faced the paparazzi.

If the threats didn't work…what *would* she respond to?

Perhaps there was another way to get what he needed.

Instead of demands, persuasion might be more effective. Didn't they say you could catch more flies with honey than vinegar?

Lucy shut her eyes and listened to the drowsy hum of bees in the garden and, below, the soft shush of waves. She was so incredibly lethargic, mind and body reacting as if, for the first time in years, she didn't need to be constantly on guard. It was easy to relax here, too easy, given she had a future to organise and decisions to make. She should—

'I thought I'd find you here.' The deep voice swirled across her nerve ends, jerking them into tingling life.

She sat up abruptly in the low sun lounger. Standing between her and the sun was her host. For a moment she saw only an imposing silhouette, rampantly male with those broad shoulders, long legs and classically sculpted head. Her heart quickened with something other than surprise.

She scrambled to rise.

'Don't move.' He put his hand out to stop her and sank onto a nearby seat.

She subsided, then gathered herself. Obviously he was here to demand she sign his contract. So much for the peace he'd promised!

She sat straight, knees together, watching suspiciously.

'I thought I'd take you on a tour of the grounds.'

Lucy stared at him, but he returned her disbelieving look blandly.

'Why?'

His black brows arched infinitesimally and ridiculously she felt a sliver of jab at her brusqueness. As if she cared what he thought of her manners. Once upon a time she'd have bantered polite words but not now. He'd forfeited her trust.

'If you're going to stay you should learn the lie of the land.'

He sounded so reasonable. So civilised.

But then he was a civilised man. Look at the way he'd invited her to sit at his table today, as if she was a guest, not the enemy. She'd seen the tension in him, had felt its echo in her own discomfort, but if he was able to bear her company she refused to let him know how confused and edgy she was in his.

'You don't want to spend time with me.' The words grated from her tight throat. 'Why suggest it?' The words sounded churlish, but it was the truth.

She waited for his annoyance to show, but his face remained impassive. What was he thinking?

'You're a guest in my villa and—'

'Hardly.' Her fingers curved around the edge of her seat. 'More a burden.'

'I invited you here.' He paused as if expecting her to interrupt. 'As your host I have an obligation. I need to ensure your safety.'

'Safety?' Incredulous, she surveyed the delightful garden. 'Don't tell me, you have meat-eating killer ants that prey on people who fall asleep on the lawn?'

Was that a smile she saw, quickly suppressed? The fleeting

hint of a dimple in that lean cheek was ridiculously attractive. Her response to it scared her. 'Or rabid guard dogs who can sniff out an ex-convict if they stray near anything precious?'

No smile now with that blatant reminder of reality. Lucy told herself she preferred it that way. The last thing she needed was to find the man appealing again.

'No animal dangers but there are things you need to be wary of, including an old well and some sink holes.' He paused, obviously waiting for her assent.

What could she say? His offer sounded reasonable, though the chances of her falling down a hole were nil.

He wanted something. Why else seek her out?

To badger her into signing his contract? She was strong enough to withstand threats.

Besides, she was curious. She hated to admit it but it still felt as if there was unfinished business between them. Surely a little time in his company would erase that unsettling notion? Then she could leave without that niggle at her consciousness. It would be a relief to banish him from her thoughts.

'If you think it necessary, by all means show me the dangers of your island.'

'Va bene.' He stood and extended a hand.

Lucy pretended not to notice. The last thing she needed was physical contact with a man whose presence threw her senses into overdrive.

She stood quickly, brushing down her skirt.

'The first thing you must remember is to wear a hat at all times.'

'Like you do?' She stared pointedly at his dark hair, bare to the blazing sun.

Again that hint of a dimple marked his cheek, playing havoc with her insides. Lucy drew herself up, quenching the memory of how his smile had once made her heart skip and her mind turn to mush.

Clearly she'd been a passing amusement. Had he laughed at her gaucheness and wide-eyed wonder at Rome? And at being escorted by a stranger so handsome and attentive he'd all but made her swoon?

'I'm used to southern summers and I've got the skin for it.' He was right. His olive skin was burnished a deep bronze that enhanced the decisive contours of his face. 'Whereas you—'

'Have been behind bars.' Her chin jutted.

He shook his head slowly. 'You shouldn't finish other people's sentences. I was going to say you have a rare complexion. Cream and roses.' He leaned closer. 'And quite flawless.'

His eyes roved her face so thoroughly she felt his regard like the graze of a hand, making her flesh tingle. Her breath quickened and something unfamiliar spiralled deep inside, like the swoop and dip of swallows on the wing.

'Your English is good but the phrase is peaches and cream.' As if she believed he meant it! Prison pallor was more like. She looked away, needing to break the curious stillness that encompassed them.

'I say what I mean.' His voice was a low rumble from far too close. He raised his hand as if to touch her, and then let it drop. 'Your skin has the lustre of new cream, or of pearls, with just a hint of rose.'

Lucy swung round to face him fully, hands on hips as she leaned forward to accuse him of making fun at her expense. She was no longer a gullible young thing to be taken in by smooth talk.

But the look on his face stole the harsh response from her lips. It stole her breath too.

There was no laughter in his expression. He looked stunned, as if shocked at his own words.

Burnished pewter eyes met hers, making her blood pound.

Something arced between them, something like static electricity that drew the hairs at her nape erect and dried her mouth.

Abruptly they moved apart.

She wasn't the woman he'd thought he knew.

Domenico watched her navigate the dusty path at the far end

of the island with alacrity, as if exploring a semi-wilderness was high on her list of things to do. Her head swung from side to side as she took in the spectacular views and the countryside he always found so restful.

What had happened to the girl who thrived on bright lights and male attention? Who hankered after expensive jewellery and the excitement of a cosmopolitan city filled with boutiques, nightclubs, bars and men?

Was she hiding her boredom? She did a good job.

She'd even forgotten to scowl at him and her face had lost that shuttered look in the last half hour. Relaxed, she looked younger, softer.

Dangerously attractive.

There was a vibrancy about her he hadn't seen since the day they'd met.

Perhaps she'd been seduced by the warmth of the afternoon and the utter peace of the place. She'd changed. The tension radiating from her like a shield was gone.

She paused, eyes on a butterfly floating past, as if its simple beauty fascinated her.

As she fascinated him.

The realisation dropped into his thoughts like a stone plummeting into a calm millpond.

How could it be? He carried Sandro's memory strong within him. Any interest in her should be impossible.

Yet why had he chosen to oversee her stay here? It wasn't necessary. A lawyer could witness her signing the contract.

The truth was Domenico was here because something about Lucy Knight made him curious even now. Something he couldn't put his finger on. Something he needed to understand before she walked out of his life for ever.

'Is that a ruined *castle*?' The husky thread of pleasure in her voice brought Domenico back to the present.

'It is.'

'Yet you built your villa on the opposite end of the island.'

He shrugged. 'The aspect is better there. This was built to defend, not enjoy.'

'Strange,' she mused as they stopped to take in the scene. 'I had pegged you as someone who'd rather rebuild the old family estate than start afresh. After all, you live in the family palazzo in Rome.'

She shifted abruptly and he had the impression she wished she hadn't spoken. The palazzo conjured memories of what lay between them.

'You think I'm bound by tradition?'

She lifted her shoulders. 'I have no idea. I don't know you.'

That was the problem, Lucy decided. She'd thought she knew Domenico Volpe. All those weeks during the trial he'd been like an avenging angel, stonily silent and chillingly furious, waiting for her to be convicted. His eyes, cold as snow yet laser-hot when they rested on her, had told her all she needed to know about him.

Yet now she found him approachable—courteous and civilised. As if his lethal anger had never existed. She caught glimpses of the man she'd been wildly attracted to all those years ago. The man who'd made such an impression that in her innocence she'd thought she'd found The One.

Lucy stole a look as he stared at the tumbled stones. His severe features held a charisma that threatened to steal her breath. Abruptly she looked away, hating her quickened pulse.

'Because I honour family tradition doesn't mean I live in the past.'

He lounged against a stone wall beyond which was a deep ravine. A moat, she supposed, staring at the castle beyond. But though she kept her eyes on the view, she was supremely aware of her companion. In faded denim jeans that clung to powerful thighs and a dark short-sleeved shirt that revealed the sinewy strength of his tanned forearms, he looked far too real. Too earthy and sexy. She'd never seen him like this.

Lucy told herself a change of clothes meant nothing. Yet

she couldn't suppress the idea that she was closer to the real Domenico Volpe than in his city mansion.

She shied from asking herself why she wanted to know him at all.

Lucy shrugged. 'I thought you'd prefer the castle.'

'To lord it over my subjects?'

She shook her head. This man didn't need external proof of his authority. It was all there—stamped in the austere beauty of his face. He'd been born to wealth but he'd grown into a man used to command.

'Since family tradition means so much, you could restore the place.'

'Ah, but this is an acquisition, not an inheritance. I bought it years ago to celebrate my first success.'

Lucy turned to meet his gaze. 'Success?'

'*Si.*' His brows rose and she caught a flash of steel in his eyes. 'Or did you think we Volpes have no need of work? That we sit on our inherited wealth and do nothing?' His tone bit.

Once she'd have thought that was precisely what his family did, after seeing the ultra-luxurious way his brother and sister-in-law lived. Pia had never lifted a finger to do anything for herself, or her child.

Instantly guilt flared, twisting Lucy's stomach. Pia might have been completely spoiled but her lack of involvement with little Taddeo had stemmed from her inability to bond with the baby. Lucy knew how much guilt and shame, not to mention fear that had caused the poor woman. No wonder she'd been insecure.

'I see that's exactly what you think.'

'Sorry?' Lucy blinked and turned, surprised to find herself so close to the man who now loomed over her.

'You view us as lazy parasites, perhaps?' His voice was low and amused but Lucy knew in her bones that amusement hid anger.

'Not at all.' She tilted her chin to meet his stare unflinchingly. 'I know your wealth began with your inheritance but you struck out on your own as an entrepreneur, risking your capital on projects others wouldn't touch. Your flair for managing risk made you the golden-haired boy of the European business world when other ventures were collapsing around you. You have a reputation for hard work and phenomenal luck.'

'It's not luck,' he murmured. 'It's careful calculation.'

Lucy shrugged. 'Whatever the reason, the markets call you *Il Volpe*, the fox, for good reason.'

'Fascinating that you should know so much about me.' His voice brushed across her skin like the touch of rich velvet. A ripple of pleasure followed it.

Instinctively Lucy made to step back, then stopped.

Never back down. Never retreat. Weakness shown was an invitation to be walked over.

'It seemed prudent to know what I was up against.'

His eyebrows soared. '*We* weren't in conflict.'

'No?' She shook her head. 'Your family's influence put me behind bars.'

His eyes narrowed to deadly slits. Heat sizzled at the look he gave her.

'Let's get this straight. My family did no more than wait the outcome of the trial.'

Lucy opened her mouth to protest but his raised hand stopped her.

'No! You imply *what*? That we rigged the trial? That we bribed the police or judiciary?' He shook his head in a fine show of anger. 'The evidence convicted you, Ms Knight. Nothing else.' He paused and she watched him grapple for control, his strong features taut, his muscles bunched.

He drew a deep breath and Lucy saw his wide chest expand. When he spoke his voice was crisp. 'You have my word as a Volpe on it. We live within the law.'

There was no mistaking his emotion. It was almost convincing.

'You don't believe me?' His eyes narrowed.

In truth she didn't know. There was no doubt she'd been

disadvantaged by the quality of her legal team compared with the ruthless efficiency and dogged determination of the prosecution. And it was obvious that sympathy lay with Pia, the beautiful grieving widow and young mother. Lucy knew that sympathy had given Pia's evidence more weight than it deserved. At Lucy's expense.

Plus Bruno Scarlatti, Sandro's bodyguard and the prosecution's chief witness, was ex-police. He'd shone in court. His evidence had been clear and precise, unclouded by emotion. That evidence had damned her and swayed the court. She was sure his ex-police status had weighed with the investigators too, though she had no proof.

'I…don't know.' For the first time confusion filled her, not the righteous indignation that had burned so long.

'I'm not used to having my word doubted.' Hauteur laced Domenico's tone.

Lucy's lips curled in a sour half smile. 'Believe me, it doesn't get any easier with time.'

His eyes widened as he realised she was talking about herself. She almost laughed, but there was nothing funny about it.

Even after all this time, bearing the burden of public guilt was like carrying an open wound. She wondered if she'd ever feel whole again while she carried that lie with her. It had changed her life irrevocably.

Now the dreams she'd cherished about starting afresh seemed just that—dreams. How could they not, with Sylvia's cruel betrayal and the eager press waiting to scoop more stories? How would she find the peace she craved to build a new life?

She turned away, her joy in the place forgotten.

'Wait.' The word stabbed the silence.

'What?' Reluctantly she faced him.

'This—' his hand slashed between them '—isn't helpful.'

'So?'

'So—' his nostrils flared as he breathed deep '—I propose

a truce. You're my guest. I'll treat you as such and you'll reciprocate. No more accusations, by either of us.'

Was this to soften her up so she'd sign his paper? Or was
it, a little squiggle of hope tickled her, because he had doubts
about her guilt?

No. That hope died as it was born. He'd shown no doubt in
court. Not once. He'd spurned her as if she were unclean. He
didn't want to absolve her, just strike an accord that would give
them peace while they shared the villa.

Peace. That was what she craved, wasn't it?

'Agreed.' Lucy put her hand out and, after a surprised
glance, he took it.

She regretted it as soon as his fingers enveloped hers. Fire
sparked and spread from his touch, running tendrils of heat
along her arm to her cheeks, breasts and belly. Even down her
legs, where her knees locked against sudden weakness.

She sucked in a shocked breath at the intensity of that physical awareness.

Did he feel it? His eyes gleamed deep silver and his sculpted
lips tightened.

His next words were the last she expected to hear.

'So you will call me Domenico, *si*? And I'll call you Lucy.'

Time warped. It was as if they were back in Rome, chance
met strangers, her heart thundering as their eyes locked for
the first time.

His gaze bored into hers, challenging her to admit the idea
of his name on her lips discomfited her. Or was it the sound of
her own name, like a tantalising caress in his rich, deep voice,
that made her pulse falter?

'I don't think—'

'To seal our truce,' he insisted, his gaze intent as if reading
the thrill of shock snaking through her.

'Of course.' She refused to let him fluster her, especially
over something so trivial.

Yet it didn't feel trivial. It felt… Lucy groped for a word to
describe the sensations assailing her but failed.

With a nod he released her and stepped away. Yet Lucy still felt the imprint of his hand on hers and her spine tingled at the memory of him saying her name with that delicious hint of an accent.

She had the uncomfortable feeling she'd just made a huge mistake.

CHAPTER SIX

THEY WERE SILENT as they walked along the beach to the villa. Late afternoon light lengthened their shadows and for the first time in weeks Domenico felt something like peace, listening to the rhythm of the sea and their matched steps.

Peace, with Lucy Knight beside him!

His business negotiations had reached a crucial phase that would normally have consumed every waking hour. On top of that was Pia's near hysterical response to the latest press reports, and his own turbulent reactions to the release of his brother's killer.

And here he was walking with her in the place that was his refuge from the constant demands on his time. Was he mad letting her in here?

Yet the stakes were too high. He had to convince her—

Beside him she stopped. He turned, wondering what had caught her attention.

In the peachy light her hair was a nimbus of gold, backlit by the sun that lovingly silhouetted her shape. She'd taken off her sandals and stood ankle-deep in the froth of gentle waves. She looked…appealing.

His pulse thudded and he realised she was watching him. Her gaze branded his skin.

Instinctively he moved closer, needing to read her expression. What he saw made premonition jitter through him. Was she going to agree to his terms? He schooled his face, knowing better than to rush her.

'Lucy?' Her name tasted good on his tongue. Too good. This was business. Business and the protection of his family. It was his duty to protect Taddeo and Pia now Sandro wasn't here to do it. The thought of Sandro renewed his resolve.

'I…' Her gaze skated away and he leaned in, willing her to continue. She drew a deep breath, straining her blouse across ripe breasts. Domenico berated himself for noticing, but he noticed everything about her. Was that an asset or a penalty?

'You?' Expectation buzzed. It wasn't like her to hesitate. She was aggressively forthright.

Her eyes met his and something punched deep in his belly. Gone were her defiance and her anger. Instead he read something altogether softer in her face.

'I never told you.' She paused and bit her lip, reminding him in a flash of blinding memory of the girl he'd met all those years ago. The one whose forget-me-not eyes had haunted him with their apparent shock and bewildered innocence. Who'd been a conundrum with her mix of uncertainty and belligerent, caustic defiance.

His belly tightened. There was no logic to the fact she unsettled him as no other woman had.

'Sorry. I'm usually more coherent.'

'You can say that again.'

Her lips twisted. Then she straightened, her jaw tensing as she met his eyes head-on.

'We agreed not to make accusations and I understand there's no point protesting my innocence.' She inhaled through flared nostrils. 'But there's something you need to hear.' She paused as if expecting him to cut her off, but Domenico had no intention of interrupting.

'I'm sorry about your brother.' Her gaze didn't waver and Domenico felt the force of her words as a palpable weight. 'His death was a tragedy for his wife and child, for *all* his family. He was a good man, a caring one.' She released a breath that shivered on the air between them. 'I'm sorry he died and I'm sorry I was involved.'

Stunned, Domenico watched her lips form the words.

After all this time…

He'd never expected an apology, though he'd told himself an admission of guilt would salve the pain of Sandro's loss.

She didn't confess, yet, to Domenico's amazement, her words of regret struck a chord deep inside. He stared at her and she didn't try to hide, even lifted her face as if to open herself to his scrutiny.

For the first time he felt the barriers drop between them and he knew for this moment truth hovered. Truth and honest regret.

'Thank you.' His voice was hoarse from grief that seemed fresh as ever. But with the pain came something like peace.

The cynic in him stood ready to accuse her of an easy lie, a sop to his anger. Yet what he saw in Lucy's face drowned the voice of cynicism. 'I appreciate it.'

Her lips twisted in a crooked smile. 'I'm glad.' She paused then severed eye contact, turning towards the sea. 'I wrote to your sister-in-law some time ago, saying the same thing. I'm not sure she even read the letter.'

'You wrote to Pia?' It was the first he'd heard of it and usually Pia was only too ready to lean on him for emotional support.

He stared at the woman he'd thought he understood. How well did he know her after all? She confounded his certainties time and again.

She made him feel so many unexpected emotions.

A day later Domenico stood at his study window, drawn from his computer by the sound of laughter.

On the paved area by the head of the stairs to the beach were Rocco's niece, Chiara, and Lucy, neat in her denim skirt and blouse. Lucy bent to mark the flagstones in a square chalk pattern and Domenico fought to drag his eyes from the denim tight around her firm backside.

Heat flared as his gaze roved her ripe curves.

Too often he found himself watching Lucy with distinctly male appreciation.

He switched his gaze to Chiara as, shaking her head, she took the chalk and drew her own patterns, circular this time. As she finished, understanding dawned. They were playing a children's game: Mondo. Watching Chiara gesticulate he guessed she was explaining her game rather than the English Hopscotch, that Lucy had marked.

'You wanted me, boss?' Rocco tapped at the door.

Did he? Domenico couldn't recall. Frustration bit. He'd been distracted all morning. Lucy and her refusal to sign his contract undermined his focus.

'Have you seen who your niece is playing with?' His voice grated as he realised it wasn't Lucy's obstinacy that distracted him. It was the woman herself—prickly, proud and, he hated to admit it, intriguing in ways that had nothing to do with the danger she posed to his family.

'They're good together, aren't they?'

Domenico frowned. 'You have no qualms about Chiara playing with a woman who served time for killing a man?'

Not just any man. His brother. Domenico's breath was harsh in his constricted lungs.

There was a long silence. He turned to find Rocco regarding him steadily. 'The past is the past, boss. Even the court said it wasn't premeditated. Besides, she loves children. Anyone can see that.' He nodded to the garden and Domenico turned to see Lucy ushering Chiara, who'd grown boisterous with excitement, away from the steps.

Domenico felt a sliver of something like shame, seeing her concern for Chiara. Even the prosecution at her trial had acknowledged she'd been a reliable carer for little Taddeo.

'Mamma trusts her with Chiara. You can't say better.'

Rocco's *mamma* was a redoubtable woman, canny and an

excellent judge of character. As housekeeper to the Volpes for over thirty years, she and Sandro between them had brought Domenico up when his parents had died.

'Maybe Signorina Knight isn't the woman you think.'

Domenico stiffened. He didn't need Rocco's advice, even if he was the best security manager he'd ever had.

Yet once lodged in his brain, his words couldn't be dismissed.

Was she the same woman he'd heard about all those years ago? Greedy, self-centred, luring his brother into indiscretion under his wife's nose? If he hadn't experienced first-hand the powerful tug of her innocent seductress routine he'd never have believed Sandro would be unfaithful.

She had been only eighteen then; had the last years changed her?

He saw glimpses of a far different woman. One with surprising depths—an inner core of strength and what he suspected was her own brand of integrity. One that reminded him a little of the golden girl who'd once snared his attention, but far, far tougher and sassy. Besides, that girl had been a mirage.

Frustration rose. He wasn't used to uncertainty, either in business or with women. Usually his instincts for both served him well.

Was he seeing what he wanted to see?

More important, did he see what *she* wanted him to see? Unfamiliar tension coiled in Domenico's belly. She'd got under his skin, inserting doubt where previously there'd been certainty.

Why maintain her innocence after all this time? Unbidden, he recalled again her inexperienced legal representative. Would the trial's outcome have been different with a better lawyer?

A twinge of discomfort pierced him.

Domenico's mouth tightened. His curiosity had as much to do with attraction at a primal level as it did the need for understanding. This was about more than gagging Lucy Knight from spreading stories that would harm his family.

The stakes were far more personal.

* * *

Lucy was walking back to the villa when a figure loomed before her.

'How would you like to come snorkelling?'

Suspicion welled as she looked into Domenico's unreadable grey eyes. True, they'd agreed a truce. True, he let her have the run of the estate, even access to the Internet so she could trawl fruitlessly for jobs—as if anyone would take her on with her history. But taking her on an excursion?

Lucy shook her head. 'I should check my email.' As if there was a chance some employer had bothered to respond to the dozens of queries she'd sent. Given the poor economic climate, attracting an employer's interest would be a miracle. Even if she managed that, there were the hurdles of character and criminal record checks.

'You can do that when we return. Come on, it will be good to get off the island.'

'Why?'

What did he want? Remembering his glowering scowl when they'd first met, a fatal boating accident seemed possible. But lately… No, he wasn't a violent man, just one used to getting what he wanted. And he wanted her to sign his contract. Was he trying to soften her up?

He shrugged and to her chagrin she followed the movement of those wide, straight shoulders with a fascination she still couldn't conquer.

'Because I'm fed up with emails and performance indicators and financial statements. It's time for a break.' His lips curved in a one-sided smile that carved a long dimple in one cheek and snared her breath before it could reach her lungs.

The man was indecently attractive.

'I really should—'

'You're not avoiding me, are you, Lucy?'

Stoically she ignored the way his hint of an accent turned her ordinary name into something delicious. It had made her weak at the knees the day they'd met.

'Why would I do that?'

His eyes sizzled pure silver—the colour of a lightning bolt against a stormy sky. She could almost feel the ground shake beneath her feet from its impact.

Again he shrugged. This time she kept her eyes on his face. 'Perhaps I make you nervous.'

He was dead right. No matter how often she told herself Domenico had no power over her, instinct eclipsed logic and fear shivered through her. A fear that had nothing to do with his wealth and influence and everything to do with him as a potently attractive, fascinating man.

She'd washed her hands of him long ago. She'd seen him in court and her heart had leapt, believing he was there for her. Instead he'd cut her dead, so sure of her guilt before the trial even began. She'd been gutted.

Why did she still respond to him?

'Why should I be nervous?'

'I have no idea.' Yet his expression was knowing, as if he read her tension.

Did he guess the shockingly erotic fantasies that invaded her dreams each night? Fantasies that featured Domenico Volpe, not as disapproving and distant, but as her hot, earthily sexy lover? Lucy swallowed hard, reassuring herself that if he knew the last thing he'd do was invite her to spend time with him.

'I don't have a swimsuit.' Her voice emerged husky and she watched his attention shift to her mouth. Her lips tingled and heat bloomed deep in her belly.

He smiled. A fully fledged smile that made her heart skip a beat and alarm bells jangle.

'Be my guest. Find yourself a new one in the pool house.'

Lucy shook her head before she could be tempted. 'No, thank you.'

'Why not? Don't you want to go out there?' His gesture encompassed the azure shimmer of sea that had lured her since the moment she'd arrived.

How she'd love to do more than paddle in the shallows for

once! She'd even toyed with the idea of a midnight skinny dip but it would be just her luck to be found by his security staff.

'I don't accept handouts.' She wasn't a charity case.

Domenico watched her for long seconds with a look that in anyone else she'd call astonished. When he spoke his voice had lost its teasing edge.

'It's not a handout. It's what we do for our guests. Rocco's *mamma* has a lovely time buying hats and wraps and swimsuits for guests. You'd be surprised how many people forget them on a seaside stay.'

Not like her. Lucy had been shuffled out of Rome in a hurry with no idea where she was heading. She wasn't like his other guests. She opened her mouth to say so when he spoke again.

'Come on, Lucy. Set your pride aside and enjoy yourself. I promise it won't make you obligated to me.'

That was what she hated, wasn't it? Feeling indebted to Domenico Volpe for this respite when she most needed it.

Of course he had his own agenda. He wanted to buy her silence.

Was she too proud? Self-sufficiency was something she'd learnt in a hard school. Did she take it too far?

The sound of the sea behind her and the tang of salt on the air reminded her that the only person to suffer for her pride was herself. Swimming in the Med was something she'd always wanted to do. When would she have the chance again? When she finally found a job she'd be too busy making ends meet to travel.

'Thank you,' she said at last. 'That would be…nice.'

Was that a flash of pleasure in Domenico's eyes? Not triumph as she'd half expected. Her brow puckered.

'Good.' He pointed her to the pool house. 'You'll find what you need up there. Don't forget a hat. I'll meet you at the boat.'

Fifteen minutes later Lucy hurried down the steps to the beach. She'd rifled through a treasure trove of designer swimwear, finally selecting the plainest one-piece she could find. No way was she flaunting herself before Domenico in a barely there string bikini. Nevertheless she felt strangely aware of the Lycra clinging to her body under her skirt and shirt. It reminded her of the flicker of heat she saw in his eyes, and her body's inevitable reaction—a softening deep inside.

So often she found him watching her, the hint of a frown on his wide forehead, as if she was some enigma he had to puzzle. Or was he calculating how long she'd hold out against the fortune he offered?

On condition she stopped proclaiming her innocence.

She set her jaw. The first thing she'd do when she found work was pay back the price of this swimsuit. Even if it took her months on the basic wage!

Lucy stepped into the boatshed, trying to calculate how much a designer swimsuit would set her back.

It was dim inside and it took a moment for her eyes to adjust. She blinked at the sleek outline of the speedboat moored inside. Was this the boat they were taking?

She turned, wondering if she should wait outside, when movement caught her eye.

On the far side of the boat a man came towards her—thickset with a bullish head and broad neck that spoke of blatant strength. He moved with surprising agility. His dark suit blended with the shadows but, as her eyes adjusted to the gloom, she caught the crooked line of a broken nose and hands the size of dinner plates.

The hair at her nape stood on end and terror engulfed her. She froze, recognition filling her.

The rusty taste of blood on her bitten tongue roused her. She drew a shuddering breath and catapulted towards the door. With every step she imagined one of those heavy hands grabbing her, capturing her, punishing her.

Lucy's breath sawed through constricted lungs as she reached, hands outstretched, for the door. Her legs seemed to slow as if in a nightmare. She knocked over some tins that clattered to the floor and almost fell but kept going, eyes on the sunlit rectangle of freedom ahead, desperation driving her.

With a sob of fear she plunged outside, blinded by light, only to find her flight stopped by a hard, hot body.

He'd never held her but she knew it was Domenico. The scent of warm spice and pine, and something else, something so profound she had no name for it, told her it was him in the millisecond before his arms came round her, hugging her close.

'Please,' she gasped. 'Watch out! He's here. He's—'

She struggled to turn, but Domenico's grip was firm. She was plastered to him, her face pressed to his collarbone. One hand held her head against him and his other arm lashed protectively around her waist.

Lucy felt heat, strength and solidity. Safety. His heart beat steadily against her raised palm and, despite her fear relief weakened her knees. Tendrils of heat invaded her ice-numbed body, counteracting the horror that filled her.

'Lucy? What is it?' His deep voice ruffled her hair and wrapped itself around her.

She shook her head. 'Be careful! He—'

'I'm sorry, sir.' An unfamiliar voice came from behind her. 'I was putting provisions in the boat. I didn't mean to scare the lady.'

Lucy turned her head, eyes widening at the man who emerged from the boatshed.

He was a stranger.

Her heart leapt even as reaction set in and her knees buckled. She clung to Domenico. His grip tightened, holding her against him as if she belonged there.

Later she'd regret clinging to him, but now she was too overwhelmed by a sense of deliverance from danger.

It wasn't him.

The knowledge beat a rapid tattoo in her blood. She took in the worried face and bright eyes of the stranger. What she'd thought a bodyguard's suit was a casual uniform of dark trousers and shirt. The man was an employee, but not the one she'd feared. Even the crooked jut of his nose was different and his eyes held none of the gleaming malice she remembered.

In face of the stranger's concern Lucy tried to summon a reassuring smile but it wobbled too much.

'Lucy?' Domenico's broad palm rubbed her back and comforting heat swirled from the point of contact. She pressed closer, arching into him.

'I'm sorry.' Her voice was husky. She turned as far as she could within Domenico's firm embrace. She should step free but couldn't dredge the strength to stand alone. 'I...overreacted. I saw someone coming towards me in the darkness and...'

'I'm sorry, *signorina*.' The big man looked solemn. 'I didn't mean—'

'No. Don't apologise.' Lucy's smile was more convincing now, though it felt like a rictus stretch of stiff muscles. 'It was my mistake.'

'It's okay, Salvo.' Domenico's deep voice was balm to shredded nerves. 'Everything's fine. You can leave us.'

With one last troubled look the man left and Lucy sagged. The rush of adrenalin was fading. She felt almost nauseous in the aftermath.

'Lucy? Come and sit in the shade.'

Suddenly, as if her brain had just engaged, she became fully conscious of how intimately they stood. The press of hard muscle and solid bone supporting her. The reassuring beat of his heart beneath her palm. The need to lean closer and lose herself in his embrace. The flare of pleasure at the differences between them—he was so utterly masculine against her melting weakness.

That realisation made her snap upright on a surge of horrified energy.

'I'm sorry.' Humiliation blurred her words as she struggled to remove herself from his hold. What must he think of her, clinging to him?

Bile churned her stomach. She knew what he must think. The prosecution at the trial had painted her as a femme fatale, using the promise of her body to win expensive favours from her indulgent boss. Domenico probably thought she was trying a similar tactic to win sympathy.

A shudder of self-loathing passed through her and she broke free. How could she have turned to him?

Her pace was uneven but she managed the few steps to the boatshed, putting her hand to its wall for support.

Stifling her shame and embarrassment, Lucy forced herself to turn. He stood, frowning, the line of his jaw razor-sharp and his grey eyes piercing.

'Now we're alone you can tell me who you thought you were running from. Who are you scared of?'

CHAPTER SEVEN

'SCARED?' LUCY GAVE a shaky laugh. Her hand dropped from the wall and she straightened. She swayed and Domenico discovered the heat curling through his belly had turned to anger.

It was a welcome change from the surge of hunger he'd known as she'd melted against him.

'Tell me, Lucy.' His tone was one his business associates obeyed without question.

Her chin jutted obstinately. 'There's nothing to tell. I saw someone coming towards me in the dark and panicked.'

Domenico shook his head. 'You don't panic.'

'How would you know? You're hardly an expert on me.'

But he was.

He'd spent the weeks of the trial trying to learn every nuance of her reactions—not that it had got him far. She'd been an enigma. But in the days since her release he'd been able to concentrate on little but her and he'd learned a lot. Enough to make him question his earlier, too easy assumptions.

'You're no coward. You faced the paparazzi.' He added quietly, 'You faced *me*.'

Her eyes widened, acknowledgement if he'd needed it, of just how hard she'd found the last several days.

He remembered her hunched on the floor in the palazzo, her hand splayed where Sandro had breathed his last. Her blind pain had been almost unbearable to witness. What strength of character had it taken to face the place? The same strength it took to face him with an air of proud independence despite the tremors racking her.

Something hard and unforgiving inside him eased. Something that had already cracked when she'd expressed regret for Sandro's death. When he'd seen her playing with little Chiara. When he'd held her close and been torn between protectiveness and an utterly selfish desire for her soft, bountifully feminine body.

'There's nothing to tell.' But her eyes were clouded and her mouth white-rimmed. Her tension reignited the protectiveness that had enveloped him as he held her and felt the waves of fear shudder through her.

'Liar.'

She flinched, her face tightening.

'I thought we'd agreed to leave the accusations behind.' There was desperate hauteur to her expression but she couldn't mask her pain.

'I'm not talking about the past. I'm talking about now. Here.' His slashing hand encompassed the scene that had just played out. 'You were scared out of your wits.'

Her pale eyebrows rose. 'Nothing scares me. After the last few years I'm unshockable.'

Looking into her unblinking gaze he almost believed her. Yet her desperate panting breath against his throat, the clutch of her hands and the feel of her body's response to overwhelming fear had been unmistakable.

Domenico stepped close and she stiffened. He kept going till he stood a breath away. Her face tilted up to his as he'd known it would. Lucy had proven time and again that she was no coward. She faced what she feared.

Until today. In the darkness of the boatshed.

His heart beat an uneven rhythm as he realised only true terror would have made this woman run.

'Who is he, Lucy?' He lifted a hand to her jaw, stroking his thumb over her silken flesh, feeling the jittering pulse. 'Who are you afraid of?'

Her eyelids flickered. She pressed into his touch and pleasure swirled deep inside.

'Bruno.' The word was a whisper. 'Bruno Scarlatti. Your brother's Head of Security.'

Domenico read her fear and knew she spoke the truth. He wanted to assure her she was safe. He wanted to tug her close and not let her go.

Because she was scared?

Or because he wanted an excuse to touch her?

He dropped his hand. 'Why are you afraid of him?'

'It doesn't matter.' Her mouth flattened.

'Did he visit you behind bars?' Had he threatened her?

'Him! Visit me? You've got to be kidding. In five years my only visitors were a couple of criminologists writing a book on female offenders and crimes of passion.' Sarcasm dripped from her voice. 'They found me such a *fascinating* study.'

She shouldered away from him, into the sun. Yet she rubbed her hands up her arms as if to warm herself.

Stunned, he let himself be distracted. In five years she'd had no personal visitors? What about her family and friends? Then he remembered the tawdry exposé interview with her stepmother. Lucy's family relationships were strained. But to be alone so long?

He felt no triumph, only regret as he read her grim tension, the way she battled not to show emotion.

'Tell me, Lucy.' His voice was gruff. 'Why are you afraid of Bruno Scarlatti?'

His gaze held hers and almost he thought he'd won. That she trusted him enough to tell him.

She shrugged but the movement was stiff as if her muscles had seized up. 'We agreed not to talk about the past. Let's abide by that. You wouldn't appreciate what I have to say.'

She turned towards the water.

There was no point trying to force her to talk. She'd proved time and again that she didn't bow to pressure.

But her terror couldn't be denied.

Something had happened. Something that frightened one of the most composed, self-sufficient women he knew.

He thought of her evidence at the trial. She'd claimed it was Bruno Scarlatti, not Sandro, who'd come to her room that night. He'd heard about the scene between Sandro and Lucy when earlier that day she'd pleaded for immediate leave to visit her sick father. Understandably, Sandro had refused, concerned that with Pia unwell and the nanny off work due to illness, they needed the au pair, Lucy. The meeting had ended with Lucy shouting she'd find a way to leave despite her contract.

Her story was that Bruno had said he'd help her persuade the boss to give her leave and she'd innocently let him into her room. Once inside, he'd allegedly attacked her, tried to rape her. Sandro had heard the noise and come to her aid, but in the scuffle with Bruno he'd knocked his head against the antique fireplace and died.

Domenico rubbed a hand over his tense jaw, remembering all the holes in her story. The court had dismissed it. There was too much evidence of her guilt.

Pia had given evidence, backed by diary notes, that Sandro and Lucy had had a passionate affair. Bruno's evidence had been the same. He'd revealed her as a seductive tease who knew her power over men and bragged about twisting the boss around her little finger. He'd seen her and Sandro together, given dates and times.

Sandro had given her expensive treats, like the exquisite jewellery found in her room the night he died. The household had heard her threaten Sandro when he'd refused to let her go.

That night he'd been drinking, torn no doubt between concern for his wife and the fight with his mistress. He'd gone to Lucy's room with an expensive gift to salve her anger. But they'd fought again, she'd shoved him and, unsteady on his feet, he'd fallen and cracked his skull. As for Lucy blaming Bruno—he had an alibi.

Pia had found Sandro bleeding to death, cradled in Lucy's arms.

Domenico shivered, recalling the moment he'd discovered Lucy's identity—the image of her in a bloodstained night-dress with a blanket around her shoulders, being escorted to a police car outside the palazzo. Sandro was dead and she'd been arrested.

Domenico hadn't even been able to blame Sandro for his fatal attraction to the young Englishwoman. He knew how difficult Pia could be and guessed that in the months following childbirth she'd been particularly demanding.

More importantly, Domenico had first-hand experience of Lucy's power. He'd fallen under her spell in just a few hours. What must it have been like for Sandro, facing such temptation in his own home every day? That didn't excuse the affair. But Sandro was only human.

Who was Domenico to judge when he'd felt attraction sizzle the moment he'd looked into Lucy Knight's eyes? That knowledge had twisted guilt deep in his gut ever since.

He shifted his focus to the woman walking along the beach. Her head was bowed and her arms were wrapped tight around her body.

Confusion filled him as he recalled the fear that had racked her as he'd held her.

Because she thought she'd seen Bruno Scarlatti.

Because he'd killed Sandro?

The thought stopped the breath in Domenico's lungs. It wasn't possible. The court had been through all the evidence, right down to Lucy's fingerprints on the expensive necklace Sandro had given her that night. It had been a lovers' quarrel. And there was a witness who put Scarlatti elsewhere when Sandro died.

And yet... Again that frisson of unease stirred. That sense that something wasn't right.

Domenico forced himself to concentrate on proven facts. The evidence supported Lucy's guilt yet she was scared of Scarlatti. Had one part of her story been true? Had he tried to force himself on her?

There'd been an avid hunger in Scarlatti's eyes whenever he'd looked across the courtroom at Lucy. Domenico had noticed immediately, ashamed as he was of his own response to her.

Domenico's hands clenched so hard he found himself shaking. Could that be it? The idea hollowed his belly.

He wished Scarlatti was here now. Domenico needed an outlet for his churning fury.

'Scarlatti no longer works for the Volpe family.'

Lucy spun to find Domenico a few paces away, eyes shaded by wraparound sunglasses. She felt at a disadvantage, wondering what the lenses hid from view.

'Why not?'

'He was dismissed years ago. Rocco found evidence that he'd...bothered one of the maids.'

'Bothered?' Why wasn't she surprised? Bruno was a slime ball who wouldn't take no for an answer.

'She complained he was pestering her. A bit of digging revealed she wasn't the first.'

Lucy bit her lip. The temptation to spill her own story about Bruno was strong. But Domenico had heard it in court. He hadn't believed it then and wouldn't now. Defeat tasted sour on her tongue.

Why should it matter after all this time that he didn't believe her? Instead of getting easier to bear, it grew harder.

Nothing had changed. She'd let herself be lulled into believing it had.

Domenico was weakening her, subtly undermining her ability to keep the unsympathetic world at bay.

'Don't worry, he's long gone.'

She nodded. What was there to say?

'Now, let's get out on the water.'

'I've changed my mind. I'll stay ashore.'

'Why? So you can hide in your room and brood?'

Lucy's eyes widened. 'I *never* hide!'

'Isn't that what you're doing now?'

She knew Domenico's tactic. He deliberately baited her, yet she couldn't resist the challenge. The one thing, the only thing she'd had on her side all these years had been her resolute strength. An ability to tough out the worst the criminal justice system could throw at her and pretend it didn't matter.

She'd forced herself to morph from a scared, desperate teenager into a woman who could look after herself no matter what.

There was more than pride at stake. It was her faith in her one tangible asset—strength in the face of adversity.

Without that, how could she face the future that loomed like a black hole? She had no family now. No friends. No prospects, as each day's job-hunting proved. If she let herself weaken she'd never survive.

Lucy met Domenico's gaze, reading anticipation in his stillness. He expected her to make a run for it, damn him.

'Where's your boat?'

Three hours later she was a different woman. The mutinous set of her mouth had eased into a smile that made Domenico's belly flip over. Her haunted expression had disappeared. Now her eyes shone pure forget-me-not blue, rivalling the sky for brightness.

He'd only once before seen a woman lit from within like this. It had been Lucy then too. Her enthusiasm was contagious.

He shook his head, unable to believe her avid enthusiasm was anything but real this time. There'd been no primping, not even a comb or mirror in the bag she'd brought. No coy looks or subtle feminine blandishments. Her focus had been on the boat and the sensation of speed as they circled the island. Her husky laughter still echoed in his ears. She'd been like a kid on a roller coaster for the first time—delighted and delightful in her glee.

'Did you *see* the size of that octopus?' She surfaced beside him, grinning as she removed the snorkel's mouthpiece. 'It's amazing, and the way it moves!'

'Do you like octopus? I could catch it for our dinner.' Like a smitten youth showing off for a pretty girl. Like the man he'd been that first day in Rome. He'd turned from a cabinet of ornate jewellery and fallen into the cerulean depths of her gaze.

Yet even that thought couldn't dim Domenico's good mood. He'd enjoyed the last couple of hours more than any he could remember in months.

She was a pleasure to be with. Her questions had stimulated rather than bored him. She'd made him see the place through fresh, appreciative eyes.

How long since he'd enjoyed such simple pleasures? Usually when he visited he was busy, finishing work or entertaining guests who were too sophisticated to get excited about snorkelling or a speedboat ride.

'No.' She reached out and put a restraining hand on his shoulder when he would have dived back under. 'Thank you, but I'd rather you let it be.'

'Squeamish about seeing your dinner before it appears on your plate?' He kept his eyes on her face though it was her slim hand on his shoulder that stole his attention.

'Maybe.' Her smile turned wistful. 'Can't we just leave him alone? Free?'

Something about the way she said that last word made him pause. Was that what she'd enjoyed so much? The freedom of their afternoon on the water?

It struck him that this was a massive change from the restrictions she'd known behind bars. He couldn't imagine such a life. How had she coped?

He wasn't in the business of feeling sorry for her. Yet seeing her so different from the touchy, self-protective woman he'd known, Domenico couldn't completely suppress a sense of connection between them.

His motive in being with her had been to soften her into accepting his deal—her silence for a big chunk of money. But somewhere in the past days he'd found himself *wanting* her company. He'd told himself he needed to understand the woman who threatened his family, but that wasn't all. Not any more.

He wanted to be with her. He wanted...

'In that case we'll leave it be.' He looked at the westering sun. 'It's time to stop. Come on.'

Lucy wrapped an oversized beach towel around herself, conscious of Domenico's gaze lingering as he'd helped her aboard. His eyes had shone silver as he took in the swimsuit moulding her body. It had only been for a second before he'd looked away, but that had ignited a slow, curling heat inside. His look had seared her to the core and shivers still rippled across her skin.

The trouble was, though they were on opposing sides, the old attraction was back, stronger than before.

Worse, she'd begun to *like* him.

He put her at ease and made her smile, and it wasn't just about him trying to persuade her to sign his contract. There was the way he was with little Chiara—like an honorary uncle instead of the man who employed half her family. The way he treated Lucy—always straight down the line. The way he'd held her this afternoon.

It scared her how much his concern had meant to her.

'Why did you never speak to me at the trial?'

Horrified, she heard the words slip out. Did she really want to break the afternoon's spell by dredging up the past? It seemed she did. 'I thought you'd talk to me at least. Acknowledge me.'

There. It was out in the open finally.

She turned her gaze on him. To her amazement, colour flushed his tanned face, rising high on those lean cheeks.

'Would it have changed anything?'

Lucy's lips firmed. It wouldn't have changed the trial's outcome but it would have meant everything to her.

'When I saw you there I thought you'd come to support me.' Her mouth twisted. She'd felt utterly alone, her family so far away. 'Until I found out who you were.'

His eyes widened, something like shock tensing his face.

'Surely you knew that already.'

'How could I? I only knew your first name, remember?'

They'd had such a short time together, less than a day. Her chest tightened. It wasn't his fault she'd fallen under his spell so utterly. That she'd read too much into simple attraction. She'd been so inexperienced. Domenico was the first man to make her heart flutter.

She looked into his stunned eyes and realised what a little fool she'd been. What had her claim on him been? An afternoon's pleasant company compared with supporting his family in crisis.

All this time she'd blamed him for not hearing her out. How could he, with Pia clinging hysterically to him? With the weight of his brother's death weighing him down?

How could she have expected him to leave those responsibilities for her, a woman he barely knew? Simply because she'd woven juvenile fantasies about him! Suddenly she felt a million years older than the immature girl who'd stood in the dock.

She raised her hand when he went to speak.

'Forget it, Domenico. It doesn't matter now.' To her surprise, it was true. Clinging to pain only held her back.

If this afternoon had shown her one thing it was that life was worth living—here, now. She intended to grab it by the throat and make the most of it. No point repining over what couldn't be changed.

'I'm thirsty. Do you have anything?'

Still Domenico stared, a strange arrested look in his eyes. 'There's beer or soft drink.' He stepped closer and now it wasn't his expression that held her.

He'd wiped the excess water away but hadn't wrapped a

towel around himself. She drank in the sight of his gold-toned body, powerfully muscled and mouth-wateringly tempting. His low-slung board shorts emphasised his virile masculinity.

'Juice?' she croaked.

He poured her a glass then collected a beer and sat down.

'We're not going ashore?'

He shrugged and Lucy couldn't help but watch the way muscle and sinew moved across his shoulders and chest. In Rome he wore a suit like a man bred for formal dress. But his tailored clothes hid a body that spoke to her on the deepest, most elemental level. A level that made her forget herself.

'Not unless you're in a rush. Sunset over the island looks terrific from here. I thought you'd enjoy it.'

Lucy had no doubt she would, if she could tear her eyes from him.

'Thank you for this afternoon,' she said brightly. 'I've never done anything like this before.' Better to babble, she decided, than to gawk silently. Why didn't he cover himself?

'You've never been snorkelling?'

'Or for a ride in a speedboat. I've never been in a boat.'

His eyebrows rose. 'Never?'

Lucy smiled. She couldn't help it. His look of amazement was priceless. 'I'm a landlubber. I've never even been in a canoe.'

'But you can swim.'

'Even in England we've got public indoor pools, you know.' She paused. 'That's why I jumped at the chance to work in Italy, to see the Mediterranean.' Pleasure rose at the sight of the azure sea, the sky turning blush pink over Domenico's island and, when she turned, the dazzling view of villages clinging to the mainland.

It was the embodiment of those fantasies she'd had as a girl: sun, sand and an exotic foreign location. Even a sun-bronzed hunk with mesmerising good looks.

How naïve she'd been, yearning for adventure.

'You lived far from the sea?'

She sipped her juice. 'Not far. But our interests were all on dry land.'

'Our?'

'My dad and me.' She paused, registering the familiar pang of loss, but with her attention on the breathtaking view, the pain wasn't as sharp as usual. 'He was a bus driver and mad about vintage cars. I spent my childhood visiting displays of old automobiles or helping him fix ours.' She smiled. 'He'd have loved that one you have at the palazzo.'

Her smile faded and her throat tightened as it often did when she thought of her dad and the precious time they'd lost. 'He died just after the trial.'

She turned to find Domenico looking as grim as she'd ever seen him. This time the shiver that ran through her wasn't one of pleasure but chill foreboding.

'I'm sorry for your loss, Lucy.' He stood and moved towards her, then shifted abruptly away.

'It's no one's fault,' she murmured, refusing to listen to the little voice that said she should have found some way to see her beloved dad before he passed on. The voice of guilt, reminding her of all she'd put him through when he was so ill.

'But you wanted to be with him.'

Surprised, she looked up and saw understanding in his eyes. Of course. He'd been overseas when his brother had died. He knew how it felt to be far away at such a time.

'Yes.' Her voice was hoarse.

'He would have known. He would have understood.'

'I know, but it doesn't make it easier, does it?'

He was silent so long she thought she'd overstepped the mark, referring however obliquely to his own loss.

'No, it doesn't.' His mouth twisted. 'I was in New York when Sandro died. I kept telling myself it would never have happened if I'd been in Rome.'

Lucy bit her lip but finally let the words escape. 'It wouldn't have made any difference.' Did he want to hear that from the woman he thought responsible?

His eyes darkened, then he nodded. 'You're right. It's just that Sandro was—' he frowned '—special. Our parents died when I was young and Sandro was more than a big brother.'

'He was a good man,' she said. He hadn't been perfect. She'd wished he'd got specialist help for his wife's depression. Yet though she didn't agree, she understood his reluctance not to upset her when she saw outside help as proof she was a bad mother.

As an employer he'd been decent. Looking back, she realised what a quandary she'd put him in with her hysterical demand to leave immediately for England. Of course he'd put his family's needs first. She'd been young and overwrought, convinced a delay of a few days would make a difference to her father.

'Sandro was the one who taught me to swim, and to snorkel.' Domenico smiled wistfully. 'And, come to that, how to drive a speedboat.'

'My dad taught me how to strip down an engine.' Her mouth curved reminiscently. 'And how to make a kite and fly it. He even came to ballet classes when I was little and too shy to go alone.'

'He sounds like a perfect father.'

'He was.'

'You never wanted to be a mechanic or a driver like him?'

'No. I wanted to be a teacher. Working with children was always my dream. But that's not possible now.' She kept her voice brisk, refusing to wallow in self-pity.

'What will you do?' He sounded grave, as if her answer mattered.

Lucy looked at the sunset glowing amber and peach, rimmed with gold, then across to the mainland, where the dying sun gilded the coastline into something fantastic. It was the most exquisite view. She stored the memory against the empty days ahead, when life would be all struggle.

'I took a bookkeeping course. I thought there'd be more chance of getting a job working with figures than with people, given my record.' Except she doubted she'd be left alone long enough to find a job. This was a temporary respite. Once she left, the press would hound her. Who would employ her?

Abruptly she put her glass down and stood. 'Isn't it time we headed back?' She needed to be alone, to sort out the problems she'd avoided while she was here. She'd been living in a fantasy world. Soon she'd face reality.

Lucy spun away. But the deck was slick where she'd dripped seawater. Her foot shot out beneath her. She flailed but was falling when Domenico grabbed her and hauled her to him.

She told herself it was the shock of almost falling that made adrenalin surge and her heart thump. It had nothing to do with the look in Domenico's stormy eyes or the feel of his hot, damp body against hers.

'You can let me go.' Her breasts rose and fell with her choppy breathing.

Lucy put her hands on his arms to push herself away. Instead her fingers curled around the tensile strength of his biceps as if protesting the need to move.

'What if I don't want to let you go?' His voice was so deep its vibration rumbled through her.

Bent back over his arm, she watched his face come closer. His gaze moved to her mouth and her heart gave a mighty leap as she read his intent.

'No!' Her voice was breathless. 'I don't want this!'

He shook his head. 'I thought we'd agreed, Lucy. No more lies.' For a moment longer he watched her, waiting for the protest they both knew she wouldn't make.

Then slowly, deliberately, he lowered his head.

CHAPTER EIGHT

DOMENICO'S LIPS BRUSHED hers in a light, barely there caress that made her mouth tingle and her blood surge. Twice, three times, he rubbed his mouth across hers, sending every sense into overdrive, till finally impatience overwhelmed caution and she clamped her hands to his wet hair and kissed him back.

There! No more teasing, just the heat of his mouth on hers. Her fingers slid around his skull, cradling him. The reality of him, the unyielding strength of bone and bunched muscle, of surprisingly soft lips making her blood sing, was everything she'd imagined and more.

His tongue slipped along the seam of her lips and it was the most natural thing in the world to open for him. For him to delve into her mouth and swirl delight through her veins. For her to respond with an honesty that eclipsed any vague thought of restraint.

She felt as if she'd waited a lifetime for this.

It didn't matter that she was a novice and he a master at this art. Eagerness made up for inexperience as she met his need with her own. Their tongues tangled, slid, stroked and goose bumps broke out across her flesh.

Domenico sucked her tongue into his mouth and her pulse catapulted. He nipped her bottom lip and Lucy sighed as pleasure engulfed her.

She leaned back, supported only by his embrace but she had no fear of falling. His arms were like steel ropes, lashing her close. His chest slid against hers and she gasped as electricity sparked and fired through her body, to her nipples, her stomach, the apex of her thighs. Behind the shocking heat came a melting languor that liquefied her bones and stole her will.

She tilted her head, accommodating him as desire escalated and their kisses grew urgent, hungry. She was burning up and so was he, his flesh on fire beneath her hands.

Yes! This was what she wanted from him, had always wanted. Even when she'd spat and snarled, she'd fought this chemistry between them.

Why had she tried to fight it? It was delicious, addictive.

Domenico tasted of the sea and dark, wickedly rich chocolate— a seductive mix. She shivered in sensual overload as he devoured her with a thoroughness that matched every long-suppressed need.

Had he yearned for this too? Had he lain awake, imagining this moment?

The slide of their bodies was pure magic. The thin fabric of her swimsuit was negligible against the heated promise of his body. Lucy pressed closer, revelling in his powerful musculature, the heady scent of his skin and a deeper, musky note of arousal.

He kissed her throat and she arched back, feeling her feminine power even as she knew herself caught in a web of desire. She was utterly open to his caresses, unprotected against his strength. Yet Lucy felt no doubt or fear. Each kiss he pressed to her skin was homage to the spell woven between them.

Rousing herself from drugged delight, Lucy pulled herself higher, rubbing her cheek against his. The friction of his sandpapery jaw sent another shaft of lightning straight to her groin and she shivered in delicious arousal.

She nipped his ear lobe and heard him growl, low in his throat. It was the sexiest thing she'd ever heard. She smiled and did it again, eager at the thought of Domenico reacting to her at the most primal level.

Large hands wrapped around her waist and he lifted her

high to sit on something. Domenico pushed her thighs apart and stepped between them, lodging himself at her core.

'Domenico.' Her voice was a rasp of pleasure as the fire spread, overriding a belated voice of warning.

She wanted him. Had done for so long. Even in the days when she'd hated him, she'd secretly yearned for this delight. This affirmation. She'd given up trying to puzzle the attraction that smouldered between them. It was enough to let glorious pleasure sweep her away.

Lucy felt the power of his erection between her legs and against her belly and her breath faltered. They felt so *right* together. It was all she could do not to rock against him, lost in the need for sensual satisfaction.

With an effort of willpower that almost undid her, she opened her eyes and met the mercurial glitter of his. Heat and shimmering silver fire engulfed her.

His hand palmed her breast and she gasped, overloaded with exquisite sensation. It was too much to bear.

She grabbed his neck and pulled him to her, wanting his lips on hers. Needing the dark mystery of their kisses. Needing *him*.

Long fingers thrust through her hair, tipping her head back as he tasted her in a long, luxurious kiss that curled her toes. His other hand teased her nipple. Darts of heat arced from the spot, making her move restlessly.

Immediately Domenico slid his hand from her scalp, down her spine, to splay over her bottom and drag her up tight against him. He kissed her hard, his tongue delving as his blatantly aroused body surged against hers.

The world tumbled and re-formed. Her blood sizzled like molten metal swirling in a crucible of pure need. Her lips moved against his and her dazed brain almost stopped functioning.

Domenico eased away a fraction as he slipped his hand over her bare thigh to brush the Lycra at the juncture of her thighs. A bolt of lightning slashed through her, jolting every

nerve end, concentrating every sense on that point of contact.
She grabbed his shoulders.

Wide-eyed she looked up. His face was pared to austere
lines that spoke of raw hunger. Gone was his sophistication,
stripped to something more elemental.

More dangerous. The words surfaced in her foggy brain as
long fingers teased the band of fabric at her inner thighs, sending whorls of fiery pleasure through her.

Desire warred with shock as she realised how far their kisses
had taken her. To the brink of fulfilment. To the brink of giving herself to the man she'd called enemy. To the point of baring herself emotionally as well as physically. *That* was what
scared her.

Her hand clamped his as he moved to insinuate his fingers
under the fabric. He froze, his eyes turning blindly to hers. His
other hand still cupped her breast.

Lucy watched realisation dawn. His eyes lost that unfocused
glitter and widened a fraction.

'I think it's time to stop.'

It was a wonder he heard. Her voice was hoarse, a frayed
thread of sound. Yet he understood. An instant later he'd
backed away, his hands furrowing through his thick hair as if
he didn't trust himself not to touch her again.

Lucy swayed, perched on the edge of the boat. Without his
support she felt bereft. She bit her tongue to stop herself calling him back. Her eyes ate him up, from the hard jut of his jaw
to the dusting of hair across his broad pectoral muscles and
the swell of his biceps as he lifted his arms. From the heavy
arousal to the storm-dark glint of his hooded eyes.

She wanted him still. Wanted him to step back and oblit-
erate her doubts with the caress of that clever mouth, seduce
her into delight with that big, hard body. Every nerve ending
danced in anticipation, undermining her resolve.

Fear surfaced. She'd never known how compelling the need
for sexual gratification could be. Domenico tempted her to forget everything. She'd thought herself strong and self-sufficient.

Yet all it had taken was one kiss to undo every barrier she'd spent years erecting.

What did it mean?

'You're right. It's late.' He turned away and, to her consternation, Lucy felt disappointment swell.

After an evening apart breakfast the next morning was full of silences and stilted conversation.

What had got into him?

Oh, he knew what had got into him. He'd desired Lucy from the moment he'd set eyes on her all those years ago.

How could he have come so close to sex, raw and unvarnished, with the woman convicted of killing Sandro? Guilt churned in his belly. Where was his family loyalty?

Gone the moment he held her. Evicted by sexual desire and the conviction Lucy Knight was a mystery he'd just begun to unravel. An enigma who'd haunted him for years. He desperately needed to understand her for his peace of mind.

It wasn't only desire she triggered. He'd been beside himself with thwarted fury when he realised she'd been attacked by a family employee. His need to protect had been as strong as if she was his responsibility. *His woman.*

A frisson of warning crept down his spine.

Yesterday's revelations had rocked him to the core.

For years he'd believed Lucy had engineered their initial meeting. How unlikely a coincidence that she'd literally bump into him, on his fleeting visit to Rome, when she already worked for his brother?

When the revelations had come thick and fast about Sandro's uncharacteristic weakness for his au pair, the way she'd twisted him round her little finger and milked him for expensive gifts, it hadn't taken a genius to work out she'd tried out the same wiles on Domenico.

He'd picked up the tension in his brother's household that very morning on his visit, only later realising it was due to a love triangle.

Or was it?

She'd said yesterday she hadn't known his identity before the trial. It was tempting to think Lucy lied but there was no reason now. Besides, he'd seen real hurt in her face when she'd asked why he'd avoided her. Hell! He no longer knew what to believe.

Could she be innocent?

His blood froze. The idea that he'd misjudged her so badly, letting her suffer for a crime she didn't commit, didn't bear thinking about.

He looked across to where she sat, eyes riveted on her breakfast as if it fascinated her.

Never before had she refused to meet his eyes.

He wanted to demand she look at him. He wanted to kiss that sultry down-turned mouth and unleash the passion that had blasted the back off his skull yesterday. Behind that reserve lurked a woman unlike any he'd known. More alive, more vital, more dangerous.

Was he out of control, ignoring what he owed his dead brother? Or were his doubts valid?

'Mail, sir.' The maid entered with a bundle of letters. To his surprise she placed an envelope beside Lucy's plate.

'For me?' Lucy frowned. 'Thank you.'

Who knew she was here? Someone she'd corresponded with via email? He forced himself to take another sip of fresh juice rather than demand to know who'd sent it.

She slipped a finger under the seal and withdrew a sheet of paper, discarding the envelope. That was when he saw a bold, too-familiar logo. It belonged to the magazine that had run her stepmother's interview.

He clenched his jaw, forcing down bile. Obviously Lucy was making the most of her opportunities, accepting his hospitality while negotiating with the gutter press for a better financial deal.

It shouldn't surprise him.

So why did he feel betrayed?

So much for the wronged innocent. How often would he let her dupe him?

'Is it a better offer?'

'Sorry?' Lucy looked up into eyes of gun-metal grey, piercing in their intensity.

She blinked, stunned by the change in Domenico. His eyebrows slashed in a V of disapproval and he looked as if he'd bitten something sour.

True, she'd shied away from contact this morning, still shocked by her response yesterday. But there'd been no venom in his voice, no ice in his stare when she'd entered the breakfast room.

'I assume from your absorption they're offering better terms than I did.'

Belatedly understanding dawned as he stared at the paper in her hand.

Pain sliced down, sharp as a blade of ice. It tore through her heart, shredding the bud of hope she'd nursed since yesterday. Making a mockery of that warm, sunshine glow Domenico had put there with his protectiveness, his acceptance and his desire.

What an idiot she'd been! How pathetically gullible.

Hadn't life taught her not to believe in miracles?

Domenico Volpe caring for her, trusting her even a little, would be a miracle. Yet against the odds she'd hoped some of the emotions she'd read in him yesterday had been real.

She'd almost given herself to him!

Lucy cringed at how far she'd let herself be conned.

Crazy, but even more than his sexual hunger or his protectiveness, Lucy missed their camaraderie as they'd snorkelled and watched the sunset. The sense of acceptance and liking. That had been precious. They'd shared things that were important to them both. Memories of their loved ones.

For those few hours Lucy had felt genuine warmth, a spark of liking. Of trust.

Fool, fool, fool. He'd buttered her up to get what he wanted.

'I said—'

'I heard.' She looked from him to the letter in her clenched fingers. There was nothing to choose between them. At least the press was upfront about what they wanted. Domenico had tried to distract her with a show of friendliness.

And she'd fallen for it.

What was one more deceit in a world of disappointment? Yet this one gouged pain in a heart she'd told herself was too well protected to hurt again.

'It's an attractive offer,' she said at last. As if the idea of selling her story to those hyenas didn't make her flesh crawl. They'd done more than destroy her reputation. They'd harried her poor dad in his last weeks. 'I'll have to consider it carefully.'

Distaste burned but maybe she didn't have the luxury of saying no any more. If she sold her story she'd get enough to start fresh. Hadn't she earned the right to profit after the terrible price she'd paid?

Maybe if she co-operated they'd leave her alone and she could pretend to be the woman she'd been before.

And pigs might fly. The press would never let her go whilst there was a story to be sold. Lucy squeezed her eyes shut, imagining lurid revelations about her attempts to live a normal life. Shocked reactions from neighbours when they discovered a killer living in their midst.

It would never end. Not for years.

She snapped open her eyes and glared as Domenico looked down his aristocratic nose at her.

A silent howl of despair rose. She'd wanted to trust him. She'd begun to open up, to believe he cared.

'Perhaps I could canvass the other media outlets and see what they're offering.'

His scowl was a balm to her lacerated feelings. Let him stew!

'You haven't already done that? Isn't that why you spend so long on the computer? Negotiating the best deal?'

'Actually, no. But of course you won't believe me.'

He leaned across the table, his eyes flashing daggers. 'If you haven't contacted the press, how do they know where you are?'

Lucy shoved her chair back and stood.

'Perhaps they took an educated guess,' she purred. 'Since they knew I was at your palazzo it wouldn't take much to suppose I'd be at one of your properties. Maybe they've written to me at each one. Who knows? Maybe this is the first of a flurry of offers.' She smiled, injecting saccharine sweetness into her tone. 'A bidding war. Wouldn't that be fun?'

He looked as if he wanted to strangle her with his bare hands. They clenched into massive fists before him.

Lucy's bravado ended as she recalled the stroke of those hands across her body. He'd touched her as if she were the most precious thing on earth.

She'd *felt* precious, desirable, special.

She forced down welling pain.

'Here.' She slowed as she walked past, letting the letter flutter to his lap. 'See what the opposition is offering. Maybe you'll increase your bid.'

Lucy strode out of the door before nausea engulfed her.

'Excuse me, boss. Have you seen Chiara?'

Domenico looked up from his email to find Rocco at the door, concern etched on his face.

'Isn't she with Lucy? They spend half the day together.'

'Chiara said Miss Lucy couldn't play today. She said she looked upset.' He paused and Domenico's stomach dipped. A finger of guilt slid across his neck as he remembered the pain he'd seen on Lucy's face when he'd confronted her.

After what they'd shared yesterday, and in light of what they'd *almost* shared, her anguish had been a knife to his gut. It made him feel like a jerk. Even though he was trying to protect his family, he'd been in the wrong.

Maybe because his anger wasn't about protecting his nephew but himself? Because he'd overreacted when he'd seen her correspondence as he'd felt his illusions shatter?

Lucy Knight got under his skin as no other woman. He'd lashed out because emotion had overridden his brain.

Certainty had become doubt. But was it because he wanted her for himself or because she was innocent? He circled again and again round the puzzling truths he'd discovered about her.

She had him so confounded he didn't know what to believe. He'd felt so betrayed this morning, discovering he couldn't rely on his instincts where she was concerned.

Then he'd read the letter and realised she'd told the truth. The magazine had taken a chance on finding her here.

He'd been boorish and in the wrong. The knowledge didn't sit well.

'Chiara didn't come in for lunch.' Rocco interrupted his troubled musings.

'That's not like her.' Domenico frowned, anxiety stirring.

'No. She hasn't been seen in any of her usual haunts for hours. I'm just about to search for her.'

'Where's Lucy?' Domenico shoved his chair back.

'She's already searching.'

Most of the staff was scouring the shoreline, though no one had voiced their deepest fears, that Chiara had got out of her depth in the water. Domenico strode along the path at the wilderness end of the island, knowing someone had to check the less obvious places. That was how he ran into Lucy. Literally. She catapulted around a curve in the track and into his arms.

Domenico grasped her close. The summer sun lit her hair to gold and he inhaled her sweet fragrance. Yesterday he'd imprinted her body on his memory and now he didn't want to let her go. Crazy at it seemed, it felt as if she belonged there against him.

'Please,' she gasped, her hand splaying against his chest. It trembled. 'Please, help me.'

'Lucy?' He tilted her head up. 'What is it?'

She was breathless, barely able to talk. Her cheeks were

flushed and there was dirt smeared across her cheek as if she'd fallen. Domenico tensed.

'Is it Chiara?'

She nodded. 'Up ahead.' She grabbed his shirt as he made to go. 'No! Wait.' She gulped in air and he forced himself to wait till she could speak.

'You'll be faster than me. We need rope and a torch. A medical kit too.'

'The well?' His heart plunged into a pool of icy fear.

'No. A sinkhole. I found her hair ribbon on the edge of it and some marbles.'

Domenico's breath stopped. If she'd been playing too close to the edge and then leaned in...

'I'll go and check it out.'

Lucy shook her head, her hands clutching like talons. 'No! I've done that. There's no sound from below. We need a rope to reach her. Every minute counts. Please, trust me on this.' He read her desperation.

He thought of the way she'd cared for Chiara as they played together, and her careful nurturing of Taddeo all those years ago.

He couldn't waste precious time. He had to trust her judgement. A second later he was gone, pounding down the dusty path to the villa.

When he returned, laden with supplies, Lucy had disappeared. He found her half a kilometre on, at the edge of the narrow hole. She was leaning down, talking. As he sprinted to her he realised she was telling a story about a brave princess called Chiara who was rescued in her hour of need.

'She's spoken to you?' He shrugged off the rope looped across his shoulder and put down the medical kit.

Lucy's face was solemn. 'No. But I thought if she comes to and hears a familiar voice she won't be so scared.' Her mouth was white-rimmed and she blinked hard. Domenico squeezed her shoulder.

'Thank you, Lucy. That's a great idea.' He wasn't sure he'd have thought of it.

'Where are the others?' She looked beyond him.

'Still at the shore. They'll be here soon. Chiara's grandmother will have got the message to them by now.' He looked around. 'I'll have to tie this to that old olive tree. You keep a look out while I'm down there.'

'No. I'll go.'

Domenico dropped to his knees and shone the torch down the hole but he couldn't see anything. His heart sank but he quickly uncoiled the rope.

'I said I'll go down.' As if he'd let her risk her neck down there. 'My property. My risk.'

'Have you seen the size of that hole? Your shoulders are too wide. You'll never fit.'

Domenico turned to scrutinise the sinkhole.

Damn! She was right. In his youth he'd done some caving but the squeezes had become difficult as he'd grown. This hole was so narrow he wasn't sure a grown woman could get down.

Nevertheless he opened his mouth to protest.

Lucy's fingers pressed his lips. He tasted dust and salt and the familiar sweet flavour of her skin. His nostrils filled with her scent. Despite the crisis his body tightened.

'Don't argue, Domenico. If I'd come out to play with her this morning this wouldn't have happened.'

'It's not your fault.' Already he was looping the rope around her, securing it firmly. 'You didn't do anything wrong.'

Deep blue eyes met his and a flash of something passed between them. Something that pounded through his chest and into his soul.

'Thank you, Domenico. But that's how it feels. Now, how do I lower myself?'

'Don't worry. I'll take care of it all.'

The next hour was pure nightmare for Lucy. She'd never been fond of small, dark places and being confined in a claustrophobically narrow hole evoked panicked memories of her first nights behind bars, when life had been an unreal horror.

She scraped off skin getting through the entrance but to her relief, the hole widened as she progressed.

Even better, she found Chiara conscious, though barely. Lucy's heart sped as she heard her whimper.

'It's all right, sweetie. You're safe.'

Nevertheless it took an age. First to undo the rope so Domenico could send down the medical kit. Then to assess Chiara's injuries—grazes, a nasty bump and a broken wrist. Then to bind her wrist and reassure her while she secured the thick rope around her.

Lucy wished she could go up and hold her close but there wasn't room for two. Finally, an age later, she tugged the rope so Domenico could lift Chiara free. Lucy bit her lip, hoping her assessment of minor injuries was right. They couldn't leave her here much longer; already she was shivering from shock and cold. Goodness knew how long it would take to get a medic from the mainland.

The shadows had lengthened and the sky clouded over by the time Lucy entrusted herself again to Domenico's strong arms. She was breathless with relief as he hauled her up to sit on the ground. A crowd of people was there, huddled around Chiara.

Lucy gulped lungfuls of sweet air, hardly daring believe she was on the surface again.

'How is she?' Her voice sounded rusty.

'She'll be fine, but she's going to the mainland for a check up.' The deep voice came from close by. Powerful arms pulled her higher then wrapped her close. A sense of belonging filled her, and sheer relief as she sank into Domenico's hold.

Weakness invaded her bones and Lucy let her head drop against his chest. Just while she collected herself. Her heart pounded out of sync as she breathed deep, absorbing the peace she found in his embrace.

How could it be? He'd berated and duped her. He'd raised

her up till she felt like a goddess in his arms, then reduced her almost to tears with cruel taunts.

Her body betrayed her. It never wanted to move again.

Dimly she became aware of noise and lifted her head to applause and cheers. They were all looking at her, smiling and clapping.

'Thank you, Lucy.' Rocco came forward and, turning her in Domenico's arms, kissed her on both cheeks. 'You saved our special girl.'

His mother came next, the friendly woman who'd been so kind to her, then a string of others, some she knew and some she didn't. One by one they embraced her and kissed her cheeks. And all the while Domenico supported her as if he knew her shaky legs couldn't keep her upright unaided.

Warmth stirred. A warmth Lucy hadn't known in what seemed a lifetime of cold, miserable isolation. It radiated out till her whole body tingled with it. Something deep inside splintered and fell away, like ice from a glacier. Its loss made her feel raw and vulnerable and yet closer to these welcoming people than she'd felt to anyone in years.

Finally they moved away, bustling around Chiara.

Lucy stayed in Domenico's arms, too exhausted, too stunned to move. A smile stretched her muscles yet she felt the hot track of tears down her cheeks. She didn't understand why she cried, but she couldn't seem to stop. A sob filled her chest then broke out, shocking her.

Domenico's arms tightened.

'It's all right, Lucy. We'll have you home soon.'

Home? Bitterness drenched her. She was the eternal outsider. She had no home, nowhere to belong. Then she stiffened. She had to get a grip.

Lucy blinked and saw Domenico looking down at her, no arrogance, no hauteur, no accusation on his face. There was an expression in his gleaming eyes that made another splinter of ice crack away. She shivered, realising how defenceless she was against him now.

'Thank you, Lucy, for saving Chiara.' He lifted his hand and wiped her cheek. She'd never seen him look more serious. 'You risked your life for her.'

Lucy shook her head. 'Anyone would have—'

'No! Not anyone. Lots wouldn't have dared. If it hadn't been for you I dread to think how long it would have been before we found her and got her out.'

His thumb swiped her cheek again, then rubbed across her lip. She tasted the subtle spice of Domenico's skin through the salt tang of tears.

'I was wrong about you.' His voice had lost its mellow richness. Instead she heard strain. 'You're not the woman I thought. What I said this morning… I apologise.' He drew a deep breath. 'Can you forgive me?'

Numb with shock, Lucy nodded.

Then sweet wonder filled her as he dipped his head. Their gazes meshed, their breaths mingled and something like joy swelled in her breast.

Domenico leaned in and kissed her gently, tenderly, with a reverence that filled her heart with delight and eased her wounded soul.

CHAPTER NINE

'OF COURSE TADDEO is welcome here as usual. Nothing will ever change that. He's my nephew and as precious to me as a son.'

Domenico thrust his hand through his hair in frustration as his sister-in-law squawked her outrage down the phone line. She was family and, for his nephew's sake especially, Domenico put up with her.

'Yes, Lucy's here. Far better she stays here away from the press than selling her story. Isn't that what you wanted?'

He eased the phone from his ear as Pia unleashed a torrent of objections. Mouth flattening, he strode to the wide terrace and inhaled deep of the fresh sea air. Pia had read about Domenico rescuing Lucy from the press and demanded to know why she was still with him.

As if he had to clear his actions with Pia!

He'd only got involved in this situation because Pia had pleaded for him to intervene.

Though this had passed well beyond a simple business negotiation. He was...personally involved.

He thought of his overwhelming relief when Lucy had emerged from that dark hole. For heart-stopping minutes panic had filled him as it seemed to take a lifetime to haul her up. Domenico tasted rusty fear, remembering.

He'd gathered her close and hadn't been able to release her even when her well-wishers crowded around. He'd needed her with him.

Domenico scrubbed a hand over his jaw. He and Lucy had unfinished business. Business he'd delayed. It had nothing to do with Sandro or Pia or the press.

'Calm down, Pia, and hear me out.'

Lucy heard Domenico as she entered the house. She stopped, not to eavesdrop but because he had that effect on her. She'd given up pretending. She might be weak where he was concerned but she refused to lie to herself.

The sound of that rich macchiato voice pooled heat deep in her body. The memory of his tender kiss, as if he treasured her, made forbidden hope unfurl.

'I understand your concerns, Pia, but she's not the woman the press have painted.'

Lucy started, realising Domenico was talking to his sister-in-law about *her*. She went rigid, torn between curiosity and protecting herself. Since the rescue it had been hard to keep him at arm's length. Yet she needed to because he could hurt her badly.

She was moving away when he spoke again.

'That was years ago, Pia. People change. *She's* changed. Did you get her letter?'

Lucy's steps faltered.

'You shouldn't have destroyed it. She wrote to say how much she regretted Sandro's death. She was genuine, Pia. I'm sure of that.'

Lucy's heart hammered against her ribs, her hand clenching on the door handle.

Domenico was standing up for her against his sister-in-law! She could scarcely believe it.

'I understand, Pia. But it's time we moved on. For Taddeo's sake.' He paused as if listening. 'We can't change the past, much as we wish it. I know Lucy wishes she could. She's genuinely sorry for what happened to Sandro.'

Lucy clung to the door handle as her knees wobbled.

'That's your choice, Pia. But think about what I've said.

Living in the present is the best thing for your son. He's a fine boy, one Sandro would have been proud of. You don't want him growing up bitter and fearful, do you?'

Domenico's voice dipped on his brother's name, reminding Lucy this was a private conversation.

She released the door and crossed the foyer. Confusion filled her but it didn't dim her smile and her step was light.

Domenico had stood up for her!

Sunlight filtered through spreading branches and Lucy leaned against her cushion with a sigh of contentment.

'More?' Domenico lifted a bunch of dark grapes with the bloom of the vineyard still on them.

'I couldn't.' She patted her stomach. 'I've eaten like a horse.'

His eyes followed the movement and fire licked her. She stiffened then forced herself to relax as his gaze grew intent. Domenico saw too much, especially now when her skill at hiding her feelings had disintegrated.

'I'll have some.' Chiara skipped across the clearing. The plaster on her wrist was the only reminder of last week's ordeal.

Lucy met Domenico's rueful gaze and realised they shared the same thought. She smiled, sharing the moment of relief, and he smiled back. It was like watching the sunrise after endless night, warming her with an inner glow.

Her breathing snagged then resumed, quicker and shorter as she watched his eyes darken. Her skin shivered as if responding to the phantom brush of his hand.

'Domi? Can't I have some?'

Domenico dragged his attention to Chiara. 'Of course, *bella*.' He handed over the bunch then leaned back on his arms. Lucy's heart pattered faster. If he shifted again they'd be touching.

Domenico hadn't touched her since Chiara's accident. That made her wonder if she'd imagined the strength of his embrace that day, or the way his hands had trembled as he held her. Her breath eased out in a sigh.

She'd never forget the magic of his kiss. Her fingers drifted to her mouth as she relived the brush of his lips.

It worried her how much she longed for him. How readily she responded now he treated her as a welcome guest. After hearing him defend her to Pia she hadn't been able to quell effervescent excitement, or the conviction that things had changed irrevocably between them.

She looked up to find his hooded eyes gleaming with heat. It arced between them, pulsing darts of sizzling awareness to her breasts, her belly and beyond.

Lucy shivered and his mouth curled in a lopsided smile that carved a long dimple down his lean cheek. She curled her fingers into the grass, fighting the impulse to reach out and touch.

'So, Lucy.' He paused, glancing across to where Chiara sat with the flowers she'd gathered. 'You approve of Italian picnics?'

'I *adore* Italian picnics.'

'You've only been on one.'

She shrugged and felt the soft breeze waft over her bare arms, the melting laxness in her bones. 'What's not to like? Sunshine and food fresh from the farm.' She gestured to the remains of home baked bread, bowls of ricotta and local honey, prosciutto, olives and a cornucopia of summer fruits. 'It's heaven. Almost as good as our picnics back home.'

His eyebrows slanted high. 'Almost?'

'Well, there's nothing like a sudden English rainstorm to liven up outdoor eating.'

He laughed, the deep rich sound curling round her. An answering smile hovered on Lucy's mouth.

Smiling had become second nature lately. Because she'd been made to feel she belonged. By Chiara's warm-hearted family and by Domenico. Gone was his judgemental frown, replaced by easy-going acceptance that banished so many shadows. He'd taken her snorkelling again, taught her to waterski and whiled away more hours than he needed to in her company, never once mentioning his brother or the story she might sell to the press. *As if he trusted her.*

Lucy could relax with him now.

No, that wasn't right. This tingling awareness wasn't relaxation. It was confidence and excitement and pleasure all rolled together.

Risky pleasure, when it lulled her into fantasy. When she found herself hoping the horrors of the past would vanish and leave them untroubled in this paradise.

A chill frisson snaked up her backbone.

It can't last.

One day soon the real world would intrude.

Lucy marvelled that Domenico had taken so much time out from what must be a heavy work schedule. He'd have business elsewhere. And she…she'd have to go too.

Regret lanced her and she twisted towards Chiara rather than let Domenico glimpse her pain.

Its intensity shocked her. It ripped through her, stealing the breath in her lungs.

Lucy pressed a hand to her chest.

'Are you okay?' Domenico moved abruptly as if sensing her discomfort.

'I'm fine.' This time her smile was a desperate lie. 'Just a little too much indulgence after all.'

Panic stirred. This wasn't just regret that the vacation was almost over. She'd known it would be tough trying to create a new life. She'd spent the last weeks facing the unpalatable facts of a future without family, friends, a job or anywhere to call home.

But the dread that made her skin break into a cold sweat owed nothing to that. It had everything to do with Domenico Volpe and what she'd begun to feel for him.

She felt…too much.

On a surge of frantic energy Lucy shot to her feet. Domenico was just as quick, his expression concerned as he broke his own unspoken rule and encircled her wrist with long fingers.

Instantly Lucy stilled, willing her pulse to slow.

'What is it, Lucy?'

'Nothing. I just wanted to move.'

Grey eyes searched her face and she held her breath, praying he couldn't read her thoughts. She could barely understand them herself. Amazing as it seemed, she *cared* for Domenico in a way that made the idea of leaving him send panic spurting through her.

'Liar.' To her addled brain the whisper sounded like a caress.

The stroke of his thumb against her wrist *was* a caress. She clamped her hand on his to stop it, looking down to see his dark golden fingers cradle her paler ones.

They held each other, fingers meshing. Strength throbbed through her. How could she give this up?

Because she must.

'You promised—'

'I promised not to revisit the past.' His breath was warm on her cheek. 'But this isn't about the past, is it, Lucy? This is about the present. Here. Now.'

Unable to stop herself, she turned her head and met his eyes. Molten heat poured through her as their gazes locked. The world receded, blocked out by the knowledge she read there, the awareness.

'I can't—' Words clogged in her throat.

'It's all right, Lucy. You don't have to do anything.'

'Domi? Lucy? What's wrong?'

Domenico looked down at Chiara and Lucy felt the sudden release of tension as if a band had snapped undone around her chest. She breathed deep, trying to find equilibrium. But Domenico still held her, his touch firm and possessive. A thrill of secret pleasure rippled through her.

'Everything's fine, little one. I've got a surprise for you both.'

The surprise was a trip to the mainland, to a town that climbed steep hills in a fantasy of pastel-washed houses. Lucy wished she had a camera. Everywhere she turned were amazing vistas and intriguing corners.

'Come on, you're so slow.' Chiara tugged her hand.

'I've never seen any place like this.' Lucy lifted her gaze past a tree heavy with huge golden lemons to the view of green hilltops above the town. 'It's beautiful.'

The little girl tilted her head. 'Isn't it pretty where you come from?'

Instantly Lucy had a vision of grey concrete and metal, of bare floors and inmates scarred by life. It seemed like a dream as she stood here in the mellow afternoon sunlight.

'Yes, it is pretty.' She thought of the village where she'd grown up. 'The bluebells grow so thick in spring it's like a carpet in the forest. Our house had roses around the door and the biggest swing you ever saw underneath a huge old tree in the garden.'

Summers had seemed endless then. Like this one. Except it had to end.

She'd have to forget trying to find a bookkeeping job. Instead she'd look for casual waitressing when she got to England. Something that didn't require character references.

'Come on.' Chiara tugged her hand again. 'Domi said we can have a *gelato* in the square.'

Lucy let herself be led back towards the centre of town. Domenico would have finished his errand for Chiara's *nonna*. He'd be waiting. Her heart gave a little jump that reminded her forcibly that it was time to leave for England.

Yet her smile lingered. For this afternoon she'd live in the moment. Surely she could afford to store up memories of one perfect afternoon before she faced the bleak future?

They were passing some shops, Chiara hopping on one leg then the other, when a shout yanked Lucy's head around.

'Look! It's her!'

A thin woman on the other side of the narrow street pointed straight at Lucy and Chiara.

'I *told* you it was her when they walked up the hill, but you didn't believe me. So I went in and got this. See?' She waved a magazine, drawing the attention not only of the man beside her, but of passers-by.

Lucy's heart sank. She took Chiara's hand. 'Come on, sweetie.'

But the woman moved faster, her voice rising.

'It's her I tell you. She's a killer. What's she doing with that girl? Someone should call the police.'

Nausea roiled in Lucy's belly as she forced herself to walk steadily, not break into a sprint. That would only frighten Chiara. Besides, fleeing would only incite the crowd. She remembered how a mob of inmates reacted when they sensed fear in a newcomer.

Skin prickling from the heat of so many avid stares, she tugged Chiara a little faster. Around them were murmurs from a gathering crowd.

The woman with the magazine came close but not close enough to stop their progress. But the malevolent curiosity on her sharp features spelled trouble. For a moment Lucy was tempted to snarl a threat to make her shrink back.

But she couldn't do it. She couldn't bear to regress to that hunted woman she'd been, half-savage with the need to escape, ready to lash out at anyone in her way.

It had only been a few weeks since her release but they'd altered her. She'd lost the dangerous edge that had been her protection in prison. Besides, what sort of example would that set? She squeezed Chiara's hand and kept walking.

'Why doesn't someone stop her?' the woman shrieked. 'She's a murderer. She shouldn't be allowed near an innocent child.'

Out of the corner of her eye, Lucy saw the picture in the magazine she waved like a banner. It was a close-up of Lucy getting into Domenico's limousine. The headline in blood-red said, 'Where Is Sandro's Killer Now?'.

Her heart leapt against her ribcage as fear battered her. The nightmare would never end, would it? Now Chiara was caught in it. She felt the child flinch as the woman screeched. Anger fired deep inside.

She stopped and turned, tugging Chiara protectively behind her.

The woman shrank back apace. 'Don't let her hurt me! Help!' Instantly others surged forward, curious.

'*Signora*—' Lucy dredged up a polite tone '—please don't shout. Can't you see you're frightening my friend? It would be much better for everyone if you didn't.'

The woman gawped, opening then closing her mouth. Then she hissed, 'Listen! She's threatening me.'

'Lucy?' Chiara's voice was unsteady, her eyes huge as Lucy turned to reassure her, stroking her hair and plastering what she hoped was a confident smile on her face. But inside she trembled. This was turning ugly.

'Grab her, someone. Can't you see she shouldn't be with that child?'

There was a murmur from the crowd and Lucy sensed movement towards her. She spun around to confront a sea of faces. Her stomach dived but she drew herself up straight.

'Touch me or my friend and you'll answer to the police.' She kept her tone calm by sheer willpower, her gaze scanning back and forth across the gathering.

The words were loud even over the mutterings of the crowd. And enough to hold them back…for now.

Domenico took in the defiant tilt of Lucy's head and her wide-planted feet, as if she stood ready to fight off an attack. But she couldn't fend them off. Her hands were behind her back, holding Chiara's.

She looked like a lioness defending her young.

A lioness outnumbered by hunters.

Something plunged through his chest, a sharp purging heat like iron hot from the forge. His hands curled into fists so tight they trembled with the force of his rage. He wanted to smash something. Preferably the shrewish face of the woman stirring the crowd.

He strode up behind Lucy.

She must have sensed movement for she swung round, her face pale.

Her eyes widened. She gulped, drawing attention to the tense muscles in her slender throat and the flat line of her mouth. She looked down, murmuring reassurance to Chiara, but not before he'd seen the fear in her eyes. Half an hour ago those eyes had danced with pleasure at the sight of the pretty town and its market stalls.

Naked fury misted his vision.

Domenico stalked the last pace towards her. In one swift movement he scooped up Chiara and cuddled her close. He looped his other arm around Lucy and pulled her to him. She was rigid as a board and he felt tension hum through her, an undercurrent of leashed energy.

'I don't know who you are,' he growled at the harridan in the thick of the crowd, 'but I'll thank you not to frighten my family.'

Beside him Lucy jerked then stilled. He heard her soft gasp and rubbed his palm up her arm. It was covered in goose bumps. *Damn him for leaving them alone!*

'But she's—'

'It doesn't matter who she is, *signora*. But I'll have your name.' His voice was lethal. 'I'll need it for my complaint to the police. For public nuisance and harassment.' He watched the woman wilt. 'Possibly incitement to violence.'

He turned and glared at the gathering, which had already thinned substantially.

'And the names of anyone else involved.'

He turned to Chiara, giving them time to digest that. 'Are you all right, *bella*?'

She nodded. 'But Lucy isn't. She was shaking.'

'It's all right, little one. I'm here now and Lucy will be fine.'

Domenico felt Lucy shudder and held her tighter, wishing

he had both arms free to hold her. Wishing he hadn't dispensed with security support today. He turned back to the street. Only a couple of people remained, watching wide-eyed. He heard the woman at the front whispering.

'He's the one in the magazine. The one whose—'

'*Basta!*' He scowled. 'One more word from you and I'm pressing charges.' He gave her a look he reserved for under-performing managers. A moment later, she and her companions had scuttled away.

'Right, girls.' He turned towards the main square, his arms tight around Chiara and Lucy, his tone as reassuring as he could make it over simmering fury. '*Gelato* time. I'm having lemon. How about you?'

CHAPTER TEN

LUCY SHOVED HER spare shoes into her bag. Just as well she didn't have much to pack. She'd be done in no time.

Then what? the little voice in the back of her head piped up. *Back to the town where you almost caused a riot simply walking down the street?*

She'd talk to Domenico—

No, not him.

She'd talk to Rocco. Surely a security expert could suggest how she could get away and lose herself in the crowds of a big city in England. Anonymity was all she asked. She had no hope of ever getting that in Italy. Not with the press hot on her trail.

Unless she gave in and sold her story.

Her stomach cramped at the idea of lowering herself like Sylvia, her stepmother. That betrayal cut deep. How could Sylvia have done it?

Lucy needed the money, now more than ever. But she needed her self-respect too.

She grabbed a shirt and slapped it on top of the shoes, fighting the hot prickle of tears.

What was happening to her? She hadn't cried in years, not till Chiara's accident. Now she wanted to curl up and blub out her self-pity. It was as if her defences had collapsed, leaving her prey to weakness she'd thought she'd conquered years before.

She looked at the winking lights of the mainland.

A few hours ago she'd been *happy*. Happier than she'd believed possible. The day had been glorious, the surroundings spectacular, and she'd basked in Domenico's approval and solicitude. She'd blossomed into a woman she barely recognised, who actually believed good things might come to pass. Who believed Domenico saw beyond the surface to the woman she was at heart, or was before the last years had scarred her.

She dragged a deep breath into constricted lungs.

He'd been kind, caring, fun. She'd enjoyed his company. More, she'd believed he'd enjoyed hers. And though he hadn't kissed her again, she'd felt the weight of it between them, a potent presence. A promise.

But there could never be more between them. She tried to tell herself he was softening her up to convince her to sign his contract. But she rejected the idea.

Why?

Because she'd fallen for him.

Her hands clenched so hard the nails bit crescents into her flesh.

Pathetic, wasn't she? As if he'd ever care for her.

Maybe those years in jail had warped her judgement—made her ready to succumb to the tiniest hint of caring. She was ready for passion and more, for tenderness, because they'd been denied her so long. That had to be the reason. How else could she explain the way she'd fallen for Domenico like a ripe plum?

She was doing the right thing, getting on with life. This time tomorrow she'd be in anonymous London.

'What do you think you're doing?'

His voice slid like a finger of dark arousal down her spine. Lucy trembled and clutched her clothes tight. Her heart pounded so hard it seemed in danger of bursting free.

'Packing.' She didn't turn. This was difficult enough already. Domenico made her weak in too many ways.

Her pulse thundered as she waited for his response. Maybe he'd turn and leave, glad to be rid of her.

When he spoke again he was so close his words wafted warm air on her neck. She shivered with longing.

'No, you're not.'

Lucy spun round, dropping clothes from nerveless fingers.

'I *beg* your pardon?' She drew herself up. 'Don't tell me what to do.'

But her defiance was hollow. Her heart wasn't in it. Especially when the sight of his arrogant, endearing, brooding features clamped a different sort of pain around her chest.

She yearned for him to pull her into his embrace as he had earlier and convince her that everything would be okay.

Except it wouldn't. Nothing could make this right.

'You're not the sort to run away when things get tough.'

Lucy's eyes widened at the compliment.

Or did he just see her as prison-tough and able to weather anything?

'Watch me!' She turned to her case but he grabbed her upper arm and hauled her round towards him.

Shock froze her. Some part of her brain rehearsed the quick, violent action that would make him break his hold, yet she made no move to free herself.

'You're not a coward.'

He was so close his words caressed her forehead. Unbidden, rills of pleasure trickled across sensitive nerve endings.

'This isn't just about me. What about Chiara? She got caught up in this.'

'You're using Chiara as an excuse.'

'Excuse?' Her voice rose to a screech as guilt and despair filled her. 'Don't you understand what happened back there?' She waved an arm towards the mainland. 'I've seen what a mob can do. I don't want Chiara or anyone else put in danger because of me.'

Lucy yanked her arm free and marched to the door, gesturing for him to leave. He followed, but only to stand before her, hands on hips and mouth stern.

'Our business isn't finished.'

'*Your* business, not mine!'

Cold washed through her as she realised that was what mattered to him. Signing that contract. Selling her soul and her chance to prove her innocence.

That was all she was. A problem to be sorted.

That was the only reason he'd been so nice to her. Nice enough for her to weave foolish dreams all over again.

Lucy thought she'd dredged the depths of despair but Domenico opened up a whole new chasm of it. She trembled on the brink of a vast void of anguish.

'I'm leaving.' Her words were clipped by welling emotion.

'You're going because you're scared.'

'Scared? Me?'

Her eyes rounded as he reached out one long arm and pushed the door shut with a decisive click.

'Oh, yes,' he purred in a low, menacing tone that made the hairs on her nape rise. 'You.' His face was implacable. Fear rippled through her.

Or was it excitement?

She stared, unable to break his gaze. What she saw unnerved her. Those hooded eyes were dark as a stormy sky, piercing as a dagger to the chest. She tried to fill her lungs and couldn't.

'*I'm* the menace to society, remember? People are scared of *me*.'

The bitter twist to her lips and the wretched, jarring note in her voice tore through Domenico's good intentions.

He pressed forward till she was flush against the wall.

Something wrenched in his gut at her retreat. He read her haunted expression, the jut of her chin and the shadows in her eyes.

Silently he cursed.

He refused to let her retreat into her shell again. She'd just let him discover the warm, vibrant woman behind the sassy attitude and touch-me-not air.

Briefly he thought of his family responsibility but nothing had the power to pull him back now. What was between Lucy and himself was every bit as important as his reverence for Sandro's memory.

'What have I got to be scared of?' It was pure bravado speaking but he heard the pain beneath. His heart clenched even as anger and anticipation surged.

'This.'

He took her jaw in his left hand, splayed his right on the wall beside her head and kissed her with all the force of his pent up fury and desire.

His senses convulsed in an explosion of pleasure. The sweet scent of her filled him, and her body against his was pure enticement. He swallowed her gasp of shock and heard it turn to a mewl of pleasure that revved his need higher. A shiver rippled through her and she arched against him, tearing away his last coherent thought.

He tasted her on his tongue, tart and sweet, like citrus and sugar syrup. Deeper he delved, needing more. Needing all she had.

The world tilted then righted itself as, with a groan of surrender, Lucy opened her mouth, luring him deep with the flick of her hungry tongue against his.

Instantly heat ignited in his groin. He pressed her to the wall, ravaging her mouth. Days of desperate longing had built need so deep one kiss couldn't satisfy. Domenico swept his hand down her arm and across to the swell of her breast. She stiffened, then desperate fingers threaded his hair, holding him to her as she kissed him with a passion that made his senses swim.

He squeezed her breast, rejoicing as its lush weight fitted his palm. His grip tightened and he wondered dimly if he should ease his hold but Lucy pressed closer, sending the last of his control spiralling into nothingness.

He was burning, fire instead of blood running in his arteries, hunger humming through each nerve and sinew.

Tearing fingers wrenched her shirt undone so he could tug her bra down beneath her breast. Her skin was silk and heat.

His hand shook as he toyed with her nipple and heard her gasp of surrender.

He wanted to feast on her breast, lave her nipple and watch her writhe in pleasure. But he didn't have the patience.

One touch had sparked the powder keg of desire he'd guarded so long. Bending his knees, he ground his hips against hers, rejoicing in the friction against the warm centre of her womanhood. Lightning filled the blackness behind his eyelids.

'More!' Lucy gasped against his mouth, her hands almost painful against his scalp as she strained higher against him.

In his arms she grew frantic, her breath coming in little hard pants as she pulled her mouth from his and nuzzled his collar aside to bite the curve between his neck and shoulder.

Domenico shuddered as a bolt of jagged fire transfixed him.

He rocked into her again and she lifted one leg, wrapping it around his thigh as she tried to climb him.

A man could only withstand so much.

Hands at her waist, he hoisted her high, satisfaction rising as she wrapped him in her thighs, locking her ankles hard as if closing a trap.

She had no need to trap him. He was only too eager. He surged, wedging her back against the wall. His skin was too tight to hold the rising tide of need.

Through slitted eyes he saw the flush of arousal on her cheeks, the long line of her throat as she tilted her head back and her pure alabaster breast, tipped a delicate rose pink.

He'd never seen anything so arousing in his life. Or so beautiful. For a heartbeat he stilled, drinking in the sight of her, tenderness vying with pure animal lust at the way she opened herself to him.

Then her hand brushed the straining zip of his trousers and his body's needs banished all else. Between them they fumbled his zip down. Somehow Domenico freed himself of his underwear, not even bothering to wrench his belt undone.

He let his palms slide up the smooth invitation of her thighs, rucking up her skirt as he went. Quickly he reached for her panties, meaning to haul them aside just enough, but he misjudged his grip. They tore and fell, leaving her completely open.

'Lucy.' His voice clogged deep in his throat but she heard because she opened heavy eyes. Her blue gaze was feverish and he couldn't mistake the desire he saw there.

Yes! *This* was what he wanted from her. Total abandonment. His blood sang with triumph.

With a last shred of sanity Domenico reached for his wallet. Was there a condom there? He wasn't into one-night stands but the habits of youth, or of caution were ingrained. Hopefully…

Lucy kissed him hard, her tongue swirling, drawing him towards oblivion as she tightened her legs. His erection surged, brushing soft hair and even softer skin.

Domenico's pulse drummed a rough staccato beat as they moved together in an age-old rhythm. Arousal escalated to breaking point. One hand at Lucy's breast, he clamped the other around her calf, loving the feel of her encompassing him.

With each slide of their bodies against each other combustible heat rose. She felt so *good*. So perfect against his needy erection. He tilted his hips, enjoying the way she shivered against his shaft. Once more then he'd reach for…

Lucy hoisted herself higher, and on the next slow surge Domenico found himself positioned perfectly. Too perfectly, he realised as he slid a fraction into tight, slick pleasure.

He gritted his teeth, moving his hands to her hips, ready to withdraw and keep them safe. All he had to do was summon the willpower to withstand temptation. It would only be for a moment and then—

Lucy moved against him again, but this time it was a jerky rock of the hips. Her legs clamped tight as a hoarse gasp of shock filled his ears. She shuddered around him. Her body convulsed and Domenico felt her muscles ripple, urging him on. His eyes snapped open and he caught her gaze as she came apart, wonder in her eyes.

Need destroyed thought. He reacted instinctively, thrusting

deep. For a teetering moment her body resisted, impossibly tight. So tight there could be only one reason for it. One that blew everything he'd heard about her out of the water. Stunned, he grappled to make sense of it.

Then coherent thought was obliterated as, with a sudden rush he was there at the heart of her, deep enough to feel the last of her shudders against his sensitive flesh.

The sensations were too much, especially with Lucy abandoned and delicious around him. With a cry of triumph he arched high and hard, pumping into her welcoming warmth.

Behind his closed eyes stars and planets whirled, whole constellations and galaxies burst into life and showered light in a dazzling, mind-blowing display. The ecstasy of release was so intense he wondered if he'd survive.

Through it all he felt Lucy's ragged breath on his face, her hands clutching as if she'd never release him.

When Lucy came to she was lying on the wide bed, under a sheet. She had no recollection of Domenico crossing the room and stripping the sheet back. She'd been dazed and disoriented by that cataclysmic orgasm. Remembering made her shiver, reawakening muscles she hadn't realised she possessed.

'Cold?' Domenico's voice rumbled from the other side of the bed.

She smiled slowly. Did she have the energy to speak?

'Lucy? Are you okay?' The strain in Domenico's voice puzzled her.

'Never better.' Her words slurred as if she'd been drinking. She felt marvellous. Wonderful. She sank into the feather pillow. This was utter bliss. Only one thing was missing. 'Hold me? Please?'

Silence.

'Domenico?'

'You should rest.'

Something in his voice made her drag her eyes open.

He stood on the far side of the bed, fully dressed, the picture of urbane sophistication but for the frown creasing his brow.

Gone was the out-of-control lover. This man didn't have so much as a hair out of place.

For the first time Lucy realised she was naked beneath the sheet. She vaguely recalled her buttons scattering as he'd tugged her shirt open. Her panties were history, a torn scrap on the floor somewhere. But the rest of her clothes? How could she not have noticed him undressing her?

Uneasily she shifted and felt moisture between her legs. Fire scorched her cheeks. She was wet from Domenico. Her belly clenched at the memory of him pumping into her. The power and stark beauty of what they'd shared overwhelmed her.

Looking at his closed face now, she saw Domenico didn't share her joy. He looked as if he'd just made the worst mistake of his life.

In a rush all her pleasure bled away.

'Good idea,' she murmured through frozen vocal cords. 'I think I'll rest.' She rolled away from him, wincing as tender muscles protested.

'Lucy?' His voice came closer. She shut her eyes. She'd never felt more vulnerable.

'Go away. I don't want to talk.'

The bed sank as he sat beside her, making her roll forwards. Putting out an arm to steady herself, she touched solid muscle beneath his cotton shirt. Instantly she dragged her hand back as if stung. She sucked in a shocked breath as skittering awareness filled her. How could that be when she was completely spent after that no-holds-barred loving?

Sex, she reminded herself. Domenico would call it sex. She refused to consider what she'd call it.

She thrust to the back of her mind the feelings she had for him. The ones that grew stronger daily. The ones that had burst into full bloom when he'd called her his family and hugged her in front of that crowd. He'd acted like a man who'd defend her no matter what it cost.

That one act had shattered the last of her fragile defences.

Her mouth trembled as she acknowledged how much he meant to her. How much his good opinion mattered.

This had nothing to do with her years of sexual abstinence and everything to do with Domenico the man.

'Lucy?' A light touch on her forehead stilled her heart. 'I'm sorry.'

'Sorry?' Her eyes popped open.

'What I did just then…'

'What *we* did.' That was the magic of it.

'I was stupid and selfish.'

'What?' She'd lost track of their conversation.

He leaned close and Lucy inhaled the addictive scent of him, layered with something warm and spicy. The scent of sex, she realised.

'I didn't use a condom.' His glittering eyes held hers as she processed what he said. 'There's no excuse for what I did. But believe me, it wasn't deliberate.'

How could she not have noticed? Not even spared a thought for her safety?

Biting her lip, she sat up, dragging the sheet with her. She thought she'd matured—no longer the naïve girl who'd made the mistake of letting a predatory male into her room. She'd prided herself on her ability to protect herself. Yet she'd had unprotected sex.

'If it's any help, I can tell you I have no infectious diseases.'

She nodded, avoiding his eyes. After what they'd shared it was stupid to feel embarrassed but she was. 'Me too.'

But that left the risk of pregnancy.

Her heart crashed against her ribs. Pregnant with Domenico's baby?

The complications would be enormous. The divided loyalties, the sheer impossibility of it. And yet… Lucy pressed her palm to her stomach. Was it even possible?

Wonder filled her and a niggling sensation that felt like hope. She'd always wanted children. Nothing had changed that, not even her stint in prison. If anything, that had consolidated her need for a family of her own now her dad was gone.

'You're not on the Pill, are you?'

The hope on his face soured her pleasure. 'No. Surprisingly, I wasn't planning on sex with the first man I met when I left prison.'

Except it was more than sex. It was liking, caring, and something she didn't want to name.

'If there's a baby—'

'Yes?' She felt herself freeze. Yet who could blame him for not wanting her to carry his child? Her heart dipped as she braced herself.

'If there's a baby you won't be alone.'

Her head jerked up and his silvery gaze snared her.

Did he have any idea how much his words meant? Imagine the scandal if she of all people bore his child! She'd half expected him to talk about a termination, not to reassure her.

She opened her mouth then found she couldn't speak. She nodded, dazzled by the warmth his words evoked. For the first time in ages she wasn't alone.

'I didn't hurt you?' His words were abrupt, scattering her thoughts.

Hurt her? He had to be kidding.

'I'm no china doll, you know.'

For a fleeting instant she thought she saw a smile, a masculine smirk of satisfaction quiver on his lips then disappear. She must have imagined it. When she reached out to touch him he shot to his feet as if scalded.

Lucy frowned, watching him pace across the room. He looked out of the window.

'But you were a virgin.' He ploughed his hands through his crisp dark hair. In a man so controlled it was a sign of major turmoil.

A presentiment of fear scudded through her.

Ridiculous! What was there to fear?

Yet why make such a big deal about her inexperience? It

hadn't stopped them. She'd wanted him and he'd wanted her and the result had been glorious.

'It doesn't matter, Domenico. Really.'

Her words made no difference. He held himself ramrod stiff, tension in every line of his body.

'It matters.' His tone was harsh.

He swung round, his expression shuttered, no sign of warmth. His eyes were steely, devoid of the connection she'd imagined there.

'I…' Her words trailed off as realisation smashed into her in a sickening blow. She pressed a hand to her belly. Her heart nosedived as her last meal surged upwards.

It couldn't be true. It couldn't!

She jack-knifed out of bed, yanking the sheet around her with shaking hands.

'Why does it matter, Domenico?' Her voice was a scratch of sound, barely audible over her pounding heart.

In vain she waited for him to assure her it didn't. That he was just concerned he hadn't hurt her.

He said nothing.

The shaking in her legs worsened.

She couldn't drag her eyes from his. Domenico's expression was impenetrable. He didn't want her reading his thoughts.

There could only be one reason for that. One reason why the knowledge of her virginity turned him to stone.

Her blood ran cold.

'You utter bastard!' She heaved in a shuddering breath. Only sheer willpower kept her on her feet. 'You wanted proof, didn't you? Proof that I was telling you the truth?' She pulled herself up as straight as she could despite the cramping pain in her stomach.

'That's what this was about! You couldn't let me leave without knowing once and for all if I lied when I said I wasn't your brother's lover or killer.' She drew a breath so sharp it sliced straight through her ribs. 'When I claimed in court to be a virgin.'

Lucy marched across the room on stiff legs, kicking aside the dragging sheet. He stood still as a graven image.

'You had sex with me to find out if I was innocent or guilty! Didn't you?'

She raised her hand and smacked him across the cheek with such force her hand smarted and her arm ached. But it was nothing to the raw, bleeding anguish of her lacerated heart.

CHAPTER ELEVEN

HE DESERVED THAT slap, and more.

Not because he'd had sex with Lucy as some test, but because of the hurt ravaging her features.

He'd known she was stretched to breaking point by what life had thrown at her. She'd confounded the odds and stayed strong despite everything. But he'd seen behind the bravado to the woman who'd faced down disenchantment, betrayal, injustice and pain. The woman who bled inside but would rather die than show it.

Her prickly defensiveness hid a vulnerability that had first intrigued but latterly worried him.

Now he'd added to her pain.

Because he couldn't keep his trousers zipped!

She spun around, the sheet flouncing as she made to stalk away.

His hand snapped out and imprisoned her wrist, jerking her to a stop.

'Let me go. Now!' She had her back to him but Domenico knew she spoke through gritted teeth.

'Not yet. Not till you've heard me out.'

'Heard you explain why it was necessary to get naked with me?' A shudder racked her. 'Oh, that's right. You didn't get naked, did you?' Her voice dripped sarcasm. 'That would be taking it too far, wouldn't it? Why go to so much effort when all you had to do was—'

'Basta!'

She whipped round to face him, her eyes burning like embers, her colour high. 'No! That's *not* enough. You can't silence me.'

'Not even to hear what I have to say?' God help him, but seeing her so passionate, so vibrant, he wanted her again. More urgently than before. Heat drenched him and his body hardened.

He wanted to smother her anger and her protests with his mouth, strip away that damned sheet and take her again and again till she was boneless and didn't have the strength to snark at him.

He wanted to conquer her even as he revelled in her strength and defiance.

Ma che cavolo! What she did to him! What had happened to his ordered, structured life, where sex was simple, satisfying and civilised?

He stepped in and saw her eyes widen. Something other than fury flickered in those blue depths. Disappointment? Pain?

His urgency deflated to manageable levels.

'I didn't have sex with you to check if you'd slept with Sandro.'

'As if I'd believe that now. You heard me say in court I wasn't your brother's lover. If you'd *believed* me it wouldn't have been a shock to you.'

Domenico swallowed. 'It's not that simple.'

'Not simple?' Her voice rose. 'Either you believed me or you didn't.'

He shook his head, for the first time he could remember, floundering.

How did he explain he'd compartmentalised his thoughts—separating his strengthening belief in Lucy's innocence from the harsh fact of Sandro's death? In his heart he'd been convinced Lucy wasn't the woman they'd all believed. Yet he hadn't followed through to formulate the alternative in his mind. He'd been too busy reacting to her to think logically.

He'd been too addled by lust and all the other wild emotions she dragged from him.

And too horrified at what he'd have to confront if she *was* innocent—the enormity of how he'd failed her.

'I knew you weren't the woman we'd thought. I knew you weren't totally guilty.'

'Totally guilty.' Her voice was flat. 'That's nice. So I was just a little guilty. Which bit? Maybe I didn't kill Sandro but slept with him for money? Is that what you thought?'

'No! Don't talk like that.' The idea of her and Sandro together had eaten like acid in his belly for too long. Even now when he knew the truth, Domenico couldn't stomach the idea of her with anyone else.

He might be bigger and stronger than her, he might hold her in an unbreakable grip, but she had him reeling.

'I wasn't thinking! All right?' Tension crackled along his spine, augmented by the hefty dose of guilt weighing his belly. 'I wasn't planning to prove anything except how good we'd be together. Satisfied?'

His belligerent tone concealed the fear he'd felt, watching her pack. The thought of her leaving had gutted him, forcing him into actions that weren't planned but driven by his soul-deep instinct not to let her go.

'No, you weren't thinking.' Her face was pale and set. 'If you had been you'd have realised my virginity—' she said the word as if swallowing something nasty '—isn't proof I'm not a killer. The court rejected my offer of a virginity test, remember?'

Fire branded her cheeks and Domenico swallowed hard, remembering the day in court when the relevance of her virginity had been debated back and forth. His stomach dropped. How hard it must have been for an eighteen-year-old innocent, with no one but an impersonal lawyer to support her.

'I'm sorry.' His touch gentled on her wrist. 'That must have been horrific.'

Lucy blinked and stared as if seeing him for the first time. 'It was like being violated while the world watched.'

He felt her skin prickle and smoothed his thumb over her wrist. Guilt soured his tongue and sliced through what was left of his self-respect. How had he got it all so wrong and let her suffer so?

'My inexperience doesn't prove I'm innocent.' She spoke softly now, as if the fire in her belly had died.

Domenico wanted to wrap her in his arms and haul her to him, but one false move would have her lashing out. His cheek still burned from that slap. Not that he cared about being hurt. What he cared about was not hurting her.

Hell of a rotten job he'd done so far.

'For all you know,' she went on, 'I was leading your brother on, like they said, holding out the promise of sex for jewellery and money. Whether I'd actually spread my legs for him doesn't matter.'

'Don't talk like that!' Domenico's voice was hoarse.

'Why not?' She tilted her jaw in challenge. 'It's what I did just now—'

'No. It's not.' She *couldn't* reduce what they'd shared to something so crude. It had been wild and out-of-control, but it had been anything but casual sex. It had been… Dammit, he didn't understand what it was, but he knew it was *something*.

Domenico grabbed her other hand, regardless of the sheet slithering to the floor between them.

Fifteen minutes ago he'd been unable to tear his gaze from her luscious naked form. Now, though his predictable body stirred, his gaze meshed with hers. She looked back with a hauteur that chilled him to the marrow. She was so furious he wondered if she even noticed the loss of the sheet.

He threaded his fingers through hers, entwining them together. 'What just happened wasn't like that.'

'What was it like then?' Her fine brows arched. 'When you didn't even believe me?'

'I believed.' Not coherently, not consciously, because he'd put such effort into hiding from what his instincts told him. He'd shied from connecting all the dots. Because if Lucy was innocent she'd suffered all these years because of a mistake and his family's need for justice.

Because he'd let himself be swayed by hurt pride into believing the worst when others claimed she'd seduced Sandro.

He'd taken the easy route and avoided confronting his doubts head-on. He'd found comfort in his cosy role of righteous brother.

He'd been too comfortable, too long.

Domenico had never thought himself a coward. Now, seeing how he'd wounded her, he knew himself less than the man he'd always believed himself. His stomach churned.

'Liar,' she whispered.

'I knew you weren't the woman the prosecution painted you.' He sounded desperate. 'I knew you were warm and caring, that your instincts are decent, not self-centred. Look at the way you saved Chiara. The way you faced down a mob to protect her rather than leave her and take to your heels.'

She shook her head. 'Not good enough.'

He knew it wasn't. Shame blistered him as he realised it was the best he could do. He should have been sure *sooner*.

He'd wanted to believe she was innocent. He'd wanted to think her fear of Sandro's old bodyguard pointed to him, not her, being responsible for Sandro's death. But Domenico hadn't made that final leap of faith. Even when he'd felt her virginal body welcoming him home the truth hadn't hit. He'd been completely absorbed in the heady pleasure of potent, white-hot sex more intense than anything he'd known. His own pleasure had ruled him.

It was only afterwards, watching her go limp in his arms that the enormity of what he knew about her struck.

It had fallen into place, everything he felt, knew and guessed about her.

Every instinct had been attuned to Lucy since she'd bent at his car door and stared at him in frozen horror. Fear of being disloyal to Sandro had stopped him seeing clearly. Or was he simply used to the world fitting his expectations? Had he grown so used to his rarefied world he couldn't see the truth before his eyes?

Heat seared his face.

Domenico gestured to the wall where the world had shuddered as they came together. 'I wasn't thinking about your virginity.' Desperation made him speak the unvarnished truth. 'All I could think about was being inside you, filling you till you screamed my name as you came. Filling you till I finally found my own release.' His lungs hurt as he dragged in air. 'Do you *know* how I've hungered for you?'

Her eyes widened as if his words shocked her. A trickle of heat circled in his belly at the idea of shocking her some more, with actions this time, not words.

It was strange how innocent she was in some ways while she was so tough and worldly in others.

'I didn't have some grand plan to seduce you.' He held her gaze, wondering if he had any hope of convincing her. 'It's you who's been seducing me all along.'

'I have not!' She jerked back in his hold. 'You make it sound like I connived—'

'You didn't have to. All you had to do was be yourself.' That was what had hooked him from the start. Her fascinating, richly layered character. Her strength and fiery independence and her warm-hearted generosity, especially with Chiara. Her courage, her pleasure in simple delights, her straight-down-the-line honesty. She was so uncompromising in her truthfulness that even now he found her a challenge. How had he ever believed her deceitful?

Because he'd wanted someone to suffer for Sandro's death.

Because in his grief and rage he'd been too ready to accept the image painted by the prosecution.

Because he'd been jealous of his brother.

'You're like those lawyers, making out I—'

Domenico tugged her to him so her naked body pressed against his. His senses jangled into overdrive.

Yet Lucy apparently felt none of the seductive friction between them. She held herself proud as a princess.

He fought to keep his mind on what mattered. 'What happened had nothing to do with the trial.' He searched her troubled gaze, frustration filling him when he couldn't read her thoughts. 'You have to believe me.'

'I don't have to do anything.'

That was the hell of it.

He had no right to expect anything, especially after what had been done to her in the name of justice. Yet he wanted her, still, again, more than before.

Any minute now she could wash her hands of him and leave. Who would blame her?

He gathered her closer, one hand shackling her wrist and the other encircling her bare back. Heroically he strove to ignore the silken invitation of her nakedness. He was torn between so many conflicting emotions.

'I know you didn't kill Sandro, Lucy.'

He felt the almighty tremor race through her at his words, saw her eyes pop wide as she stared up at him.

'You can't know it.' She shook her head emphatically, distrust in her gaze. 'You have no new proof. Nothing. I told you, the fact that I didn't sleep with Sandro—'

'I understand.' He released her hand and lifted his fingers to her cheek, hesitating a moment before sliding his fingers into her hair. 'Technically it doesn't prove your innocence.'

But he knew in his gut, with every instinct, that she was innocent. Finding that she was a virgin had simply been the shock that made the pieces fit together.

No wonder he'd been plagued by doubts. Nothing about the woman he'd come to know fitted with the woman the prosecution had portrayed in court.

'I won't ask you to forgive me for doubting you so long.' That would be asking too much. 'But you must know I'm sorry for what happened. More sorry than I can say.'

He recalled how she'd watched him in court, waiting for him

to go to her. And he, blind fool, had been so wrapped up in prejudice and hurt pride, he'd spurned her instead of listening to his instincts. Even though an extramarital affair was out of character for Sandro, Domenico had believed it because Lucy had knocked him off his feet and he was scared by the conflicting emotions she aroused. In his neat world, no woman had the power to unsettle him.

'And I'm going to prove you didn't kill Sandro.' That wouldn't erase the last five years, but he owed her.

He read something that might have been wonder in her face. Hope dawned on her fine features. Her lips trembled and she swallowed hard. His throat dried as he saw her struggle with emotion.

How alone she'd been, with no one on her side. She deserved better.

Then she blinked and her mask of indifference dropped into place. The one she used to keep the world, and him, at bay. The one he was beginning to hate. He wanted to strip it away and smash it, so she couldn't hide from him any longer.

His pulse drummed at the intensity of what he felt.

He was so caught up in his thoughts he didn't move to stop her when she backed away, scooping up the sheet and wrapping it tight around her.

He tried not to notice the way the cotton moulded her ripe breasts and pebbled nipples. Impossibly, the flimsy cover only made him more aware of her delectable body beneath.

'Why would you try to prove my innocence?' Suspicion filled her voice and he was struck anew by how hard it was for her to trust.

'Because of the wrong done you.' Wasn't it obvious?

'That's not your problem.'

Domenico frowned. Didn't she want his help?

It didn't matter; she was getting it whether her pride revolted at the idea or not.

'I should have questioned earlier. Instead an injustice has

been done in the name of my family. To ignore that would be cowardly. Not to act would bring shame on my family and me. I owe you.'

Lucy looked up into that dark, proud face, honed by a centuries-old aristocratic gene pool and the assurance born of success, wealth and privilege.

Despite the intimacies they'd just shared—maybe because of them, with him smartly dressed and her naked beneath a sheet—she felt the yawning chasm between them more than ever.

He spoke of family honour as if that was all that mattered.

Her heart dived. She'd thought for a moment his concern was for *her*. Instead it was for the precious Volpe name. She knew how devoted he was to it after he'd gone to such lengths to preserve it. He'd even brought her from prison to his home.

He hadn't done it for her. It was for his family.

She'd been right. He'd had sex. He hadn't made love.

'I'm not interested in preserving your family's honour.'

His eyes narrowed to glittering slits. 'This is about clearing *your* name. Rehabilitating you in the eyes of the world.'

Despite all logic, hope leapt in her chest. But only for an instant.

'That's something even you can't do.' If she'd had evidence to prove her innocence she'd have used it.

His head reared back as he folded his arms over his broad chest, the epitome of male confidence. 'Watch me.'

He spoke with the assurance of a man who took on disastrous financial markets and won. Who'd built an empire against all known trends. Who succeeded where so many others crashed and burned. A man who never failed.

But he'd learn as she had. The task was impossible. She'd hoped to clear her name but she'd accepted now she couldn't.

'Good luck with that, Domenico. But I don't care to stay around and watch you fail.'

Fire sizzled in those slitted eyes. Anger or challenge?

He paced towards her and to her horror Lucy found herself retreating.

'One way or another we're going to reintroduce you to society. You will *not* be on the run from troublemakers like that harridan this afternoon.' She opened her mouth to protest but he kept right on talking. 'If it's humanly possible, I'll find a way to overturn the court's ruling.'

Lucy wrapped her arms around herself, torn between wanting to believe he meant it and worry that he did. She didn't have the strength to keep fighting, much less go through another bout with the criminal justice system. The thought of it made her flesh crawl.

'You're not going anywhere, Lucy, till we've made this right.'

That's what he was good at, wasn't it? Fixing things, overcoming obstacles. Look at the way he'd risen to the challenge of keeping her from selling her story.

Only now he saw it as family duty to rectify the wrong done in their name. He'd do what he could to put things right because honour demanded it and then... What?

He'd walk away.

Better to make the break now, while she could. For no matter how she tried to deny it, her emotions were engaged. What she felt for Domenico petrified her.

'You haven't thought this through.' She wrapped the sheet more securely and walked to the bed where her case now rested on the floor. She lifted it onto the bed. 'Any scheme to "rehabilitate" me will attract press attention. The media circus would get worse and your family privacy would be a thing of the past.'

Guilt or no guilt, that would make him leave her alone. In a contest between family and the woman he'd lusted for briefly, family would win every time.

She bit her lip and reached for a shirt to put in the case. To her horror, her hand shook visibly.

A long arm reached around her and took the shirt from her

grasp. He stood so close behind her she felt the blazing heat of his body warm her. Lucy stiffened.

'I don't care.' His words brushed her nape and shivered around her. 'I have to do this, Lucy. Don't you understand? Everything has changed.'

She stood transfixed as his words sank in.

How she wanted them to be true.

His hand wrapped around hers but this time his touch was infinitely gentle. Slowly he turned her towards him. For the life of her, Lucy couldn't resist.

When he demanded, she could stand up to him. But his tenderness? It undid her.

'Nothing has changed. Don't you see?' Her chest was too tight as she looked into eyes the colour of soft mist in the morning. 'I've lived with this. I *know*.'

'Cara.' The simple endearment stole her breath, or maybe it was the way he looked at her. As if he saw only *her*, not some debt of honour. 'You have to trust me, at least for a little longer.'

'I—' His thumb brushed her bottom lip as he cradled her jaw, the heat of his hand pure comfort after the inner chill she'd battled so long. It made her forget that she no longer knew how to trust.

'Let me help you, Lucy. Let me try to make amends.' He leaned forward till his mouth almost brushed her cheek. Her eyelids grew heavy as that riot of sensations started up inside. 'Please?'

The rich timbre of his voice detonated explosions of delight across her senses. Her head swam.

Domenico leaned closer, his lips brushing hers with a tenderness that almost undid her. Lucy's heart pounded and she jerked her head back.

'Don't do that!' If only she sounded as if she meant it. 'I don't want you to kiss me.' She shoved her palm against his chest but that only brought her in contact with his muscled heat.

'Liar,' he whispered in her ear, sending sensual pleasure

spiralling through her. His mouth grazed her cheek, then his lips were at the corner of her mouth.

'I said no!' With a supreme effort she pulled out of his hold to stand, panting with exertion as if she'd run a marathon. That was how strong the sensual current of awareness she fought. 'You don't have to seduce me, remember? You already know all about my sexual experience. You've got nothing else to prove.'

Meeting his eyes was one of the most difficult things she'd done. Lucy felt stripped bare, the memory of her passion, her complete sexual abandon, glaringly proclaiming her weakness for him.

'You have no idea, do you, *cara*?' He shook his head, his mouth a grim line. 'This isn't about proving anything, except how much I want you. How perfect we are together.'

In a sudden, shocking movement, he tugged his shirt free of his trousers, pulling it over his head and away.

Lucy's throat narrowed and the air hissed from her lungs as she surveyed his chest—a dusting of dark hair over golden skin, a torso full of the fascinating dips and bulges that proclaimed his body's muscled power.

'I want you, Lucy. The same way you want me.' He kicked off his shoes and bent to strip away his socks before she could formulate a reply.

She stepped back, horrified, as her resistance crumbled at those simple words. Was that all it took to make her putty in his hands? The backs of her legs hit the mattress. Dazed, she thought of escape, but couldn't summon the energy to try.

Or maybe she didn't want to. The memory of ecstasy held her still.

As she watched, he made short work of his belt and zip, only pausing to retrieve his wallet before letting his clothes drop to the floor.

She'd seen him in bathers, with water plastering the fabric to his strong thighs and taut backside. But she'd never seen him naked. She wanted to reach out and trace the lines of his body. She wanted…

Domenico let the wallet drop and tossed a foil packet onto the bedside table. The sight of it made her skin prickle and heat swirl deep in her womb. He swept her bag off the bed and, dazed, she saw her belongings scatter across the floor.

She couldn't believe she stood, unmoving, waiting for his touch.

Except it was what she wanted—Domenico's passion and warmth. She craved the sense of being linked not just bodily but soul to soul. It almost didn't matter that it was an illusion. What he did to her was magic and, despite every argument common sense mustered, she couldn't turn her back on it. On him.

Not yet.

'Carissima.'

He took her in his arms as if she were fragile gossamer. Only the glitter in his eyes and the tremor in his touch revealed how hard it was for him to take his time.

Yet take his time he did, learning her body with a thoroughness that made her squirm in ecstasy and increasing desperation. Along the way she discovered some of his weaknesses. When she trailed her fingertips across his hip and down to his groin he sucked in his breath. When she nipped at his throat he groaned aloud and when she took his shaft in her hand he rolled her onto her back and pinioned her with the full weight of his body. She revelled in the sense of his powerful frame blanketing her.

'Do that again and this will be over in seconds,' he growled.

'Don't treat me like a piece of porcelain.' She stared up into stormy eyes, loving that she'd made him lose his cool. 'I want you. Now.'

Domenico's sudden feral smile should have scared her. Instead, fire licked her veins. She wriggled, her thighs opening wider, and he sank onto her.

His smile faded and her breath hitched.

What followed was testament to Domenico's iron control and sexual prowess. He brought her to not one but several peaks of ecstasy, till she thought she'd die from the force of the pleasure pounding through her.

Then at last he joined her, reaching his climax just as Lucy's world shattered in a whirling kaleidoscope of fractured colours and pleasure-drenched senses that surely would never recover from the onslaught.

For the longest time they clung together, hearts pounding in sync, gasps mingling and bodies so entwined it seemed they were one entity.

Lucy never wanted it to end. She never wanted to let him go.

She squeezed her eyes shut, imprinting the moment on her memory, knowing this couldn't last.

Finally, mumbling about being too heavy, Domenico rolled away. Instantly cold invaded her body. Even when he hauled her close, his arm around her and her head pressed to his thundering heart, she couldn't recapture that moment of perfect communion.

Lucy reminded herself that sexual pleasure was fleeting. The sense of let-down was natural.

But it was more than that.

She listened to Domenico's breathing slow, felt his heart beneath her cheek return to its normal beat. But even when her pulse slowed too, she felt anything but normal.

That was what petrified her.

She'd lost part of herself to Domenico Volpe. A part she could never get back.

CHAPTER TWELVE

'I STILL THINK this is a huge mistake.' Lucy stood in the vast dressing room of Domenico's master suite in the Roman palazzo, staring at the plastic-draped clothes lining one wall.

Exquisite designer clothes. All for her.

She clasped her hands as nerves snaked through her. This wasn't just a mistake, it was looming catastrophe.

'How could you even *think* this would help?'

'Because attack is the best form of defence, didn't you know?' Domenico's voice came from the adjoining bathroom. She gritted her teeth at his casual tone.

Didn't he know how much she risked, being seen in public with him?

Of course he did. When this backfired it would smear his name as much as hers. The thought made bile churn and she pressed her hand to her stomach.

She had to find calm.

Calm! The last three weeks had been anything but calm.

Lucy fought down the pleasure that always hovered at the memory of Domenico's loving. Anyone would think they'd be sated now, worn out by the amount of time they'd spent naked together.

Instead she felt energised. When she was with him she almost believed she could take on the world. Especially as she'd decided to make the most of each precious moment.

This interlude couldn't last. When he'd done his best to

clear her name they'd go their separate ways. If she'd learnt anything in scouring the press reports it was that he moved in a world far beyond hers. One that collided with hers only due to the circumstances of Sandro's death.

Domenico favoured elegant brunettes who fitted that world as she never could. Socialites and celebrities who took luxury as their due.

Lucy had no illusions. She was a novelty, a wrong to be righted. Domenico felt only lust, guilt and a determination to do right. Tellingly, he never spoke of a future for them beyond that.

When he failed, as inevitably he would, he'd turn to some gorgeous woman from his own rarefied world and Lucy would go far away to start again. All she'd have was memories.

Pain seared, banishing her nerves.

Who knew how long she had with Domenico? Tonight could be the beginning of the end.

Lucy tried to tell herself it had been worth it, these weeks of indulgent delight. She'd made her choice and settled for fleeting joy. She was strong and aware of the consequences. She simply chose to enjoy pleasure while it lasted, rather than wallow in self-pity.

Time for that later.

There could be no future for them, even if she did...*care* for Domenico.

Lucy grimaced at the way she avoided even thinking the alternative word.

What choice did she have? Domenico might be a wonderful lover, passionate and heart-stoppingly demanding. He might be single-minded in pursuing proof of her innocence, but that was guilt at work and his obsessive drive to make things right.

He might be tender with her but only in the way a man treated his current temporary lover. He never spoke of *them*, or of the future, only of clearing her name. He felt guilty because he hadn't trusted her all those years ago.

Domenico was a decent man, a good man, despite his arrogant certainty that the world would bow to his will, but there was no chance he could ever love her.

'Still not dressed?'

Lucy whipped around to find him leaning against the door-jamb, resplendent in a dinner jacket, his fresh-shaved jaw pure temptation to a woman who couldn't get enough of him.

She curled her fingers into fists and looked away, ignoring the inevitable jangle of awareness that cascaded through her.

'I still think this is nonsensical. What will it achieve, being seen in Rome with me? Nothing but more scandal.'

'What it will achieve—' he crossed to stand beside her '—is to prove I'm proud to be with you. That the past is the past. That's a first step.' He dragged a finger across the sensitive skin beneath her ear and she shivered.

'But it will do no good, don't you see?' She looked up at him. 'There'll be a rash of stories about me moving from one brother to the other.' She swallowed hard, trying to rid herself of the bitterness on her tongue.

'Ah, but there'll be far more revealed, just you wait and see. Soon things will seem a lot brighter.' He looked suspiciously pleased with himself.

'What do you know? Is there something?' She couldn't help the surge of hope that dawned.

'Soon, *tesoro*. I promise you, soon this will all be over.'

Logic told her there could be no proof unless Bruno confessed. But Bruno Scarlatti had been happy to let her bear his punishment. That wouldn't change.

Besides, Domenico was right. If by some miracle he did prove her innocence all this would be over. Not just the public burden of guilt, but their time together.

He stroked her again, lingering where the neckline of her T-shirt dipped. His eyes turned smoky dark and Lucy's pulse accelerated. One fleeting touch and she wanted so much more!

It was the knowledge of her neediness that gave her strength to step back.

'You don't trust me with your news?'

The sexy smile curving his mouth died. 'It's not that. I need to have it confirmed. It should be soon.' He paused, raking her face as if searching for something. 'But there is *some* definite news. As soon as you're ready we'll go downstairs and you'll hear all about it.'

'Why don't you tell me now? It's my name you're trying to clear, damn it!' She jammed her hands on her hips. She wasn't used to standing back and relying on others. It made her uneasy.

Domenico leaned in, the glint in his eyes pure devilment.

'Because I know, *cara*, that if I don't give you a reason to get changed and come downstairs, we'll have another argument about you accepting my charity.' He waved a hand towards the wardrobe stuffed full of expensive clothes. 'But now you know the only way to discover what I've found out is to do what I want…'

His smile was all arrogant male satisfaction. Exasperation filled her.

Lucy pressed her hand to his dinner jacket, feeling the steady beat of his heart. She let her fingers slide down the lapel, her fingers brushing his shirt. His muscles contracted beneath her touch.

She let a knowing smile play on her lips. The sort of smile she'd learned from *him*. It hid her skittering fear. Fear that she wanted too much from him.

'I wouldn't say it's the only way I could find out.' Her voice dropped to a husky note as she rose on tiptoe and pressed her lips to a point at the corner of his jaw.

He couldn't hide the way his muscles clenched tight, or the slight hitch to his breathing.

'Witch!' He stepped back, putting space between them.

'Coward,' she purred, pleased more than she should be. Sexually, there was no denying her power over him.

'A wise man knows when to retreat. I'll wait downstairs.' He made for the door then turned, his mouth curling in a piratical smile that turned her knees to jelly. 'But there'll be a reckoning later, *cara*. You can be sure of that.'

* * *

Domenico looked up at the sound of heels tapping on the travertine floor. He moved to the door of the drawing room, only to stumble to a halt.

Shock slammed into him. Shock and what felt remarkably like awe.

He knew every inch of Lucy's delectable body, each dip and curve and enticing hollow. Her face was the last thing he saw at night and the first thing he saw in the morning.

And yet she had the power to stun him.

Per la madonna!

A fine sweat broke out on his brow and heat misted his vision.

He thought he'd known, but he'd had no idea!

A vision stalked towards him in killer heels that made her hips sway in an undulating rhythm that took his pulse and tossed it into overdrive. A full-length gown in glittering gold clung like sin. It scooped low from tiny jewelled shoulder straps to skim the upper swell of her high breasts. The skirt accentuated the long, delicious curve of hip and thigh, hugging close before swirling out around her ankles.

Domenico hitched a finger inside his collar to loosen its suddenly constricting pressure.

'Lucy.' The word was a croak of shock. 'You look…' words failed him '…beautiful.'

More than beautiful. She was luminous. Her eyes were bigger than ever, her lips a glistening, tinted promise of pleasure to come.

He wanted to haul her back to bed.

What was he thinking, planning to show her off to the hungry wolves of Roman society? What madness possessed him?

'I told you it was too much.' She gestured to the dress as she stopped before him and he read the doubt in her eyes.

How could she doubt for a moment how fabulous she looked?

But he'd learned the woman behind the bravado was full

of surprises. His chest tightened at the lack of confidence her words revealed. Only now was he beginning to understand how imprisonment had scarred her.

His belly hollowed with guilt.

How could he ever make it up to her?

Domenico reached out and took her cold hand, raising it to his lips as he held her gaze. He turned her hand and pressed a kiss to the soft underside of her wrist, then another, and was rewarded by her shiver of pleasure. Colour tinged her cheeks and her eyes turned slumberous.

'You look perfect,' he murmured in her ear. 'The most beautiful woman in Rome.'

And even now she might be carrying his child.

He'd relegated the idea to the back of his mind, but seeing her so beautiful yet vulnerable loosened the guard he placed on his thoughts.

A surge of protectiveness filled him.

He forced himself to step back.

Looking into her stunned face, Domenico had an unsettling feeling he'd strayed out of his depth. He'd never experienced anything like it.

He thought he'd known what he was getting into but at each turn Lucy confounded him. Uneasily he banished the suspicion that he, not she, was the one who needed help.

'Come, there's someone here to see you.' He hooked her hand through his and covered her fingers. 'And remember, I'm with you.'

His hand closed around hers in a gesture of reassurance.

She couldn't drag her gaze from his. For the first time ever she felt truly beautiful, because of the admiration in his eyes.

Domenico ushered her into the spacious sitting room. Walking in breakneck heels was much easier with his support. She could get used to—

Lucy stumbled mid-step, her hand clawing his arm. Her spine set as she fought a primitive instinct to flee.

How could he have done this to her?

'You remember my sister-in-law, Pia.' His voice was smooth, his manner urbane, as if he hadn't just introduced the woman who'd once screamed abuse at her for killing her husband.

Lucy swayed. Her knees weakened and she feared she'd crumple till Domenico wrapped an arm around her.

His hold was all that kept her upright.

Pia was pale and perfect, from her expertly cut dark hair to her exquisite designer shoes. Huge dark eyes surveyed her as if trying to read her soul. Slowly she crossed the room.

Lucy tried to drag in air. She couldn't breathe. Maybe the oxygen had been sucked from the room by the intensity of Pia's stare.

The other woman raised her hand and Lucy flinched.

It took a lifetime to recognise the gesture. A handshake? From Pia Volpe?

Hysterical laughter rose and Lucy bit her lip to stop it bursting out. She shook her head in disbelief.

'You won't shake my hand?' The other woman's face was tight as she shot a look at Domenico. 'I told you, didn't I?'

'Don't be hasty, Pia. Lucy's surprised. She didn't know you were here.'

Because if she'd known she'd never have agreed to come!

Lucy couldn't look away from the face of the woman before her. 'What's going on?' Her words were a rough whisper but at least her larynx worked.

'Come and sit down.' He urged them towards a group of leather sofas. 'There's no need for formality.'

Again that inappropriate gurgle of laughter threatened. He thought they could be casual? She and the woman who blamed her for her husband's death?

Yet she found her legs moving stiffly. A moment later she plopped onto a sofa as her knees gave way. Domenico held her, his body crammed close. If she had the energy she'd elbow him away, but she was hollow with shock.

Pia subsided gracefully into an armchair. She didn't look happy.

'Pia, perhaps you'd explain why you're here?' Domenico's voice was smooth but held a note of steel. Lucy watched Pia shift and realised it hadn't been her idea to come here.

What was going on?

'I came to…' The brunette darted a look at Domenico then turned to Lucy. Her fingers went to her throat in a nervous gesture. 'To apologise.'

Lucy's breath stopped but her heart pounded on. She opened her mouth to speak but nothing came out.

Pia crossed her legs then uncrossed them, clearly ill at ease.

'I don't understand,' Lucy croaked.

'Domenico told me what he'd found out.'

Lucy jerked in shock, her head swinging round to Domenico. He *couldn't* have told her, could he? Fire scorched her face at the idea of him informing Pia she'd been a virgin.

As if reading her thoughts he shook his head. 'Not that,' he whispered. His hand closed on hers but she shook it off.

'He explained there was new evidence,' the other woman went on, 'about Bruno being the guilty one.'

Lucy darted a look at Domenico but his face was inscrutable.

'I never liked him, you know,' Pia said. 'He was always a bit too smooth. But I never thought…' She shook her head. 'You must believe me, Signorina Knight. I didn't know he lied. All I knew was Sandro was in your room, with you cradling his head, and he was dead.' She sobbed and lifted a handkerchief to her eyes.

'It's all right, Pia. Lucy understands you didn't know the truth.' Domenico's hand touched Lucy's again and this time she was too distracted to move it.

'Of course,' she said, trying to digest this news.

What new evidence?

'You understand?' Pia looked up through tear-glazed eyes.

Lucy nodded. 'I didn't know what Bruno was really like either. If I had I'd never have let him into my room.' She shuddered, thinking how gullible she'd been.

Domenico squeezed her shoulders and she had no desire to shake him off.

Pia's hand went again to her throat. 'It was a shock when Domenico told me the truth.' Her mouth curled in a trembling smile as she looked at her brother-in-law. 'You gave Sandro back to me with your news. You have no idea what that means after all this time.'

'It took me too long.' Domenico's voice was grim. 'I should have thought of it years before.'

Lucy looked from one to the other, curiosity mounting. 'Thought of what?'

The other woman turned to her. 'My jewellery, of course.' Her eyes widened. 'Domenico, you didn't tell her?'

'No one has told me anything.' Frustration rose. Everyone knew more than her!

'I thought Lucy would appreciate hearing it from you,' he said.

Lucy bit down a demand for someone, anyone, to tell her what was going on.

'Domenico found the artisan who made my jewellery.' Pia extended her arm. On her wrist was a bracelet of enamelled flowers, exquisitely executed and interspersed with lustrous pearls.

Lucy leaned forward, identifying primroses and forget-me-nots in a design she'd never expected to see again. Her stomach clamped down as icy fingers danced on her spine. Nausea rose and she breathed hard through her mouth, forcing it down.

Abruptly she sat back, shutting her eyes in an effort to regain control.

When she opened them she saw Pia's hand caressing the matching necklace at her throat. Lucy had been so preoccupied she hadn't recognised it.

'That was the necklace they found in my room.' Lucy's voice was hoarse. Stupid to be so affected but it brought back that night in too-vivid detail. More, it evoked memories of how it had been used against her in the trial. 'I didn't know there was a bracelet too.'

'Nor did I,' Pia said, smiling as she looked at her brother-in-law.

Lucy turned in his hold. Domenico's eyes were fixed on her with an intensity that banished the cold prickling her backbone. 'You knew there was a bracelet?' Why was that important? She still didn't see.

'No, I just tried to track down the maker. I was desperate for any leads that might give me a better picture of what happened back then.' His hand tightened on hers.

Her heart dipped. He'd tracked the maker down because he'd sought the impossible—something to prove she wasn't a killer.

'The police were only interested in the fact you had the necklace, not where it was made.'

'Because everyone assumed he'd bought it for me.' Lucy shivered, remembering how the prosecution had made so much about the match between the enamelled flowers and the colour of her eyes. Plus the fact that, beautiful as the piece was, it was nothing like the glittering emeralds and rubies Sandro had previously given his wife. The implication was that he'd got something expensive for his new lover, but nothing to rival the grandeur of the jewels he'd bought his wife.

'But they were wrong. See?' Pia undid the bracelet and held it out.

Lucy couldn't bring herself to touch it. Instead Domenico took it and laid it across his broad palm, revealing the engraved lettering on the back: *To my beloved Pia, light of my life. Always, Sandro.*

'I don't understand.' Lucy's head whirled.

Domenico passed the bracelet back.

'Sandro had commissioned a matching set but only had the necklace the night he was killed. According to the maker, when he came to collect them he decided to have the inscription engraved on the bracelet, but he didn't want to wait to give the necklace to Pia. He took it and said he'd be back for the second piece. When he didn't return and the artisan discovered he'd died, he didn't know what to do with the bracelet. He had no idea of its significance to the case. He thought of removing the inscription and selling it on, but was superstitious enough to think it might bring bad luck.'

'Why didn't your brother wait for both pieces?'

'Because of me.' It was Pia who spoke. The glow of happiness dimmed and her features were sharp with pain.

'I wasn't...well.' Her eyes met Lucy's before shifting away. 'I didn't know at the time. It wasn't till after that night, much later, that Domenico arranged for me to get help.' She swallowed and Lucy felt sympathy surge for the other woman's obvious pain.

'I...' Pia paused and dragged in a deep breath. 'I wasn't myself after Taddeo was born. I was...troubled.' She worked the bracelet on her wrist. 'I was so miserable I accused Sandro of not caring for me and of infidelity.'

Guilt-filled eyes rose to meet Lucy's.

Lucy remembered how difficult and moody Pia had been all those years ago. How she hadn't liked it when Lucy could calm little Taddeo so easily, and how she'd jumped to conclusions when she'd found Lucy and her husband talking together. Poor Sandro had been worried about his wife and son, checking with Lucy about his concerns. He'd been torn between placating his wife and getting help for what Lucy thought could be Pia's severe depression.

'At the trial I said things about you and Sandro.' Pia sucked in a shaky breath. 'Things I believed at the time, but things that looking back I realise I didn't *know*.'

Like stating emphatically that Lucy had been Sandro's lover, saying under oath she'd found them in compromising positions.

'It wasn't till Domenico came to me with his news, and *this*—' she looked at her bracelet '—that I realised what I'd done.' She paused. 'Sandro and I met in spring, you see. For all his money, Sandro courted me with primroses and forget-me-nots. When he ordered this he was trying to remind me of those early days when we were happy. He was bringing the necklace to me that night, not you. It must have fallen from his pocket when he…when he…'

Lucy leaned across and touched the other woman's hand. 'Your husband must have loved you very much. It was there in his face whenever he mentioned you.'

Pia's eyes filled but she smiled. 'I know that now. But at the time I was so unhappy. That's why I said those things—'

'It's all right, truly.' Even at eighteen Lucy had understood enough to realise Pia hadn't deliberately slandered her. She'd been hysterical with grief and misery, falling easily into supporting Bruno's damning evidence that tied so well with her own imaginings. He'd painted Lucy as an immoral opportunist, no doubt feeding Pia's worst fears. 'I'm sure it made no difference to the case.'

'You think so?'

No. Lucy wasn't certain. She'd seen the court moved by the beautiful grieving widow. But pity was stronger now than any desire for revenge. Pia's regret was genuine, as was her joy at rediscovering her husband's love.

Would Lucy ever know love like that? Her heart squeezed. 'I know it,' she murmured.

'Thank you.' Pia took her hand. 'That means a lot.'

A third hand joined theirs. Then Pia's touch dropped away as she sat back in her seat and Domenico's fingers threaded through Lucy's. Warmth spread from his touch. Not the fire of physical desire but something more profound.

Was he congratulating himself on the reconciliation? One step closer to the day he could wash his hands of his obligation to her?

He looked up at the antique clock above the mantelpiece then rose, tugging her to her feet. 'Come on, ladies. It's time we left.'

Pia rose and reached for a gossamer-fine wrap. It was left to Lucy to ask, 'Where are we going?'

'To the opera, then supper.' He tucked her hand into his elbow. 'We have a reservation at Rome's premier restaurant.'

'But the press! They'll see—'

'They will indeed,' he murmured. 'They'll see that far from shunning you, you're our guest. It will prime them for more news to come.'

CHAPTER THIRTEEN

'It's not as bad as I expected.'

Lucy's murmured comment made Domenico smile.

He surveyed the ultra modern restaurant that was Rome's latest A-list haunt and thought of the other women he could have brought here. Women who'd toy with the exquisitely prepared food while making the most of the chance to see and be seen. Who'd have spent the day getting ready to come here.

By contrast he'd had to force Lucy into her glamorous new clothes. She shunned the avid gazes sent their way, concentrating on her food with an unfashionable enjoyment that would endear her to the chef.

'I'm glad you think having supper with me isn't too much of a burden.'

Her gaze darted to his face and her lips quirked in the first genuine smile he'd had from her all night. He couldn't believe how good it felt, seeing that. He'd even wondered, for about half a minute, if he'd done the wrong thing, thrusting her into the limelight again.

Earlier at the opera with Pia, Lucy had stood stiffly as they mingled in the foyer, sipping champagne and chatting with the many acquaintances who'd approached them. The three of them had been a magnet for attention. Yet only he, holding Lucy close, knew what it cost her to appear at ease in the glittering crowd. She'd projected a calm, slightly aloof air that fitted the setting perfectly and she'd held her own with a poise that made him proud.

She truly was a remarkable woman.

'If you're fishing for compliments you're out of luck, Signor Volpe.' But her eyes sparkled. 'It's not *you* I was worried about. It was everyone else.'

'You handled them beautifully.'

She laid her spoon down and licked a stray curl of chocolate from her upper lip. Desire twisted in Domenico's belly, sharp and powerful, and he sucked in his breath.

She aroused him so easily. Each time he had her he wanted her again. Every day he needed more, not less.

How long would it take to have his fill?

'*You* handled them beautifully, not me. No one dared say anything outrageous with you beside me. But they wondered what was going on.'

Domenico spread his hands. 'Of course they wondered. What do we care for that? Tonight is about making it clear the Volpes accept you. That's why Pia came to the opera. If we champion you, who in society will deny you?'

'It's not Roman high society I'm worried about. It's everyone else. The press, for a start.' She reached for her water glass and drank deeply. It was the only outward sign that she wasn't completely at ease.

'Let me take care of the press, Lucy.' Strange how he found himself deliberately using her name so often. As if he got pleasure from its taste on his tongue.

'Don't you see?' She leaned forward, face earnest. 'You can ward them off with your bodyguards. But when I'm on my own it will be different. They'll bay for my blood even more than before.'

Domenico covered her hand. 'It will be all right. You just need to be patient. If all turns out as I intend, soon you won't have to worry about the press.'

The media would have another victim in its sights. There'd

be a spike of interest in Lucy as victim, rather than criminal, but eventually it would die down.

Triumph filled him. After weeks of intense work, they were on the brink of success.

This particular success brought a satisfaction greater than any business coup. Because his pleasure in this was *personal*.

It would salve his battered conscience, clearing Lucy's name. The Volpe family would pay its debt by redressing the wrong done her. More specifically, it would be some small recompense for the way he'd rejected her out of hand.

But there was more. He'd been surprised at how tonight's meeting between Pia and Lucy had affected him. How he'd felt both women's pain.

He'd always thought Pia over-emotional and needy. Now he realised her belief in Sandro's betrayal had fed that neediness. She really had loved his brother. Believing Sandro no longer loved her had undermined her fragile self-worth. Now perhaps she could face the world with a little more confidence.

As for Lucy—he watched her watching him from under lowered lashes and his hold tightened possessively. It might have been responsibility, obligation and guilt driving him to clear her name. But he wasn't just acting out of duty.

He felt *good*, knowing Lucy would be in a better place when this was over.

In the past he'd confined his philanthropy to large charitable donations. Maybe in future he'd take a more hands-on role. He'd discovered he enjoyed righting wrongs and seeing justice done.

But there was another, more personal dimension to this—an undercurrent that flowed deeper and stronger than any do-gooder intentions.

Domenico stroked his thumb across Lucy's palm and felt her shiver. Her lips parted. He wanted to kiss her with all the pent up passion he kept in check.

But he preferred privacy for what he had in mind.

He stroked her palm again, this time drawing his finger

past her wrist and along her forearm, watching with satisfaction the tiny telltale signs of her pleasure.

'What do you think you're doing?'

He loved the way her voice dropped to that husky note when she was aroused.

'Nothing.'

He looked up and her sultry gaze caught him. His heart thudded and urgency filled him.

'Liar,' she whispered. 'I know your game.'

'Good.' He drew her from her seat. 'Then you won't mind leaving the rest of your dessert.'

She leaned forward so her breath feathered his cheek. 'Not if you're offering something better.' She turned, collected her shimmering evening bag and headed towards the door with a slow, sexy sway that drew every male gaze.

Domenico was torn between appreciation and dog-in-the-manger jealousy that she flaunted herself in front of others.

In mere weeks she'd blossomed from artless innocent to a siren who turned him into a slavering idiot.

She really *was* remarkable.

Eyes glued to her, he summoned a waiter and had the bill put on his account.

He smiled as she slowed to wait for him at the door.

What more could he want from life? He had the anticipation of success, the satisfied glow that came from redressing past wrongs, and the bonus of Lucy in his bed.

Life was excellent.

It was over breakfast that news came.

Lucy was enjoying a platter of summer fruit when she heard Domenico on the phone. She looked up as he entered the room. Their eyes met and, as ever, her skin tingled.

'I see,' Domenico said into the phone, his eyes dark with secrets. Images of their loving last night surfaced and she felt an unfamiliar blush rise.

Last night had been…phenomenal. She tried to tell herself

it was just reaction, having survived the evening without falling in a heap or being accosted as a criminal. But she knew the magic came from far deeper feelings.

The efforts Domenico went to in order to clear her name were amazing. She owed him a debt she could never repay. He'd achieved more in a few short weeks, with his discovery of the jewellery, than the police had. Presumably because they'd been only too ready to accept Bruno's evidence and blame the outsider—her.

More, he was the one who'd cracked open the brittle shell she'd built to separate herself from the world. It was scary being without it, but wonderful too. These last weeks had been crammed with precious pleasures she'd remember all her life.

She looked away from those penetrating grey eyes.

If only she could feel simply gratitude. But she felt far more. Domenico touched her deep inside. He'd changed her for ever.

'When did this happen?' He paused and Lucy's head jerked up at his tone. 'Excellent. You've done well.' A smile split his face and Lucy caught her breath.

Domenico put the phone down and sat, looking smug.

'What is it? What's happened?' Even as she spoke something tempered her impatience, an atavistic fear of upsetting the good life they shared. Tension scrolled down her spine, like a premonition of cold, hard change to come.

'Good news. The best news.'

Yet, unaccountably, Lucy felt that tension eddying deep inside. Slowly she wiped her fingers on a linen napkin.

Domenico raised his eyebrows as if expecting her to burst into speech.

'The police have taken Bruno Scarlatti in for questioning in the light of new evidence. They're reviewing the investigation into Sandro's death.'

Lucy's heart pounded. 'New evidence?'

'Remember Scarlatti had an alibi for the time of Sandro's death? A colleague who claimed to have been with him on the other side of the palazzo?'

'How could I forget?' Lucy clasped her hands together, old bitterness welling.

'That colleague has come forward, saying he'd got the times wrong. He was with Bruno fifteen minutes earlier rather than at the time of the killing, as he said. There was always forensic evidence Bruno had been in the room but only your word for it he'd been there before Sandro died, not just later.'

'The witness admitted to lying?' It seemed too good to be true.

Domenico shrugged. 'He was young. Bruno was his mentor and friend. He thought he was doing him a favour, giving an alibi for a crime he couldn't believe Bruno committed.'

'You know a lot about this.' Lucy felt strangely disconnected from the news, as if it affected someone else.

'Rocco tracked the witness down and filled him in on Bruno's record since then.'

'He's got a record?' That was news.

'A conviction for assault and a string of complaints. Plus dismissal for questionable behaviour.'

Lucy sat back, her mind awhirl at the implications. 'You did all this.' It boggled her mind.

She waited for elation to hit.

'It was nothing. I had the resources to uncover the truth, that's all.'

Lucy shook her head, her heartbeat loud as a drum. 'It's more than anyone else did.'

'But I knew the truth. That made it easier.' He reached out and took her hand. His felt hard and capable. She looked into his eyes and read satisfaction there. The satisfaction of a man who'd solved a puzzle no one else had. The satisfaction of a man who'd achieved justice, no matter how belated. Who'd restored his family honour by redressing the injustice done in their name.

She slid her hand from his grip and laced her fingers together in her lap.

Dazed, she grappled with what he'd told her. She'd be able

to reclaim her good name. It was what she'd longed for and fought for all this time.

Yet instead of euphoria, a sense of anticlimax enveloped her. It all seemed too...easy.

'So you threw resources at it and hey presto, the truth is revealed?' She couldn't hide her bitterness. 'If only the police had done that in the first place—really *listened* and investigated thoroughly...' She shook her head, a wave of anger and frustration engulfing her. '*Five years* of my life gone. Five years in hell.'

When Lucy looked up it was to see Domenico's grim expression.

'You're right. It should never have happened like this. Can you forgive me?'

She frowned. 'Forgive you? I'm talking about the way the investigators latched on to Bruno's evidence and didn't want to hear anything against it because he was one of them, ex-police.'

Domenico's mouth tightened. 'If I'd taken time to hear you out instead of assuming your guilt it would have been different.' His shoulders rose and fell in a massive shrug that spoke of regret and pain.

Suddenly she saw him clearly, right to the shadows in his soul. He expected her condemnation.

So it was true, his actions had been driven by guilt all this time. She sucked in a breath, trying to find calm.

Domenico was many things but, she knew now, he wasn't responsible for her conviction. That notion had been a sop to her anger and pride in the dark days when she'd needed it most.

She didn't need it now. She'd held on to anger and cynicism for too long and she didn't like the woman it had made her.

'Don't talk like that.' Her voice was husky. 'You're the man proving my innocence.'

'But too late. I should have—'

'No, Domenico.' She raised her hand. 'It devastated me when you cut me loose but it didn't make a difference to the trial. It hurt.' She faced him squarely, letting him read the truth.

'But that's all. No one could blame you for doubting me in the face of the other evidence.'

For a long moment searching grey eyes held hers. 'You're some woman, Lucy Knight. Thank you.'

She smiled, though her heart wasn't in it.

She told herself this was the beginning of the rest of her life, the beginning she'd wanted so long, but with it came sadness that her dad hadn't survived to see her innocence proven. And welling dismay over what this meant for her and Domenico.

Lucy rubbed her forehead, trying to ease the ache beginning there.

'Lucy? What is it? Are you all right?'

She looked down at the luscious fruit on her plate and her stomach roiled.

'Of course. I'm just…stunned. It's taking a while to process.'

Could she be pregnant? Was that what made her nauseous and maudlin instead of happy at this brilliant news? The possibility had sat at the back of her mind ever since she'd learned he hadn't used protection that first time.

Joy and fear filled her at the idea of carrying Domenico's child. Despite his assurances, she knew he wouldn't be happy. Innocent she might be, but it had become clear last night, seeing the glitz of the rarefied world he moved in, that she didn't belong. She'd had to call on every ounce of courage to face the calculating gazes of the uber-wealthy and the paparazzi.

She'd even been gauchely enthusiastic about her first opera when the rest of the audience displayed only polite appreciation. She'd been so obviously an outsider.

'It's okay, Lucy.' His tone was encouraging, kind. 'We achieved what we set out to do. It's all over now.'

Her gaze darted to Domenico's face. In it she read self-satisfaction that, melded onto his superbly sculpted features, gave an air of ingrained superiority.

It's all over.

Hadn't she told herself that what they shared would end soon? She could barely call it a relationship, despite the blind-

ing moments of connection. It was based only on sexual pleasure and convenience. Not once had he spoken of a future
beyond 'rehabilitating' her.

As if she was some project instead of a woman with feelings!

Feelings. Oh, she had those in spades.

She tried to dredge up gratitude. Instead a writhing knot of
emotion wedged in her chest.

'Thank you,' she said finally. 'Without you, this would never
have happened.'

He gestured dismissively. Obviously it had been nothing
mobilising vast resources to revisit every aspect of the prosecution case.

Lucy swallowed, not wanting to ask, but needing to know.
'What now, Domenico? What will we do?'

Last night, basking in his closeness, she'd let herself dream
what it would be like if he truly cared for her. If he *loved* her.

She snatched in her breath on a desperate gasp. Until now
she hadn't used the L word. Coward that she was, she'd avoided
even thinking it. But she couldn't pretend any longer. She
wanted to be more to Domenico than a project.

She wanted to be in his life permanently. She wanted his
laughter, his tenderness, his loving, the way he made her feel
precious and special. She wanted to be the woman she'd become on his island, where she'd learned about compassion and
trust and...love.

Her stomach dipped at the enormity of what she wanted.
She'd gone from total, self-absorbed isolation to knowing she
wouldn't be whole without him.

She swallowed hard. She'd fallen in love.

'Now?' His brows drew together.

'Now it's over.'

She waited, longing for him to tell her it would never be
over. That he felt this overwhelming sense of belonging with
her too, despite the differences between them.

'Nothing more is necessary. The legal experts can take it
from here.' He gave her a reassuring smile that did anything

but. 'We'll continue the strategy of showing you out and about, accepted by the family and everyone who counts. My security staff will protect you.'

'Of course.' She felt like an inanimate object to be exhibited. Lucy told herself she was unreasonable. It didn't help.

'There'll be a spike in interest once it's clear you're innocent. But in the long run I'm hopeful you can start that new life you want so much.'

His smile was benevolent, like an adult giving a child a long awaited treat.

Except she didn't want it as she once had. Not if it meant leaving Domenico.

But it wasn't her choice to make.

She waited for him to say more. To talk about *them*.

He said nothing.

She read the satisfaction in his eyes and the way he sprawled in his chair. He'd done what he'd set out to do against the odds. Wasn't that his speciality? Succeeding where everyone failed? She'd been one more challenge to a man who revelled in beating the odds.

Lucy's stomach clenched. She wanted to be more.

'Where will you be, Domenico?' She was proud of her even tone when inside she shook like a leaf in a gale.

'Me?' He looked surprised she'd ask. 'I'll stay in Rome for a while to help you through the media attention. You won't have to cope alone.'

No, he'd made it his business to look after her. She told herself she should appreciate it more. She *did* appreciate it, except she felt like a problem to be managed rather than the woman in his life.

Miserably, she reminded herself she'd never really been his woman, just conveniently available.

'And after that?'

He shrugged and reached for his coffee. 'I've got business in New York I've delayed for a couple of weeks.' Delayed because of her.

'And then?' She laced her fingers, willing him to say something, anything about *them*. About coming back to her or taking her with him. 'What about after that?' Even a promise to see her in England would be something.

Domenico frowned, clearly not used to being quizzed.

'It depends on a number of things. Perhaps Germany for a week or two.'

'I see.'

Finally, she did.

This *was* the end.

She'd known it was coming. How could she not, when despite the precious moments of communion, she didn't fit in his world or he in hers?

He'd support her for a week or two more, squiring her and protecting her from the press. And he'd be happy, no doubt, to share his body with her, while he was in town.

After that she was on her own.

Pain stabbed, transfixing her. She breathed slowly through her mouth, willing the searing heat, like a red-hot knife in her midriff, to ease. It didn't, but she couldn't bear to sit here with him surveying her like his latest trophy of success—proof that Domenico Volpe could achieve anything he set his heart on.

When she'd set her heart on—

No! She'd known this couldn't last. She'd resolved to enjoy every minute Domenico gave her and not look back. It was she who'd broken the rules by wanting more.

She prayed she still had the power to hide her feelings from him.

'I never believed you could do it, Domenico.' She let his name roll around her mouth, savouring it one last time. 'Thank you.' She met his gaze, felt that familiar sizzle of heat, then looked at her hands threading together in her lap. She'd have to do better than this if she was to leave with dignity.

'It was my pleasure, Lucy.' The rumble of his voice reminded her of the intimacies they'd shared, not just in bed, but when they'd laughed together, talked, and played with Chiara.

Her shiver of response was the catalyst she needed. She could stay but each day would draw her further into his thrall till she wouldn't have the strength to go. She couldn't wait for the day he decided it was time for her to leave.

Lucy's chair scraped the polished floor as she stood.

'If you'll excuse me I'll go and pack.' She lifted her head and looked at a point just over his shoulder. 'I appreciate your help, but I'd rather not stay in Rome.'

Domenico froze, his coffee halfway to his mouth.

'*Prego?*' What did she mean, she'd rather not stay?

'It's time I went home. I'm sure you understand.'

The cup rattled as he put it down. Understand? Like hell he did. As for going home, he knew as well as Lucy that she had no home. Her she-wolf of a stepmother had sold Lucy's privacy for a fistful of cash.

'No, I don't understand! Perhaps you'd explain.'

How could she be so eager to leave? Indignation stirred and with it male pride. Only hours ago she'd lain in his arms, crying out his name as they found bliss together. Heat stirred, remembering.

She didn't meet his eyes.

Fear prickled the hairs on his nape. He didn't understand it, but he did trust his instincts. Something was wrong. Badly wrong.

'I'm English, Domenico. I want to go to England.'

'You haven't mentioned returning in weeks.'

She shrugged. 'Because it was obvious I'd be hounded by the press. You gave me a place to lie low and I appreciate it.'

Was that all he'd given her? She short-changed them both implying it was.

'I've been in Italy since I left prison. I want to go home.' Her hands twisted. 'Do you realise that, even out of jail, I haven't chosen where I stayed? Not even for a night?'

She complained about the way he protected her? Or did she

complain about being with him? Domenico's mind whirled. It wasn't possible. She'd welcomed him into her bed so eagerly.

'You'd rather I'd left you to the press?' He spoke through gritted teeth. He told himself he didn't want her gratitude but he sure as hell expected better than this. Anger stirred. 'You know it was for your own good.' Even if at first it had been for his convenience.

She nodded. 'I appreciate all you've done. And the way you came to my aid that day we went ashore. But it's time I stood on my own two feet.'

Domenico's jaw jammed shut. He hated that note of finality in her voice. He wanted to rail at her and tell her she couldn't leave.

But what right had he to stop her?

Only the fact that he wasn't ready to let her go. Not while the passion they shared burned so bright.

Didn't she feel it too?

Or had she simply taken advantage of what he offered, ready to discard him as it suited her?

Domenico's jaw tightened.

Never had a woman dumped him. And never had one left with such little regret. He hated this dark roil of emotions. They made him feel...alarmingly out of control.

He strode around the end of the table, ready to reach out and grab her, only to stop when she faced him with that cold mask of disdain he'd thought she'd ditched for good.

'I'm a free woman now and it's time I acted like one.'

'The press will be after you.' She needed him, couldn't she see that? Something akin to desperation racked him. 'With the case reopened the press will be more eager.'

'I don't care. At least now they won't call me a murderess. They won't stop me getting a job.'

'You want to work?'

Her eyes, like blue stars, met his head-on and the impact rocked him back on his heels.

'Of course I want to work. What choice do I have?' Her expression was dismissive.

'You could always sell your story. They'd pay even higher money for your inside story now you've been in my bed.'

Even as he said it, Domenico regretted the words. She'd goaded him into a quagmire of bitter, unfamiliar emotions, announcing she was leaving. He felt betrayed and he lashed out.

Lucy looked at him as if she'd never seen him before. Her eyes were laser-sharp as they raked him, scraping his flesh raw. Had he really imagined she cared for him?

'Perhaps I will. After all, I didn't sign that gag contract of yours, did I?'

It was a physical blow to the gut, watching her turn back into the ice-hard woman she'd once been.

He wanted to beg her not to do it. But Volpes never begged. Besides, she was beyond listening to him.

'Goodbye, Domenico.' She spun on her foot and left.

CHAPTER FOURTEEN

AUTUMN CAME EARLY to London. Wind gusted down the city street, grabbed Lucy's second-hand jacket and flapped it around her.

The chill didn't bother her. She'd grown used to feeling cold, ever since that day in Rome when Domenico had washed his hands of her.

She tilted her head down and put one weary leg in front of the other. It had been a long day and she needed this short break to regroup before her busy evening shift. Jobs weren't easy to come by, not even casual waitressing jobs, and she had rent due. She couldn't afford to be anything but on the ball when her shift began again.

A cup of tea and twenty minutes with her shoes kicked off beneath a table would be bliss.

She was calculating if she had enough cash for food too when a dark figure loomed before her. Automatically she stepped to one side. So did he. Lucy stepped the other way to find he'd made the same manoeuvre.

That was when she took in the glossy, beautifully tooled shoes blocking her path.

Her nape prickled as she raised her gaze over an exquisitely tailored suit and cashmere overcoat. She gasped and sucked in a spicy scent she'd never forget if she lived to be a hundred.

'Domenico!'

Gun-metal grey eyes met hers from under straight black

brows. The shock of him in the flesh rocked her back on her heels. She'd imagined him often, dreamt about him every night, but had forgotten how incredibly magnetic that deep gaze was.

Hungrily she took in those high cheekbones, the strong nose and hard jaw, the sensuous mouth. So familiar, so dear. Her heart bumped then catapulted into a gallop. She buried her hands deep in her pockets lest she reach for him as she did in her dreams.

He looked utterly gorgeous, but there were lines of strain around his eyes and the groove in his cheek scored deeper than before. He'd been working too hard.

'Lucy.' Just two syllables and her nerves danced a shimmy of delight. No one said her name as he did. No one made it sound half so appealing.

'What are you doing in London?'

'I have an important meeting.'

Of course he did. Domenico's world was full of important meetings. She'd followed his progress in the press these last couple of months, from the USA to Germany, China and back to Rome. Nothing had stopped his spectacular business success. Certainly not regret over her.

Still she couldn't bring herself to move. She stood, drinking him in, like a shaft of Italian sunshine on this grey English day.

'With you.'

'Sorry?' She'd lost the thread of the conversation.

'It's you I'm here to see.'

She shook her head. Of course she wanted to see him, but self-preservation cautioned it could only lead to catastrophe. She didn't have the willpower to say goodbye again. Getting over Domenico Volpe was even harder than she'd feared.

'It's true.'

'How did you find me?'

His eyebrows rose and she thought of the vast resources he'd used to find the truth about her past. He'd probably just clicked his fingers and hey presto!

'Why track me down?' What could he want after all this time?

Then it struck her. Domenico put family above all. He was big on duty and making things right. Why else would he come?

She made herself meet his eyes, not letting him see her disappointment. 'You don't have to worry. You didn't get me pregnant.'

Domenico stared into her brilliant blue gaze and felt a knife slash of pain. The chances had been slim but still he'd hoped.

He made himself nod as if her news hadn't all but gutted him. 'Thank you for telling me.'

Crazy to have hoped so hard. He should have known nothing about this would be easy.

Looking into her wary face, having her so close, was more difficult than he'd imagined. She looked the same, more beautiful if possible, but the warmth was gone from her gaze and there was no sign of that rare wondrous smile he'd come to believe she saved for him. No sign of the cheeky, confident woman who'd brought him to his knees with her sexy flirting. Lucy held herself back as if expecting more pain.

Something plunged deep in his belly. Guilt sharpened its claws on his vitals.

'So there's no reason for us to meet.' She gave him a cool smile but he saw beyond it to her bewilderment. Either her mask of unconcern wasn't as good as it used to be or he was getting better at reading her.

Yet it was far too early to feel anything like hope.

'But we have things to discuss.' He reached for her elbow. 'Come. My hotel is just around the corner. We can talk there.'

He breathed in her honey and sunshine scent and pleasure slammed into him. His fingers tightened on her arm as he drew her along.

'I don't want to talk in your hotel suite.'

He should have known she'd resist. When had she made things easy? Nervous tension battled pleasure at her familiar obstinacy.

'Fine. We'll use the public rooms.' He managed a smile, despite the nerves tightening his belly. Surely if she didn't trust the privacy of his suite it was because he could still tempt her? The notion charged his hopes.

He eased his grip and he tucked her arm in his. She didn't resist and anticipation rose as he led her around a corner towards a familiar brick building decorated with flags.

'Signor Volpe. Madame.' The top-hatted doorman welcomed them and they stepped inside.

Instantly Domenico felt Lucy stiffen. He liked the quiet and the excellent service here but he took for granted its hushed opulence.

'We can go to my rooms if you'd prefer.' His lips brushed her hair as he leaned close. The scent of her drove his careful plans into a tangle of lust and nerves. He prayed she'd say yes.

'No. This is fine.' He felt her stand taller, taking in the elegance of the area before them. It reminded him of her spunk when faced with the glitterati at the opera in Rome. Lucy had stiffened her spine, kept her head up and won the admiration of many.

Minutes later they were seated in a secluded corner of the vast reception room. The décor was opulent—huge arched mirrors, enormous pillars with gilded capitals and the scent of hundreds of roses from the massed arrangements. Yet here at their small table, seated comfortably in the glow of a nearby lamp, they had an illusion of privacy.

Lucy avoided his gaze, rubbing at a stain on her black skirt.

Domenico dragged his eyes from the short skirt that revealed her stunning legs. He had to focus.

Panic stirred and he forced it down. This was the most important negotiation of his life and he couldn't let nerves wreck his chances.

'Your stepmother contacted me.'

Lucy jerked her head up. 'Why you?'

He shrugged. 'She'd read about me collecting you from prison, and you being with me in Rome. It was the only place she could think of to reach you.'

Wariness was writ large on Lucy's face. 'What did she want? Money?'

'No.' He paused, remembering that difficult conversation. 'She wanted to talk with you.'

Lucy shook her head. 'I can't imagine why.'

'Apparently she wants to apologise.'

'And you believed her?' Lucy's face was taut with outrage but with something else too. Something that might have been hope.

Domenico's heart lightened. Lucy tried so hard to be tough and cold, yet always she responded with a good heart. Look at the way she'd taken to Chiara and the way she'd let him into her life. She'd given Pia a second chance. Maybe she'd do it again.

'I believe she was genuinely sorry for that article. She said she needed the money and thought she could handle the media. According to her, the reporter twisted most of what she said and conveniently removed any positive comments.'

He paused, waiting for her to consider.

'She said she didn't want to talk with you before because she felt so ashamed of what she'd done.'

Lucy gnawed her lip and he wanted to reach out and stop her. But he didn't have the right. She'd walked away from him and who could blame her? Even now he couldn't believe he'd let her go. Twice now he'd missed his chance with Lucy. Finally he'd learnt his lesson!

'I'll think about calling her.'

'Good.' He nodded and sat back as a waiter appeared with their afternoon tea. He was glad for a distraction despite the urgency coiling his belly tight. For the first time he could remember he was *scared*, not able to predict the outcome of this meeting.

'So, is that all?' Her tone was brisk, yet she cradled her celadon-green cup as if needing warmth. He didn't even bother taking his tea. He wouldn't be able to hold it steady. Too much rode on this and he'd lost the facility to pretend it wasn't important.

'No. There's more.'

Her brows arched. 'What? Is there something wrong with the case against Bruno?' For the first time she looked truly shaken.

'Nothing like that. It's all going smoothly.'

Her relief was palpable, yet it struck him that she hadn't looked directly at him. Not since that moment on the street when he'd read shock and something he couldn't name in her eyes.

'And so?'

'And so.' He swallowed and leaned forward. 'I want to talk about us.'

'There is no *us*, Domenico.' Her expression was cool. Yet the way she said his name in that scratchy voice gave him hope. He might be fooling himself but he'd take all the encouragement he could get.

She put her cup down and he snatched her hand up. It trembled.

'Liar,' he whispered. 'There's always been an us. Even when I didn't trust myself to believe what I felt for you in the beginning. I felt the world crumble around me because I wanted you so much it hurt. I wanted you so much I cursed my brother for having you first. Can you believe it?'

'Domenico!' Her voice was a hoarse gasp. 'You can't be serious. Back then you hated me.'

'I thought I hated you because of the bolt of emotion I felt whenever I looked at you. It shook me to the core and it wasn't just lust. It was a…link I couldn't explain. A link I pretended didn't exist because I let myself be swayed by lies and my own jealous pride.' He heaved in a tight breath.

'You felt it too, didn't you, Lucy?'

Her eyes were huge in her pale face. With her blonde hair long enough now to brush her shoulders, she looked more like the innocent who'd stood in the dock all those years ago and stolen his soul.

She shook her head. 'No. I knew you hated me and I felt…'

'What? What did you feel, Lucy?' Urgency made him grip her hand harder.

'I can't explain it.' She looked away. 'A link, I suppose, from the start. But it wasn't right. It was just lust.'

Was that what she thought? He grimaced, knowing it was his fault she believed it.

'No, *carissima*, it wasn't just lust.'

She tugged her hand. 'Please, let me go.'

'Not until you look at me, Lucy.'

Reluctantly she turned her head and he felt again that blast of heat surging through his veins as their gazes melded. Domenico lifted her hand and kissed it. He turned it over and pressed his mouth to her palm and felt her shiver delicately.

With a sigh he released her hand and watched her cradle it in her lap as if it burned her. Just as his lips tingled where he'd caressed her sweet flesh.

'I was a fool to let you leave, Lucy. I've regretted it from the moment you went.'

'It wasn't a matter of you *letting* me go. It was my decision.'

'Only because I couldn't see what was before my eyes.'

'What are you saying, Domenico?'

'I'm saying what's between us is more important than lust. It always was, though I was too shallow to trust my instincts. I'm saying I want you with me, Lucy. In Rome, or here in Britain if you prefer. I want you in my life.'

There. He'd said it. He'd never asked that of any woman.

'I don't believe you.'

She looked like a queen surveying a troublesome subject. So proud. So feisty. So hurt. Seeing the pain etched around her pursed lips, shame rose.

'I was a fool to let you walk away but I was too proud to plead with you to stay.'

'I can't imagine you pleading for anything.'

'Can't you?' His lips twisted bitterly.

'No. You're too arrogant. Too sure of yourself.'

'Remind me never to come to you for a character reference. You know me too well.'

'What is it you want, Domenico? Is this some sort of game?'

'I was never more serious in my life.'

'Domenico?' Her eyes rounded as he slipped from his chair and knelt before hers. 'What are you doing?'

'Pleading, *carissima*.' And the hell of it was he didn't give a damn who saw him. All he cared about was convincing Lucy.

'I don't understand.' She blinked, her eyes overbright and he reached to take her hand.

'Nor did I, in Rome. I was too full of myself. Too pleased with my success in setting things right, and too full of relief that finally I was doing right by you after all those wrongs. I didn't question what was happening between us.'

For the first time since he'd known her Lucy looked lost for words.

'I thought I had it all—the satisfaction of seeing justice done, and you in my bed, in my life.' He paused, the words harder now. 'I thought that was all I wanted, to enjoy the moment, to have your company and the phenomenal sex, as long as it lasted.'

Her hand clenched in his. 'I hadn't thought past that. When you called me on it I wasn't ready to face what I really wanted. Because what I wanted scared me.'

'Liar.' The whispered word shivered through him. 'You're never scared.'

Again he lifted her hand to his mouth, inhaling her warm scent, absorbing her taste. He couldn't bear the thought of not being allowed to touch her again.

'I was absolutely petrified. So petrified I couldn't think straight. It wasn't one of my finer moments. But when you reminded me you hadn't really been free from the moment you got out of jail, how could I stop you? You deserved the right to the life you wanted.'

He searched her face but couldn't read her thoughts. Fear

coursed through his bloodstream and his breathing came in short, hard stabs.

'Cut to the chase, Domenico. What *is* it you want? Do you want me as your lover while you're in England? Or in Rome—' she paused as if searching for words '—till you've had enough?'

'No! I want more. I want everything. I fell for you years ago on one magic day in Rome. Then later you were so beautiful and so stoic in the face of all that horror, I couldn't get you out of my mind.'

His heart pounded as he pressed her palm to his chest. Her touch gave him courage to go on.

'When we met again I fell for you all over again.'

She shook her head. 'You're talking about sex.'

'That too.' He smiled at her prim expression, remembering her in his bed. 'But actually I fell for the woman who made me feel like a new man.'

He sliced his free hand through the air. 'I can't explain, but with your honesty, your generosity and your pleasure in everything around you, I became different too. A man who didn't calculate every last item, who remembered what it was to enjoy life and to *feel*. I learned there's more to life than balance sheets and takeovers. There's caring and forgiveness.'

His words echoed into silence. His pulse drummed a staccato tattoo that surely convinced her as nothing else could, that he was genuine.

'I want to be with you. I want to live my life with you, wherever you are. I want to make a family with you and be with you always. I love you, Lucy.'

Finally the words ran out. He'd bared himself utterly. In his former life where control meant everything, that would have been unthinkable.

'Lucy? Say something.' His voice was hoarse.

'I say you're very long-winded, Signor Volpe. But I wouldn't have missed a moment of it.' She leaned forward and there were stars in her eyes. 'You could talk the birds from the trees if you wanted.'

Hope spilled as he saw her glorious smile. 'You're the only one I'm interested in. Will you have me, *tesoro*? Will you be mine?'

'Domenico—' she murmured his name as if savouring each syllable and every muscle cinched tight '—I've been yours for so long I can barely remember what it was like before you burst into my life.' She sighed and whispered in his ear, 'I love you, Domenico.'

'Carissima!'

Finally he was free to do what he'd longed to from the moment he'd seen her in the street. He scooped her into his arms and kissed her so thoroughly he almost forgot to breathe. Breathing was overrated. With Lucy in his arms, who needed oxygen?

Eventually something, a faint noise, caught his attention. He lifted his head, smiling at the beatific glow on his beloved's face, and turned.

'Champagne, sir?' The waiter held a vintage bottle of his favourite bubbly.

'Excellent idea. In my suite. Now.'

The waiter nodded and melted discreetly away.

'Lucy?'

'Mmm?' She snuggled into his arms as he lifted her. 'How do you feel about having our honeymoon right here?'

Eyes the pure blue of an Italian summer sky met his and a pulse of emotion beat through him. 'I think first you need to persuade me to marry you.' Her smile was that of a temptress.

Domenico turned and carried her out of the room, oblivious to the stares and smiles of the other patrons. The world had never been so right.

'Ah,' he whispered in her ear. 'You know how I like rising to a challenge.'

* * * * *

MEDDLING WITH
A MILLIONAIRE

BY
CAT SCHIELD

Cat Schield has been reading and writing romance since school. Although she graduated from college with a BA in business, her idea of a perfect career was writing books for Mills & Boon. And now, after winning the Romance Writers of America 2010 Golden Heart® for series contemporary romance, that dream has come true. Cat lives in Minnesota with her daughter, Emily, and their Burmese cat. When she's not writing sexy, romantic stories for Desire, she can be found sailing with friends on the St Croix River or in more exotic locales like the Caribbean and Europe. She loves to hear from readers. Find her at www.catschield.com. Follow her on twitter @catschield.

To my daughter, Emily. Thanks for believing in me.
I couldn't have done it without you.

One

Sighting his quarry at last, Nathan Case dodged a waiter carrying a tray of champagne and navigated around a chocolate fountain. Twenty feet ahead, Emma Montgomery slipped through the cream of Dallas society gathered to celebrate New Year's Eve. Ever since arriving at her father's home an hour ago, Nathan had been searching for Emma, contemplating exactly what he intended to do when he tracked her down.

His options ranged from kissing her to throttling her.

He had yet to decide which way to go.

As if sensing the intensity of his thoughts, she glanced over her shoulder. A strand of hair caught on her lush lips as she scanned the party guests. Delicate fingers brushed long sable bangs back from her forehead, exposing the frown that pulled her brows together. She looked like a wild creature caught out in the open, unsure of where to flee. Then, her chocolate eyes locked on him.

Quick as a rabbit, she ducked around a potted palm and disappeared.

His heartbeat surged as he picked up his pace. He'd had women play hard to get before. The game sweetened their ultimate surrender. But Emma had taken the maneuver to a whole new level. If he didn't know better, he would think she was avoiding him.

Ridiculous, given what he'd learned today.

He passed the library where a rollicking sing-along was taking place, with two dozen people crowded around the grand piano to belt out Sinatra tunes.

He caught sight of Emma just before she ducked into the room and followed, glad to leave behind the throng drinking Silas Montgomery's booze and gawking at the mansion the oil tycoon had built as a testament to his wealth and power.

The two-story library with its cherry paneling and wall of bookshelves was more intimate than the colossal great hall they'd left behind, but not quiet enough for Nathan. He intended to have Emma to himself by midnight. He had no intention of letting anyone but him kiss her incredible mouth.

She stopped dead as he cut off her escape route. The noise level was too high for conversation, but Emma had little trouble communicating her impatience as he herded her toward the piano and nudged her into a narrow space between a blonde in a red halter dress and a short balding man whose attention was riveted on the woman's cleavage.

Nathan surveyed the blonde without interest. Although he appreciated a half-naked woman as much as the next guy, he wasn't a fan of augmented breasts. He preferred curves that jiggled. Emma's in particular.

His lips hovered just above her ear as he softly sang the lyrics that accompanied the romantic tune. He put his hands on the gleaming black instrument, trapping Emma between his arms. She stepped closer to the piano to avoid contact with his body.

With her luscious frame calling to him, Nathan locked his elbows to prevent himself from pressing his lower half against her round rear end. He almost groaned at the memory of cupping those sexy curves in his palms. Desire roared in his ears, drowning out the music. He lowered his head and inhaled her perfume. The scent wrapped around his libido, causing momentary amnesia. Why was he angry with her?

Then he remembered.

In the pause between songs, he whispered in her ear, "Your father and I had an interesting chat this afternoon."

Emma lifted her shoulder as a barricade. "Cody mentioned that you had a proposition for Daddy."

Nathan had a proposition for her as well. A proposition of a very different nature than what he'd discussed with Silas Montgomery.

"Did your brother tell you what we discussed?" he quizzed.

"No."

"Aren't you curious?"

"Should I be?"

Leaning down, Nathan nuzzled Emma's temple. "Your name came up."

She jerked away from his lips and glared at him, but before she could voice the protests roiling in her eyes, the man tickling the ivories played the first bars of "Come Fly With Me" and conversation became impossible.

What was going on? Emma certainly wasn't acting like a blushing bride-to-be. But he was convinced she'd been behind the terms her father had presented earlier that afternoon. Silas Montgomery couldn't resist giving his little girl anything her heart desired, and Nathan knew Emma wanted him. She'd certainly demonstrated that after he'd stolen her away from the Christmas party they'd been at three weeks ago. So why had she bolted the instant she'd set eyes on him tonight?

Across the piano, a round, middle-aged woman frowned at him, an expression made all the more dramatic because it looked as if she'd used a black marker to drawn on her eyebrows. He met her gaze hard, silently warning her to mind her own business. She shifted her attention to the bald man, who was now captivated by Emma's cleavage.

Nathan sucked in a breath and counted to eight before he mastered the impulse to bare his teeth at the guy like some overzealous guard dog. Instead, he focused on the familiar music, relaxed into the romantic lyrics that had caused generations of women to swoon, and contemplated the knockout he must marry if he hoped to do business with her father.

Nathan and her brother, Cody, best friends since college, had often talked about business opportunities that sparked their interest, but they hadn't discovered any worth pursuing until recently. When he and Cody had first discussed the idea of a joint venture between Montgomery Oil and Case Consolidated Holdings, Nathan hadn't anticipated marriage to Emma as part of the negotiations, but he couldn't say he was completely surprised that Silas had made it a key factor in the deal. The project would be a long-term undertaking, requiring huge amounts of capital from both companies. Cementing the connection between Case Consolidated Holdings and Montgomery Oil through marriage ensured that both sides were totally committed to the venture.

Emma would know that. And use it to her advantage. He should be flattered that she wanted him so much that she'd cooked up the scheme and persuaded her father to go along with it. And why wouldn't Silas agree? Once Emma was married, she became someone else's responsibility.

"You have an amazing voice," the blonde to his left told him. She smoothed her left hand across the piano's glossy surface, showing off the huge diamond adorning her middle finger. The bare ring finger proclaimed her availability. "And you know all the words."

Across the narrow space separating their bodies, Emma's spine stiffened at the blonde's blatant flirting.

"My mother loved Sinatra and played his music all the time while I was growing up. She used to call me her very own Rat Pack member. Although, I think her meaning had less to do with my singing and more to do with my knack for troublemaking."

The blonde gave a throaty laugh.

"You're trouble all right," Emma muttered.

Nathan grinned. He liked her humor. She was a terrific package: sexy and funny.

Thinking he had smiled at her, the blonde rotated her upper body toward him. Her low neckline gaped farther as she extended her right hand. One shapely leg slipped between the long slit in her skirt and grazed his thigh. "My name is Bridget."

"Nathan." He clasped her hand while annoyance radiated from Emma like fallout from a nuclear disaster. "How do you know Silas?"

He didn't catch Bridget's answer because his arm no longer blocked Emma's exit, and she'd seized the opportunity to run. As she turned to go, her chest brushed against the bald man's shoulder and his eyes almost popped out of his head. Oblivious to the commotion she'd caused, Emma offered him a brief apology as she slipped past.

Nathan gave the blonde a what-can-you-do shrug. Her smile became a pout as he turned to follow Emma.

She didn't get more than three steps beyond the library before he caught her. Nathan slid his hand around her waist and altered her direction, guiding her to the one place on the first floor where they wouldn't be disturbed by party guests.

"The last time we met I got the feeling you were looking

for a little trouble," he murmured near her ear as he herded her down the hallway to her father's study.

She eyed him as warily as a colt sensing the approach of a mountain lion. Perhaps she'd guessed what was on his mind. No man pursued a woman the way he had without wanting her naked and horizontal.

"Maybe I was," she said. "But that was then."

"And this is now."

At the end of a long corridor, Nathan opened a door, and ushered Emma inside. Dark paneled walls absorbed the single light source: a lamp perched on one corner of a massive antique mahogany desk. In a home office of normal size, a piece of furniture like this might have overwhelmed the room, but this house had been built to impress. A leather couch, with flanking chairs, sat before the carved marble fireplace. Texas landscapes adorned the walls, painted by one of Nathan's favorite artists of the early twentieth century. Unlike the delicate French antiques decorating the rest of the mansion, this room's rugged lines and leather furnishings suited the Texas oil magnate who lived here.

Nathan shut the door, caught Emma's arm and spun her around. Before she offered a protest, he backed her against the door. On the other side of the panel, voices and music blended into hazy, indistinct murmurs. Alone at last.

He leaned his forearm above her shoulder, letting his intent settle over her like a silk sheet. "Aren't you curious why your name came up?" he questioned, returning to their earlier topic.

"Not in the least."

"It seems that your father is shopping around for a husband for you."

"Damn." Her head fell back against the door, and the fight whooshed out of her. "He's been trying to marry me off since college."

"Why?"

"Because I'm a handful of trouble he wants to dump into someone else's lap." Bruises developed in her eyes, put there by her father's harsh opinion. "He's got this idea stuck in his head that I need someone to take care of me."

Being the pampered daughter of a billionaire was part of her charm. Nathan was looking forward to spoiling her rotten.

"What's wrong with letting someone take care of you?" he asked.

"Because the assumption is that I can't take care of myself." Her chin came up. Fire returned to her eyes, but her voice gained a ragged edge. "And that's completely unfair."

In the interest of keeping the conversation civil, Nathan resisted arguing that point with her. Even though he didn't see her brother, Cody, much since he'd gotten married, they kept in regular contact, and Nathan had heard all about Emma's escapades. The near-engagement to a fortune hunter, a sentence of community service after she'd been caught holding a friend's purse containing drugs, and a totaled Mercedes from driving home after a party in the middle of an ice storm.

Granted, she appeared to have settled down in the last few years, but her impulsiveness with him three weeks ago made him question whether she had truly grown up, or whether she'd just gotten better at keeping her activities a secret from her family.

"Have you told your father how you feel?" he asked.

"Yes." She expelled her breath in a rush. "For all the good it did me. When Daddy sets his mind to something, it stays set. He wants me engaged by Valentine's Day. Whether I like it or not."

And whether Nathan liked it or not.

He needed this joint venture with Silas to seize control of the family business from his half brothers. Neither Sebastian nor Max had any faith in his vision for their company. That's why the partnership with Montgomery Oil was so important. Not only would the new venture's cutting-edge technology put Case Consolidated Holdings on the map as an innovator, the future profits would ensure that the balance of power in the company would shift to Nathan. His half brothers would hate it, and there would be nothing they could do about it.

But first he needed to make the deal happen.

On a sudden whim, Nathan quickly unfastened Emma's diamond and sapphire earrings from her ears.

"Give me back my earrings," she demanded as he dropped them into his pocket

The last time he'd stolen her away from a party, she'd fought the chemistry between them, driving him half mad in the moments before her complete surrender. Afterwards, she'd raced off, leaving nothing behind but the evocative scent of her perfume on his skin. Tonight he intended to keep something she'd want to reclaim.

"Not yet."

Artfully arranged wisps of sable curls framed a heart-shaped face with exotic high cheekbones and a slender nose. Tonight she'd tamed her sumptuous brown waves into a fancy, upswept hairdo that drew attention to her elegant neck. Although he liked the way the style bared her lovely golden skin and the hollow of her throat, he preferred her hair loose around her shoulders, tousled by his hands.

He removed the pins holding her hair in its fancy updo. A rich, satiny curtain tumbled about her bare shoulders, stripping away another layer of sophisticated veneer.

"Nathan, what are you doing?"

"I should think it was pretty obvious." He feathered the tips of his fingers along her gown's neckline, grazing her skin.

"Can't we just talk?" she gasped, putting a hand on his chest to hold him off.

The heat of her touch seared through his shirt, igniting a thousand fires. His powerful need for her unsettled him. She made him wild. No other woman turned him on as fast as she did, or made him lose control so completely.

He sifted his fingers through silken waves of sable, twirling one curl around his hand. "If you'd bothered to call me back, we could have talked numerous times in the last few weeks. Right now I have other things on my mind."

"Here? In my father's study? Are you crazy?"

Lust surged at the notion of taking her hard and fast against the door, but he had no intention of doing that again.

Three weeks ago, his first glimpse of her in a dozen years had knocked him off his game. He'd gone to the holiday party, looking to relax and reconnect with another college buddy of his and Cody's. A couple of hours at one of Grant Castle's parties offered him the opportunity for some casual flirting with beautiful women. In fact, he'd been surrounded by five lovely ladies, all vying for his attention when Emma had strolled through the front door, her long, shapely legs bared by a black minidress that shimmered.

Her gaze had shot to him as if he'd released the wolf whistle hovering in his mind. When their eyes locked, all casual thoughts went out of his head. He targeted her like a jungle cat sighting a leggy gazelle and had her out the door and in his car before an hour had passed.

He'd kept his hands to himself until they arrived back at his condo. But once inside, his lips captured hers. He'd been caught off guard by their first kiss. He'd expected more expertise, not the tentative, sensual attack of her fingers against his face, through his hair. Emma acted like a woman who hadn't been kissed in a long time, or at least not one who had been kissed properly.

He'd gone slightly mad then. Nothing else could explain why he'd been too impatient to carry her to his bedroom and take the time to savor every inch of her skin. He'd burned for her and she'd matched his intensity. It amazed him that they hadn't set the foyer on fire.

The next time they made love it would be on a mattress, with her naked and sprawled out to await his pleasure—and hers.

She was a woman worth appreciating.

"Shall I tell you what I'm going to do to you?"

Her breath caught on a quick inhalation. "No."

Yet despite her denials, she didn't push him away. So he capitalized on her ambivalence, using words as a prelude to action.

"First, I'm going to strip you out of your very sexy dress." He grazed his knuckles along her side where the zipper started below her armpit and ended at her hip.

She made a grab for his hand, but he brushed her fingers aside. Her attempt to stop him had been halfhearted at best. Already her resistance was dissolving beneath the heat of this thing between them.

"Then, starting with the spot on your shoulder that drives you crazy when I kiss it, I'm going to take my time with you." He hoped this was working on her because he was driving himself crazy. "You're not getting away until I put my hands and my mouth on every inch of you."

He shifted his grip lower, drawing her tight against the unruly tension in his loins. His breath slipped out in a half sigh, half groan as she rotated her hips against the pressure of his hands.

"Are you wearing the black thong and strapless bra again? Or something different?"

His palms itched, and his fingers tingled as he remembered the way her nipples had hardened as he learned the shape of her full breasts. Tonight's midnight-blue dress seemed equally infatuated with her figure because it clung to her lush form with adoration.

"Let's have a peek," he cajoled, only half-serious. Last time, half the fun of their brief encounter had to do with how flustered she'd gotten at his teasing.

"No." The word broke from her lips in a passionate moan somewhere between protest and plea.

Her hand slid against his chest, finding his heartbeat. He wondered what she'd make of its increased tempo.

He cradled her face while he turned up the volume on her shivers and smiled against her skin as she tipped her head into his palm, giving him better access to her neck.

"Come on, let's go somewhere we won't be disturbed." He drifted his lips along her cheek, devouring her with languid, sultry slowness.

"I'm not going anywhere with you." Her objection ended in a murmur of pleasure as he leaned his chest against her breasts, pressing into her slowly. She stretched like a cat, rubbing against him, a dark, husky rumble deep in her throat.

It amused him that she continued to deny him. They both knew he would get his way in the end.

His lips descended until they were a hairbreadth from hers. "Why not? We were incredible together." One hand swallowed the curve of her buttock, coaxing her against the aroused hardness below his belt. "Feel how hot I am for you. I know you're just as hot for me."

The hand on his chest became a fist. "You have any number of women hot for you."

Is that why she'd been dodging his phone calls?

He smiled indulgently. "But you're the only one I want."

Emma lost the ability to breathe. His words intensified the ache inside her, a potent craving that left her shaky. And tempted. Oh, so tempted.

Flirting with him at Grant's party three weeks ago had seemed like a harmless lark. After all, he'd had no trouble resisting her ten years ago. At twenty he'd been broad of shoulder and delicious to look at, with a cocky charm that dried her mouth and left her at a loss for words. She'd pulled out every trick in her sixteen-year-old arsenal in hopes that he'd look her way. To her shock, it seemed to work.

Until the devastating one-two punch to her ego.

Her cheeks blazed anew at the memory of the day she'd put on her shortest skirt, a brand new pair of stiletto heels and borrowed one of her mother's push-up bras. She'd cornered Nathan in the kitchen and practically begged him to help her become a more experienced woman.

Then, he did exactly as she asked. Only not in the way she wanted.

Expression hard, gray eyes shot through with flashes of lightning, he'd held her at arm's length, laughed and told her to go wash her face and stop playing at being grown-up. And once he finished trampling her self-esteem to dust, he'd sauntered out of the kitchen. The following day he'd left for Las Vegas and hadn't returned to Texas until a few months ago.

She'd been thrilled to see him, believing she'd mastered the skills needed to cope with his vast reserves of sex appeal. Oh, how little she'd learned.

"I'm the one you want right now," she countered.

"You have no idea," he murmured, coasting gentle kisses across her eyelids.

If she let him have his way, how long before he moved on? Could she stand to spend every second of their time together waiting for the other shoe to drop? No. Better to leave things exactly as they were. The memory of their one night together would have to be enough. For both of them.

"Let's go back to my hotel." His hands flowed from her hips to her waist, the firm pressure fitting her more fully against his unyielding torso. "If you can resist screaming my name for an hour, I'll never bother you again."

An hour?

Anticipation swelled, drowning anxiety, as she remembered all too well the roller-coaster ride of screaming thrills awaiting her at his hands. She rubbed her thighs together to combat a mounting frustration. The way she felt right now, she'd climax before he had her clothes off.

He'd win. He knew it. Worse, he knew she knew it. Hell, she was ready to scream his name right here and now just to make the building pressure go away.

"Nathan, I'm not going to sleep with you again."

"Again? You didn't stick around long enough to sleep with me the last time. I'm looking forward to waking up with you in my arms."

His hand was warm and compelling against the small of her back. She lifted her chin while he nuzzled her temple. When his lips brushed the corner of hers, soft as a butterfly's wing, golden light spilled into her veins. If he had any idea how much she'd wanted to end up like this tonight, alone with him and poised to surrender, she would be doomed.

Don't do this. A rational voice shrilled in her mind while her bones melted, and her skin flushed. *You'll never get a chance to marry for love if you let him seduce you again.*

"You're afraid to give into this thing between us," he murmured. "Don't be."

"I'm not."

Letting go had been fun. She'd fantasized about him for years. But not one sizzling daydream had prepared her for the thrilling hard press of his muscles or the urgency of his kisses. He'd cajoled and demanded and she'd happily surrendered.

It was the aftermath that had terrified her. The treacherous longing to surrender control and let him dictate where the relationship went and how long it lasted. Discovering how fast she became putty in his hands had made it easy to avoid his phone calls.

His lips trailed wildfire kisses down her throat to the hollow where her pulse fluttered madly. "I promise to take it slow."

"How thoughtful of you," she said, injecting irony into her

tone. He couldn't find out how much she wanted to give in. "But I think you're getting the wrong idea."

"The wrong idea about what?"

"About what I want."

"And what is that?"

A man who would love her forever.

"Three, two, one…" voices shouted in enthusiastic unison. Noisemakers and horns generated a cacophony, almost drowning out cries of "Happy New Year!"

Listening to the party on the other side of the door, Emma wondered what the coming year would offer.

"Happy New Year," she whispered.

This was his cue to kiss her, but he didn't. He had such sexy lips, well-shaped with a fullness that teased and a wicked quirk that enticed. Anticipation lashed at her. She couldn't stop trembling.

"Happy New Year," he echoed, a smile in his voice. "Have you made any New Year's resolutions?"

"Just one."

"And that would be?"

She shook her head to clear the sensual net he wove around her with so little effort. "I'm resolved to be less spontaneous."

He chuckled. "And how is that working for you so far?"

"Not very well." She kept her tone dry, determined to master her nerves. "How about you? Have you made any resolutions for the New Year?"

"Just one," he said.

She lifted her hands to his face, sliding her fingers over his bold, masculine bone structure and sharp, well-defined jawline. Even in the darkened room he had an arresting face.

He tugged his bow tie loose and left it dangling, drawing her attention to his impressive chest. Heat poured off his long torso, seeping into her skin and setting fire to her better judgment. Her fingers tingled as she traced the muscles beneath his white shirt. He radiated power and vitality. The sensation of all that caged energy weakened her knees.

"What is it?"

His mouth brushed against hers, lingering just long enough to blend their breath. She tried to catch his lips, to compel him to kiss her hard and deep, but he pulled away.

"I'm going to spend the rest of my life making love to you."

Her heart fluttered against her ribs like a startled canary.

"That's a pretty big commitment," she said, unsure what to make of his declaration.

"On the contrary." His breath tickled her ear, redirecting her focus. She turned her head toward the lips hovering beside her cheekbone, but he pushed back, taking away temptation. "I can't wait to make you Mrs. Nathan Case."

Two

At his words, her heart hit her toes. Mrs. Nathan Case?

"What?" She wheezed, unable to breathe. "Have you lost your mind?"

Her hands left his chest and settled on her temples, where a jackhammer had started drilling into her brain.

"Hardly."

"This isn't because of the other night, is it? Because I assure you, one night of sex does not require a noble gesture on your part." She leaned forward and stage-whispered, "I wasn't a virgin."

A low chuckle rumbled out of his chest. "You sure didn't behave like one."

She let his comment pass unanswered while scrambling to make sense of what he'd just proposed. Unfortunately, she found it almost impossible to think rationally while the scorned sixteen-year-old inside her whooped with triumph. She smothered young Emma's enthusiasm and concentrated on reality.

Marry Nathan? Impossible. His ability to make any woman feel special did not make him marriage material.

"My father put you up to this, didn't he?"

"It's what we talked about this afternoon." Nathan's eyes narrowed. "He thinks it's past time you married."

"To someone I choose."

White teeth flashing in a cocky grin. "Got anyone in mind?"

Understanding dawned. She gasped in horror. "You thought I chose you?" An unsteady laugh escaped her. Oh, the humiliation. "I don't want to marry you," she said, keeping her tone slow and deliberate so he wouldn't misinterpret her meaning. "I don't want to marry anyone. Not right now."

Not without love.

"Your father seems pretty determined."

"You have no idea," she muttered. "But it's not happening."

Looking past Nathan's imposing shoulders, Emma eyed her father's enormous study and wished they were using more of it for this discussion. Speaking sensibly about all the reasons why they shouldn't get married would be easier without Nathan's gorgeous, muscular body trapping her against the door.

In an instant, she plummeted back in time to three weeks ago, when she stood pinned against a different door, her heart thudding madly, her senses alive while he thrust into her. With absolute authority, he had stripped her defenses, made her crazy with wanting and done things to her body that left her in a panting, spent puddle, craving more.

Emma pushed away the memory, locked her knees when they threatened to buckle and marshaled her resentment.

"Why would you agree to something like this?" she demanded.

"Case Consolidated Holdings wants to do business with Montgomery Oil."

"Daddy made our marriage a condition of the deal."

A business deal. She might have guessed. A howl rose in her chest. She clenched her teeth together to contain it. How could her father do this to her again? Hadn't he learned anything from the last time he tried meddling in her love life?

The summer she graduated from college she'd been engaged to an up-and-coming executive at Montgomery Oil. Imagine her surprise when she discovered that the reason for Jackson Orr's rapid advancement had to do with the deal he had struck with her father when he'd first started dating Emma. Jackson would move up the food chain in exchange for marrying her. When she'd found out, she'd broken her engagement and determined never to repeat her mistake.

"It must be one hell of a business deal," she grumbled, reaching over to flip on the lights.

Floor lamps chased away shadow. She blinked as her eyes adjusted to the brightness.

"The biggest one I've ever done."

"Then I guess marrying me is a small price to pay." The bitter taste of the words gave her tone a sharp bite.

"What's wrong?"

Her spirits drooped still lower. With a big business deal on the line, Nathan wouldn't be receptive to her pleas to turn her father down.

"I don't want to marry you like this."

"Like this?" he echoed dryly, picking up on how those last two words had betrayed her. "Is there some other way you'd like to marry me?"

Emma ignored the gleam in his eye. "I don't want to marry *anyone* like this." She didn't want to marry a man her father could manipulate. She couldn't respect such a man, and she knew she'd never trust him. "I resent being used as a bargaining chip in my father's deal with you."

"And I don't like being a pawn in your father's attempt to

control you," Nathan countered without heat, speaking as if he found the whole mess completely reasonable. "However, I suggest we make the best of the situation we find ourselves in."

His eyes burned with sexy intent as he located her gown's side zipper and slid it down. Before she voiced a protest, he stroked the straps off her shoulders. Her breath rushed out as she caught the dress before it fell. Her dress. Her defenses. Let one drop and the other would follow.

"Let me remind you how amazing we are together," he coaxed, sliding his lips into the spot on her shoulder he'd mentioned earlier.

"I don't need reminding, Nathan." Anxiety and anticipation fluttered in her midsection like drunken fairies. Although she couldn't shake her misgivings about his reasons for marrying her, the memory of his body mastering hers proved a powerful aphrodisiac. Marriage to Nathan would be like bronco riding: dangerous, exhilarating, uncertain. He would trample her heart, oblivious to the damage he'd inflicted, then race off to take on his next challenge. "But great sex isn't enough to base a marriage on."

He reached out and took her chin in his fingers to turn her face toward him. "It is if we don't indulge in unrealistic expectations."

She almost laughed.

In her darkest moments, when she'd contemplated her life if forced to go along with her father's plans, she'd pictured herself living the way her mother had, married to a businessman who worked long hours. She'd imagined herself spending her mornings shopping, followed by lunch at the club. Eventually, she'd indulge in a torrid affair with her golf coach or her daughter's French tutor. From observing others in their social circle, she'd assumed that she and her husband would live completely separate lives, coming together for business dinners and parties. Sex would be infrequent and only if she became sufficiently tipsy.

That was not the life she would have with Nathan Case, a man who left her weak-kneed and wanting with a look. For him, she'd pore through lingerie catalogs and work out at the gym to make sure she maintained her perfect figure. She saw herself planning luscious dinners for two and vacations to exotic locales. He would become her life, her obsession.

Emma shivered.

And what would she get in return? Would he be a faithful husband? Or would he indulge in extramarital affairs that would drive her to become like her father: Suspicious and watchful to the point where she drove him away? She'd watched her mother grow more and more miserable until Emma's junior year of high school, when she'd filed for divorce and moved to Los Angeles. She'd never remarried, and Emma often wondered if her mother was less afraid of losing her alimony than she was of risking her heart again.

Recalling his flirtation with the blonde in the library, doubts marched in and rang a warning bell.

"Unrealistic expectations?" she echoed. "Such as fidelity?" There, she'd said it.

"I intend for this to be a real marriage, Emma." Lightning danced in his gray eyes. His fingers slipped whisper-soft against her cheek. "You will be the only woman in my bed."

But what about his heart? How could a marriage be real without love?

Emma fought the panic trembling through her as she considered what sort of emotional seesaw awaited her as Nathan's wife. When her father had barred access to her trust fund ten months ago, complaining that the amount she spent on clothes and shoes proved she had no grasp of fiscal responsibility, she thought he was just trying to teach her a lesson. She never truly believed he'd force her to marry someone.

Reaching to fidget with her jewelry, Emma tugged on her earlobe and recalled Nathan pocketing the sapphire and diamond drops. They were one of her earliest designs. She'd dabbled at making jewelry since graduating from college, but a two-year stint as a goldsmith's assistant had dampened her enthusiasm for executing other people's designs. But when her father cut her off, she'd stubbornly decided to live on what she could make selling her own line of jewelry.

She realized after six months of slow sales that even if she lived without luxuries like designer fashions and spa visits, making enough to pay her mortgage, put gas in her car and food in her refrigerator would require her to work a lot harder than she ever had. And not just for a year, but for the rest of her life.

Or she could get her trust fund back. If she did what her father wanted and got married. Within one year. It was the one condition he'd put on restoring her funds.

She was tired of fighting. Fighting her father's will. Fighting the temptation to spend money. Fighting to pay her bills. This year had been hell. It would be so easy to quit. To do what her father wanted. Marry Nathan. Let him take care of her. No more eyestrain or aching muscles from sitting at her worktable for hours at a time. No more fretting over whether she could afford to keep her membership at her favorite yoga studio.

Emma straightened her spine. "May I have my earrings back?"

"I think I'll hold on to them for a little while."

"Why?"

"You disappeared out of my life three weeks ago without looking back. I want to make sure that doesn't happen again."

"I didn't disappear." But she had. The flash fire of desire

between them had sent her scurrying for cover like a startled rabbit. "Please, Nathan, can't we talk about this tomorrow? I'm tired, and I need time to think. Let's meet for breakfast in the morning."

Her weary defeat must have reached him because his hands fell away. He backed off enough to let her open the door and watched in silence while she zipped up her dress.

"I'll pick you up here at ten." Powerful and confident, dangerous and sexy, the combination sabotaged her resolve to walk away without a backward glance.

"Ten. Sure." She fled before he could stop her. She didn't think she had enough strength to resist him one more time. She had to get out of here. Tonight.

Racing up the back stairs, her heart pounding in fear that he might change his mind and follow her, she reached the second floor and paused to catch her breath when she was confident he'd let her go.

The wide hallway in front of her wrapped around the four-story great hall, circling upward to a dome painted with clouds. Her father had spent $50 million to re-create a little slice of French drama on the two-hundred-acre estate north of Dallas. The forty-thousand-square-foot mansion took its inspiration from Versailles both in style and grandeur with pastel walls and ornate French antiques throughout. It had taken almost three years to build, thanks to her father's obsessive need to oversee the tiniest detail, but it had kept his mind off his divorce from his fourth wife and granted Emma a respite from his nosing into her life.

Unfortunately, nothing good lasts forever. And when the last piece of furniture had been delivered at the beginning of February, Silas had once again turned his attention to his only daughter.

"And he complains about my spending," she grumbled.

The party didn't sound as if it was winding down. She neared the rail and peered below. A moving, brightly colored mosaic of elegant gowns and glittering jewels made her dizzy. Emma backed away and placed her hand over her churning stomach.

"There you are."

Emma turned in the direction of her father's voice. He strode along the hallway in her direction, his long legs eating up the distance between them. At sixty-three, he had the athletic build and energy of a man twenty years younger. He used his height as well as his strong personality to intimidate business associates and family members alike.

"I saw you and Nathan together." Her father eyed her mussed hair. "Have you talked?"

"Oh, we talked all right," she muttered, her cheeks warming.

"Wonderful. Come downstairs. I want to announce your engagement."

Emma hated confrontation. Growing up, she had learned to keep her head down in the ongoing battle between her parents. Clasping her hands together, Emma gathered her resolve.

"Not tonight, Daddy. I'm tired."

"Nonsense. It will just be a quick announcement and a toast to the two of you."

As much as she hated taking on her father, she was determined to stand her ground on this issue. "There is no engagement."

Silas Montgomery's blue-green eyes blazed. "Didn't he ask you to marry him?"

"He told me we were getting married. I told him we weren't." Resentment burned, giving her courage. She had to find some way to escape her father's plans for her. Whatever it took, she had no intention of becoming Mrs. Nathan Case. "I'm not going to marry him as part of some business deal between you two."

"Last Valentine's Day, I gave you a year to find someone

to marry. That time is almost up, and you haven't settled on anyone. So I found someone for you."

"I don't want to marry Nathan." Her father and Nathan were evenly matched in stubbornness, arrogance and lack of concern about her feelings in this matter. "In fact, he's the last man in the world I would pick to marry."

Her father frowned at her aggrieved tone. "That's not the impression I got from the conversation between you and Jaime at Christmas."

Emma groaned. As if this entire night wasn't humiliating enough, now she'd learned that her father had overheard her telling her sister-in-law about leaving Grant's party with Nathan and what had happened afterwards?

"You were eavesdropping?"

"You weren't exactly keeping your voices down."

"I thought we were alone in the house."

"I came back to get some papers." Her father's handsome face reflected little compassion. He was dealing with her with the same ruthless determination he brought to all his business dealings. "I know you've liked Nathan for a long time. I remember how you behaved when he used to visit from college.

So did she. Emma's cheeks burned. "I was sixteen. I didn't know what I wanted."

"And now you're twenty-eight. It's time you figured that out." Her father tugged on his cuffs, signaling the end of the discussion. "Nathan will make a good husband for you."

"I don't love him. He doesn't love me."

"But he will marry you."

"Because you're blackmailing him the same way you're blackmailing me." The edges of Emma's vision began to darken. She focused on her father's bow tie to keep from being swallowed up by helplessness. "Don't do this. It's not fair to either of us."

"You need someone to take care of you. Nathan is the man to do it."

"I don't need someone to take care of me."

"Yes, you do. You've never worked, and because you've never earned your own money, you spend without thought. I hate to think what would happen if you weren't limited by an allowance. And from what Cody tells me, your loft in Houston is a disaster. I've looked out for you for twenty-eight years, it's time I turn the job over to your husband."

Her loft wasn't a disaster. It just needed a master bathroom, a new kitchen, all new wiring and plumbing. She'd bought it shortly before she'd lost access to her trust fund. Her jewelry business barely covered her necessities. She had nothing left for remodeling.

"I don't need a husband. I can take care of myself. My jewelry business is taking off." A major exaggeration, but necessary if she was going to convince her father to give up on marrying her off.

"How much do you have left of the $100,000 I gave you last February?"

"Most of it." Emma refused to be more specific. She'd been in denial the first few months after being cut off and hadn't yet learned to be frugal. Giving an accurate number would reinforce her father's opinion about her frivolous spending.

"More like two-thirds of it," her father countered.

A mad, ridiculous notion sparked. "What if I had all of it?"

Her challenge ignited a speculative look in her father's eye. He loved making deals. "What do you mean?"

Yes, what did she mean? She wanted to retract her words, but it was too late. Backing down now would only give her father more reason to think she was flighty. "You say I can't take care of myself and earn a living. I say you're wrong." Emma gathered a deep breath and plunged forward. "What if I replace the entire hundred thousand by Valentine's Day?"

"How are you going to do that in six weeks?" Her father laughed.

"By selling my jewelry."

He shook his head. "You'll never do it. You're good at spending money, not making it. You don't have the drive to work hard and succeed."

Her heart constricted. Paralyzed by his scornful words, she felt smothered by all the mistakes she'd made in her life. Was it too late for her to change how her father perceived her? And what if she didn't try? It was either a loveless marriage to Nathan or learning to live on what she earned. Both sounded dreadful.

"But if I do," she persisted, her voice strengthening as her determination grew, "will you give me back my trust fund?"

Her father snorted. "I've seen the balance in your account. You won't be able to put the money back."

He was probably right, but she had to try. "I can and I will." She hoped she was displaying a great deal more confidence than she currently possessed. The task she'd set for herself made her stomach twist with anxiety. "One more thing. When I replace the entire hundred thousand, you'll also agree to stop meddling in my life." She stuck out her hand. "Deal?"

"As long as you don't borrow the money from anyone to bring the account balance up, we have a deal." Her father swallowed her hand with his and squeezed gently. His smile softened. "I'm only doing what I know is best for you."

"It's what you think is best for me," she retorted, pulling free. "And you're wrong." Her insides felt like jelly. What had she just agreed to do? "Now, you'd better get back to your guests."

"Are you coming down?"

Emma shook her head. "I'm driving back to Houston tonight."

"It's too dangerous to be on the roads at such a late hour."

It was far more dangerous for her to stay. "I'll be careful."

He frowned. "Emma—"

"One way or another, in six weeks I'm no longer your responsibility, Daddy," she said. "It's past time you start letting go."

"Of course it is." He kissed on the top of her head and retreated down the hall.

In her bedroom, Emma stripped out of her dress, being extra careful with it even in her haste. She'd borrowed both the dress and her shoes from Jaime, and would never forgive herself if she returned the designer original with any damage. As she zipped the gown into its protective bag, she contemplated her shift in perspective. A year ago she wouldn't have taken such care with her clothes. Any tear, stain, sometimes even a single wearing would prompt her to shift the outfit to the back of her closet. Funny…what Jaime had given her with so little concern, Emma now treated like a magical gown from her fairy godmother.

Thank goodness this dress hadn't disappeared at the stroke of midnight. A wry smile formed despite her turbulent emotions.

She donned jeans and a sweater, and then tossed the rest of her clothes into her overnight bag. Until her encounter with Nathan, she'd intended to stay the night, but after what had almost happened between them again, she needed some time to think, and the four and a half hours back to Houston would be just about right.

She didn't worry about falling asleep at the wheel. The encounter with Nathan ensured that the adrenaline pumping through her veins would keep her awake. As for being sober, she'd wanted a clear head in case he'd shown up tonight and hadn't allowed herself a single sip of champagne.

Feeling like a cat burglar, she hugged the wall as she descended the back stairs. She pictured her earrings resting in Nathan's pocket. What a lousy thief she would make, coming away from the house with lighter pockets than when she'd arrived.

Not until she turned left out of the driveway and followed the moonlit road back to the highway did the pressure in her chest lessen. Whatever it took, she'd put the money back in her account. She'd prove to her father that she could take care of herself and avoid the marriage net he'd woven to snare her. Nathan Case would have to figure out some other way to do the deal with Silas Montgomery.

"What do you mean she's not here? When did she leave?" Nathan glared around the quiet, empty cavern of a foyer that showed no signs it had been occupied by party guests a few hours earlier.

The maid clasped her hands before her. "I'm not sure."

"Hey, Nathan." Cody Montgomery trotted down the grand staircase. Dressed in jeans and a navy sweater, he advanced with a huge smile. "What are you doing here?"

The maid faded away as Nathan shook his best friend's hand. "Your sister and I were supposed to have breakfast this morning."

"Are you sure? Dad told me she headed back to Houston last night."

"Quite sure," Nathan said, indulging in a frustrated exhale. She'd disappeared on him again. He should have listened to his instincts last night and persuaded her to go back to his hotel room with him. "We had some things to discuss."

"Like setting a wedding date?" Cody chuckled as Nathan raised his eyebrows. "Dad told me you two are getting married. Never thought I'd see the day when you'd finally admit my sister has had you wrapped around her finger since she was sixteen."

Nathan held a growl between his clenched teeth while his best friend had a good laugh at his expense. "I wouldn't go that far."

Cody frowned. "But you love her."

Nathan wasn't surprised by the question. After five years of marriage, Cody and Jaime were still crazy about each other as they awaited the birth of their first child. Nathan wasn't sure what sort of water the two were drinking, but he intended to stick with whiskey.

"You know how I feel about love," Nathan said. He wasn't looking to fall into that trap. "It's never going to happen for me."

"But you're getting married." Cody gaze shifted away from Nathan. With a glance over his shoulder, he edged Nathan toward the front door, but didn't speak until the two men stood outside in the brisk January wind. "Does Emma know you're not in love with her?"

Nathan wasn't going to lie to his best friend. "She knows."

"I can't believe it's okay with her. After watching her mother's marriage to Dad fall apart, she's pretty determined not to marry unless the guy's crazy in love with her."

Cody made no secret of his belief that Silas's third wife had married her billionaire husband for financial rather than romantic reasons.

"She'll come around."

Cody shot his friend a skeptical look. "I don't think she will. You've been on her radar since she was a teenager, but she's got this whole fairy-tale happily-ever-after thing going. She's not going to marry you unless she thinks you're madly in love with her."

"Have a little faith in my powers of persuasion." Nathan offered his friend a slow grin.

A grin that faded as he strode to his car and gave his best friend a farewell salute. Cody's words poked at him like a burr long after the wheels of the BMW 650i coupe hit the main road.

Love.

Emma wasn't going to marry without it. Nathan wouldn't marry with it. Stalemate.

He wasn't sure when he'd decided that he'd never let himself go down that path. Had it been the Christmas morning when his mother burst into tears because he'd asked why his father didn't spend any holidays with them? He'd been eight that year. Or maybe when he turned ten and Brandon Case's wife had shown up to see for herself what sort of "whore" her husband had taken up with. His mother had cried for three hours straight after that. The next day she'd slapped him when he said he hated his father and hoped he rotted in hell.

Love made people miserable. It led to expectations. Expectations led to disappointment. Disappointment led to infidelity. Infidelity led to divorce. Except for Cody, all his friends had cheated on their wives or been cheated on. And they'd all started out madly in love.

He was an hour south of Dallas when his cell rang. He engaged the car's hands free system. "Hello."

"Hey, Nat, how'd it go?"

Hearing Max's voice, Nathan restrained a snarl. He could tell from his older brother's overly cheerful tone that he'd called expecting to hear that Nathan had failed. "It went fine."

"So, Montgomery is doing the deal?" Max's voice lost some of the good humor.

If his half brothers found out about the strings Silas had attached to the deal, Nathan would never hear the end of it. He intended to get the contracts signed without that happening.

"There are a few bugs to work out, but I'd say things look pretty good." Nathan relaxed his death grip on the steering wheel.

In his early twenties, he'd spent almost a year on the

poker tournament circuit, learning how to read people and to hide his thoughts. In the championship game, he bluffed two of the best poker players in the country and won half a million dollars. The skills he'd picked up during that time had come in handy these last six months working with his half brothers. He'd learned a long time ago never to let them see him sweat.

"But you don't have a signed contract," Max persisted, regaining his cockiness.

Nathan ground his teeth. Leave it to the middle Case brother to point that out. "As I said, there are a couple details still under negotiation."

"You were pretty sure you'd come back with a signed contract. Wasn't Montgomery impressed with your proposal?"

Nathan bristled at the implied insult. His brothers had developed their business acumen in the boardrooms of Corporate America. Nathan had taken an entrepreneurial approach. He'd grown his millions in the stock market and from venture capital investing. No matter how legitimate his investments, Max and Sebastian refused to give him credit for having a strong business sense. They couldn't get past the fact that his fortune had grown from the seeds of his poker winnings.

"Silas is looking over the numbers. He'll have an answer for me in six weeks." Valentine's Day. He hadn't understood the significance of Silas's choice of date until Emma explained her own deadline to him.

"That long? He's probably no more comfortable with the risk than Sebastian and I are. Two hundred million is a big chunk of our assets. If you're wrong, we stand to lose everything."

After their father's retirement, Sebastian and Max had changed Case Consolidated Holdings' business strategy from high-risk to ultraconservative. Nathan would be the first to admit that their father's obsession with huge profits had led him to make some dicey deals, but his brothers had overreacted.

And because they had, Nathan's ideas for moving forward by joining with Montgomery Oil to create a new company instead of continuing to buy existing companies had been met with skepticism.

"I'm not wrong," Nathan said.

He'd been a fool to let his father talk him into coming to work with his brothers. Brandon Case had been out of his mind to think Sebastian and Max needed him. They only needed each other. And their safe little strategies.

"You feed on taking risks," Max said. "It's like you get high from it."

"Any risks I've taken in business have come after a lot of careful analysis."

Max snorted. "Is that what you did at the poker table? Careful analysis?"

Nathan hated having his hard work reduced to little more than fortuitous circumstances, but he wasn't going to brag about his accomplishments. He intended to demonstrate to Max and Sebastian how wrong they were to underestimate him.

"Face it, Nat," Max continued. "You're not going to get the deal with Montgomery done. Silas is just leading you on. Which brings me to the reason I called. We heard from Lucas Smythe. He's willing to take a meeting."

Max's news infuriated Nathan. Sebastian had been eager to bring Smythe Industries into the fold for a couple years. Buying the family-run business would further diversify Case Consolidated Holdings' portfolio. It was the perfect move for his risk-averse brothers.

"Why now? A year ago he turned us down flat."

"He didn't say and it doesn't matter. Sebastian and I like Lucas's company. There's not as much risk involved."

Or as much reward. "All I need is six weeks to get the details ironed out." He left the specifics deliberately vague. "If you give me time, I can make this deal happen."

"This isn't about you." Max's voice hardened. "It's about what's best for Case Consolidated Holdings. Stop acting like a lone wolf and prove to us that you can put the company's best interests before your ego."

"That's what I'm doing."

The unfairness of the criticism hit Nathan hard. He'd always been the one on the outside. His mother's long-term affair with Brandon had robbed Nathan of any chance for a normal family life. After her death, when he'd been twelve, he'd gone to live with the Case family. Neither the wife Brandon had cheated on, nor her overprotective sons had been happy to share a roof with the living proof of Brandon's infidelity. Sebastian and Max were thirteen months apart, with Nathan a mere six months younger than Max. But while his brothers were as tight as twins, they shut out Nathan completely.

"It's hard to act like part of the team when I've been treated like the opposition."

Silence followed Nathan's statement. When Max spoke again, he sounded colder than ever. "We'll see you in the office tomorrow."

"Sure."

"I'll set up a meeting with Sebastian in the afternoon. You can bring us up-to-date then."

Without waiting for Nathan's answer, Max disconnected the call. Nathan muttered a string of curses and inserted a CD. While Dierks Bentley reminded him that good things happen, Nathan contemplated his situation. The last six months had been hell. He probably wouldn't have lasted this long if he didn't love a challenge so much.

Nathan rested his elbow against the door and propped his head on his hand. Unbidden, the sexy image of Emma wearing the black thong and matching strapless bra rose in his mind as he thought back to the night of Grant's party. Her skin had been like hot silk beneath his fingers as he'd stripped her underwear off. She was exactly the sort he went for, all sultry sophistication and flashing sable eyes.

Her brother, Cody, had been his best friend in college. The first time Nathan had laid eyes on her, she'd been sixteen. The four-year difference in their ages made her jailbait, but she'd stalked him, her curiosity fully engaged on her journey from girl to woman.

An attractive, cheeky brat, she'd worn red lipstick to draw attention to her lush mouth, batted her long lashes and flaunted her shapely golden body in a string bikini every chance she got. She would arch her back and lift her wet hair so the breeze would catch the damp strands.

Amused by her kittenish play, he'd let her practice her feminine wiles on him. Keeping his distance, however, grew increasingly difficult as she got bolder. Then came the afternoon she caught him alone in the kitchen. In an insanely short skirt and high heels, she'd strutted past him, plying his libido with her sassy smile.

If he'd caught wind of her intentions, he'd have been out of there fast, but he never dreamed that she'd back him against a counter and set her full, rosy mouth on a collision course with his lips. For two sluggish heartbeats he'd stared at her pretty face, long lashes painting ebony half moons on her flushed cheeks, and been tempted to teach her a lesson on the dangers of flirting with older men. Instead, rattled by her detrimental effect on his good judgment, he'd rebuffed her without much finesse, cut his visit short and hit the highway.

Twelve years later she was no longer forbidden fruit.

Three weeks ago, he'd had his first taste, and it left him hungry for more.

With an impatient, disgusted snort he shoved the provocative pictures away and focused on the problem at hand:

convincing Emma to marry him. Because he couldn't do the deal with her father and take control of Case Consolidated Holdings away from his half brothers unless he did.

Three

Emma sat in the middle of her walk-in closet. Surrounded by empty hangers and four plastic garbage bags filled with the last of her designer clothes, she fought an overwhelming sense of hopelessness. She needed to replace $35,000 and had about five weeks to do it. The amount staggered her.

Her cell phone rang.

"I was calling to invite you out to dinner," Addison said, her tone brisk. "Paul's taking the kids to basketball practice tonight so I've got a couple hours free."

Emma pictured her best friend sitting in her beautifully decorated home office, going over the details for whatever event she was organizing. For the last five years, Addison had been growing her party planning business, working long hours, setting goals and achieving them. With a tireless work ethic and an abundance of determination, she inspired Emma's entrepreneurial drive and at the same time made Emma feel guilty that she didn't work harder.

"I don't know if I can make it," Emma said, when what she

really meant to say is that she didn't know if she could afford it. Thanks to her father's actions a year ago, she'd gone from spendthrift to penny pincher. The transformation had been humbling, but she recognized that it had also been a good lesson to learn. "I've been going through my closet to see what I can sell."

"Are you crying?"

Emma shook her head and dashed the back of her hand against her damp cheek. "No."

"You sound like you are. Why don't you just let me lend you the money?"

"You and Paul can't afford to do that. And I wouldn't take it anyway. I've got to do this on my own." She'd never get her father to stop meddling if she didn't beat him at his own game.

"You aren't going to make enough money in five weeks by selling your clothes. Have you heard from the people running the art and design show?"

A couple months ago, Addison had badgered her into applying for a spot at a prestigious art and design show in Baton Rouge. Unsure how her work would be received, Emma's nerves had been tied up in knots. Yesterday, she'd been accepted.

"I'm in. But I don't have enough inventory to take to the show. Almost everything is consigned at Biella's." By her calculation, she had at least $50,000 tied up in unsold jewelry. Almost all of it decorated the cases in Biella's, Houston's most prestigious jeweler.

"So, go there and get it back. It's not as if they've sold more than five or six pieces in the last six months. I think the Baton Rouge show's your best bet."

"But can I make enough?" Emma dumped a garbage bag out onto the floor and began sliding hangers back into her clothes. "Daddy says I don't have the drive to succeed. Maybe he's right."

"He's not right. I know you can do this and, deep down, so do you."

Did she? Emma wasn't so sure. Being independent and financially responsible was hard work. And, right now, the enormity of the task before her made her want to crawl back into bed and pull the covers over her head.

"Besides," Addison continued. "Don't you want to see the look on your father's face when he realizes he has to turn your money over to you? It should be priceless."

Addison's enthusiasm bolstered Emma's sagging confidence. "What would I do without you?"

"Fortunately, you'll never have to know. Now, put on some Prada and get going."

An hour later, Emma stepped into Biella's, and paused just inside the glass doors. Fidgeting with her gold hoop earring, she scanned the large space. The exclusive downtown Houston jewelry store had been split into two parts. Diamonds and precious stone rings occupied one side, while necklaces, bracelets, watches and men's jewelry filled the cases on the other. Tones of cinnamon, gold and slate cradled the expensive collections. Copper-toned mirrors lined the walls behind the displays, reflecting the golden light from crystal chandeliers. Emma's feet sank into plush, dark gray carpet as she circled the room.

Little had changed since she'd honed her skills here as an apprentice goldsmith five years ago. The ambiance remained luxurious and elegant. The store owed as much of its success to the quality of the shopping experience as to the uniqueness of its merchandise.

An eager, smiling sales associate appeared ready to offer the knowledgeable assistance expected at Biella's. The redhead must be a new hire; otherwise, she'd recognize Emma and realize she wasn't a customer.

Emma approached the cases, drawing the sales consultant like a shark to fresh blood.

"Aren't these beautiful? A local artist does the work. Is there something you'd like to see up close?"

Thinking that she'd seen each and every piece up close already, Emma smiled at the clerk, appreciating her enthusiasm. "I was wondering if Thomas was around."

Thomas McMann was Biella's manager, and Emma's former boss. He'd been the one to propose the idea of consignment; Emma had hoped to sell the pieces outright. She understood his reluctance to take on so much inventory. Considering her lack of reputation, the price she'd assigned to each piece and the quality of the designs, he might not want to take a chance on such untraditional items.

"I'll see if he's available."

"Thanks."

While the girl disappeared into a back room, Emma counted the pieces in the display case to see if anything had been sold. Another two of the smaller pieces were missing. She breathed a sigh of relief. That meant another $3,000 in the bank.

It would make a little dent in the $35,000 she still had to put back. It was a huge amount to earn in five weeks, and she'd be lying if she said she wasn't daunted by the prospect, but failure meant she couldn't show her father and Nathan that she was a capable, independent woman who deserved to make her own choices about who she married and when.

Too bad she hadn't known about her father's plans for Nathan five months ago. She might not be in her current predicament. When her father first cut her off, it took her two months to go through a quarter of the money, and another thirty days before the reality of her troubles began sinking in.

She enjoyed designing and creating jewelry, but she'd never considered pursuing it as a career. It had been Addison who'd suggested that Emma could make enough money to keep herself afloat if she stuck with creating spectacular, one-of-a-kind pieces.

Unfortunately, setting herself up with the equipment and supplies she needed put another dent in the hundred thousand, and another thirty days melted away before she'd produced enough pieces to show the manager of Biella's what she could do. In the end, her hard work had paid off, and the first dollars she'd earned by selling what she'd made had given her a huge thrill.

"Hello, Emma," a soft nasal voice greeted. Tall and as thin as a cartoon rendering of Ichobod Crane, all elbows and skinny legs, Thomas McMann had a beak for a nose and incredible bedroom eyes framed by sumptuous eyelashes that belonged to a cover girl. "Did you see we sold three more pieces?"

"Three?" She rechecked. Sure enough. A little glow blossomed around her heart. She recognized it as confidence, something she'd been sorely lacking for the last eleven months. "That's terrific." She took the envelope he extended, resisting the urge to tear it open and see the size of the check.

"I hope you've brought us some new pieces."

"Actually, I was hoping to take these back." She pointed to the jewelry in the case. "I was invited to participate in an art and design show, and you have all my inventory."

"Oh. That's a problem." He looked at her somberly. "Your jewelry is really starting to sell, and we have two months left on our contract."

By that he meant he wasn't willing to give up the forty percent commission he took from each piece. Emma chewed on her lower lip.

"I'll return whatever doesn't sell at the show, and I'll design some new pieces as well."

A quarter-inch of glass and one man's stubbornness separated Emma from the glittering collection of jewelry she'd designed and crafted. Regaining possession of the necklaces, earrings and rings, embellished with diamonds and precious gems, was crucial to her plan.

"You can have whatever we haven't sold in two months." From his tone, he wasn't yielding. Thomas had always been a stickler for rules. It's what kept him in charge of Houston's top jewelry store for the last ten years, and why she'd left.

With her heart crushed to the size of a peanut, Emma blew out a breath and decided she'd better come up with plan B if she hoped to escape her father's marriage trap.

After leaving Biella's, she decided to stop by Case Consolidated Holdings and retrieve her earrings. If she hoped to have enough to sell at the show, she might have to sacrifice some of her personal favorites. She would need the earrings Nathan took.

Standing in the elevator, she watched the floor numbers light up one by one in the display panel beside the door. Her stomach gave a little lurch as the elevator slowed. She smoothed her simple beige silk dress, recognizing the nerves behind the gesture. More than nerves, she amended. Her heart thudded almost painfully in her chest. Panic better described it.

Until that moment, she'd forgotten that she'd stood him up for breakfast on New Year's Day. For the last few days she'd been so focused on her finances that she hadn't considered how annoyed he would be that she'd dodged him yet again. But how could she do otherwise when she'd almost given in and let him have his way with her a second time?

Just thinking about him, recalling what he'd said to her, the way he'd known exactly what would drive her crazy, she was hot and ready for a repeat performance of their one time together. Of course, there wouldn't be a repeat performance.

Emma entered the offices of Case Consolidated Holdings, immediately distracted from her mission by the original artwork hanging on the lobby walls. She stepped closer to one particular painting. Her eyes widened as she recognized the work of Julian Onderdonk, one of the most highly acclaimed Texas artists of the twentieth century.

He'd always been a favorite of Emma's because his work captured the subtle beauty of south Texas. She'd encouraged her father to purchase three of his paintings. He'd hung them in his study and often remarked that although they hadn't appealed to him when he'd first bought them, he came to appreciate the landscapes more every day.

"Can I help you?" the young woman at the reception desk inquired.

"In just a second." Emma moved on to the next painting.

Adrian Brewer, she mused. Painted in the late twenties. Emma admired the field of bluebonnets that drifted off into the expansive Texas horizon. Someone with a discerning eye shared her appreciation for early Texas artists. Who was the collector?

"Do you have an appointment?" the receptionist continued, her brisk tone disturbing Emma's reflective mood.

Art always had a powerful, soothing effect on her, and right now, she needed all the calm she could muster.

"I think she's here to see me," a familiar, masculine voice replied.

Nathan came to stand behind her right shoulder, close enough for her to feel the tension in his muscles. The hair on her arms lifted as if she stood in close proximity to a lightning strike. She froze, dazzled by the effect the man had on her.

How easy it would be to lean back against him and be enfolded in his arms, to let him take away her worries and drown her doubts in deep, drugging kisses. She inhaled his scent, a subtle blend of sandalwood soap and lavender shampoo, and recalled how his hair had felt between her fingers as she'd gripped him tight and encouraged him to feast on her. A groan collected in her throat. She eased her eyes shut to capture the memory and hold it tight.

"I always considered Julian Onderdonk the master of the bluebonnet," she said, grateful to hear the steadiness of her voice. Now if only she could count on the rest of her body to follow suit. "But after seeing Brewer's interpretation, I might have to change my mind."

"I wouldn't know anything about that," he retorted, clipping off the words with an impatience that banished her sensual daydreaming. "We buy purely for investment purposes."

Emma's eyes flashed open. She glanced up at his forbidding profile. He appeared preoccupied with the painting. Despite his grim expression, she detected a hint of softness in his lips. The gentleness vanished a second later as his flat, gray eyes slashed to her. Her pulse jerked.

Seizing her by the elbow, he drew her down the hall that stretched away from the receptionist's desk. The speech she'd prepared vanished at his touch. She was at a loss for words, wishing his impersonal grip didn't affect her so acutely.

The hall buzzed with activity, but Emma might have been blind and deaf for all the attention she paid. She couldn't concentrate on anything but Nathan and the annoyance radiating from him. Clearly, this had been a mistake.

He steered her into a huge office and abandoned her in the middle of the space. While he crossed to his desk, Emma glanced around. The walls held more artwork, this of a modern flavor, by artists whose work she didn't recognize. Half a dozen canvases sat propped against an end table. Yet as compelling as her curiosity about the art was, the man who owned it captivated her more.

Nathan stood before the wall of windows, hands clasped behind his back, and surveyed downtown Houston. The broad shoulders she'd caressed and clung to appeared no less intimidating encased in a charcoal-gray suit coat that matched his eyes. Sunlight stabbed through the window and drew forth the gold in his brown hair.

"To what do I owe the pleasure of this visit?" he asked.

It dawned on her that she'd used the excuse of retrieving her jewelry to see him again. "I came to collect my earrings."

"They're at my condo," he said. "We could go and pick them up."

Him and her alone in his condo would only lead to one thing. "I wouldn't want to put you out. Why don't you just bring them here tomorrow and I'll pick them up?"

"How about dinner tonight?" He countered.

Dinner with him sounded like a prelude to seduction. "How about breakfast tomorrow?"

For the first time since entering the room, he turned and faced her. "But if we started with dinner tonight, breakfast tomorrow will be inevitable."

The air sizzled with the power of his magnetism.

"I already have plans for dinner," she hedged as he advanced toward her. Emma backed up. If she didn't get out of here fast, he'd figure out how effortlessly he made her pulse race and her willpower waver. "How about we meet at nine tomorrow morning after my yoga class?" Preferably at a place where she couldn't be persuaded to take her clothes off. "I go to Carley's Café quite a bit."

"I don't think so." He shook his head. "You stood me up for breakfast once."

Emma doubted that he'd ever been stood up before. Cody had regaled her with enough of Nathan's conquests for her to recognize that he kept a woman around as long as it suited him to do so. *He* determined the length of the relationship, not the other way around.

She'd understood that three weeks ago when she'd left the party and gone to his penthouse condo overlooking downtown Houston. But that didn't mean she had to wait for him to grow tired of her, like all the other women who fell for his charms.

She shrugged. "Sorry about that. I had to get back to Houston right away."

"And the reason you didn't call and give me a heads-up?"

What could she say to that? "Because you don't take no for an answer."

"Funny," he murmured, his gaze trailing over her features, "that doesn't stop you from saying no to me."

With her heart thundering in her ears, she pressed her lips together to keep from spilling the truth. In the weeks since he'd taken her hard and fast against the front door of his condo, she'd been consumed with a crazy, irrational desire to see where dating him might lead. She'd been on the verge of returning his phone calls when her father had interfered and saved her from making a huge mistake.

"Until three weeks ago, you never gave me the chance," she said, immediately regretting both the statement and her aggrieved tone.

"I didn't realize you were that interested," he said, taking a step toward her.

His predatory intent induced Emma to take a step back. "I wasn't."

"No?"

Emma's pulse kicked up a notch, intensifying her need to retreat. When her back collided with something solid, she brushed aside her bangs in acute frustration. She'd misjudged her direction and missed the doorway. The wall kept her from escaping.

"Look." She tugged on her earring. "The night of Grant's party was nice."

"Nice?" he echoed, his tone neutral.

"It gave me closure."

He set his hand on the wall above her shoulder and leaned in. "Closure?"

"I wondered what…being with you would be like." She took a deep breath. "Now I know, and…"

His nostrils flared. "Let's see if I have this straight. You'd been curious what sex with me would be like? And now that you know, you're done with me?" Gray ice melted as heat blazed in his eyes. The rest of his expression remained frozen, but his searing, penetrating gaze heated places that would inspire her to surrender if she wasn't careful. "Well, let me set the record straight. I'm not done with you."

Traitorous impulses surged through Emma's body, undermining her resistance. She shoved Nathan's business deal with her father to the furthest reaches of her mind and gathered handfuls of his lapels, but before she could draw him closer, a tall brunette breezed into the office as if she belonged there.

"Nathan, I hope you're free to take me to lunch."

At the interruption, Emma's hands fell to her sides. Nathan shifted his gaze to follow the newcomer across his office and pushed away from the wall.

He smoothed his tie and straightened his suit coat. "Gabrielle, what are you doing here?"

"I've been craving Rolando's crab bisque all morning." The brunette set her purse on his desk and pulled out a compact, appearing oblivious to the charged atmosphere.

A wave of nausea pounded through Emma. She'd been a fool to think for even one second that she was the only woman Nathan was interested in. Scanning Gabrielle from her elegant haircut to her expensive shoes, Emma recognized that Nathan's taste in women ran to sophisticated, pampered brunettes with large bank accounts.

Nathan looked from her to Gabrielle and back again. Was he comparing his women? Who would he choose? The tense, pale girl in a simple beige dress or the accomplished flirt in the pencil-slim skirt, cowl-neck halter top and Manolo sandals?

"Nathan?" the brunette asked, sensing that she hadn't captured his complete attention. "Are you listening to me?" She turned around and spotted Emma. "Oh, is this your new assistant? I'm glad you finally listened to Sebastian and hired someone. Tell her to make reservations for us at Frey's."

"Gabrielle, this is Emma Montgomery. She is not my new assistant. Her father is Silas Montgomery of Montgomery Oil."

"Really?" Gabrielle turned the full power of her aqua-marine eyes on Emma and perused her appearance with amusement. "Well, my daddy is chairman of the board and CEO of Parker Corporation."

What was this, battle of the spoiled heiresses? And adding to Emma's humiliation, Nathan had introduced her as if she was the daughter of a business associate instead of his… What? Lover? Girlfriend? Well, wasn't she?

Emma unclenched her jaw and forced her lips into a polite smile. "Nice to meet you, Gabrielle," she said, not meaning a single word. It was long past time to go. She slid sideways along the wall until she found the doorway, then practically fell on her behind when the gap appeared. Dodging the hand he reached out to her, she muttered, "Carly's Café at nine. Bring my earrings."

Beset by the sense that something had just gone very wrong, Nathan stepped into the hall. He watched Emma race away, fighting the urge to chase after her. His mood worsened when he reentered his office to find Gabrielle ensconced in one of his guest chairs, her skirt hiked up to show off her great legs.

"Ready to take me to lunch?" she demanded, her lower lip pushed out in a sulky expression she wore way too often. "I'm starving."

"See if Max is free."

"I don't want to have lunch with Max." Which meant they were arguing again. Gabrielle and Max had an on-again, off-again thing going. Nathan didn't understand it. There were plenty of women in Houston eager to help a guy scratch an itch. Why did Max put up with Gabrielle's demands and temper? "I want to have lunch with *you*."

She only wanted his company because she thought it bugged his brother. It didn't.

"I don't have time. I'll give Max a call for you."

"I'll bet you would have gone if she'd asked you." Gabrielle wasn't ready to give up. She leaned forward, running her hand along her shin to draw attention to her best asset. "What's up with her, anyway? And where the hell did she get that dress? I would expect someone with her kind of money to have better taste in clothes."

"I thought she looked fine."

Indeed, the dress's scoop neck had shown off a hint of cleavage and the hundred tiny buttons running from neckline to hem had awakened an urgent desire in Nathan to unfasten every one, or give up and rip the garment right off her. Arousal lashed him like an unexpected storm. He dropped into his leather desk chair to keep Gabrielle from noticing.

Picking up the phone, he dialed. "Max, Gabrielle wants to have lunch with you."

She squawked in protest and got to her feet.

"Great," he continued. "I'll let her know.

"He's on his way." Nathan replaced the phone.

Hoping this would be the last time he'd see Gabrielle at Case Consolidated Holdings, Nathan flashed her a broad grin. Maybe Max would send her packing, the way he had sent the last dozen packing, with a full stomach and a firm, noncommittal goodbye. Gabrielle had been bragging of late that she'd succeeded in enticing the elusive Max Case from his bachelor ways. Nathan almost felt sorry for her.

The next morning, a heated discussion was taking place in Sebastian's big corner office.

"I've looked at Smythe's numbers. It seems like a pretty solid deal," Sebastian said, as cool and unflappable as Max was hot and animated. "Which means we're not going to be able to do the deal with Montgomery Oil."

Nathan tapped his pen on his yellow legal pad to keep his temper from flaring again. "I put in a call to a buddy of mine in Chicago in investment banking. He's got the inside scoop on Smythe. The guy is not going to sell."

"And we're just supposed to believe your *buddy?*" Max demanded.

Nathan shrugged. "It doesn't change the fact that if Smythe does sell, we won't have nearly the potential for profit as we would if we did the deal with Montgomery." His temper slipped. "And if you two would stop acting like a couple of old women, you might understand the value in taking a little risk."

"Don't lecture us about taking risks," Max shot back. "You're nothing but a hotshot who wouldn't be here if Dad—"

Max had always doled out his criticism with boisterous, taunting directness. Sebastian chose a quieter, deadlier approach.

"I'm sure Nathan understands his position in this company."

Yeah, Nathan understood his position all right. He was an outsider. It didn't matter that he bore their last name. His mother had been Brandon Case's mistress. He wasn't their "legitimate" brother, and they resented that they'd been forced to share their father with him. And now their company.

"Don't give up on the deal with Montgomery," Nathan said, letting the subtle and not so subtle jabs slide off him. He would get nowhere if he continued to agitate his brothers. "I told you I have a couple things to iron out in order to get things finalized. Give me a few more weeks. You owe me that."

"Forget it, Nat," Max said. "You took your shot and lost."

I didn't lose. "Don't be an idiot. You've seen the numbers.

The technology is poised to explode, and if we get in on the ground floor, we'll make a killing." He leaned forward. "Look, I get that you're angry that Dad didn't consult you when he brought me on board. You want me gone, but that's not going to happen. So you might as well quit playing games."

"What's that supposed to mean?" Sebastian exchanged a look with Max.

"Ever since we were kids you two have ganged up against me. I get why. I was the illegitimate one. The proof that your father had cheated on your mother. Well, that was a long time ago. My mother's been dead twenty years. Don't you two think it's time you let it go?"

Both his brothers looked surprised by his vehemence. They turned to each other and another of those nonverbal exchanges passed between them. Nathan hated how their closeness shut him out. It renewed his determination to take control of the company away from them.

"What do we really know about this technology you want to invest in?" Max grumbled, his body language and expression broadcasting his skepticism. "We're out of our depth here."

Nathan stared at his brother. "I'm not."

"Well, excuse me if I'm having trouble taking your word on this."

Sebastian silenced his younger brother with a sharp gesture. "Nathan has given us solid numbers on this, Max. Until this thing came up with Smythe, we agreed to give him a chance to approach Montgomery about their joint venture. Silas hasn't made a decision. I think we should at least give Nathan until the middle of February. If he's right about Lucas, we can afford to wait."

"I never thought you'd be up for this kind of risk, Sebastian," Max said, his eyes narrowing. "That sort of gambling is better left to the experts." A great deal of sarcasm went into the last word.

Nathan sidestepped the urge to react to his brother's taunt, but it rankled. He didn't have an MBA or their business credentials, but he'd made a hell of a lot of money on his ability to research up-and-coming companies and glimpse their potential.

"Why don't you discuss it?" Nathan glanced at his watch. He was going to be late if he didn't get going right away. "I've got a breakfast meeting. Let me know what you decide."

Leaving his brothers to make their decision, Nathan grabbed his coat and headed out. Carley's Café was a three-block walk, and he let the chilly winter air cool his anger as he strode along the sidewalk. For the first time in months—maybe even years—he had a project he could sink his teeth into. He would not give up because of his brothers' timidity and lack of imagination.

He hadn't completely banished his ill humor by the time he pushed into the tiny restaurant, but his pulse kicked up in anticipation of seeing Emma again. At this hour, there was only one table available. He stripped off his coat, ordered coffee and settled down to wait.

When the waitress offered to refill his cup a second time, he glanced at his watch. Where the hell was she? It was already half an hour past the time she'd promised to meet him. He tossed money on the table and donned his coat.

Cody had given him her address weeks ago. After their encounter at his condo, he'd considered sending flowers, a balloon bouquet, something foolish and romantic. The impulse disturbed him. He wasn't the foolish, romantic sort. In the end, he hadn't done anything, and after she'd ignored his phone calls, he was damn glad.

Nathan walked the five blocks to her building and slipped in without having to warn her of his arrival, thanks to the woman who exited the secure front door just as he arrived. He crossed the newly remodeled lobby to the refurbished freight elevator, imagining Emma's shock when she answered the door.

On the fourth floor, Nathan found Emma's unit and rang her doorbell. When no one answered, he tried again. While he considered that she might refuse to let him in, he doubted that she would be hiding inside, pretending she wasn't home. He tried the doorknob and, to his surprise, found the door unlocked. Entering the unit, he called Emma's name.

The only noise that reached his ears sounded like someone being violently sick.

He crossed the living room, absently inventorying the size of the place and the abundance of renovation projects left incomplete, and headed down a narrow hallway, following a hunch. At the end of the hall he hit pay dirt. What he found dismayed him.

Someone had taken a sledgehammer to the master bathroom and completely gutted the space. The walls and ceiling had been stripped down to the studs, exposing the wiring and plumbing. Where the shower should have been, he noticed rotten wood, mottled with black stains. The only fixtures in the entire room still intact were the sink and the toilet. And that's where he found Emma, hunched over the bowl, her eyes wide and incredulous in a face the color of chalk. She wiped her mouth with the back of her hand.

"Nathan?" She closed her eyes, and her face twisted into an expression of agony. "What are you doing here?"

Before he could answer she had leaned over the toilet and heaved. Concern for her overrode his earlier irritation. He knelt beside her and soothed his hand over her shoulder, buffeted by an all-too-familiar feeling of helplessness. How many times had he sat by his mom after her chemo treatments and struggled with the frustration of not being able to help her?

"I came to see why you stood me up again."

"And now that you've seen why I couldn't make it, you can be on your merry way."

Her rejection didn't faze him at all. "And leave you like this? Not likely." He cast around the dismantled space looking for a towel. "I'll be right back."

He retraced his steps down the hall and entered her tiny kitchen. The ancient cabinets and outdated appliances indicated that her renovation project hadn't gone far. That was probably for the best if her bathroom was any indication of how badly the remodeling was going. He found a kitchen towel and ran it under the cold water. He squeezed out the excess and returned to the bathroom. Emma sat where he'd left her.

"Here, this should make you feel a little better." He applied the wet towel to her cheeks and forehead, peering at her in concern. "What were you celebrating?"

She had enough strength to glare at him, but not enough to fight his ministrations. "This is not a hangover. It's food poisoning. Go away."

He sat down on the floor beside her, not caring that the torn-up flooring would ruin his expensive suit. It bothered him to see her in these sorts of surroundings. No wonder her father wanted her married off. She obviously needed someone to take care of her.

Something reached through his concern and stunned him with its possibility.

"Is there something else?" she demanded. "Because I'm not really feeling up to entertaining you."

He pushed a lock of hair behind her ear. "Are you sure this is food poisoning?"

"What else could it be?" Her brows came together.

"Well, it's been almost a month since we were together." His voice trailed off as he scrutinized her expression.

Emma eyed him through her long bangs. "And?"

"Are you pregnant?"

Four

Pregnant? Emma's queasiness now originated from a whole new source. Foreboding surfaced like a rash. Her focus narrowed to the irritation of a persistent itch that wouldn't go away, no matter how long or hard she scratched.

She had food poisoning. Nothing more.

"We used protection," she reminded him, her voice a noon shadow.

"It's not one hundred percent effective."

Oh, and wouldn't he love that. He'd have even more leverage to get her to marry him if she turned out to be pregnant. Closing the door on her doubts, she glared at him. "Go away."

"I'm not leaving you like this," he said. "I'm going to get you some water."

"No, please." While she acknowledged that her body could use some fluids right now, she didn't want Nathan around while she felt so weak and helpless. It was just too easy to lean on him, let him handle things. And before she knew it, he would have her agreeing to marry him. "Just leave me in peace."

"You can't afford to get dehydrated."

She hid her face in her arms. "I really don't think I could keep anything down."

Although exhausted by her rough morning, Emma suspected that Nathan wouldn't leave until she proved that she could take care of herself. Hoping her stomach could take it, she began pushing to her feet. Before she could stand upright, Nathan bent down and swept her into his arms. Too shocked and too weak to protest, Emma gripped his shoulders for stability. The short walk to her bedroom reminded her how many times in the last three weeks she wished she'd stayed at his condo that night. Would he have carried her to bed like this?

He set her on her feet and kept one arm around her waist as he swept the covers aside. "For the last month I've been looking forward to getting you into bed," he said, the grim, unyielding businessman morphing into a handsome snake charmer. "But this isn't exactly what I had in mind."

She quashed the amusement his comment produced. Gorgeous, cheeky and way too sexy for his own good, she resented that he seemed to know exactly what to say to make her forget that she'd been up and sitting within arms' reach of the toilet since just before five o'clock when she had been overcome by nausea.

"I'm in no condition to flirt with you," she told him as a wave of dizziness hit her.

His wry grin faded as he pulled the covers over her. "Can I get you anything?"

She clutched the edge of her comforter and stared up at him. Her stomach flipped in a way that had nothing to do with food poisoning.

"No. I'll be fine." She probably should thank him for taking care of her, but he'd entered her home uninvited and had stumbled upon her in the most humiliating of moments. No, she didn't have to feel one bit grateful. If only he'd go. "I'm going to sleep for a while."

She shut her eyes, to block out the concern tangling with humor in his dark gray eyes, and hoped he'd take the hint. Retreating footsteps told her that he'd left her room, but she couldn't relax while sounds of him moving around the loft reached her ears. He returned to the bedroom and placed something on the nightstand beside her. She spied a glass of water within easy reach just as she heard the front door to the apartment open and shut. Although every muscle protested, she slipped out of bed and slowly crossed the living room to slide the dead bolt home.

Her legs shook with the effort of retracing her steps across the expansive space. She caught at the door frame leading to her bedroom as her vision darkened. Gulping air, she shuffled five steps and dropped into bed, pulling the covers over her. As her body went limp, sleep claimed her at last.

When she woke late that afternoon, the food poisoning seemed to have run its course. Feeling weak and shaky from low blood sugar and lack of water, Emma swung her legs out of bed and sat up. While her head swam, her stomach barely reacted at all. With a faint, relieved smile, she headed for the kitchen. A piece of toast and a cup of herbal tea sounded like heaven. The smell of cooking brought her up short.

Emma pushed her sleep-tossed hair out of her eyes and gaped at the man standing in her kitchen. Nathan had replaced his expensive business suit with thigh-hugging jeans and a long-sleeved blue sweater that emphasized the capable strength of his torso.

His gaze swept over her. She'd caught a glimpse of herself as she'd passed her dresser mirror. It wasn't pretty. She waited for his expression to reflect disappointment. But as he perused her ancient but comfortable cotton pajama bottoms and lingered over the fact that she wasn't wearing a bra beneath her equally worn T-shirt, only appreciation altered the curve of his lips.

Her nipples tightened, driving a spike of longing straight to her core. She crossed her arms over her chest a fraction too late. His smug grin confirmed that her body's involuntary response hadn't gone unnoticed. Why couldn't he disapprove of her appearance just this once? It would give her a firm base to build resentment on. Instead, she felt all mushy and weak-kneed.

"I see you're up." He stirred something in a pot on the stove, something that smelled heavenly. "Feeling better?"

"You left."

"I went out and bought some supplies. I figured you'd be hungry when you woke up."

"I locked the door."

"I anticipated that and took your keys with me."

Damn the man for having all the answers. She retreated to her room to put on a robe and comb her hair. Using the water he'd left beside her bed, she brushed her teeth. A quick rinse with mouthwash, and she returned to sit on a stool at her breakfast bar and scowl at him.

"You certainly have made yourself at home," she groused. "I don't recall issuing you an invitation to dinner."

"You were in no shape to issue any sort of invitation." His slow smile increased the room's temperature. "But I've always had a knack for anticipating a woman's needs." He nudged a teacup toward her. "It's peppermint. Good for nausea."

Wondering how he'd know something like that, Emma sipped the tea. "Are you sure it was my needs you were anticipating and not yours?"

"I assure you, I thought only of you."

Skepticism rumbled in her throat. Emma nodded toward the stove. "What are you cooking?"

"Chicken soup. My mother's recipe."

Now this was too much. "From scratch?"

"That's the only way. Would you like to try some?"

"How could I resist?"

Nathan dished up two bowls and pushed a plate of crackers toward her. Emma inhaled the soup's aroma and her stomach growled impatiently. The first spoonful of smooth chicken broth slid across her tongue, stimulating her taste buds with cilantro, lime and a hint of onion.

"This is delicious."

"It's not bothering your stomach?"

"Not at all. What a relief."

Nathan finished his soup and set his bowl in her sink.

"Are you feeling strong enough to tell me what happened to your bathroom?"

"I had a leak in the shower."

"Looks like overkill for a leak."

"The plumber I hired found mold. I had him rip everything out so we could see how bad it was."

Her explanation made him hiss in exasperation. "How long has it been like this?"

"A couple weeks."

"You need to get this taken care of."

She resented his assumption that she needed him to point that out to her. "It's the holidays and everyone I called is busy until the end of January."

"Mold is dangerous. You can't stay here."

"I've been living here for a year. I can survive another month." Besides, she had no place to go.

"It's dangerous," he repeated. "Why didn't you check into a hotel?"

"I can't afford to."

"Why not?"

It was time to explain what was really going on. "Last February, Daddy cut me off from my trust fund and gave me a hundred thousand to live on for the year."

"Why a hundred thousand?"

Emma grimaced. "It's what I spent on shoes the year before." Seeing the grin tugging at Nathan's lips, she rushed on. "New Year's Eve, Daddy and I made a deal. If I replace the hundred thousand in my account by Valentine's Day, he's promised to sign over my money and I don't have to marry you." She loaded the last bit with enough satisfaction to wipe the amusement off his face, but her smug words had no effect.

"Let me guess how much you have to replace." He cocked an eyebrow. "Fifty thousand?"

"Thirty-five."

His smirk made her blood boil. Why had she told him about the deal with her father? Over the years, Cody had probably regaled Nathan with assorted tales of her spending sprees. But she wasn't the same frivolous girl she'd been ten months ago. She'd learned to budget. She'd spent long hours designing and making her jewelry. And she'd figured out the best way to market it.

"The earrings you took. I need them back."

"Are you planning on selling them?"

"As a matter of fact, I am. I've started a business. I design fine jewelry. Expensive, original, one-of-a-kind pieces."

Except her father didn't take what she did seriously. And from the look on Nathan's face, he didn't, either. The harder she worked, the more she wanted her father to recognize her talent. How could you claim to love someone and not get them? Replacing the hundred thousand had become as much about proving to her father that she was great at something as it was about getting her trust fund back.

"I'm going to put the money back in my account," she said.

Instead of appearing concerned that she might succeed, he shrugged. "You don't seriously think you can do that in five weeks."

He sounded just like her father. When he looked at her, he saw only failure. Wouldn't he be surprised when she demonstrated just how capable she was? "I have a big art and design show coming up. I'll make more than enough money."

Naturally, she left out the part about lacking inventory to sell and how buying the supplies she needed would mean dipping back into the account she was trying desperately to replenish.

"I'm sure you make very nice jewelry," he told her in a patronizing manner that made her grind her teeth. "But you don't seriously expect to make enough money at some craft fair."

"I can do it," she declared, annoyed with him for echoing her own doubts about her plan. "You'll see."

"In the meantime, you can move into my condo while your bathroom is fixed."

"Move…" In with him? Emma stared at Nathan. "Absolutely not."

"Well, I'm not going to let you stay here," Nathan retorted, brisk with impatience. "I'll find someone to come in and take care of the mold and get your bathroom working again. It shouldn't take more than a couple weeks. In the meantime, you can stay with me."

"I'd appreciate your help with a contractor, but I'm not staying with you."

A sly smile softened his sculpted lips. "Afraid you might like it too much to leave?"

His question aroused memories of New Year's Eve, reminding her how close she had come to succumbing to his charms. She began to tingle beneath the molten steel in his eyes. As he watched her struggle for an answer, his eyebrows lifted.

"I'm not afraid," she retorted, crossing her arms over her chest. Oh, but she was.

She craved his hands on her, his mouth claiming hers, and it robbed her of sanity, just as his knowing grin stole her breath. What would it be like to fall asleep sheltered by his arms each night? To be awakened every morning by the sensual slide of his naked muscles against her skin? Just thinking about it nudged her into the realm of an addict. If she let herself fall into his trap of seduction, she'd never be able to escape.

He shook his head. "I think you are." His eyebrows dropped back into their customary position, his lips curved ironically and he peered at her askance. "What are you fighting so hard to prove? You and I both know you aren't the independent sort. You'll be happier once you're married and have someone to take care of you. Your father knows it, too. That's why he's so determined to see you settled."

Growing up, whenever Emma had played with her dolls, she imagined they were falling in love and living happily ever after. By eighteen, she had her life all planned out, something her college friends had teased her about incessantly. She would get married shortly after college, to a man who adored her. She would be pregnant with her first child three years later. Between socializing with her friends, dinner parties with her husband's business associates and charity events, she would be blissfully happy. But her ex-fiancé, Jackson, had spoiled her innocent dreams.

Having to guard herself so vigilantly against making another mistake in love while longing to let go and take the plunge was a tug-of-war that took its toll. And the longer she fought, the more resistant she became to the trust she needed in order to let herself fall in love. Surrendering to her emotions became a thing of her past. Until Nathan Case had reentered her life.

"I thought you understood that I'm not going to marry you because of some business deal." Finishing the last of the tea, she leaned over the breakfast bar and put the cup in the sink.

She fixed a steady gaze on Nathan as he moved out of the kitchen in her direction. "Someday I will marry, but on my terms—not my father's."

He stepped between her thighs and caught her face in his hands. The instant he entered her space, her senses filled with the scent and power of him and her bones melted.

"Marry me," he coaxed. "You won't regret it."

Her heart jolted as he regarded her somberly. With his proposal ringing in her ears, she gripped his sweater, and then hesitated, uncertain as to whether to push him away or pull him close.

"Nathan." His name left her lips in a low plea for him to stop, to continue. He swooped into her moment of indecision and took charge. Dipping his head, he grazed her lips with his. The action froze them both.

"Sweet heaven," he murmured.

An astonishing tumult fluttered in her breast as he dragged his mouth over hers, absorbing her breath, teasing her with the promise of passion. Emma lost herself in the pliant caress of his lips. A sigh broke from her throat.

Then shock dimmed, replaced by a sweet wildness. Her heart plummeted to her toes only to rebound into glorious rapturous flight. She opened to the questing fire of his tongue, and the whirling increased, forcing her to hang on for dear life.

Hard arms came around her, binding her so close to his chest, their hearts beat in time. She wanted control of her body. She wanted control of her mind. Emma got neither. Nathan's kiss seduced reason from her world.

She slid her fingers into his hair, savoring the caress of softness against her skin. His hands moved slowly down her spine, unleashing an earthquake of trembling. Every nerve ending came alive with rollicking, shivering delight. Behind her eyes, stars sparkled.

No one but Nathan made her feel like this.

So much.

So fast.

Buffeted by emotion too strong to resist, she watched dry land recede. Protecting herself in a harbor might be dull, but she wouldn't drown in heartache. But it was too late to turn back. She was adrift in a stormy sea of passion. She would have to trust Nathan to guide her safely home.

Releasing fear, disregarding the promises she'd made to herself, Emma locked her legs around his thighs, holding him close with her soles pressed against his calves. His kisses became more demanding. With her arms wrapped around his neck, she surrendered to his strength, needing his mastery, yielding to his passion.

By pressing his hips toward hers, he made her aware of his arousal. His need. The hard length of him nudged against her core, already lava-hot. Her blood pooled and pulsed between her thighs, awakening a hunger that could only be slaked by this man.

He swept scorching caresses up her sides, edging the fabric of her T-shirt up. She moaned as he swallowed her breasts in his palms, fingers gliding along her skin, measuring and caressing, driving her crazy as he circled her hardening nipples.

"Emma." He rasped her name, half entreaty, half demand. "Look at me."

Losing herself in the sensations raging through her would be a lot easier with her eyes closed. She could concentrate on his deft touch and pretend that Nathan caressed her with emotion as well as passion.

"I don't think that's a good idea."

"You can't run from this."

No, but she could hide.

A sigh slipped from between her lips as she opened her eyes and met his gaze. The expression on his face warned her that he intended to devour her. "I'm not going anywhere."

She couldn't. Her longing for him trapped her as effectively as the steel bars of a cage.

"Good."

When he ducked his head, Emma watched him swirl his tongue around her breast and she arched her back, pushing into the caress, as aroused by his touch as she was by the sight of what he was doing to her.

His hand slipped beneath the elastic of her pajama bottoms. Her breath emerged in a frustrated groan as his fingertips dipped between her thighs and stopped short of where she wanted him. She pressed herself against him, gyrating in a manner that demonstrated her need.

"Touch me," she pleaded, long past caring how smug he might be at the depth of her desperation. All pride and every hesitation flew out the window whenever he touched her.

She moaned as he obliged, her body shuddering as his clever fingers slid against her.

"Oh baby, that's it," he crooned before claiming her mouth again. "Let go."

His mouth claimed hers again. She rocked against his hand, while urgent, encouraging sounds emanated from her throat. Her muscles tensed as she mindlessly sought the pleasure that danced just out of reach. Every sense was trained on the man making her body sing. She filled her lungs with the scent of his cologne. He tasted like chicken soup and peppermint tea, comforting and soothing. His deep voice, murmuring erotic suggestions in her ear, drove her crazy and made her want to laugh with joy at the same time.

And then there was the pleasure. The indescribable, building pressure that threatened to take her head off when it blew. She panted, her breath coming in irregular gasps. With his name on her lips, she climaxed. His mouth crashed down on hers, taking her cries into him, capturing her pleasure as his own.

As the fog cleared from her brain, Emma tugged on his

sweater, needing the feel of his skin. He obliged her by sweeping it off. She explored the ridges and texture of his gorgeous torso. A contented purr rumbled out of her. She craved the feel of his bare chest sliding over the hot skin of her breasts.

Nathan was of the same mind, because he murmured, "Naked." His fingers flexed into her hips, the bite causing a spike in her urgency. "I need you naked."

"Okay."

Something stirred in the depths of Nathan's eyes, swirling like smoke. Satisfaction? Triumph?

While nerves fluttered in her midsection, Emma bit down on her lower lip. A low noise rumbled in his chest. Nathan bent his head, his tongue soothing the dents left behind by her teeth. Breath catching, she tangled with him in a sexy kiss that reawakened her appetite, and then groaned in protest when he tore his mouth from hers.

"This is going to happen fast," he said, his voice dark and gritty. "Do you want it here or in bed?"

"Bed," she whispered, sliding off the stool, only to find that her legs could barely support her.

Five

Satisfaction exploded in Nathan's chest as Emma swayed across the meager inches between them, her fingers fanning against his bare chest. He liked how it was between them. Hot, sweaty, all-consuming and sexual. Easy to succumb. Mindless in its intensity. A feast for the senses.

He wrapped his arm around her waist and bent to sweep her feet off the floor. She gasped as he lifted her, and her fingers dug into his shoulders. Her liquid-chocolate eyes sought his. Despite her earlier passion, she looked somewhat uncertain. Needing to seal the deal before she had second thoughts, he turned toward the bedroom.

He'd taken one step when her doorbell rang. Nathan saw immediately that the interruption had startled the sensual glow from her eyes. A frown appeared between her finely arched eyebrows as she looked at the door. She bit down on her lower lip, even white teeth contrasting against the passion-bruised darkness of her mouth. He growled.

"Ignore it," he said, his long strides carrying him away from the sound of the intruder.

"I can't."

He was within ten feet of the bedroom door when the pounding began, followed by a feminine shout.

"Emma, are you all right? I've been calling all day. Emma, can you hear me?"

"It's Addison. I missed our yoga class this morning and never called her." Emma began to squirm. "Put me down."

Her words splashed cold water over his ardor. Muttering curses, Nathan set her back on her feet and watched in disgust as she raced to the door without so much as a backward glance. He retraced his steps at a much slower pace and scooped his sweater off the floor.

"Have you been home all day? I've been worried sick." A tall, thin woman, dressed casually in ultraexpensive designer clothes and radiating intense concern, burst through the door Emma opened. With a long, narrow face, aristocratic nose and sharp cheekbones, she was elegantly beautiful. Her long, straight red hair blew back from her shoulders as she spun to give Emma a thorough once-over. As concern for Emma faded, her voice became as voluptuous as her body was angular. "I suppose you were working and turned off the phone."

"I'm sorry I didn't call you, I spent most of the day in bed." Emma's gaze flickered in Nathan's direction.

He offered her his most salacious grin. Even across the room he could see the color that flooded her cheeks.

"Were you sick?" Addison glanced over her shoulder in the direction of her friend's gaze and her perfect cupid-bow lips dropped open at the sight of Nathan standing half-naked beside the breakfast bar.

He let the woman's pale blue eyes drink their fill of his bare chest and obvious arousal before he casually slipped the blue sweater over his head. Sliding it into place, he strode forward and held out his hand.

"Hello, I don't think we've met. I'm—"

"Nathan Case," she finished for him, extending her hand. "Addison Clements."

Either she was one of those women who didn't believe a firm grip was feminine, or her astonishment at finding a half-naked man in her friend's loft left her dazed, because she scarcely put any effort into the handshake.

"He stopped by to check on me, too. We were supposed to have breakfast this morning, and I missed our meeting because I was sick." Emma emphasized the last three words, to deflect her friend's obvious curiosity. "I think I had food poisoning from dinner last night. Were you okay? I meant to call, but I felt so awful."

"I've been fine," Addison murmured, unable to take her eyes off Nathan.

He could see more than curiosity in her almond-shaped eyes. He glimpsed speculation as well.

"I'm sure you ladies have a lot to talk about," he said, catching Emma's hand and dropping a kiss into her palm. She quivered. "I'll be going. Nice to meet you, Addison."

Addison walked toward the kitchen, giving them some privacy. Emma followed Nathan to the door. Emotions whirled and churned through her as she tried to process what had almost happened again with him. How had he overridden her better judgment so easily?

Before she realized his intention, his hand slid along her hip, pulling her firmly against him. He dipped his head and claimed her lips, drowning her protests in a sensual assault. Her spine remained rigid for all of two heartbeats. Wrapped in the spicy scent of his cologne and the soothing warmth of his skin, she sagged against his chest.

With her surrender complete, Nathan eased his mouth

from hers. While his hands spanned her back, thumbs moving rhythmically, he spent a long moment nuzzling her temple.

"I'm going to send movers for your stuff tomorrow."

Despite his unsteady breathing, he sounded unaffected by the kiss. Humiliated that she'd fallen back into his arms so quickly, she applied pressure to his chest. He pulled back but was slow to release her. Her heart hammered against her ribs as his hands eased down her back and over her hips.

"I already told you I'm not going anywhere." She flinched at the breathy, disturbed timbre of her voice. It was bad enough that she dropped her guard any time he touched her—did she have to broadcast it?

"You have mold in your bathroom. And who knows where else. It's dangerous for you to stay here."

"That might be true but—"

"I have a perfectly nice condo and you can have your very own room." He smirked at her, undaunted by her temper or her refusal to cooperate with him. "Unless, of course, you'd like to share a bedroom with me."

She clenched her teeth to suppress a sarcastic retort. Why rise to the bait when that seemed to be exactly what he wanted? "I'm not moving in with you."

"She can stay with Paul and me," Addison called from the kitchen, where she'd obviously been eavesdropping.

Emma heaved a sigh, disliking the way they were ganging up on her. "You don't have room."

"The boys can share for a couple weeks. It won't kill them."

"The way those two argue, it might. Besides, I need to get ready for the show and that means I have to be here to work, so moving out doesn't make sense." Her shoulders felt as if a thirty-pound weight had been draped across them. "I'll be fine."

"You can move your worktable and equipment into my spare room," Nathan said.

Their combined logic beat her back like a phalanx of soldiers intent on conquering enemy territory. "Why don't we wait and see what your contractor has to say about the mold?"

"And if he recommends that you move out?" Nathan prompted.

"Then I will."

"That's my girl."

Setting his hand beneath her chin, Nathan tipped her head up. What she saw in his wolf-gray eyes set her heart to pounding. A slow, sly smile curved his sculpted lips.

She sucked in a sharp breath. "I'm not your girl."

"Sure you are." He kissed her on the nose. "You just don't want to admit it yet."

With that parting shot, he set her free and turned to go. His possessive declaration annoyed her. She didn't belong to him. Not yet. Not as long as she kept him at arm's length.

She leaned her hot cheek against the doorframe and watched his progress down the hall, appreciating the way his broad shoulders tapered to a narrow waist and his worn jeans cupped his perfect butt. Unruly cravings surged anew. Her fingers tightened on the door. Addison's arrival had been a lucky break. Convincing Nathan that she wasn't going to fall for him would have been that much harder after he completely transformed her into a moaning, writhing hedonist.

Catching her watching him, he flashed a cocky grin before stepping onto the elevator. Furious with herself for staring after him like some infatuated idiot, Emma slammed the door shut.

"Well, I obviously interrupted something," Addison said from the kitchen. She snagged a bottle of water from Emma's refrigerator. "Sorry."

Addison didn't look anything of the sort. Emma made a face at her.

"You didn't interrupt anything."

"Nice try," Addison said. "But he wasn't wearing a shirt and your eyes are wearing that half-dreamy, half-hungry look you get when you talk about him."

"I do not."

"Oh please. You've had a thing for him since you were sixteen. And from the way he kissed you just now, the feeling's obviously mutual."

Emma ignored her friend's last remark. "He's only interested in me because he wants to do a deal with my dad."

"I doubt that's the only reason." Addison waved away the beginnings of Emma's protests. "Yes, I know, your father is a controlling nightmare, blah, blah, blah. But you keep saying you want to fall in love and get married, yet you're so afraid that every man's going to be another Jackson that you don't give anyone a chance."

"Did you ever think that maybe I had good reason to keep my guard up?" Addison's lecture slid like needles into her insecurities. Irritated, she decided her oh-so-smart friend needed a better grasp on the situation. "And, for your information, Dad made marrying me a condition of the deal between his company and Nathan's."

Addison remained unfazed by Emma's revelation. "From everything I've heard about Nathan Case, he isn't anything like Jackson," she said, her tone calm and confident. "He's not going to marry you to get on your dad's good side."

"It's the only reason he wants to marry me," she shot back.

"So, say no."

"I'm trying."

Addison's lips twitched. "Not very hard. I obviously interrupted something pretty hot and heavy between you two."

Emma dropped her forehead onto the breakfast bar with a groan. "It's as if I spontaneously combust every time he touches me." Her head came up. "But that's not enough. I need more than sex." Incredible. Fabulous. Mind-blowing sex.

"Are you sure? Seems like you haven't been getting a lot of great sex lately. Or any sex, for that matter."

Emma didn't want to think about great sex with Nathan. Because if she thought about great sex, or any sort of sex with the man, she was going to have a hard time not having it with him again.

"Positive."

"I saw the way you two looked at each other," Addison said. "Maybe this thing between you two could lead to something more. It might be worth the risk. You haven't taken many of those lately, either."

Could it? Temptation tangled her resolve with a whole host of possibilities and left her adrift in confusion. She claimed that she wanted to fall in love and get married, but wasn't that all about taking chances? Was Addison right? Did she use her father's meddling in her life and her past naiveté as far as Jackson was concerned to guard her heart? Was she her own worst enemy when it came to finding someone to spend the rest of her life with?

After a moment, Emma shook her head. "Nathan approaches marriage like a business arrangement. I want to marry a man I love and who loves me in return. I want the fairy-tale ending. What's wrong with that?"

"Women get rescued in fairy tales," Addison pointed out. "Cinderella, Snow White, Rapunzel, Sleeping Beauty. All rescued. I thought you were trying to prove to your father that you can take care of yourself."

"All the more reason not to get involved with Nathan. He thinks exactly the way my father does. That I need him to look after me." She huffed. "And I don't."

Into the silence that fell between them, Addison added one last bit of advice. "I hope whatever decision you make, you don't regret it."

On that, Emma wholeheartedly agreed.

* * *

True to his word, Nathan sent a contractor to her loft the following morning. The stocky man had a brisk way of talking and a competent air as he inspected her bathroom.

"No wonder you've got problems." He wore a disgruntled expression as he surveyed the plumbing job done by the previous owners. "I've never seen such poor workmanship."

Emma set her hands on her hips. "But you can fix it?"

"Sure, but first we've got to get rid of this black mold," the contractor explained. "It's the most toxic variety there is. Can cause headaches, dizziness, difficulty concentrating. Not to mention runny nose and itchy eyes, and it could irritate or damage your lungs. I'd recommend that you vacate until we can get the problem taken care of."

His pronouncement nettled her. Was he telling her that because she was truly in danger or because Nathan had prompted him to do so? "For how long?"

"Let me make a couple calls."

While he took measurements and talked on the phone, Emma retreated to the small second bedroom where she'd set up her equipment. She could spare no time or energy debating whether or not she should stay in the loft. After Addison had left yesterday, Emma had gone through her inventory to get an idea of how far she would need to dip into her account to make enough jewelry for the show.

She pulled out her design pad and flipped through the sketches she had made over the last few months. Something tugged at her, an elusive notion of what the designs were missing. She turned to a blank page and let her pencil flow across the paper.

The contractor found her in the room a short time later. "I have someone who can come by tomorrow to take a look at your bathroom. His schedule's pretty full but he can probably get a crew here in ten days or so. Do you have someplace you can stay until the mold is removed?"

"That long?" She blew out a breath. "Do I really need to move out?"

"I definitely think it's a good idea."

Emma walked the contractor to the door and returned to her workroom. She didn't want to deal with packing up and moving. Especially not to Nathan's condo where prolonged exposure to his sex appeal would weaken her determination not to tumble into bed with him again.

She resumed flipping through her sketchpad, hoping to recapture her creative spark. Frustration filled her as focus eluded her. She couldn't stop thinking about Nathan's intoxicating kisses yesterday. Her skin tingled. Blood raced hot and frantic through her veins, pooling in the sweet spot between her thighs. She shifted on her stool, willing the impatient urges away.

She didn't have time to be distracted. With three weeks until the show, she would need to be focused on her jewelry every second. That meant no thinking about a certain handsome millionaire businessman who drove her crazy in every possible way.

Shaking her head, Emma told her traitorous pulse to settle down and picked up her pencil once more. Sometime later, her phone began to ring, waking her out of a creative fog. As the call rolled to voice mail, she sifted through all the new designs she'd come up with and smiled.

Her stomach growled, so she headed into the kitchen to heat up the leftovers of Nathan's soup for lunch. While she ate, Emma gazed around the outdated cabinets and appliances. She'd heard a great deal of criticism from everyone who'd seen the loft, but despite all the negative comments, Emma loved the space—imperfections and all—and the possibilities it represented.

She'd bought it a year ago, loving the high ceilings and the industrial feel of the exposed ductwork and brick walls. The front door opened into a large space she used as a combination living room and dining room. Shortly before she'd moved in, she'd had the hardwood floors refinished and they gleamed as they stretched across the inviting space. She'd furnished the living room with a comfortable gray couch and two blue armchairs the shade of Texas bluebonnets. The same blue broke up the expanse of white walls in the form of landscape photographs.

Her phone rang again as she washed her bowl and glass by hand. The dishwasher had died two months ago. Yet another thing that needed fixing.

She let this call go to voice mail as well. She guessed it was Nathan calling to badger her about moving in with him again. Well, that wasn't going to happen.

Returning to her workroom, she surveyed her equipment and the supplies scattered around the space. It would take her a day or more to get everything organized to move. She didn't have that much time to waste.

Nathan was just going to have to accept that she wasn't going to pack and she wasn't going to move. He wasn't her boss.

With a dismissive snort, she returned to her project and banished a tall, hunky millionaire from her mind.

"What do you mean she refuses to go anywhere?" Nathan barked into his cell phone. The mover he'd hired sputtered excuses as Nathan strode through Case Consolidated Holdings' parking garage toward his car. Two days ago his contractor had told her it was dangerous for her to remain in the loft, exposed to the mold.

Stubborn woman. He'd been all set to head home and find Emma all settled in, only to hear that she continued to defy him.

Nathan unlocked his car and tossed in his briefcase, breathing deeply to calm down. He was taking his frustrations out on the wrong person. "Why don't you guys grab dinner on me while I sort everything out?"

Ten minutes later he advanced down the hallway toward her loft. When Emma answered his impatient summons, she actually looked surprised to see him. Then, a mutinous expression settled over her beautiful face.

"What are you doing here?"

Despite her unfriendly question, his nerve endings sizzled and popped. She'd pulled her long, dark hair into a ponytail. Worn denim hugged her hips and a baggy sweater dipped off one golden shoulder, baring a purple bra strap.

He leaned his shoulder against the wall, realizing that he'd rather hear "no" from her than "yes" from any other woman.

"Nice to see you, too," he purred. Arguing with her was getting him nowhere. He needed to switch tactics. "Get changed. I'm taking you to dinner."

"I don't have—"

"Time. Yes, I know. But you have to eat, and I doubt there's anything edible in your refrigerator. Take a little break. You'll feel more up to working when you get back."

"And spend the whole meal being bullied by you into doing what you want me to do? No thanks."

"How about we only talk about the things you're interested in?" He offered her a neutral smile.

"No badgering?" she prompted. "No attempts at persuasion?"

He raised his right hand as if he was swearing in a court of law. "None."

"Oh, all right," she muttered ungraciously. "Give me a couple minutes to change."

While Emma retreated into her bedroom, Nathan called the movers and gave them new instructions.

For two days, he'd spent a good chunk of his time imagining the changes she would make in his life. His decision to marry her might have been born out of necessity, but lately he found himself thinking less about business and more about pleasure.

Unfortunately, standing in the way of those days and nights of unbridled passion was her stubbornness and this ridiculous wager with her father that she couldn't hope to win.

There was no way she could put the money back in her account by Valentine's Day, but that wouldn't stop her from trying. And he had his own deadline to worry about. He'd convinced his brothers to give him until the middle of February to secure the deal with Montgomery Oil. He couldn't do that without marrying Emma. The best way to do that was to make sure she had no way to win her wager. And the best way to do that would be to keep her too busy to work.

His groin stirred at the notion of all the things he would do to her once he moved her under his roof. She'd been without a decent bathroom for quite a while. Wait until she set eyes on the whirlpool tub in his master bathroom. It was made for long, romantic soaks. With candles burning, he'd even let her put bubble bath in the water. Hell, he'd do whatever it took to encourage her to join him.

He was still grinning ten minutes later when she crossed the living room toward him, her hips swaying in that natural motion that drove him crazy.

She'd donned a narrow, caramel-colored skirt with a wide ruffle that kissed her knees and a blouse of cream lace that revealed flirtatious hints of her creamy skin. Her brown hair had been twisted into a loose knot atop her head. She carried a brown velvet jacket that matched the color of her eyes.

"Where to?" she asked, fastening intricately woven earrings of gold wire studded with green freshwater pearls to her earlobes. They tapped against her neck, drawing Nathan's attention to the tender, sensitive skin.

"It's a surprise," he answered.

She didn't press him for details as he took her keys and

inserted them in the dead-bolt lock. She didn't utter a word until they were in his car, heading away from downtown. Then, she took hold of the conversational reins and steered them toward a safe topic.

"How do you like working with your brothers?"

"That question might take me all night to answer," he retorted.

"We don't have all night," she reminded him. "So you'd better get started now."

"We could have all night."

As her gaze played hide-and-seek with his from beneath her long bangs, he tightened his grip on the steering wheel to resist the urge to brush the sable locks away from her eyes. He had the crazy idea that if he looked deep enough, he would find that they wanted the same things, only she was too afraid to admit it.

"How long have you worked at Case Consolidated Holdings?" she asked, avoiding being pulled into flirting with him.

For the moment Nathan gave up trying to provoke her into a sexy repartee. He knew two ways to convince her that marriage between them made sense: to get to know her better and to get her back into bed. Since the latter was out of the question at the moment, he decided to focus on something that held equal appeal, making a connection.

"Six months."

"What did you do before that?"

So it was to be the third degree. Nathan split his attention between the road and the sexy lady sitting beside him. "I was in New York."

"That answers where you were, not what you were doing."

"I was making money in the stock market and attending auctions."

"Is that where you learned so much about art?"

"I had some good teachers. One woman I met loved the galleries and supported quite a few new artists. She had an eye for gifted young talent."

Emma hummed knowingly. "And were you one of the talented young men she had an eye for?"

"Are you asking if we were lovers?" he asked, amused by her perception of him as an innocent youth being corrupted by an older, more experienced woman. "No. She wasn't my type. I like curvy brunettes, remember?"

"And she wasn't either of those things?"

"No, Madeline had the look of a half-starved jungle cat. And she could be equally dangerous. Lucky for me she took a shine to my Texas accent and deep pockets. We were great friends. She had a ball trying to polish all my rough edges."

"I can't picture you in New York."

She squinted at him as if trying to put him in different clothes. He'd prefer if she'd just strip him out of the ones he currently had on. That pesky desire stirred again.

"I didn't blend in well," he agreed.

"Is that why you left?"

"No, I left because my father had a heart attack earlier this year and his doctor told him if he didn't slow down, the next one might kill him. He asked me to come work with Sebastian and Max. He thinks all three Case brothers belonged at the company our grandfather built." A thread of self-disgust ran through his explanation. "They certainly belong there. However, they're not convinced that I do."

"And why is that?"

He looked askance at her, wondering how much she knew about him. "Sebastian and Max are my half brothers."

"Cody said your father was having an affair with your mother and that you came to live with your father and half brothers after she died."

Just like that, his past was on the table, and his illegitimacy didn't seem to bother Emma one bit. "I was twelve when she died. Sebastian and Max weren't exactly thrilled to find out they had a half brother."

"I'm sure it was hard on all of you." There was understanding in her voice and comfort in the hand that covered his. "I'm sorry you lost your mom so young."

Something unraveled in his chest. Her sympathy exposed a place he'd walled up the day his mother died, a place he guarded against intruders. For a split second he wanted to share with her how much it had hurt to lose the one person in the world who'd loved him.

Instead, he shrugged.

"My brothers made my life hell. I moved out when I turned eighteen, kept moving after college."

"I'm surprised you came back after all these years."

"I wouldn't have if Dad hadn't called me."

Her eyes narrowed as she gazed his way. "I think there's more to it than that."

Did she see how much he wanted to best his brothers? To wipe Max's smirk right off his face and know he was responsible for the defeat in Sebastian's eyes?

"Maybe I want a chance to prove they've been wrong about me all these years. To make them admit I'm the one who should be running the family business. That's why this deal with your dad is so important."

Her hand fell away from his. Watching her knit her fingers in her lap, Nathan knew he shouldn't have resurrected the idea that his reasons for pursuing her were more practical than personal. But her compassion had touched a tender spot, and he'd flinched.

Nathan passed a semi and returned to the right lane. Time to change the subject. "How did you get into jewelry making?"

"I have a degree in sculpture from the University of Houston. I knew I wanted to make jewelry from the time I was six and I got one of those bead kits for Christmas. I drove everyone crazy with my necklaces and bracelets. I made one for my father. He even wore it once."

Nathan tried to imagine Silas Montgomery, the stiff, forceful businessman, wearing a necklace of bright-colored plastic beads around his neck. "So that's how you know so much about early Texas artists. I'm assuming your curriculum included a little art history."

"It did. But you've made me realize that I need to expand my knowledge base."

"I'd be happy to take you to an auction at Sotheby's. We could retrace my plunge into the dissolute world of art collecting."

"A trip to New York to gallery-hop." Her voice softened with longing. "That sounds like heaven."

Nathan glanced at her and wished he hadn't. The dreamy expression on her face reminded him of how she'd looked moments before her friend had interrupted them. His chest tightened. His groin stirred. And he heaved a sigh.

Tonight, whether she was ready for it or not, he was going to make something memorable happen.

Six

Emma watched Nathan navigate the Houston traffic and tried to harden her heart against the lost boy she'd glimpsed a moment earlier. An impossible task now that she understood a little bit more about what made him tick. He wasn't the unfeeling businessman who thought only of money and deals. But that didn't mean he wouldn't ruthlessly stomp all over her heart in pursuit of his agenda. Which meant, the more charming he became, the more she needed to be wary.

"Where are we headed?" she asked, her stomach seizing up with hunger pangs and anxiety.

He'd been a little too nonchalant about her continued determination not to move out of the loft. She knew he'd arrived tonight because she'd stonewalled the men sent to remove her things, but he hadn't mentioned it, and that aroused her suspicions.

"I thought we'd try Mark's American Cuisine."

Knowing their destination was a public place didn't settle her nerves the way it should have. She'd been convinced he was taking her to his condo to ply her with red wine and sex appeal until her resistance dissolved. To her immense shock, she was disappointed that he had no such nefarious plans.

"I haven't been there," she admitted. "But the food is supposed to be wonderful."

"I hadn't heard about the food," he said, casting a wry grin her way. "I was taking you there for the ambiance."

Mark's had been voted Houston's most romantic restaurant. "Is that so?" she quizzed, her tension unraveling beneath his flirtatious smile.

"That's so."

At the restaurant she waited while he came around the car and opened her door. As he pulled her to her feet, her heel caught in a hole. Unbalanced, she stumbled against his long frame. He caught her by the shoulders. Her heart stopped as the heat of his body enveloped her.

He hummed. "You know, we could grab some takeout and head back to my place."

Now, that was the Nathan she knew and...

"You were bringing me here for the ambiance," she reminded him, her eyes half closing as his warm breath stroked her cheek.

"My place has a great ambiance. Perfect for just the two of us."

And she wanted to go. So much. Despite the warnings from her rational side. Giving in now would signal Nathan that he'd won. He'd become even more relentless.

Her earrings tickled her neck as she shook her head. "Now that we're here, nothing could persuade me to leave without tasting Chef Mark's food."

"What about a chance to taste me?" The dare in his quicksilver-gray eyes touched her like a caress. She trembled.

What madness had led her to believe she could master her

attraction to Nathan? It throbbed in her body like a drumbeat, insistent, steady, increasing to a heady climax.

"You can be dessert," she whispered.

His eyes widened at her response. "After dinner we'll stop and buy some whipped cream."

Gulping, she grasped at something to defuse the sudden influx of sexual tension. Teasing him seemed to be the best way. "You don't think you're sweet enough for me?"

His grin blindsided her.

"Not by a long shot."

Emma gave him a shaky smile in return and lifted onto the balls of her feet to kiss him on the chin. "Then bring on the whipped cream."

"Dammit, woman," he muttered, guiding her inside the restaurant. "How the hell am I supposed to enjoy dinner when all I can think about is dessert?"

He sounded as disturbed as she felt. Emma's head spun at the notion that she had some power over him. He wasn't completely in control. Knowing that leveled the playing field a bit and relaxed her.

"You'll just have to manage," she said, squeezing his arm. "This is beautiful."

Located in a renovated church, the restaurant lived up to its reputation for romantic dining. The soaring cathedral ceiling, awash in golden light, arched over candlelit tables with white tablecloths and elegant place settings. A graceful staircase curved upward to what had once been the choir loft, now open to the tables below and edged with simple wrought-iron railing. The ceiling's line was echoed in the detailing above the doorways, drawing the eye upward.

The dining experience was everything she expected it to be. Won over by the candlelight, her charismatic dinner companion and way too much food, Emma set down her fork and spread her fingers over her stomach.

"That was delicious," she said, feeling sleepy despite

turning down the wine Nathan had ordered. Although the evening had taken on an enchanted glow, she needed to return to her loft and get back to work. Alcohol would have made that task impossible. "I can't recall the last time I ate so much."

"I have to admit, I do enjoy watching you eat. There's something so very sexy about it."

She made a face at him.

"Did you save room for dessert?" their waiter asked.

Emma welcomed his arrival because it kept her from having to answer Nathan. "I'm afraid I couldn't eat another bite."

Then she remembered her earlier dessert conversation with Nathan and her cheeks warmed. She glanced his way. A silver flame kindled in his eyes. Despite the large amount of food he'd consumed, there remained a hungry look about him. He appeared ready to devour her. A slow, steady heat crept through her, moving with determination to the parts of her most vulnerable to the persuasive power of desire.

"About dessert," she began, sounding unsteady and breathless.

The way his eyes slid over her made her quake. Traitorous longings weakened her resolve to go back to work tonight. Nathan Case, covered in whipped cream, was too much temptation for her to resist. And Emma had never been one to deny herself something she wanted. Hence, her current predicament.

She cleared her throat and tried again. "I really have a lot of work to do tonight. I should get back to my loft. There's so much to be done for the show. I'm starting with almost no inventory. The more pieces I make, the more I will have to sell and the better the show will go." She was babbling, but stopping the words from flowing off her tongue was nearly impossible, pierced as she was by those quicksilver eyes dancing with carnal promises.

"I understand," he said. "As long as you promise to give me a rain check on dessert."

With his hand warm on the small of her back, Emma let him guide her between the tables and out the door. "I'm not sure if a rain check is such a good idea."

As they waited for the valet to bring the car around, Nathan turned her toward him and cupped her upper arms in his hands. "Shh. Don't say something you'll regret."

Amusement fought with annoyance at his arrogance. She was trying not to *do* something she would regret.

Suddenly, Emma wondered why she was resisting the pull between them. Maybe she should just get him out of her system, and let him get her out of his. Then this business of her father's could dry up like a creek bed during a drought.

Once they were in Nathan's car, he turned left out of the parking lot instead of making the right that would take them back toward her loft. Emma got that funny feeling in her stomach again.

"Where are we going?"

"I thought we'd swing by my condo so I can return your earrings," he said as if this hadn't been his plan all along. "You said you wanted them back."

To claim otherwise would make him wonder why she was so skittish about the detour. Maybe he had no ulterior motives. Emma glanced at Nathan's profile. His lips had softened into a sensual curve. Excitement raced along her nerves as she recognized his expression. Oh, he definitely had ulterior motives.

Her breath shortened as anticipation seized her. Struggling to quell her body's thrumming need, she tore her attention from Nathan and watched the city slide by her window. By the time he drew up in front of his house, she was a tangled mess of sizzling hormones.

"Can't I just wait here while you get them?" she asked as he opened her car door. "I really have work to do."

He shook his head and held out his hand. With a gusty sigh, Emma let him pull her from the car. He slid his palm into the small of her back as they crossed the elegant lobby and ascended in the elevator. Her heart thumped hard enough to hurt as she recalled the last time she'd gone to his condo with him.

If his thoughts ran along the same lines, Emma couldn't tell from his bland expression. She half expected him to close his front door and pin her against it the way he had a month ago. Of course, last time, they'd both known why they'd come to his condo. The chemistry between them had been hot and inescapable. This time, Emma stepped into his foyer with a cooler head.

She didn't realize that she was holding her breath until they reached the condo's main living space. Letting the air flow out of her lungs, she stepped away from Nathan's tempting presence and scanned the room. A leather sectional occupied one end of the large open-concept floor plan; beyond that, a dining table was surrounded by ten chairs.

"What do you think?"

"About what?"

"My home." He smirked at her. "The last time you were here, we never made it out of the foyer."

Her cheeks burned as she recalled how he had taken her by storm. His urgency had thrilled her. Never in her life had a man wanted her with such intensity. Half closing her eyes, she relived the sensation of him sliding into her. The memory flushed her skin hot, arousing her.

She took in the view of downtown Houston visible through the floor-to-ceiling windows.

"It's very nice. But I'm not staying. I just came up to get my earrings."

He circled her like a tomcat on the prowl, his shoulder brushing across her back, his chest grazing her breasts as he stopped in front of her. Leaning forward, he whispered in her ear, "Are you sure that's the only reason?"

"Of course," she retorted, all the desire he aroused reducing her voice to a husky rasp. She had to get out of here. But her knees wobbled too much to let her escape.

"Because I was hoping I could get you to stay for a drink," he said, his hands sliding around her waist.

He nuzzled her neck, zeroing in on the spot that made her gasp. Her nipples tightened into hard beads of sensation. Her breasts felt heavy, ready for his possession. She swayed into his body, sighing as he flattened his palms against her butt, lifting her onto her toes, aligning her curves against his hard planes.

"I really shouldn't," she told him, her body liquefying as wave after wave of longing washed over her. "I've got work to do." She was beginning to sound like a broken record.

"Later," he growled against her lips before flicking his tongue against hers, stealing her breath and her sanity.

Sliding her hands up his chest, she buried her fingers in his hair and held on as he deepened the kiss, plundering her mouth, demanding that she respond without reluctance or hesitation. She surrendered to the hands that molded her body, the fierce seduction of his mouth stripping away her reservations about the lovemaking to come.

Lust ravaged her, destroying her last qualm. Her body belonged to him. He'd proved that the last time. And she trusted that he would be the perfect guide on this excursion into carnal delights.

"Tonight, we're going to do this slowly." He slipped his lips over her chin, her cheek, her eyes, her nose. "Last time you rushed me. That will not happen again."

Her head fell back as his teeth nibbled her earlobe. His ministrations ripped an airy giggle from her throat. "Not too slowly, or I might change my mind."

"I have no worries about that," he murmured, sounding

smug, the way a man with an armful of wanton woman would.

"Oh, for heaven's sake," she sighed, rubbing her pelvis against him in restless frustration as his palms kneaded her hips. Only with Nathan did she experience such riotous sensations. "I have so much pressure inside me, I'm going to burst."

She demonstrated the serious nature of her distress by moving against him in a manner that aroused her more than it eased her suffering. Nathan's mouth collided with hers as their hips began to rock together in a pantomime of what was to come.

"You have no idea what you do to me, Emma."

His words stoked the flames higher. Emma increased the abandoned gyrations of her body, too caught up in the heady turbulence to want a slow seduction. She knew he wanted their next time together to be in bed, but she was ready to throw him to the couch and straddle him.

Eager to see every gorgeous inch of him, she tugged his shirt free of his trousers, frantic to feel the warm silk of his skin. Nathan eased the pressure on her mouth long enough to aid her.

Together they dispensed with his buttons. With his shirt gone and her fingers against his skin, Emma purred with satisfaction. Urgency became awe as she skimmed the smoothness of his shoulders and the lean brawn beneath.

"You are beautiful." Hard muscles shifted beneath her exploring caress.

"I've never been called beautiful before."

"You are," Emma assured him, trailing her fingers across his chest and boldly tracing the path of rough hair to the place where it disappeared beneath his pants. "Now take everything off."

Nathan groaned as her provocative words and saucy tone impacted on the one area of his body he couldn't control. If he had been hard from the moment they'd stepped into the condo, he was ready to burst his seams after that comment.

She leaned forward and stroked her tongue against his collarbone, grazing his shoulder with her teeth.

"You first," he said. He couldn't trust his voice any more than he could count on controlling the rest of his body.

His desire for her ran fierce and resolute through his veins, but he bound it with relentless control. She deserved a slow, sensual ride. He wanted to bring her the same wild, unbridled pleasure her touch promised him.

"So, let's start with this." Emma stripped off her jacket and reached for the hem of her lace top, lifting it over her head, disturbing her careless topknot as she did so. She emerged from the cream material and gave her head a vigorous shake.

Nathan's breath caught. Long brown hair tumbled about her shoulders, framing a face of vulnerable beauty. He considered the wide-eyed darkness of her chocolate-hued eyes and the thoroughly plundered redness of her mouth.

Had he only kissed her? She looked positively drugged by passion.

"Now, that's more like it," he said an instant before her hands snaked out and caught his belt to tug him closer. He bent his head and answered her urgent call for a kiss.

Her lips clung to his when he lifted his head. She breathed in a rapid, unsteady manner that made him smile as he surveyed the wholly sensual look on her face, put there by his caresses.

Groaning low in her throat, the animalistic sound fanning his desire, she slid her palm downward. Before she could touch him, Nathan caught her wrist and pulled her hand away. "None of that right now. I promised you a night to remember," he growled, sweeping her off her feet and into his arms. "Not a quickie on the floor in my living room."

When he set her on her feet once more, his king-size mattress bumped the back of her knees.

"A quickie," she murmured, fumbling to unfasten the belt and the top button of his trousers. "Yes, make love to me now."

He tumbled her onto the bed. "If you insist."

"I insist." She arched, catlike, as he rolled her beneath him.

Nathan dipped his tongue in her ear and elicited a disturbed shudder, and then he leaned back to consider her smooth, pale skin and the provocative charm of her rose-tipped breasts, glimpsed through the lace of her bra.

"You are so soft," he sighed against her throat, trailing his tongue down her chest and across the delicate fabric of her bra.

She arched and offered her breasts. He felt her nipple harden after he raked his teeth across it. Her breath rasped in and out of her lungs, keeping time with the disturbed movements of her hands in his hair and across his shoulders.

"I've never felt anything like this before."

Her muted, feminine voice entered his system like the resonance of pure crystal, brightening his mood. "Good."

He rolled onto his back, taking her with him. With a hand on each thigh, he positioned her on top of him. He held her head and devoured her mouth, plunging his tongue deep to tangle with hers. As she gave him back all the passion he demanded, Nathan found his control slipping a little further from his grasp.

He'd intended to seduce her slowly, to ply her body with all the expertise at his disposal, but she moved against him frantically, her thighs tightening on his hips. Desire raked long talons across his senses. He was dangerously close to letting the urge to take her hard, deep and fast dictate his actions.

Without warning she broke off the kiss and sat up. She

rubbed her thumb across his lower lip. He nipped at the pad. Her lips curved in a satisfied smile as she stroked lower, sampling the shape of his chin, the sensitivity of his ears and the pulse throbbing in his throat.

"You have a very nice chest," she told him, drawing provocative circles in ever-tightening swirls around his pectoral muscles.

"I was thinking the same thing about you."

He lifted one hand to skim across her breasts just above the lace edging of the bra. Their pale roundness moved enticingly with each shuddering breath.

When he grazed her nipple through the satin fabric, she mimicked him. The sensation startled him. His erection prodded her through their clothes, insistent, relentless.

She shook her head, sending her long hair cascading around her face. Leaning down, she brushed the brown silkiness against his chest, tickling him, tantalizing him and hiding her expression.

"How does it feel when I touch you like this?" she asked, raking her nails over his nipples and down his abdomen.

"Incredible. How about when I touch you like this?" He swallowed her breasts in his hands and gently kneaded.

She threw back her head and arched her spine, putting her hands behind her and pushing into his caress. "Amazing."

Inspired by her husky, awed comment, he slowly rid them both of the rest of their clothes, taking the time to slide his hands and mouth over each new inch of her flesh he bared, until they were both naked and shaking uncontrollably. Emma's lashes veiled the expression in her eyes as Nathan drew the tip of one finger along the curve of her breast to her nipple. He watched her shiver as he slowly bent his head to capture the hard bud in his mouth.

"Oh, Nathan," she whispered his name as his mouth tugged at her breast.

"Are you cold?" he questioned, kissing his way down

her stomach to dip his tongue into her navel. Emma's gaze remained riveted on him as he lifted her thigh so that he could kiss the inside of her knee.

"No." Her voice broke as he opened his mouth and sucked on the sensitive flesh a little higher up. She rocked her hips, enticing him to touch where she ached.

"You're trembling."

"That's your fault."

"Let's see what I can do about it then."

His tone might have been affectionate and teasing, but his chest tightened with driving need. He eased his fingers along her thigh, aiming for the source of her pleasure. He caught and held her gaze while he brushed the brown curls at the juncture of her thighs. Her lashes fluttered, but she bravely watched. This open, visual lovemaking would drive him mad. Ah, but what a way to go.

The swirling pressure in his groin built into a knot of searing demand as Nathan slid his finger against her warmth, focusing her pleasure where he wanted it. Her eager reactions filled him with fierce satisfaction. He intended for her to feel the same wildness that was clawing him.

Her head moved restlessly against the pillow as he stroked her, pushing her toward the beckoning promise of fulfillment. She gripped the sheets, tension riding her curvaceous frame. The sounds of pleasure she made told him exactly how to increase the sensations roiling her.

"That's it, love," he crooned as she fragmented, her body rocked by a powerful orgasm. He held her while she gasped for breath, soothing her with long, sweeping caresses.

She tugged on his arm, urging him up beside her, and threaded her fingers through his hair. He kissed her nose and traced the line of her lower lip with his tongue, his body tight with need.

"Nathan?"

"Yes, Emma?"

"That was incredible." She parted her legs and rotated her hips until he was trapped in the sexy cradle between her thighs. "But I need more."

Her heat called to him, drove him mad with wanting. He kissed his way down her neck. "What's the rush? We have all night."

"You want to make me yours," she reminded him, nipping at his chin. Her breath hitched as he eased his lips over her skin. "Please do that."

He closed his eyes as her pleading eroded his willpower. "I want you fully satisfied before I do so. I don't think I've fulfilled my end of the bargain."

His voice shook with harsh urgency, but he couldn't control that any more than he could stop the trembling in his muscles as her fingers caressed his chest and moved lower. He wanted her so much he thought he might die from the ache.

"I won't be fully satisfied until you're inside me."

Nathan sucked in his breath as her fingers found his shaft and measured him in a series of provocative, fluid strokes.

No more words were needed. He eased forward. Her hips lifted to find the hardness of him and her hands cupped his buttocks to urge him into her. Trapped between her heat and the soft determination of her hands, he had no choice but to give her what she wanted.

Bracing his weight on his arms, he slipped inside her a little at a time. She groaned in pleasure as her body absorbed all of him. The sound almost pushed him over the edge, but he sucked in a deep, steadying breath and focused on her face.

"Tell me what you're thinking," he said, taking a long moment to savor the passion-drugged sleepiness in her heavy-lidded expression.

"I'm thinking..." she answered in a soft, cautious voice, digging her nails into his butt. Nathan's body jumped in response to her provocative caress. "That I've never been so turned on before."

"That's good."

He eased out of her as slowly as he had entered and watched her eyes round and darken until they were all pupil. She bit her lip. He clenched his teeth together to keep himself from slamming into her repeatedly and gaining the exquisite release his body craved. When he came, he wanted her with him.

The satisfying friction as he moved in and out of her blew huge, gaping holes in his willpower, but he started replaying multiplication tables in his head and held on.

She increased his tempo much sooner than he wanted. Her soft cries and the frantic movement of her hips destroyed the control he had fought so hard to maintain. The shattering of his heart began the moment he felt her release. Nathan gathered her into his arms and pounded his way to his own climax, enthralled by the way she kept pace with him. Together, they stormed into the brilliance of pleasure so acute he couldn't breathe.

As his name left her lips, as her fingers dug into his shoulders, as his chest tightened with the intensity of his emotions, he banded her to his body and shook in reaction, dazzled by their turbulent lovemaking.

In the aftermath of the fire, Nathan stroked a strand of hair away from her cheek and placed a gentle kiss on her lips, sensing that, at last, he'd found the woman who could curb his restless nature.

Seven

According to the digital clock on the nightstand, it was a quarter after five. Emma yawned. Falling asleep had been a mistake. Already she could feel herself falling under Nathan's spell. Spending the night and following that up with morning lovemaking would set a precedent Nathan would exploit to the fullest.

Although he hadn't mentioned marriage or even referred to an unofficial engagement between them last night, Emma knew his mind-set. He needed the deal with her father and would do whatever it took to persuade her to marry him, including seduce her limp and senseless over and over until she could refuse him nothing. But she had more immediate concerns.

Easing from beneath Nathan's arm proved difficult for several reasons.

Huge muscles were heavy.

His big naked body held as much temptation relaxed in sleep as it had aroused.

And he'd worn her out with the most incredible lovemaking she'd ever experienced.

As she swung her feet to the floor, Nathan stirred and reached toward her. She scooted off the bed and glanced over her shoulder, wondering if he'd awaken. He slumbered on, face half-buried in her pillow, his muscular torso sprawled across the space she'd so recently occupied. Ignoring the voice in her head encouraging her to wake him up for one last hurrah, Emma searched the dark room for her discarded clothes.

She nearly tripped over her skirt. Her bra lay three feet away. When had she kicked off her shoes? She paused to drape Nathan's pants across the foot of his bed. His shirt followed after she put the garment to her nose for a deep hit of the cologne he wore. The same scent emanated from her skin. She smiled, wondering if the hands he'd smoothed over every inch of her skin smelled like Donna Karan's Cashmere Mist.

A groan gathered in her throat. Why hadn't she honored the promises to herself and stayed out of Nathan's bed? Who was she kidding—the instant his mouth settled on hers, stealing her breath, demanding her surrender, she'd been putty in his hands. He'd wrung impassioned moans from her throat, sexy encouragement from her lips and uncontrolled writhing from her body. Her cheeks burned hot as she thought about all the things she had let him do.

She stared at the bed, eyeing the tangled sheets that bared his back and most of one butt cheek. Shockingly, the space between her thighs tingled. She bit down on her tender, well-kissed lips, fighting temptation. How could she possibly be ready for more?

Quit stalling. Get yourself dressed and get out.

The urge to pause for one last look at the slumbering man fought with her practical side. Hadn't she already over-indulged? Emma slipped on her lingerie and skirt, zipping it on the short walk into his living room, and dangled her shoes by the straps as she made her way to the door.

As each mile of the taxi ride home took her farther away from Nathan, her body came down off a sensual high. She felt the first twinge of a withdrawal headache as she put her key in the lock. By the time she swung the door open, her nerves were showing distinct signs of exposed edges. She felt strung out and weary beyond words.

Flipping on the lights, she stared at the empty room. Adrenaline surged, banishing any fatigue. What the hell had happened to her stuff?

She advanced into her loft and stopped where her couch should have been. Her heart jumped in her chest. Next, she pushed open the door to her workroom and stared at the bare space. No equipment. No supplies and finished pieces. Half-dazed, she crossed the hall to check out her bedroom. Furniture. Clothes. Everything she owned. Gone.

Emma closed her eyes. Her fingers tightened into fists.

Nathan.

He'd lured her out for a romantic dinner with assurances that he wouldn't persuade or bully her to move out of the loft. He'd plied her with flirtatious conversation until she'd fallen back into bed with him. Emma growled. All the while his movers had been busy clearing out her things. He must have had a good laugh at her expense tonight. What an idiot she was.

Thank goodness it was too early to call Addison. Emma wanted nothing more than to run to her best friend, borrow a pair of pajamas and curl up on her couch to whine about Nathan. Three months ago she would have done just that.

Her father's belief that she lacked drive wasn't a notion he'd pulled out of thin air. As a pampered and spoiled heiress, Emma was never expected to accomplish anything. As a result, she'd never taken charge of her life, just drifted through it.

But her expectations for herself had changed. And if she

intended to produce $35,000 worth of jewelry, she would have to go to Nathan and demand her equipment back.

She dug her car keys out of her purse and marched out the door. At half past five o'clock in the morning, few cars were on the road as she sped through town on her way back to Nathan's condo. She didn't bother to call him again, not wanting him to know she was coming. By the time she pulled into his parking lot, she'd worked herself into a fine fury.

Standing outside his door, she listened to her pounding heart and some of the urgency left her. She wasn't good at confrontation. Probably because she'd spent so much of her childhood surrounded by it. Her parents fought all the time. Fire from her mother. Ice from her father.

Nathan answered the door almost before she lifted her finger from his doorbell. Dressed in pajama bottoms, his muscular chest looming bare and magnificent before her eyes, he leaned his forearm against the doorframe and looked her up and down. "Well, hello. Did you run out for coffee and doughnuts?"

That he continued to play games with her, after taking her to dinner under false pretenses and then making love to her as if she was the most important woman on earth, revived her anger.

"Where's my stuff?"

He stepped back and gestured her inside. "Some of it's in storage. Some of it's here."

"I told you I didn't want to move." She crossed the threshold and pulverized his grin with a hard look. "Not in here with you. Not anywhere."

"Despite everybody telling you that staying in your place was a health hazard?" He shook his head.

She set her hands on her hips. "So you decided to steal all my stuff?"

"I didn't steal it." His measured tones infuriated her as

he tugged her deeper into the condo. "I moved it so the contractors I hired could get to work."

"You hired contractors?" she demanded, annoyed at how control over her life was slipping from her grasp. "It's my loft. I should be the one doing the hiring." She narrowed her eyes at his easy shrug and trailed after him as he headed into the kitchen. The scent of brewing coffee made her nose twitch with interest despite herself. "And I don't understand why everything is gone. Surely they don't need all my furniture removed to clean up a mold problem."

Nathan poured two cups of coffee and handed her one. "After leaving your loft yesterday, I realized that you can't sell it the way it is now."

"Sell it?" Emma wondered if she'd just heard him properly. "Why would I want to do that?"

"Because after we're married we'll live here."

The words *after we're married* reverberated through her head. He was taking a lot for granted. "I thought you understood that I'm not going to marry you because of some business deal."

"But you are going to marry me."

The man was insufferable.

"No, I'm not," she fumed. "And I'm not moving in with you, either."

He sipped coffee and watched her over the rim of the cup.

Emma stared back at him, matching his silence while her thoughts churned. How was she supposed to get all her pieces finished in time for the show? Then, it occurred to her that this had been his plan all along. If he stopped her from working, she wouldn't make enough to replace the money in her account and she'd be forced to marry him. Her heart skipped a beat. Was he that diabolical?

"Where's the equipment and supplies from my work-room?"

"In storage. Your clothes are in my guestroom."

Hadn't he heard a word she said? "I'll stay with Addison until the mold is cleaned up, then I'm moving back into the loft. Call your contractors and cancel them. I'm not going to do any remodeling on the loft because I'm not going to sell it." Her jaw hurt from clenching her teeth, but she managed to add, "I'll have someone in here either this afternoon or tomorrow to move my things out."

"And where do you plan to work? You'd better not go back to the loft."

"I'll find studio space I can rent."

"You can work here."

His offer was grudging at best. He didn't want her working at all. And Emma couldn't imagine getting anything done with his presence distracting her.

"You don't need to worry about me," she said, and wished her words would convince him.

"How can I help it?"

"Easy. Just remind yourself that I'm not your responsibility."

His dark eyebrows arched. "Not yet."

"Not ever."

"We'll see."

Nathan realized that he'd been staring at the set of financials for half an hour without making any sense of the numbers. In fact, he'd been distracted all morning. After five days of searching, Emma had been unable to find space to work. Desperate and running short on time, she'd ungraciously reconsidered her refusal of his spare bedroom as her studio, but spent her nights at her friend's house.

Despite knowing that he was her last option, he'd been pleased that Emma had stayed within his grasp, even if she'd wrung a promise from him not to sabotage her jewelry or interfere with her workspace.

This meant the only way to keep her from working would be to distract her with kisses and lovemaking, but like the shoemaker's elves, she was both industrious and elusive. In the four days since she'd been working in his condo, he had yet to catch sight of her.

Every night when he arrived home, he went straight to the spare room where her equipment was set up and noticed new sketches pinned to the walls and glittering works in progress scattered across her worktable.

And the more jewelry she finished, the more likely it was that she would make good on her threat to sell enough at the show to meet her goal. He needed to slow her down. An impossible task with all the long hours he was working at rehashing the numbers for the venture with Montgomery Oil.

Maybe he should take work home. Lord knew he could use a break from the office. His brothers' negative attitudes were getting on his nerves more than ever. For the last week, he'd been as surly as a bear awakened in the middle of winter.

He checked his watch. He could head home for lunch and surprise her with a little afternoon delight. Decision made, he grabbed his keys and the tube containing the architect's plans for her loft that he'd commissioned. Anticipation kicked him hard as he headed for the door. He dodged the implication that not seeing Emma was what accounted for his foul mood, but it dogged his heels in a relentless bid for attention.

He was moving briskly down the hall when Sebastian called after him. "Nathan, got a minute?"

Hissing in exasperation, Nathan turned and spied his older brother standing just outside his office. Sebastian must have seen him going by. "Sure," he said, retracing his steps. "What's up?"

"Max and I are heading out to meet with Lucas for a couple days." Sebastian gestured Nathan into his room. "I wondered if you had any input for us before we go."

Nathan noticed that he hadn't been included in the meeting. Resentment burned. They'd regret cutting him out of the decision-making process. He'd make sure of it. "I don't see the point. You won't like what I have to say."

Sebastian's mouth tightened at Nathan's sarcasm, but he wasn't as reactive as Max. "Maybe you should come along and say it in person."

Sebastian's offer surprised Nathan. Obviously, he and Max were still determined to persuade Lucas to sell his company, but it also appeared that they were willing to listen to Nathan's analysis of the business.

Or at least Sebastian was. Max hadn't voiced his opinion. But if Nathan could get one Case brother on his side, chances were the other one would come around in time. Divide and conquer.

Or was it possible that they were interested in finding some middle ground and starting a dialogue?

"When are you thinking of going?" Nathan asked, curious as to what his brothers were up to.

"We thought we'd go this week," Sebastian said.

He really should stick around Houston and prevent Emma from having uninterrupted access to her equipment and supplies at his condo.

"Set up the meeting," Nathan said. "Let's see what Lucas has to say."

"Earth to Emma."

Distantly she heard her name and blinked to redirect her focus from the necklace on the worktable. Nathan lounged in the doorway, his shoulder propped against the frame. Dressed in a navy suit, pale blue shirt and red tie, he looked every inch the powerful executive in his prime. Emma's traitorous pulse lunged like a racehorse from the starting gate.

She'd been very careful to avoid him, keeping the hours she spent at the condo short to leave for Addison's before he arrived home. At first she hadn't wanted to run into him because she was still furious over the way he'd tricked her into moving out of her loft. Then, as her anger faded and the night she'd spent in his arms played repeatedly in her mind like a steamy foreign film, she'd steered clear of him out of a desire for sheer self-preservation.

She didn't trust herself to be alone in the condo with him and not succumb to his sizzling kisses again. Just the thought of him and her and an empty condo got her hot and bothered. He needed to believe that she wasn't going to fall for his winning charms and let him boss her around anymore.

Sifting through a pile of sapphires, she did her best to ignore the throb of awareness pulsing through her. If only he'd stop eyeing her as if she was a juicy apple he was dying to sink his teeth into. She almost groaned at her body's sharp reaction to the notion of his mouth on any part of her.

With the back of her hand, she brushed her bangs off her face. "How long have you been standing there?"

"A couple of minutes. You certainly seem preoccupied by what you were doing." He gestured with the long tube he carried.

"I have a lot to do and only ten days to get it done." She held up a half-finished necklace for his inspection, pleased by how well her design looked in gold. The light clipped to the side of her worktable made the diamonds sparkle. "But I'm doing some of my best work ever."

He cocked his head as he surveyed the necklace. "I'm glad to hear that."

Her insides twisted into an uncomfortable knot. To her dismay, she realized that she'd expected his eyes to light up with pride at her accomplishments. She wanted him to appreciate her craft and to understand how important this show was to her, not just because she needed to restore the money to her account, but also because it would prove that she could take care of herself by doing something she was great at.

What an idiot she was. Bad enough that he whipped her into a sexual frenzy with his lazy smiles. She'd really be setting herself up for heartache if his opinion of her started to matter.

Nathan tapped a roll of blueprints out of the tube he was holding and spread them across her worktable, using pliers, the box that held her loose stones, and the necklace she'd shown him to weigh down the corners.

"I brought you some sketches for the remodel on your loft."

She shook her head. Exhaustion dragged at her shoulders. "I don't have the money or the time to think about remodeling my loft right now."

"Let me do it."

"No." Emma bristled. He wanted to fix up her place to sell it. "Why won't you listen to me?"

Instead of reacting negatively to her sharp tone, Nathan left the sketches and circled her worktable. He'd come within reach before she caught the intent in his eye. Back against the wall, surrounded by equipment, she had no place to flee. She held up her tweezers.

Ignoring her defensive stance, he spun her around on her stool. His hands settled on her shoulders, thumbs rolling deep pressure into her muscles. Rather than feeling sexual, his touch pleasured her on a whole different level. She groaned her appreciation and let her head drop forward.

"You should take some time off," he told her, massaging his strong fingers down either side of her spine. "You're working too hard."

"I have to get ready for the show."

"You'll concentrate better if you're not so tired."

Did he know she wasn't sleeping? Crashing on Addison's couch wasn't ideal. Between staying up late to sketch new designs and her best friend's early-rising brood, she was lucky to snag four hours of shut-eye. The first few nights it hadn't been bad, but now, in the second week, she was feeling the effects of weariness. She'd messed up an important piece yesterday afternoon for that very reason, but she couldn't stop, much less slow down.

"I'll sleep when the show's over," she said, pulling away from his invigorating massage before he convinced her to take a break. His hands on her back made her long for him to apply that healing touch to other parts of her body, parts that were achy for reasons having nothing to do with jewelry-making. She fussed with the gems on her worktable. "Until then, I intend to work until I drop."

"Take five minutes and look at what my architect came up with."

Exhausted and awash with conflicting desires, she gave him a taste of her frustration. "What part of 'I'm not going to sell my condo' aren't you getting?" she muttered crossly. "Did it ever occur to you that I don't like being told what to do? You bullied me into moving out of my loft and now you tell me that you're going to remodel it so I can sell it because we're getting married. You've never once thought about what's best for me." Emma's chest heaved as she drew breath for her next onslaught of temper. "Go away, Nathan, and take your plans with you."

She indicated the ones he'd spread over the table, but really meant all his plans—the ones for her loft, the ones for her future and, most important, the ones for her heart. She moved the weights that held the floor plans flat and they curled up on themselves.

Emma returned to sorting sapphires, her hands shaking hard enough that she could barely pick up the pink gem she intended to place into the gold setting. Although Nathan was a difficult man to ignore, she put her heart and soul into it. He stood beside her for a long moment, impatience rolling off him, before he dropped a perfunctory kiss on the top of her head and walked out of the room.

An insistent ringing disturbed Nathan's grim thoughts. The meeting with Lucas Smythe had gone worse than he'd expected. The guy was definitely considering selling his company and offering Case Consolidated Holdings first crack at it. Sebastian and Max were full of smug delight and Nathan was fighting hard to stop them from shutting down his venture with Montgomery Oil. With three weeks to go until Valentine's Day, the only thing keeping his deal with Silas alive was the fact that Smythe was not one hundred percent ready to let go of the business his family had owned for the last hundred years.

Glancing at his cell phone's display, he took the call. "Hey, Dad."

Brandon Case's rich chuckle filled Nathan's ear. "Don't you sound cheerful. Your brothers giving you trouble?"

Nathan gestured to the bartender to bring him another whiskey and stared at the hockey game on the television behind the bar. "You know they are."

"How's the deal going with Montgomery?"

"We're talking a couple times a week. He's got his people confirming our financial forecast. Cody's looking into possible locations for the production facility."

"Sounds promising."

"Yeah." Nathan knew his dad couldn't possibly miss the lack of enthusiasm in his voice. He was under the gun from two quarters. His brothers were awfully enamored of Smythe's company. How long before they convinced the guy to sell? Nathan had little trouble imagining a scenario in which he convinced Emma to marry him, and then couldn't do the deal with her father because his brothers bought Smythe Industries. "But it all might be a big waste of time."

"Let me guess—Lucas Smythe's company?"

A cheer went up behind Nathan. Someone must have scored.

"It balances our product mix and provides Case Consolidated Holdings with conservative but steady growth," he muttered.

"I was right to convince you to come home. I love those boys, but neither one has any instincts when it comes to taking risk. Too much education."

Nathan rolled his head from side to side in an attempt to loosen the knots in his shoulders. "I don't think having advanced degrees in business makes Max and Sebastian risk-adverse."

"It's because they take after their mother," Brandon said. "Whereas you take after me and your mother. Never met anyone as strong and brave as Marissa."

It wasn't the first time Nathan had heard his father's tone grow wistful when he spoke about Marissa Connor, but it was the first time Nathan asked a particular question. "Did you love her?"

He had no idea what had prompted him to delve into the relationship between his parents after avoiding the topic for so many years. Maybe he'd been thinking too much about Emma this trip and pondering how to overcome her determination to marry for love. He'd called her each day he'd been gone, getting her voice mail and leaving messages both times. She'd returned his calls, but he'd been in meetings and she hadn't left a voice mail. He craved the sound of her voice right now. It bugged him just how much he wanted to talk to her.

"Love her?" Brandon sounded surprised. "I adored her."

Was that true? Or was it a man's fond remembrance of the woman he'd lost before he could grow tired of her?

"I only wished I'd met her before Susan and I got married," Brandon continued. "I would have saved everyone a lot of heartache if I'd held out for the girl of my dreams instead of deciding it was time to settle down."

His father's words were like a left jab that came out of nowhere. His father had settled for marriage without love and lived to regret it. Nathan lurched back from the uncertainty that had appeared before him like a sinkhole. "But you didn't leave Susan."

Brandon sighed. "I wanted to, but Marissa wouldn't let me. She said I had a family who needed me."

Unexpected pain blossomed in Nathan's chest. What about him and his mom? They'd needed Brandon, too. "You're lying," he growled. "She loved you. She'd smile and hum for days after you visited. Why would she tell you to stay married?"

"Because she was stronger than me. Than Susan. Than your brothers. You both were." Brandon's voice grew melancholy. "They needed me. You didn't. Not really. Together the two of you could take on the world. It's why I wanted you to work with your brothers. They need your strength. Your confidence. The three of you will do great things with the business."

"Maybe, but we have to learn to work together first," Nathan muttered bitterly.

"Do you want me to talk to them?" his dad asked, his voice gaining an edge. "They need to understand you're an equal partner."

Nathan knew his father was feeling restless since retiring. Brandon liked keeping tabs on the business and voicing his opinions. He didn't understand how much that irritated his eldest son.

"Thanks, Dad, but this is something I need to handle."

After hanging up, Nathan sipped his drink and let his thoughts drift toward Emma as they'd been doing all too often lately. Never before had he struggled so hard to keep his attention on business.

From the moment he'd boarded the plane in Houston, it had occurred to him that he was worried about leaving her to her own devices. Her inability to understand the limitations of her energy and strength irritated him. In the last glimpse he'd had of her before leaving on this trip, he'd seen that Emma was driving herself toward exhaustion.

Until he'd surprised her over lunch, he'd assumed that the only work she'd been doing had been at his condo, but seeing how pale she'd become since he'd moved her out of her loft, he'd gotten her to admit that she spent her nights crafting her designs.

Things were going to change when he got back. He was going to convince her to move in so he could keep an eye on her and make her slow down. It was past time she started accepting that her future was with him. Once they were married, she wouldn't need to make jewelry or worry about money. He would take care of her the way she deserved to be cared for.

Eight

"You have to eat something," Nathan said, standing bare-chested before her worktable, his dark hair wet from the shower. Worn denim rode low on his hips, and he'd brought the scent of lavender into the spare room.

He'd returned home from his business trip an hour ago, more grim than she'd ever seen him, and commenced badgering her to take a break as soon as his overcoat hit the hall closet.

Avoiding Nathan's gaze, Emma eyed the plate he held. Although the fat strawberries tempted her, her stomach shifted uncertainly. She hadn't been interested in food lately. She blamed it on anxiety. Progress was much slower than she'd anticipated, due to the intricate nature of her newest designs. Of course, the finished product made the extra hours worthwhile, but she was overwhelmed with the amount of work still to be done.

"I ate before you came home." Fatigue threatened to tip

her off the stool. She'd been perched on it so long her behind had gone numb.

"What time?" he demanded.

"What time is it now?"

Nathan glowered at her. "Seven o'clock."

That meant she'd been sitting at her worktable for twelve hours straight with only bathroom breaks and a quick snack sometime around one. For the last three days, she'd been practically living in this room, taking advantage of his absence to execute one piece of jewelry after another. Never in her life had she put so much effort into anything. It was as exhilarating as it was exhausting.

She'd jump for joy if she could summon the energy.

"A couple hours ago."

"You are many things, Emma Montgomery, but a skillful liar you are not."

"I'll eat in a minute." In truth, she was afraid to stop working. Afraid, because she was so exhausted, that she might never start again. The long hours were taking their toll on her mind as well as her body, but she had a significant inventory of jewelry to show for all her effort. Yet, so much remained unfinished and with the clock ticking down, her nerves were stretched as thin as onionskin.

"You keep saying that and yet you don't." Radiating frustration, he arched his eyebrows at her. Crossing his arms over his chest made his biceps bulge. "I'm not leaving here until I see you eat every bite of that sandwich."

"Which I'll do as soon as I finish this ring." Her hands trembled as she struggled to fix a tiny diamond into place on the platinum band she was working on. She hissed a curse. "I promise."

Tears gathered in her eyes. If the stupid diamond didn't settle into the cradle she'd crafted for it, she was going to scream.

The ring blurred. She blinked away the weariness eating

into muscle and bone. Just a couple more hours, and she could knock off for the night. A couple more hours and she could stumble back to Addison's couch.

All too aware of Nathan's keen watchfulness, she clenched her teeth against a yawn. The struggle was brief, and in the end, she lost.

"Enough. You're dead on your feet." He circled the work-table, handed her the plate and plucked her off the stool as easily as if she'd been a child.

"Put me down."

Her stomach growled while she glared at him. "I don't have time for this. I need to work."

"You need to eat and rest." He swept her out of the room and strode down the hall, passing the guestroom he'd repeatedly offered.

Her heart bounced fretfully in her chest as he passed the living room and kept going. "Where are you taking me?"

"Bed."

"Not your bed."

His answer was a slow smile.

She made her displeasure known by spouting objections and shoving the heel of her palm against his steely shoulder, but despite her resistance, desire awakened and banished her earlier tiredness. How could she continue to want him with such intensity when he acted like such a domineering oaf? Yet, even as she fought for independence, the heat of his skin penetrated her annoyance and a sensual longing defused her protests.

By the time he lowered her to the bed, she'd relaxed her fists, sent her palms coasting along the silken skin of his upper back and let her fingers tangle in his dark hair.

Catching the change in her mood, he joined her on the mattress, and reclined on his side. She set the plate between them.

He picked up a strawberry and offered it to her. "Please eat."

Emma pushed herself up on her elbow and opened her mouth. He set the fruit between her lips, approval and lust glowing in his eyes as her teeth sank into the ruby flesh. Luscious and sweet, it exploded on her tongue like a sensual bomb, awakening her senses. She licked juice off her lips as he picked up another strawberry. Long before she finished the last one, she had a thundering need to get her hands on the erection straining against Nathan's zipper.

Putting the uneaten sandwich on the nightstand, she brushed her fingers down the front of his jeans, watching his pupils dilate and his nostrils flare. Wicked delight rippled through her as she drew her nails upward along the same path. His hips shifted as she plucked at the button that held his jeans closed. Thrilled by his harsh breathing, she found the tab of his zipper and began to slide it down, one millimeter at a time.

"Emma." Her name erupted out of him like a plea.

"Yes, Nathan?"

Pushing her hands away, he unzipped and stripped off his jeans. In turn, she shimmied out of her shirt, sweatpants and underwear, flinging them aside in her impatience. In less than a minute they knelt on the mattress facing each other, naked, inches apart, lungs burning with the rush of air that flowed in and out.

Emma was the first to move. She reached down and took Nathan's hard length, sliding her hand up, then down. A roar rumbled in his chest. His shaft pulsed in response to her caress. Satisfaction blazed as he threw back his head and bared his teeth. Raw need poured from his throat, arousing her still further.

Longing to give him the same sort of pleasure he'd given her, she lowered her head. Before she could put her mouth on him and taste the silken texture of his erection or run her tongue around the head and up the sensitive vein on the underside, Nathan tumbled her onto the mattress.

Startled, Emma scraped the hair away from her face and searched his expression. Nathan knit their fingers together and rested their joined hands on the pillow beside her head. His stillness left her awash in uncertainty. Need pulsed through her. Days apart made her frantic for his long, deep kisses. Hungry for the possessive caress of his hands against her hot skin. She craved their joining as she had craved nothing ever before. Didn't he want that, too?

Something in Nathan's half-lidded gaze held her transfixed.

Emotion.

He dropped his lips to hers and made slow work of exploring her mouth. Lost in the stroke of his tongue, the sweet seduction of his breath against her neck, his teeth on her earlobe, she realized that it wasn't all about physical desire for him. He cared for her. Maybe not to the point of love, but this was neither casual nor forgettable for him. She'd tasted the truth in his kisses and the way he made sure she was completely satisfied before he took his own pleasure.

A knot formed in her chest. Pretending this was just sex between them was going to be a lot harder with what she'd just realized. And her heart was more at risk than ever. Because hope had been awakened. Hope that caring could become more. Could become love. Anything less would shred her heart.

Shoving away her worries, she concentrated on the heat building in her loins as his tongue swirled around her breast in languid circles. A gasp tore from her throat as his mouth settled over her hard nipple and suckled her. Pleasure shot straight to her core. His hand followed, stroking down her body, sweeping away her last coherent thought. He explored her with delicate care, finding a host of sensitive spots that inflamed her yearning for him to touch where she burned.

Nathan had always been a considerate lover, but today she

was too impatient, her desire too fiery, spiraling out of control. She wanted him to take her hard and fast.

"I need you." Emma's fingers bit into his shoulders. His weight pinned her to the mattress, but she could wiggle her hips, make him notice her hunger. "Inside me," she gasped as his fingers slid between their bodies and found her heat. "Now."

He obliged by shifting between her parted thighs, his knees against hers, opening her for his possession. Murmuring words of encouragement and appreciation against her hot skin, he braced his hands above her shoulders and rocked his hips forward, penetrating her with a quick, deep thrust. She arched her back and gripped his wrists as her world exploded in a dazzling shower of sensation. She opened her soul to the shattering wonder of their coming together and groaned in pleasure as her body expanded to accommodate his size.

When he was completely encased in her, he stilled, and dropped his cheek against hers. "Woman, you feel marvelous. Are you okay?"

With his weight pinning her to the mattress, their bodies fitted together as nature designed, she knew she'd never been better.

"Perfect." She breathed the word reverently and rocked her hips, taking him even more deeply inside until he rested against her womb. She felt a flutter of delight. The first promise of her climax to come.

He slid one hand beneath her, cupping her derriere in his palm as he began that incredible slide in and out of her body. Pressure built faster than she thought possible and lifted her high into the sky where she fractured and rained back to earth in a thousand pinpoints of light. She returned to her body, drawn back by Nathan's deep kisses.

"Next time we'll go together," he promised, resuming the long, slow thrusts that had pushed her over the edge the first time.

"I promise to try to be more patient," she panted, soothing his cheeks with her fingers. "It will help if you don't make me wait so long next time."

"Make *you* wait?" he growled, moving powerfully against her, driving deep into her core with spectacular results. "You've been avoiding me—" A groan escaped his lips as she tightened her internal muscles and felt him shudder in response.

It was so easy to please him. Everywhere she touched invoked a reaction. He seized her lips in a passionate kiss as their lovemaking became more and more frenzied. Then, a guttural roar proclaimed his own release as he surged into her one last time, before collapsing onto her.

With her arms wrapped around his shoulders, her legs around his hips, Emma savored the peaceful aftermath of their lovemaking, knowing the cease-fire wouldn't last. Soon he would slip out of her body and move away from her embrace, shattering the fragile intimacy created by the compelling attraction that exploded between them in bed.

Too soon, she would return to work and he would renew his efforts to distract her, but for now, she surrendered to the moment, feeling lazy and oh so very satisfied.

"Now, can we talk about how *I* made *you* wait," he murmured, kissing his way down her neck.

Despite being exhausted from the long hours she'd spent hunched over her worktable, Nathan's touch aroused her all over again. She'd spent so much time imagining the things she wanted to do in this bed. She had a dozen fantasies to live out.

"I'm not feeling much like talking," she said, rolling him onto his back and straddling him. Her breath hitched as he reached up and gently weighed her breasts in his hands.

"In other words, just enjoy this?"

She bent forward, her lips hovering just above his, and smiled. "Exactly."

* * *

Now this was more to his liking.

Nathan listened to the deep, steady breathing and inhaled the warm scent rising off the skin of the soft, naked woman sleeping in his arms. He took a long moment to savor the press of her full breasts against his chest and the tangle of their legs beneath the covers. Then, he opened his eyes and feasted on her passion-bruised mouth and long lashes. In the predawn light, with her mussed hair and naked shoulders rising out of the sheets, she appeared well-loved. His lips curved in a satisfied smirk.

When he'd first awakened, any thought of moving had been immediately rejected. The need for activity that drove him relentlessly had been tempered by the previous night's lovemaking. He wanted nothing more than to enjoy having Emma stretched out beside him. Parts of him, however, proved to have an abundance of energy. Blood surged into his groin, signaling a lust he'd thought well-sated.

Nathan slid his hand up her thigh and across her backside. He spread his fingers over the curve, applying pressure to ease her against his hard-on. Her lashes flickered, telling him she was awake. He nuzzled her temple.

"I have to go," she murmured, her muscles tensing as she braced to move.

He tightened his grip. If he let her escape, his contentment would go with her. What was happening to him that he could think of nothing better than spending the entire day in bed with her, just reading the paper or enjoying the feel of her body against his?

"Just stay a little longer."

"I've stayed too long already," she retorted, squirming against his grip, arousing him still more with her wriggling. "I've got work to do."

"Forget about the show. You'll never make your father's deadline."

"I'll make it." She glared at him and wedged her hands between their bodies to push him away. "I will make it."

"Why don't you just give up and marry me? You know I'll take care of you the way you were meant to be taken care of."

"I don't want to be taken care of."

Says the girl who wants a fairy-tale marriage, Nathan thought. If she'd give him half a chance, he could change her mind on that score, show her how thoroughly he could spoil her.

"Why are you fighting this so hard? We're great together. Last night was amazing."

Nathan rolled her beneath him, pinning her wrists above her head. Her muscles melted, body yielding. But her lips thinned in mutiny, and a resentful tempest darkened her eyes.

"Last night was about sex. That's not what I'm looking for in a marriage."

"It had better be or your husband will wander," he teased, nuzzling her neck, enjoying her skin.

"What I mean is sex isn't all I'm looking for in a marriage. I need love, too."

"Love doesn't last."

"Sometimes it does."

Feeling the tension in the slim body beneath his, Nathan released her wrists and shifted his weight off her. She slid out of bed.

His body ached as he watched her walk toward her discarded clothes. Was there anything sexier than a woman's back, he wondered, linking his fingers behind his head. The sheet slid to his waist, stopped from going farther by his morning erection. A cold shower would take care of that. In the meantime, he savored the dimples at the small of her back on either side of her spine, the sexy swoop of her narrow waist, and the flare of her heart-shaped derriere. She bent to retrieve her underwear, and he sighed as the action shoved her luscious tush into the air.

Keeping her back to him, she stepped into her pale pink panties. Watching her slide the scrap of lace into place was almost as sexy as watching her remove it. Everything about her turned him on. When she was done hooking her bra, she pivoted to face him.

"The man I marry will want me because of who I am, not because of who my father is."

Nathan leaned forward, running his eyes roaming over her half-naked form, filling the room with his desire for her. "I do want you."

"But you don't love me."

Could you?

The question peeked at him from beneath her long lashes. In her expression, he saw the barest hope that he might someday change his mind about love.

Cody's words came back to him. She wanted a fairy tale. A happily-ever-after. Is that what his mother had hoped for? His father's wife? His brother, Sebastian, whose marriage had disintegrated after two short years? Probably. Instead, they'd gotten heartbreak.

Her lips curved downward as the silence between them stretched out. He hated seeing her unhappy, but it wasn't fair to lead her on.

Finally, she got fed up with his lack of an answer. "I didn't think so," she muttered, scooping her shirt off the floor.

As much as he didn't like to be the source of her pain, she deserved his honesty. She needed to understand that she'd have his respect, his fidelity, his affection, just not his love.

And in the end, both of them would be happier for it.

"Love isn't what makes a marriage last," he said. "Or there wouldn't be half as many divorces. You need mutual respect and shared goals."

"I agree that marriage takes work," she said. "Supporting

each other's hopes and dreams. Listening and compromising. But wouldn't those things be easier with an emotional bond? Something powerful and all-consuming that keeps you together no matter how many curveballs life throws at you?"

The raw certainty in her eyes speared through him. A fervent crusader, she'd made a convincing argument for love. It might work on another man, one who hadn't seen the ravages of love up close and personal.

"And what happens when that powerful and all-consuming emotion dies?" he countered.

Hands on her hips, she pressed her lips together and glared at him. "I'll bet you think you're better off not letting anyone in. That way you don't get hurt. But isn't that awfully lonely? Don't you ever wish you could let someone take care of you for a change?"

And risk being disappointed when she stopped? "I'm a big boy," he said. "I haven't needed anyone for a long time."

She slipped the shirt over her head. "I'm sorry to hear that," she murmured and with one last searching glance, strode from the room.

Nathan threw off the sheet and stood, irrationally annoyed. He didn't need her pity. Or her love. He just needed her hand in marriage and her body in his bed.

Dismissing what felt suspiciously like regret, he headed for the shower.

Emma knelt on the floor, surrounded by the jewelry she'd made, and assessed a month's worth of work. Ten necklaces, a dozen pairs of earrings, fifteen rings and six bracelets. It wasn't enough. But it would have to do. In two days she was on her way to Baton Rouge for the art and design show. Her four weeks of exhausting work were at an end. This weekend would determine how the rest of her life would play out.

In the living room, Nathan sang along to a Sinatra tune.

The romantic music wrapped around her like a comfortable sweater and Emma found herself smiling. As much as she'd protested against moving into Nathan's condo, she had to admit that it had probably helped her prepare for the show. Left alone in her loft or staying at Addison's, she would have driven herself into the ground way before her deadline. Being forced to rest and eat, she'd met all her goals and crafted better jewelry. If she had a profitable show in Baton Rouge, she could credit a lot of that success to Nathan.

"So, this is where you've been hiding out." Addison appeared in the workroom doorway. She'd called an hour ago to say she was stopping by. "How is it going?"

"See for yourself." Emma gestured toward the pieces she'd recently finished.

Addison sat beside Emma and let her fingertips drift along a ruby-and-diamond necklace. "This is gorgeous."

"Here's the piece I created for the silent auction." Emma pulled a square flat box off her worktable and handed it to Addison. "I hope it makes up for the fact that I wasn't able to help you with the gala this year. I feel terrible about that."

For the last five years, she and Addison had co-chaired the committee in charge of a big event that raised money to fight juvenile diabetes. It was a labor of love for Addison, whose sister had been diagnosed with the disease at the age of five. How Addison managed a career, family and all her volunteer activities, Emma didn't have a clue. Her friend seemed tireless.

Emma was always happy to help, but this year her free time had been eaten up by her jewelry business and both her show and the gala fell on the same weekend.

"Don't worry about it," Addison said, popping the lid and gasping at the sparkling necklace that lay on the bed of black velvet. "This is incredible. And way more than you should be donating."

"You're sweet to say that. Here I was thinking I wasn't doing nearly enough."

The women hugged. Emma felt the burn of tears behind her eyes. She exhaled a shaky breath. Lately her emotions had been uncomfortably close to the surface. Frustration. Happiness. Desire. Anger. Emma's moods had been on a merry-go-round without end.

"I've missed having you around," Addison said. "But I can see why you decided to move in here."

"What are you talking about?" Emma stretched her lower back and grimaced as pain lanced through her muscles.

Addison eyed Emma. "You're sleeping with him, aren't you? Not that I blame you."

She wasn't ready to talk about how Nathan had swept her off to the bedroom every night for the last week or how the previous evening he'd plied her with a soothing massage that put her out for almost five hours. Damn the man.

As if her thoughts had conjured him, Nathan appeared in the doorway with a glass of wine he handed to Addison and a plate of cheese, bread and fresh fruit he placed on Emma's worktable.

"See if you can't persuade her to eat something," he said. "All her wonderful curves are disappearing."

Ever since she'd stopped making the trek to Addison's house every night, he'd been badgering her to eat and rest. After the first couple days, she'd stopped telling him that she could take care of herself. Why waste her breath when he wasn't listening to her anyway? And then three days ago, something awful had happened. She'd discovered that having him fuss over her was wonderful.

So much for Miss Independent.

"I'm not hungry," Emma said, frowning at him.

Tonight he wore a black T-shirt that clung to his chest and shoulders. The color emphasized the bad-boy gleam in his eyes and made her pulse hitch. All she wanted to do was lay her head against his broad chest and close her eyes.

"He won't stop fussing," Emma complained to Addison after he left. She popped a grape in her mouth and followed it up with a slice of Brie on fresh French bread. "It's not as if I need him to take care of me."

"But isn't it nice that he does?"

Addison's sly question hit a little too close to the mark. No one would believe Emma could take care of herself unless she demonstrated that she could. "I was doing okay before he came along."

Nathan returned with a glass of water for Emma. The ice cubes tinkled in the glass as he set it down. "Dinner will be ready in a half an hour. Can you stay?" he asked Addison.

Addison looked from one to the other. "I can't. I promised Paul I would be home for dinner tonight."

Emma watched him go, her gaze following his sexy posterior until it disappeared around the corner.

"For a woman who claims she's not interested, you are emitting some smoking-hot vibes." At least Addison waited until Nathan returned to the kitchen before her accusation burst forth. "I half expected to see scorch marks on his backside the way you were staring at him just now."

"It's awful." Emma massaged her stiff shoulders. "I can't stop myself. It's like handing a two-year-old a cookie and telling her not to eat it. He's impossible to resist."

"And given the way he looks at you, I think you'd better dust off your platinum card and buy yourself a trousseau. That man's got marriage on his mind."

Emma nodded. Pity that it was for all the wrong reasons.

Nathan covered his yawn with a fist as he parked Emma's borrowed van in the lot next to the Baton Rouge River Center. He blinked to bring moisture to his dry eyes. The clock on the dashboard told him it was a little before 9:00 p.m. Five hours earlier, he'd arrived home from a quick business trip to Chicago, anticipating a romantic reunion with the object of his desire and found her about to get behind the wheel of this dilapidated vehicle. Appalled by the idea that Emma intended to drive to Baton Rouge in something that had obviously seen more than its share of the open road, he'd overridden her objections and insisted on driving.

After the week he'd had, the last thing he'd wanted to do was more traveling. Not to mention that this was the worst possible moment for him to take time off. His brothers' interest in Lucas Smythe's company was taking on a life of its own. His location scouting near Chicago had not been as productive as he'd hoped. He really should be in the office tomorrow phoning Cody about other facility locations. What good would it do to win Emma and sign contracts with Silas if they had no production space?

Instead, he was in a van, almost three hundred miles away.

Nathan turned to the woman sleeping beside him. She'd napped almost the entire trip, confirming that he'd been absolutely right to insist on driving her to Baton Rouge. He'd never have forgiven himself if she'd fallen asleep at the wheel. And it wasn't as if his brothers would notice if he was out of the office another day.

She looked so peaceful. During the drive he'd contemplated how much he'd enjoy having her in his life on a permanent basis. Although he hadn't been blind to the perks of being married to Emma—the companionship, the incredible sex, the sense of purpose he'd felt these last ten days—he hadn't expected that she'd arouse such protectiveness in him, or that he would so completely enjoy something as simple as watching her sleep.

He liked taking care of her and sensed that as much as she resisted, she liked having him do so. Soon, she would realize they had all the elements for a solid marriage.

Everything but love.

The thought emerged out of the conversation with his father. Hearing Brandon praise Marissa for her strength and voice his regrets that he'd settled too fast into a marriage of convenience, Nathan had noticed doubt creep into his opinions on love. His father's words rang in his head, keeping him awake at night while Emma toiled down the hall, and forced him to notice a hole in his chest, a suspicion that something was missing.

Did he want Emma to love him the way his mother had loved Brandon? No, that couldn't be right. His mother's love hadn't made her happy. He wanted Emma to need him, lust for him, like him even. Nothing more. No unrealistic expectations mucking up what promised to be a satisfying blend of friendship and sex.

Nathan turned off the van and rubbed the back of his neck as he considered the woman asleep beside him. She'd lowered the seat back and turned on her side toward him. With one foot braced against the floor, she'd bent the other and her skirt rode halfway up her smooth thigh. He imagined running his hand up her leg until he reached heaven. He sighed. She was too tempting to be believed.

One hand pillowed her cheek. She'd draped the other across her middle. He reached out to grab her shoulder and shake her awake, but the soft skin beneath the denim jacket distracted him. Before he knew what he intended, Nathan slid his hand under the fabric and cupped the side of her neck, his thumb brushing her cheek. Mesmerized by the warmth and soft fragrance of her skin, he leaned down and swept his lips against hers.

Trapping a groan in his throat, he dipped his head again and lingered long enough to taste her. She stirred, her hand lifting to coast inside the open V of his cotton shirt. Placing her palm against his chest, her lips parted.

Nathan lost himself in the lazy press, slide and retreat of

his mouth against hers. He rubbed her lips with his, coaxing forth a soft murmur of delight. Her hand moved to the back of his neck, fingernails raking through his hair. Peace filled him. What was it about kissing Emma that made the world and his problems melt away?

Her perfume reminded him of springtime. He loved the season for all the possibilities it offered. The opportunity to build on past successes. A chance to grow in new directions. To take new risks.

Risks. In business. But not in his personal life.

Struck by the contrast, Nathan broke off the kiss. When it came to his heart, he shared his brothers' aversion to risk. It was the one way he didn't take after his father. Brandon had been bold in business *and* in love.

Memories surfaced. His father sitting on the worn couch in their tiny house, Marissa's feet in his lap. Marissa and Brandon washing dishes. Him kissing her neck. And laughter. Always laughter. His parents had been happy together, Nathan now realized. Devoted to each other. It wasn't being in love with his father that had made his mother unhappy. It had been their time apart that had hurt her. Funny how anger and resentment had tarnished his recollections of that.

Cupping Emma's face in his hands, he set his forehead against hers. "We're here."

"What time is it?"

"Close to nine. How long will it take you to set up?"

"A couple hours, I think."

"Are you hungry? We missed dinner. We could go grab something before getting started. You should probably keep your strength up."

"I'm too keyed up to eat. Maybe later, after we're done we could catch a late, late dinner." The hand that had been playing in his hair dropped to her lap. "Thanks for driving and letting me sleep."

"After almost a three-hour nap you probably won't feel

much like sleeping tonight," he said, kissing her brusquely on the forehead and setting her away from him. "I, on the other hand, feel like I could sleep for a week."

He caught the clear confusion on her face. The tender kiss they'd shared made him feel vulnerable in a way he'd never known with a woman. New insights into his parents' relationship made him question what he'd told Emma he wanted from her. He wasn't used to doubting his decisions. He wasn't used to feeling off balance.

He was no longer convinced that marrying without love was a good idea.

He just wasn't sure marrying for love was.

Nine

Emma half trotted to keep up with Nathan's long stride. She shot a glance at his profile, her chest tightening at the thoughtful frown pulling his brows together. He seemed miles away, and with longing tight and sharp beneath her skin, Emma felt all too present. What had just happened in the van?

Waking to the tenderness in his kiss had been her undoing. The memory of it yanked at her heart. His passion she could dismiss as lust and not let it into her soul, but gentleness—she had no protection against that.

In those seconds before he broke off the kiss, the last of her defenses crumbled to dust. Had Nathan noticed? Is that why he'd stopped kissing her? Did he realize that she'd lost the will to deny him? That he'd gotten her right where he wanted her?

She'd been working so hard this last week to keep her emotions separate from the incredible sex. It was getting harder and harder to resist the pull of longing that had nothing to do with how great he was in bed. She was hip-deep in trouble and sinking fast. Soon she'd enjoy being there.

Emma's hands clenched into fists, but there was no fighting the push and pull of excitement and anxiety that slid through her. She had to make enough money this weekend to escape the trap her father had laid for her. If Nathan was going to own her heart, she wanted to make sure he had to work for it. The only way to get on even footing with him was to take her father's meddling off the table. Being trussed up like a Christmas turkey and served to Nathan on a silver platter would put her at a distinct disadvantage.

Nathan was a silent, compelling presence beside her as she checked in with the show coordinator. With his help, she found her number on the poster board that displayed the layout of the show.

"I've got a great booth," she told Nathan, her finger on the square she would occupy for the next three days. "Look. It's on the main aisle and right in the middle of all the action."

Her enthusiasm must have been contagious because he grinned. "Let's go see it."

They struck out across the exhibition hall. Already most of the booths had been set up. An assortment of glass, pottery, metalwork, textiles, jewelry and wall art in a variety of mediums created a jumble of color and texture in the huge space. She'd been juried into this show and she knew the other artists here had been selected for their fine work as well. This was her first foray into the world of one-of-a-kind art, and her emotions overlaid one another, a hodgepodge of excitement and apprehension. So much rode on how she did here this weekend.

Emma slowed as she approached the space she'd been assigned. According to the map, her booth was on this corner. Instead of finding a blank slate, awaiting her personality and vision, the space contained a rather odd collection of sculptures depicting ugly old women in period clothing. On closer inspection, she saw they were made of small beads. While the detail impressed her, Emma couldn't quite get past the unattractive forms.

"Isn't this where you're supposed to be?" Nathan frowned as he surveyed what the area contained.

"Yes."

Her earlier excitement faded. Although she wanted the prime location, she couldn't bring herself to ask the artist to move his displays at this late hour. Disappointment seized her.

"Then he needs to move." Coiled energy radiated from Nathan.

She stepped between Nathan and the space she'd been assigned. "It's late. I don't want to be a bother."

"Don't be ridiculous. This is your booth. It's a great location. You should have it." His hard, gray gaze moved over her features and lingered on her worried frown. "Let me help you."

She closed her eyes to better resist his cajoling. "You've already done so much."

"You say that like it's a bad thing."

"It is." Her eyes flashed open. "I could get far too used to this."

"Then get used to it."

"I can't let myself. It's not who I am any longer. Not who I want to be."

Nathan wrapped her in a strong embrace, his breath warm against her temple as he sighed. "There's no reason you can't be independent and let me take care of you at the same time."

"Really? Because nothing you've done these past couple weeks has shown me that's true." She pushed against the unyielding wall of his chest. "Maybe if you stopped telling me what to do, I might let you take care of me a little."

Her tart speech had no effect on Nathan whatsoever.

He held her until her muscles loosened and she sagged against him. She liked letting him be her knight in shining armor. After a lifetime of being pampered, asserting her independence was hard work. Especially when she had a determined man tempting her to take it easy, to let her be spoiled.

But she'd be doing both of them a disservice if she meekly accepted what he offered and let him think it was enough to satisfy her.

"How about if I back off a little?" He pushed her to arm's length, his expression set into solemn lines. "Will that make you happy?" When she nodded, his grin flashed, smug and wicked. "Good. Now let me deal with this guy."

So much for him backing off.

He strode into the space, aiming straight at a young man with gel-spiked, short hair. "Excuse me. I think you've set up in the wrong spot. This space belongs to her."

The man shrugged. "She's late. I didn't think she was coming so I moved in." He turned his shoulder toward Nathan, clearly making the mistake of underestimating the tall, muscled man in faded jeans and casual white oxford shirt. "She can have my booth." He gestured to the empty space ten feet away.

"She doesn't want your space," Nathan said, his low voice firm, but polite. "She wants the booth she was assigned. This one."

"But I'm already set up here."

"But you don't belong here." Nathan pointed. "You belong there. Now, we're going out for dinner, and when we return, I expect that you will have vacated this booth."

He smiled, a slow, dangerous baring of teeth, and stepped toward the younger man. Although Nathan didn't make a single threatening movement, the other man's eyes widened, and he licked his lips nervously.

"Are we clear?"

"Yeah. Yeah, okay."

With a satisfied nod, Nathan pivoted on his heel and strode away, catching Emma's hand as he went. She turned to accompany him, knowing he would tow her along in his wake if she hesitated.

"What makes you think he'll move?" she demanded, her heart going all gooey at Nathan's demonstration of power and confidence.

He loosened his grip and slid his palm against hers, meshing their fingers. The warm, intimate clasp made her pulse dance.

The hard expression on his face melted into amusement as he glanced down at her. "He'll move."

She laughed breathlessly, warmed by the humor swirling in his eyes. "You can be very intimidating when you set your mind to it."

"Shall we stop by the show coordinator's table and point his transgression out to them?" he asked.

"Sure, maybe he'll move faster. Now that we're here I want to get everything set up."

He didn't relinquish her hand as they paused to mention their trouble to the coordinator. Nor did he let her go until he dropped a kiss on her knuckles and helped her into the van. Emma watched him through the windshield while he circled to his side and told her wayward hormones to behave. Avoiding the way he made her feel had been relatively easy while she'd been buried in her workroom, but she'd let her guard down with that fairy-tale wake-up kiss earlier and felt helpless against the pull of attraction between them.

"Are we going to sit down and eat or go to a drive-through?" he asked, starting the engine.

"Drive-through, but you knew that, didn't you?"

Nathan put the car in gear. "I suspected you'd want to get back as soon as possible."

* * *

On the second morning of the show, Emma sat opposite Nathan in the hotel restaurant and watched him tuck into a breakfast of steak and eggs. The man could certainly eat. Of course, he'd worked up an appetite last night after the show closed. She ducked behind the newspaper she'd bought, hiding a grin. The man could certainly make love, too.

Emma sipped coffee and nibbled on a piece of bacon. For the first time in weeks, her stomach wasn't churning from nervous tension. Maybe that was because, for the first time in weeks, a light had appeared at the end of the tunnel. The first day of the show had been surprisingly busy for a Friday. She'd made as much in one day as she'd made at Biella's in a month, and from what she'd gathered from the seasoned veterans at the show, she could look forward to the weekend being even busier.

"Look at this." Nathan reached out and snagged the paper from her hands and replaced it with a different section.

Emma stared in amazement at the huge photo of her necklace on the front of the entertainment section. "I can't believe it."

"I told you that reporter was going to do a piece on your jewelry," Nathan smirked.

"This is incredible publicity. Do you know what this means?"

"It means you'll be very busy today." Nathan signaled the waitress for their check. "And you owe me dinner. I'll provide dessert. I seem to recall that you like strawberries."

And what happened if she was busy? And successful beyond her wildest dreams? She'd thrown every bit of energy and focus into her jewelry, but until this instant, she hadn't truly believed it would save her. Now it looked very much as if it would.

That meant she would regain access to her money without having to marry Nathan. What were the chances that he'd stick around if he couldn't do the deal with her father? Would he disappear out of her life again?

"Do you want them dipped in chocolate or covered in whipped cream?" Nathan asked as he guided her out the door.

Emma blinked and shook her head. "What are you talking about?"

"Dessert. Strawberries. Chocolate or whipped cream?"

Laughter bubbled. "Since we're celebrating. How about both?"

Valentine's Day dawned overcast and cold. Nathan stood in his office and stared out the window at the rain falling on downtown Houston. The gray landscape was a complete contrast to his mood.

Ten days had passed since he and Emma had returned from Baton Rouge. The change in their relationship, sparked by that kiss in the van, continued to bemuse him. Never one to initiate their lovemaking, she now greeted him at the door each night, her ardent kisses providing the perfect appetizer.

Their time together, previously shadowed by mistrust and tension, had begun to approach the sort of domestic bliss his parents had enjoyed. He now understood why his father had always helped wash dishes even though the dishwasher functioned. Tangling with Emma's fingers in the soapy water had been both sexy and soothing for Nathan.

Neither one had brought up the topic of marriage. She kept mum about how she'd done at the show. A week went by. He was certain that he'd lost her. Lost the venture with Montgomery Oil.

When she'd first stated her intention to return the money to her account and thereby circumspect her father's plan to marry her off, Nathan had laughed at her efforts. Who would have guessed she had the talent to create such amazing jewelry or possessed the determination to work the long hours needed to get ready for the show?

The writeup in the paper had garnered her a great deal of attention. The traffic in her booth had been brisk. She'd charmed her customers with her salesmanship and dazzled them with her intricate jewelry. With each piece that disappeared out of the case, Nathan had seen his business deal with her father slipping through his fingers.

Then, a couple days ago, she'd admitted that she hadn't sold enough.

So Nathan knew she'd say yes when he popped the question tonight. She might prefer a marriage based on fanciful, unrealistic emotions instead of one built on respect and admiration, but she understood that what she needed was someone to take care of her.

The only thing that was still a mystery was whether his motivation for proposing remained the same as it had been six weeks ago, or if he'd decided he couldn't contemplate his future without her in it—business deal or no.

He shied away from the question, relieved that he'd never have to answer it. An hour ago, Sebastian had stopped by to say that Lucas Smythe needed a few more days to evaluate the offer he'd received from Case Consolidated Holdings. By this time tomorrow, Nathan would be engaged to Emma and his venture with Montgomery Oil secured.

"I've got a couple tickets to the Rockets that I can't use tonight. Interested?"

Nathan spied Max in the doorway. Although resentment still bubbled inside him at all the hoops his brothers were making him jump through, Nathan appreciated Max's attempt to reach out.

"Can't. Got plans."

"Me, too."

Max didn't leave Nathan's doorway. "Sebastian said he gave you the numbers for the Smythe purchase."

"I haven't had a chance to look them over yet."

"If you're still holding out for the Montgomery Oil deal, you're wasting your time. Chances are it's not going to happen."

"It will." Nathan's irritation rose, but he leashed his tone, striving for civility. "In fact, I'm set to close tonight."

"Have you really thought about what you're getting us into? We could stand to lose everything if the technology doesn't pan out." Max regarded him, his jaw jutting forward.

"Or we could stand to make a fortune."

"Is this really about the money, or are you just trying to destroy the family business?"

Long ago, after realizing that Sebastian and Max would never accept him as a brother, he'd put a cork in his frustration and decided that if he couldn't join them, he'd beat them. As alike as they were, he'd had no choice but to become an individual. Embedded habits were hard to break.

But at least *he* was trying.

"Do you really think I'd do that?" Nathan demanded, breathing hard. "Don't you see that I'm as much a part of this family and this business as you are? Of course you don't. You never let me be a part of anything you and Sebastian did. Frankly, I don't know why I'm busting my ass to bring this deal to Case Consolidated Holdings when I could do it on my own."

He stopped speaking, his hands clenching with the force of the rage that had risen up in him. The intensity of his emotions shocked him. He used to be cool under pressure. What had happened to the guy who bluffed professional gamblers with nothing but a two of hearts and a five of spades in his hand?

"So do the deal without us." Max shrugged. "You don't like it here anyway. I don't know why you don't just head out on your own."

This is exactly the sort of ultimatum he'd wanted to avoid

since returning to Houston and coming to work with his brothers. Max had tossed down the gauntlet.

"What's going on in here?" Sebastian entered the room and stood between Max and Nathan. He glanced from one brother to the other.

"Max doesn't seem to think I belong at this company," Nathan explained, unable to wrestle his bitterness to manageable levels. "And I'm starting to agree with him."

"Why is that?"

"I have a different vision for the company's future."

"And because you show up out of the blue—"

Nathan interrupted Max with a low growl. "I was brought in by Dad."

"So that gives you the right to push us to make changes. The company was profitable before you showed up. It will be profitable after you leave," Max shot back.

Around and around again with the same old arguments. The three of them could accomplish a hell of a lot more if they just stopped antagonizing each other.

Nathan pinched the bridge of his nose. "Look. We agreed that I'd have until today to get the deal done. If it doesn't happen, you'll never hear me mention Montgomery Oil again."

Valentine's Day had started out gray and overcast, but the sun had made an appearance by the time Emma let herself into Nathan's condo. She juggled three bags from expensive downtown boutiques and kicked the door closed. Shopping had never been less fun. Would she ever again spend money without thinking of all the hard work that went into earning it? She was no longer the overindulged girl she'd been six months ago. She'd learned the lesson that her father had intended.

Not that it mattered. Despite how well she'd done at the Baton Rouge show, she was almost $10,000 short of her goal. She'd screwed up her chance to prove to her father that she could support herself and lost the bet she'd made with him. Honor demanded that she marry Nathan.

Sure, she could renege and walk away a free woman. Losing her trust fund no longer bothered her. The last six weeks had demonstrated that she could take care of herself. But she'd like her word to count for something. And if she'd won and her father lost, she'd expect him to live up to his end of the bargain. She could do no less.

As to how she felt about becoming Mrs. Nathan Case…

Emma stripped off her clothes and stepped beneath the shower, her thoughts locked on Nathan. On the long drive back from Baton Rouge, she'd had lots of time to think. Since moving in with him, some shift in her perception had occurred.

As hot water cascaded over her body, she shut her eyes and imagined his hands roving over her, his long, muscular frame sliding against her bare skin, awakening her desires, his deep voice crooning encouragement as they moved together. He did things to her body she'd never experienced before.

And he made her happy. He took care of her needs both in and out of bed. Feeling cherished and fussed over had opened the door to her considering Nathan's opinions about marriage. She'd learned enough about him in the last couple weeks to decide that he'd make a great husband. He was committed to their relationship and concerned about her needs.

Still, she knew passion would never be enough for her. But what if it was combined with respect and affection? Emma wasn't sure. Marriages failed even when the couple loved each other. Could she and Nathan make it without a strong emotional bond?

Emma exited the shower and dried her hair. It was Valentine's Day. Her day of reckoning. Although Nathan hadn't mentioned the deal with her father since they'd returned from Baton Rouge, she knew he was gearing up for a romantic evening with a marriage proposal at its core.

Was it reasonable to surmise that she could continue to be happy with Nathan, knowing he would resist losing his heart to her? He sang joyful songs of love and forever, but he didn't believe a single word. Yet each chorus, every verse spoke to her, seduced her into believing that he could fall in love if he found the right woman.

And more than anything, she longed to be that right woman.

Her heart stopped. Something inside her clicked into place. The final piece of a puzzle that made the picture whole.

No wonder she was considering marrying him when she'd determined from the first that she wanted a fairy-tale ending. That she deserved to marry a man who adored her.

She loved Nathan.

What she'd feared would happen had come to pass. She'd fallen for him. Hard. And Nathan wasn't ready to let her in. To love her. He might never be. Was she really prepared to settle for that?

Her cell phone rang. She plucked it from her purse and answered it.

"Are you done with your errands?"

Despite the long hours spent stretched out in bed beside him, beneath him, on top of him the previous evening, hearing Nathan's voice awakened that familiar ache in her body.

"All done."

"Can you meet me in an hour?"

"What did you have in mind?" Despite her somber mood a moment ago, salacious thoughts began a slow striptease in her head. It did no good to wallow in misery when just talking to Nathan aroused her.

"I had been thinking about lunch, unless you had a little afternoon delight in mind."

"Why couldn't we do both? Surely there's a hotel some-where nearby your office that offers room service." A picture formed in her mind. She took a moment and savored the fantasy while Nathan's voice rumbled in her ear.

"Are you listening to me?"

"No, sorry. I was mentally undressing you. What was that you were saying?" she asked.

A muffled curse filled her ear. "Pack a bag. I've booked a suite at the Four Seasons."

"I'm on my way."

Emma ended the call and touched her lips, fingertip gliding from one end of her wide grin to the other. She should be worried that the man made her wild with anticipation after just a phone call. He was a heartbreak ready to happen, but she'd promised herself no more worrying about the future. Just live in the moment.

Easier said than done, but an hour later she strolled into the hotel lobby and spotted Nathan. He sat on one of the comfortable couches, reading the newspaper and looking every inch the corporate executive. For a moment she stopped and stared at him, her heart pounding.

Gone was her sexy seducer in jeans and bare chest. In a custom-tailored navy suit with a crisp white shirt and butter-yellow silk tie, he'd become a tycoon once more. The exact sort who'd be in business with her father. Her heart hit her toes.

Nathan looked up and caught her staring at him. His eyebrows rose slowly, giving her blood a chance to heat. The lazy smile that followed became her undoing.

"Hello, handsome," she said, sauntering over on shaky legs to sit beside him on the couch. She angled her body toward him and crossed one leg over the other, trying her best to look seductive. She'd worn an emerald-green sheath that skimmed her curves and bared her arms. "Come here often?"

His gaze toured her ankles and calves before taking in the rest of her Dior-clad body. By the time he reached her face, she buzzed with desire. He folded the paper and used it to tap her bare knee.

"Obviously not often enough if you represent their clientele. I have a suite reserved. Could I interest you in a drink?"

"While that sounds lovely, I'm afraid I'm waiting for my lover. We rendezvous every Thursday at one. He is very handsome and very sexy."

"And very late. It is already five minutes after one." Nathan flicked his cuff over his watch and his lips curved in a his-loss-my-gain smile. "Have a drink with me. A man should never keep a beautiful woman waiting."

"Well, since you put it that way."

Emma laughed as Nathan pulled her to her feet.

He sent a bellboy to fetch her things. In the suite, while Nathan tipped the man and sent him on his way, Emma pulled out the room service menu and flipped through it. Nathan came to stand behind her, his fingers grasping the zipper at her nape.

"Hungry?" He slid the zipper down her back and bent to kiss her shoulder.

Emma turned in his arms, letting the dress fall to her feet. "Dessert first."

Wrapped in a plush towel provided by the hotel, Emma dried her hair and regarded her reflection. Her eyes sparkled with secret delight and an irrepressible smile lifted the corners of her mouth. She glowed the way a woman who'd spent the afternoon being the object of a man's adoring caresses ought to. Thank goodness it wasn't illegal to feel this wonderful.

Just thinking about the exquisite way Nathan had plied her body made her shiver anew at the realization that they had all night to indulge in more such perfect loving. Of course, if they continued at their current pace, she might be dead of exhaustion by morning. But what a way to go.

"What are you thinking about?" Nathan returned from the

bedroom where he'd been ordering room service. He stepped behind her and met her gaze in the mirror.

"You," she replied, her smile turning salacious. "On the dining table in the other room, covered in whipped cream and chocolate sauce."

His brows rose. "I think it's your turn." His hands snaked around her waist to loosen the robe's belt.

"We can't," she protested, turning off the hair dryer so she could clutch the robe closed. "Dinner first. I've got to eat to keep my strength up."

"You don't need strength for what I have in mind. Just lie back and let me do all the work." His grin was pure wolf.

She laughed, but continued to defend herself from his questing hands. Breathless with rising desire and from resisting his efforts to separate her from the robe, she was only half-relieved when a knock on the door announced room service.

While Nathan went to let the waiter in, Emma quickly checked her voice mail. She was hoping for a call from a woman who'd been interested in commissioning a piece of jewelry from her. Granted, it was too late for her to use the money toward winning the wager with her father, but this sort of business would provide a whole new source of income.

She wondered how Nathan would take the news that she intended to keep designing and producing jewelry after they married. He'd told her over and over that he wanted to take care of her, but she'd proved that she could take care of herself. She was proud of the business she'd started and the success she'd had. She had no intention of giving it up because she no longer needed the money she made from it.

Two messages had come in during the afternoon. One from Addison, wishing her good luck on her evening with Nathan. The second was from Thomas McCann at Biella's. She'd called him earlier, hoping against hope that he'd had some luck selling the pieces that hadn't sold at the Baton

Rouge show. He'd been out, so she'd had to leave a message. Crossing her fingers, she listened.

"Emma, I'm glad you called. I have good news. We've sold all the new stuff you brought us. The buyers mentioned seeing your work at a recent charity event. I have a check for almost $11,000 waiting for you. And we'd really like it if you'd bring us more of your jewelry."

In stunned disbelief, Emma ended the call. She set the phone on the dresser, scarcely able to wrap her head around what she'd heard. She'd done it. She'd met her goal by the deadline.

She would get her trust fund back. She could remodel her loft. Buy new equipment. Secure studio space. Market her designs and grow her business.

She was no longer obligated to marry Nathan.

Emma's stomach muscles clenched in distress.

She loved Nathan. She might not have come to terms with marrying a man who couldn't or wouldn't love her, but she'd accepted that she was going to honor the bet with her father.

Now everything was different. She was free to choose whether or not to marry Nathan.

In some ways, things had gotten much worse. Free will left her wide open to mistakes.

Before coming here tonight, she'd accepted that he didn't love her and had grown accustomed to the idea of marrying him anyway. No, more than that, a part of her wanted to be his wife. She couldn't imagine living without him.

But if she followed her heart and married him, would she eventually grow dissatisfied and spend the rest of her life angry at herself and resenting him? All she needed was some sign, some admission, that his feelings for her were stronger than affection.

And if he didn't love her? Was she prepared to walk away?

She stared around the bedroom. Nathan had staged the

perfect romantic scene with roses, candles and chocolate-covered strawberries. She took in the unmade bed, where they'd spent the afternoon in sensual decadence, and the red roses on the dresser.

Instead of opening into full blossoms, the buds drooped on their sturdy stems. Emma knew the flowers were dying. They'd looked so beautiful, so perfect this afternoon when she and Nathan had first entered the lavish suite. But their loveliness had been an illusion. They were never going to last.

Was that a sign that she and Nathan weren't going to last, either?

Ten

Wondering what could be keeping Emma, Nathan reentered the bedroom and found her standing, lost in thought. Taking her by the hand, he drew her into the suite's main room, where dinner awaited. Candlelight sparkled off the cut-crystal glassware and highlighted the gold pattern on the china.

Nathan pulled out a chair and Emma sat down. His heart bucked as he knelt beside her chair, but other than that, he felt remarkably calm. This was the moment he'd been anticipating all day. "I have something for you." Still holding her hand, he turned her palm up. "Marry me."

Silence filled the room while Emma stared at a magnificent diamond glittering on her palm. Despite the uncertainty in her eyes, her lips twitched. "Most men propose with a ring."

"I figured you'd rather design your own."

"You'd be right."

"You haven't answered my question," he prompted.

She closed her fingers, trapping the diamond in her fist. "Funny, I didn't hear a question." She raised her chin and met his gaze. The hope and wariness at war in her dark brown eyes didn't ease the tightness in his chest. "It sounded more like a demand."

And it had been. Nathan immediately recognized his mistake. She was a fanciful girl who believed in fairy tales. He'd offered her practicality. He turned over the hand clenched around the diamond and dusted a reverent kiss across her knuckles. "Emma Montgomery, will you marry me?"

"Can you promise me I'll never regret it?"

"No."

At last she smiled. But it was a pale representation of true happiness. "You could have lied and told me yes."

"I'd rather be honest with you." He cupped her face in his hands. "I want our marriage to be based on respect and trust."

"But if there was no deal with my father you wouldn't be marrying me."

"Deal or no deal, if I didn't want to marry you, I wouldn't."

An intense light entered her eyes. Her whole body vibrated with tension. "Do you think you could ever love me?"

Here was the question he'd been dreading. The businessman in him counseled lying to her, but that would mean he would spend the rest of his life living a sham. He needed to be truthful, even if he risked losing her.

"I can't promise you a happily-ever-after, but you'll never question my commitment to you or our life together." He released her chin to coast a gentle caress against her cheek. "Marry me."

She deflated beneath his words. "I don't have to."

"What do you mean?" he demanded.

"My jewelry sold at Biella's. It's enough to replace all the money in my account. I won the bet with my father." Her voice shook. "I no longer have to settle for a marriage based only on trust and respect."

"You want love." He dragged his hand though his hair. A muscle ticked in his jaw.

"More than anything." Her warm chocolate eyes cooled as his scorn struck her.

"There is no such thing as a fairy-tale ending, Emma."

"Not for us," she whispered. "Not if you can't love me. But maybe someday for me if I don't marry you."

"You're a fool."

She pushed his hands away and stood. "No, I'm not."

Nathan got to his feet as well, but slowly, uncoiling one muscle at a time while he fought to keep his frustration in check. "You'll spend the rest of your days chasing rainbows only to have them fade before you catch them. That's what love is. An illusion."

"You're wrong. Love is what keeps us together through the worst life throws at us. It's hope and faith. It makes us strong. And you'd see that if you'd just stop expecting to be disappointed."

"You're the one who's wrong if you think I don't feel something for you."

"Not love—" She gasped as he caught her upper arms and pulled her flush against him.

A long silence followed her statement, punctuated only by their ragged breathing. Despite being angry with her, desire sank long talons into him. He could take her to bed and make love to her until she stopped thinking. He'd bring her to the edge of orgasm over and over until she admitted that he was the only man she would ever belong to like that.

But eventually they would have to leave the bed and the arguments would begin all over again. He wouldn't compromise, and neither would she. Round and round with no hope that either one would bend.

"I guess we're at an impasse then," he said. His hands fell away. She'd gotten what she wanted. She had no reason to marry him, which made his deal with her father null and void.

He had nothing more to fight for. "I hope you don't regret this decision."

Emma turned her back to him, but not before he saw her mouth twist into a grim line. "Why would I?"

"Because with me, for better or worse, you know exactly what you get. Will you be so sure of the next guy?"

When she didn't answer, Nathan retreated to the bedroom to gather his things. He dressed quickly and came to stand before her. She hadn't moved while he was packing, but now, her hand lifted toward his sleeve.

Before she touched him, he spoke. "Goodbye, Emma."

He gave the words a ring of permanence. He wanted her to understand that he was leaving her for good. No turning back.

"Goodbye, Nathan. Be happy."

Snarling at her parting words, he walked out of the hotel suite and out of her life.

The second half of February was busy for Emma. Unenthusiastic about tackling the major remodeling job it needed, she put her loft up for sale, marketing it as is, and moved her things into a tiny two-bedroom apartment. With her jewelry selling well at Biella's, she expanded into a couple stores in Dallas and Austin. Losing herself in work might not be a cure for heartbreak, but driving herself to exhaustion was a boon to her jewelry inventory.

Nathan never showed up at her door. She wasn't surprised. She'd refused to marry him. His deal with her father was done. So he was done with her.

She forced herself to eat even though her stomach protested at the mere thought of food. Every morning as she brushed her teeth, she confronted her ghost in the mirror. If she'd had the energy, she would have laughed at the contrast between the glowing, animated woman she'd been at Nathan's condo and the shadowy creature she'd become.

But nights were the worst. Questions haunted her. Had refusing Nathan been the right thing to do? Was a lifetime of heartache worth her self-respect? Did he think of her? She wanted to marry for love. By standing up for what she believed in, she'd gained her self-respect and lost her heart.

Only time would tell if she'd made the right choice.

March rolled in, bringing sunshine and warmer temperatures. A day came when Emma dressed in jeans and her favorite purple blouse and went shopping. She needed groceries and one special item.

An hour later, Emma stood in her bathroom and stared at the pregnancy test in her hand. The instructions on the box said the test was ninety-nine percent accurate, but Emma wanted to be absolutely positive—scratch that, confident about the results.

What if she was pregnant?

Horrified brown eyes stared back at her from the mirror.

Pregnant with Nathan's baby.

After the way he'd walked out on her, she knew he never wanted to hear from her again. A pregnancy would bring him back into her life. What would that mean?

She took the test, set the stick on the toilet tank, and left the bathroom in a daze. She needed to talk to someone, and with Addison out of town, she picked up the phone and dialed her sister-in-law, Jaime.

"Hi, stranger," Jaime said. "Haven't heard from you lately."

"I've been sort of busy. How are you feeling?"

"I'll be better in a week when the baby comes. Ouch. He's active today. Lately he gets restless at night."

Emma lifted her shirt and fanned her fingers over her still-flat midsection. She stared at her navel.

Was she going to be a mother?

"I had hoped to be in our new house before he was born, but it's not going to work out," Jaime continued. "I can't wait to get out of here. Living with your father means living where there's no privacy and no peace. He tells Cody what to do about everything. It drives me crazy. I don't know why I let that husband of mine talk me into moving in here while our house was being built. We'd have been better off in a hotel."

"I'm sure the maid service isn't nearly as good at the Lancaster as it is at Chateau Montgomery."

"True, but at least I could have my husband to myself." Jaime continued her one-sided conversation, then must have noticed she no longer had an audience. "Emma, are you okay?"

"I think I'm pregnant."

"Pregnant?"

Emma winced as Jaime's voice shrilled in her ear.

"Emma, pregnant? Are you sure?"

"No, I'm not sure. I'm taking the test right now. And could you please keep your voice down?"

"Is it Nathan's baby?" Jaime whispered. "Of course it is. Are you going to marry him now?"

"No."

Being pregnant didn't change anything between them. He still didn't love her. But it gave her an excuse to lie to herself and say that no longer mattered. She was pregnant with his child. An illegitimate child. It had been hard for Nathan to grow up an outsider in his father's household. Would he let his son suffer the same way?

"How long has it been since you took the test?"

Glancing at her watch, she realized that time was up. Emma raked an unsteady hand through her long hair. "About ten minutes."

"Go check."

Emma retraced her steps to the bathroom. She picked up the stick and closed her eyes. With a deep breath gathered in her lungs, she looked at the pregnancy test.

"Positive." Emma sat down on the bathroom floor. "I'm pregnant."

"I'm sure he'll be thrilled." Jaime's tone rang with conviction. "Cody said Nathan's had a thing for you for years."

Hope curled around Emma like a snake, slowly strangling her good sense. "If by *thing* you mean he wanted to get me into bed, then I agree. I know I'd be wasting my breath to ask you to keep this from your husband. But please tell Cody not to say anything to Nathan. I need to figure out what I'm going to do. And for heaven's sake, make sure he doesn't tell Daddy."

"Call me later in the week and tell me how you're doing."

"I will."

"And if you need anything, you know Cody and I will be here for you."

Tears pricked Emma's eyes. "Thanks."

"Sorry to interrupt your meeting." Missy, Sebastian's executive assistant, stuck her head through the door and smiled in apology. "But I thought you should know that Cody Montgomery is here to see Nathan."

Sebastian and Max looked at each other then locked their gazes on Nathan. "I thought you told Montgomery Oil that we passed," Sebastian said.

"I'm sure it's a social call."

"Social?" Max demanded. "Since when are you so cozy with the Montgomerys?"

"Since Cody and I went to college together."

"That's why you were so damn confident you'd get to do the deal. You had an in with the old man."

Annoyance briefly flared at Max's accusation. Then, Nathan shrugged. Why bother defending himself? Let his brothers think what they wanted. Nothing held any appeal for him these days—not besting his brothers, not making money, not even the opportunity to purchase an Onderdonk painting he'd wanted for ten years. Since he'd walked out on Emma, all roads led to regret.

Nathan lifted his feet off the coffee table and strode out of the room. Lately, everything fed his restless streak, from his brothers' uninspired decisions about the business, to sitting in his office where nothing stirred his interest, to going home to his empty condo.

He hated his life. It was lonely, dull and he'd never been more miserable. He'd failed to impress his brothers with his business savvy. In fact, he'd further aggravated his relationship with them by being surly and distant for the last two weeks. And he'd turned his back on the most amazing woman he'd ever met. He deserved to be miserable.

He found Cody pacing the lobby. "What are you doing in Houston?"

"I met with a couple of our board members this morning, but we got done early and I wondered if you had time for lunch before I head back."

Nathan glanced at his watch. "The restaurant downstairs doesn't open for another twenty minutes. Are you sure you have time to hang out in Houston? Isn't your wife due any day now?"

"We've got a couple days to go." Cody grimaced. "Although she'd probably be happy if it happened sooner." He glanced around and noticed the paintings on the wall. "Hey, those look like the ones Dad has in his office."

"Onderdonk." Nathan nodded, wondering what was up with the Montgomery family and his art collection.

"I thought so. I think Emma got him to buy them. And speaking of my sister, what's going on with you two?"

Cody's blunt transition from paintings to Emma warned Nathan that this wasn't a casual visit. "Let's go talk in my office." He gestured down the hall. "Nothing is going on between us."

The look Cody shot him reminded Nathan of Emma. Pain

lanced through him. He didn't want to hurt. When his mother died, he'd sworn never to let himself yield to loving anyone again. Yet Emma had wriggled her way beneath his guard and he'd begun to open his heart to her.

"Any reason you can't pick up the phone and see if she's all right?" Cody's aggressive tone caught Nathan by surprise.

Had something bad happened to Emma? No, if it had, Cody would have led with that.

"The last time we spoke, she made it pretty clear she doesn't want to hear from me."

"You might be wrong about that."

Nathan's spirits perked up. "Did she say that?"

"I haven't spoken with her."

"Then how do you know she wants to hear from me?"

"She and Jaime talk. Jaime talks to me." Cody shot him a dark look. "You need to talk to Emma."

Nathan didn't know what to make of his friend's sharp tone. "What you're saying makes no sense."

They passed Sebastian's office, and Nathan caught his brothers watching them with keen interest.

He gestured Cody into his office. "What's going on?"

Cody glanced pointedly at the open door until Nathan shut it. "Dad's not giving Emma back her trust fund."

Nathan's gut tightened as he pictured her living in her half-renovated condo. She deserved better than that.

"Why?"

"Because she didn't marry you."

Remorse twisted in Nathan's gut like a meal of bad shell-fish. "I don't understand. She told me she had the hundred thousand she needed."

"But apparently she needed to have it back in her account by the fourteenth and it wasn't there until the next day."

"Ridiculous." Nathan shook his head. "She had the money. So what if it wasn't in some account?"

"That's the old man." Cody shrugged. "And speaking of

the old man, he said that the deal's still good if you marry Emma."

All at once Nathan realized that he wasn't interested in the venture with Montgomery Oil because he no longer wanted to take the business away from his brothers. He wanted to be in business with his brothers. He wanted to be accepted as part of the family.

"She already said no."

"Perhaps you went about it the wrong way," Cody countered.

Nathan crossed his arm over his chest. "Perhaps I did."

There was no *perhaps* about it. Emma needed the sort of fairy-tale romance he couldn't give her. She hadn't been happy with his passion and promises of fidelity. She wanted him to love her. She thought that would make her happy. Ridiculous. Love only led to disappointment and heartache. Look how his mother had suffered as the mistress of a man who would never truly be hers. Look at how he'd been ostracized by his brothers. Look what trying to be accepted by them had done to his life. Love wouldn't make anyone happy.

"Try asking her again. Things are a little different for her these days."

"Because she's broke?"

Cody stared at Nathan like he was the biggest idiot on the planet. "Because she's pregnant."

"Pregnant?" Nathan echoed. The floor shifted beneath his feet. "Are you sure?"

"As sure as a pregnancy test can be." Cody put his hand on Nathan's arm. "You look like you need to sit down."

Nathan dropped into a chair. "Emma's pregnant? Why didn't she tell me?"

"I figured she had."

Nathan pinned his best friend with a hot glare. "And you thought I wasn't going to do the right thing by her?"

Cody shrugged, but before he could defend himself against

Nathan's accusation, his cell phone rang. While Cody took the call, Nathan leapt from the chair and began to pace.

How long had Emma known she was pregnant? Why hadn't she called or come by to let him know he was about to be a father?

A father. Nathan was lightheaded with relief.

He stared at the art on his walls. He and Emma were permanently linked now. She would marry him. He wasn't going to give up until she agreed. No child of his was going to grow up illegitimate.

"Looks like I don't have time for lunch after all," Cody said. "Jaime's water just broke. You've got to talk to my sister."

"Tell me something I don't know," Nathan muttered.

After Cody left, Nathan grabbed his car keys and headed for the elevator. He got no farther than Sebastian's office.

"What did he want?" Max demanded, stepping into the hall and blocking Nathan's path.

"He came to have lunch."

"That's it?" Sebastian stepped from his office and exchanged a glance with Max.

Their nonverbal communication grated on Nathan. He wrestled with the resentment that had become such a part of him and the revelation that he wanted to work *with* Max and Sebastian instead of against them. But how was he going to make that happen when they shut him out? They'd always had each other. They didn't need him. Disappointment made him surly.

"And to deliver a message that Silas is still interested in going forward."

"We've already decided that we're out," Max said.

"I've got some friends who would jump at the chance to get in on this with me."

Sebastian looked disappointed. "Are you considering it?"

"Any reason why I shouldn't?" He looked from one to the other.

"Is that what you want?" Max demanded, frowning.

"I thought you came back to Houston because you wanted to work with us," Sebastian added.

"And you sure haven't made that easy for me, have you?" Nathan shot back and abruptly ran out of steam. "Truth is, I'm no longer interested in working with Montgomery Oil."

"Why not?" Sebastian asked.

"I came back to Houston because I wanted to be a part of this company, a part of this family." He gave the last word a bitter jab. "Ever since we were kids you two have been in a club I could never join. After Dad called and asked me to come back and join the company, for the sake of family, I let you two shoot down every idea I had. I figured that eventually you'd get over whatever problem you had with me and realize that I know what I'm doing. The venture with Montgomery was my chance."

Sebastian gestured with his head toward Max. "And we stopped it from happening."

Max shrugged before saying, "Maybe we've misjudged you a bit."

"We've let pride get in the way of family," Sebastian added.

For the first time since returning to Houston, Nathan had a glimmer of hope that what he'd come back to find might be within reach. A powerful emotion swept him, locked up his chest and made him want to grin like an idiot. "I'm willing to work together if you are."

"Smythe is waffling," Sebastian said. "If this venture with Montgomery Oil is still on the table, I think we should go for it."

Nathan shook his head. He no longer had anything to prove to his brothers and everything to prove to Emma. "Let's hang in there with Smythe. The company is solid. It's exactly what we need to diversify our holdings. Lucas will come around."

"You sure this is what you want?" Sebastian asked.

"I wouldn't have it any other way."

Eleven

Armed with one of Nathan's dress shirts that she'd *accidentally* packed when she'd left his condo, Emma stepped off the elevator into the lobby of Case Consolidated Holdings. Since moving out on her own, she'd taken to wearing it to bed at night, comforted by the familiar cologne that clung to the cotton. Newly laundered, it no longer contained his scent.

She missed him.

Ached for him.

Had it only been two weeks since Valentine's Day? It felt like a year.

Emma's polite smile for the receptionist faded as the woman told her Nathan wasn't in. Relief and disappointment tumbled through her. She'd been preparing for this meeting for a couple days, running a hundred different speeches through her mind, even practicing a few in front of the mirror.

In the end, it all came down to, "Nathan, I'm pregnant."

Funny. It didn't get easier with repetition.

"Do you want to leave him a message?" the receptionist asked with a bright smile.

"Did he say when he was going to be back?" Now that she'd summoned the courage to tell him, she wanted to get it over with. "Maybe I could wait."

"He didn't say."

"I'll try back later." Unless she talked herself out of it.

Earlier, when she'd organized her day, she'd planned to stop at Biella's first because they'd called to say a check awaited her, but once she'd parked, she'd been overcome with the need to see Nathan and had selected this daunting errand to run first. Now she'd have to get up the nerve to make this journey all over again.

Anxiety snacked on her poise as she returned to the elevator. Before she could press the down button, the door opened and Emma found herself staring into Nathan's eyes.

"What are you doing here?" he demanded.

All her carefully prepared greetings evaporated as her stomach flipped like a frisky dolphin. She shoved the shirt she held toward him.

"I brought you back your shirt. It got mixed up in some of my things, and I packed it by accident."

"And you made a special trip to deliver it." His voice took on the sexy rumble that always had her out of her clothes in record time. "I'm glad."

Nathan took the shirt and tossed it onto one of the nearby lobby chairs. Then, he slid his fingers around her arm and pulled her into the elevator. His free hand coasted over her hip and in one smooth move, he pinned her between the wall and his lean muscles.

Giddy with delight at being crushed against his rock-solid frame, she put her hand on Nathan's chest, feeling the steady, soothing thrum of his heart.

"It was no bother. I was in the neighborhood."

"And here I was looking everywhere for you," he said.

Beneath Nathan's intense regard, Emma's cheeks heated. Then her blood. "You were? Why?"

"I've missed you."

Emma's nerves began to purr. She half closed her eyes and peered at him from beneath her lashes. Although she longed to hear a different set of three words from Nathan, these ran a close second. Was it possible that he felt something more for her than simple lust? Could his emotions be more complex than she thought?

"Not enough to call." She reached deep for a breezy smile and found one. No reason he had to know how heavy her heart had become.

He stroked a strand of her hair off her cheek. "You made it clear that we were done."

She'd made it clear? "You walked out on me, remember?"

"I was a fool to do that."

"But you did. What's changed?"

"We're meant to be together. Don't you feel it?"

Did that mean he loved her? Was it possible? Breathless with hope, she lifted onto her toes. As his lips covered hers in a slow, coaxing kiss, Emma dug her fingers into his back and stopped fighting his web of sensual entanglement. Beneath his intoxicating kisses, it was easy to let the last two weeks, and all her heartache, become a vague memory.

For so long, she'd fought to keep from losing herself in him, fearing he would never feel the same way about her. But he was so hard to resist, and she'd slipped further beneath his spell. It had taken all her willpower not to confess, over and over again, that she loved him. She could no longer fight what was in her heart.

"I love you," she said when his lips eased off hers. Once the truth came out, admitting the rest seemed inevitable. "I have for a long time."

"But you won't marry me."

Was marriage even on the table?

"I thought the deal with my father fell through."

"It did."

Her heart swelled with joy, but she remained cautious. "Then there's no reason for you to want to marry me."

"There are lots of reasons," he said, but as the elevator gently decelerated and the doors opened, he left them unvoiced.

Taking her by the hand, Nathan towed her past the crowd waiting to get on the elevator and into the office building's big, bright lobby. With her emotions a melting pot of worry and glee, she was only half aware of the voices, laughter and clink of dishes that echoed through the two-story atrium.

"Let's go to lunch," he said.

One of downtown Houston's best restaurants occupied the open space and drew large crowds to sample the widely reviewed cuisine. Emma balked. She wasn't eager to confide in Nathan about her pregnancy in a crowded restaurant.

"I have an errand to run. How about we meet in an hour?"

Nathan shook his head. "Now that I have you, I'm not letting you go. We'll run your errand together, and then I'll take you to lunch."

"Somewhere quiet?"

"Anywhere you want."

They headed outside. After days of rain, the sun had decided to make a brief appearance. Emma savored the warmth against her skin and inhaled the scent of dampness that clung to the pavement and plants. Nathan laced their fingers as they strolled along the sidewalk, his presence a solid, dependable strength by her side. She curled up in the crook of his arm and leaned her head against his shoulder.

For the first time in weeks she felt happy.

"Where are we heading?" he asked.

"Biella's. I'm bringing more of my jewelry for them to sell."

At the word *jewelry,* Nathan lifted their clasped hands and grazed his lips against her bare ring finger. "Did you ever make your engagement ring?"

She thought of the black, velvet-lined box in her purse. "Why bother when there is no engagement?"

Despite her tart tone, he grinned at her. "Can I see it?"

Was she really that transparent? Heaving a sigh, she fished out the ring box and dropped it into his outstretched hand. He popped it into his pocket without opening it. Emma's heart thundered and vertigo struck her again. She must have wavered because Nathan stopped and turned her to face him.

"Are you all right?" He cupped her cheek, thumb stroking her skin in a soothing rhythm. The concern shadowing his eyes made her long to rest her head against the powerful expanse of his chest.

Instead, she grabbed his hand and pulled it away from her cheek. "I'm fine. Just a little dizzy from not eating breakfast this morning."

"We should have stopped for lunch first."

"Biella's is right there." She pointed to the store. "This will only take a second."

As they waited for a sales clerk to get the manager, Nathan surveyed her jewelry. "There's not much here."

Thinking that he didn't recognize her older designs, Emma peered into the case. Delight seized her as she counted. Another five pieces had sold.

Thomas McMann appeared across the case from them, smiling. "Ms. Montgomery, how nice that you came by. As you can see, your designs are in high demand." He handed her an envelope containing her check. "I hope you brought us some more of your work."

"I have these." Emma pulled from her bag the newest pieces she'd created.

"And there's this." Nathan placed the ring box on the counter.

Before Emma could stop him, Thomas McMann snatched the box and opened it. He smiled with delight. "This is lovely. Do you have more engagement designs? I do a lot of wedding business. White gold or platinum?"

"Platinum. But it's not for sale." She shot Nathan a sour look.

He responded with a shrug. "I don't see why not. You're not going to wear it. You might as well sell it and make some money."

Emma met the challenge in Nathan's gaze and grappled for something to say.

"Unless, of course, you've changed your mind about marrying me."

"Why would I do that?" She sounded breathless and as uncertain as she felt.

She'd come to his office today, knowing he wouldn't want his child growing up without a father, and willing to marry him for that reason. But in the elevator, she'd started to think that maybe he'd fallen in love with her a little. In fact, in the space of a few heartbeats, she'd pinned all her hopes and dreams on it. She searched his expression for some sign that she'd been right.

"I thought maybe something had changed."

All at once it hit her. Sparkling lights appeared before her eyes. She flushed hot from head to toe. "You know."

"Know what?"

She didn't buy his innocent act for a second. He knew she was pregnant. That's why he wanted to marry her. Not because he was starting to love her.

Awash in dismay, Emma gripped the counter, mortified to realize that Thomas McCann watched their exchange with obvious curiosity. She blinked, mustered a polite smile and scooped up her engagement ring.

"I'll bring by some wedding sets next week. I think you'll love the designs. Have a nice day."

With that, she shot Nathan a hard look, pivoted on her heel and marched out of the store. Annoyance fueled her pace, and she reached the sidewalk before he caught up with her.

What a fool she was.

"Slow down." Nathan touched her arm, but she shook him off. "Where are you going?"

Where was she heading? For a moment Emma couldn't recall where she'd parked her car. Frustration made her grind her teeth. How could she shake Nathan and go lick her wounds in private if she couldn't find her car? A lump blocked her throat. She swallowed, but it wouldn't go away.

"Emma, please talk to me."

She shook her head.

"Let's go have lunch."

She shook her head again.

"You have to eat. It's important to keep up your strength."

She stopped dead in her tracks. "You know I'm pregnant." Emma pointed at him in warning as he opened his mouth to dance around her statement again. "Don't you dare deny it. Who told you?"

Nathan gave a resigned sigh. "Cody came by this morning."

Disappointment stabbed through her. "And the deal with my father?"

Nathan's expression became a neutral mask. "It doesn't matter." He caught her arm when she spun away, stopping her flight. "You are pregnant with my child. And you will marry me."

Since Valentine's Day, she'd been beating herself up for letting him walk out of her life, wondering if by proposing with a diamond instead of a ring, he did realize how important her jewelry-designing was to her. That maybe he understood her at last.

Sure, he'd downplayed the emotional side of their arrangement, but considering how much he mistrusted love, she'd hoped that with time he'd come around. She'd gone to his office to tell him about the baby, eager to see if he'd missed her half as much as she'd missed him only to find out he had and that he still wanted to marry her.

Now, after learning that he'd only wanted to marry her because of the baby, she was heartbroken all over again.

"Nothing has changed, Nathan," she said. "I want a real marriage."

"Everything has changed. I'm not going to let my child grow up illegitimate." Nathan pulled her close. "And I'm not going to let another man raise my son or daughter."

The power of his conviction made Emma's knees wobble. Why couldn't he love her half as much as she loved him? It would make everything so simple. Even a hint of love would be enough for her to fling herself into marriage with him.

"I can't marry you knowing you don't love me."

"You can't raise this child on your own, Emma."

His lack of faith in her cut as deep as his inability to love her. She twisted free. "I'll be better off without you or my father telling me how I can't take care of myself. I'll continue to grow my jewelry business. Maybe I'll even open a shop."

"You don't need to work that hard." He set his hands on his hips and glowered down at her. "Marry me. I'll take care of you and the baby."

Emma stared at him for a long moment, her entire body aching to be held in his arms. It would be so easy to forget all her worries about money and raising a child on her own and accept his marriage proposal.

But she wasn't a practical person. And a marriage for practical reasons would break her heart.

She shook her head. "I'll take care of me. And the baby."

Twelve

We'll be just fine.

Emma's words reverberated through Nathan's head as he watched her disappear into the lunch-hour crowd. He didn't doubt for one second that she would be just fine as a single mother. She'd thrive the same way his mother had. They were both strong, capable women.

But what about him?

He wasn't going to be fine without her. Not one bit. For the first time in twenty years he needed someone more than he needed to breathe. Emma had become the center of his universe. For the last two weeks, he'd dwelled in a black hole of misery, deprived of her ready smiles, her sizzling looks and even her frowns. Instead of cradling her naked, soft, sweetly scented body in his arms, he spent his nights wide awake and wondering how everything had gone so terribly wrong.

Nathan took off after Emma, but it was too late. She'd vanished. Retrieving his car, he headed to her loft. But when he arrived, she wasn't there. Nor was she answering her cell phone.

He slammed his hand against the steering wheel. Dammit. Why did the woman have to be so stubborn? He could give her a wonderful life. They would be happy if only she'd stop holding out for something he couldn't give her.

After a fruitless visit to Addison, he called Cody and left a message. Out of options, Nathan headed home rather than returning to work. Knowing she was pregnant. Knowing he'd screwed up with her again. There was no way he could concentrate until he'd made things right with her.

He paced his empty condo for hours, watching the sun set, then rise. At seven, he seized his cell phone to try Cody a second time when it came alive in his hand. He answered the call without checking the number.

"Emma?"

"Not even close," his best friend said, sounding giddy and half out of his mind. "I got your message. Sorry I didn't get back to you sooner, but I've been a little busy watching my son being born."

Cody's words hit Nathan like a baseball bat. A son.

Was Emma carrying a boy, too? His lungs constricted as he considered all the things he'd miss if he couldn't convince her to marry him. He wouldn't be around when she felt the baby's first kicks. He wouldn't be there to fetch her all sorts of edibles in the wee hours of the morning as cravings hit her. And what if she didn't let him participate at the birth?

"Congratulations," he garbled into the phone, reeling at the unexpected punch of reality.

Misery tied his midsection in knots. *I love you*. Her words drilled into his head. A wake-up call he couldn't ignore.

She loved him. And he'd done nothing to deserve it.

She loved him. And all he'd offered her was a marriage based on logic and reason.

She loved him. And he'd not once admitted that he felt the same way. And he did. He loved her. Very much.

What a fool he'd been not to realize it before this. She'd enthralled his body and captured his heart, and he'd been too caught up in business schemes and ancient family history to see what was really important.

"Have you heard from Emma?" Nathan asked.

"She drove up last night."

Then Nathan was heading for Dallas as well. "What hospital are you in?"

He jotted down the address and threw some things in an overnight bag.

Four hours later, he left the car in the hospital parking lot and took a deep breath before heading up to the maternity ward. Finding Jaime's room, Nathan hesitated on the threshold and surveyed the tableau before him.

Cody sat on the edge of the bed, his back to the door, his attention split between the tired but radiant woman propped up by pillows and the bundle of blue cloth in a rolling bassinet. The pastel walls vibrated with the couple's happiness and jealousy rocked Nathan hard.

Emma was not in the room, and he was about to see if he could go find her, when Jaime spotted him and nudged her husband. Grinning like a lunatic, Cody left his wife's side to greet Nathan with a crushing handshake.

"How are you coping with fatherhood?" Nathan flexed his hand and scanned his friend's appearance, noting the dark circles beneath his eyes, the spot of throw-up on his shoulder.

"I've got the diaper-changing thing mastered."

"He's sleep-deprived," Jaime said, tossing her husband a fond smile.

Cody might be exhausted, but he looked happier than

Nathan had ever seen him. Which said a lot. Cody embraced life with more enthusiasm than pragmatism.

"Nathan, I'd like you to meet Evan Michael Montgomery." Cody scooped his son out of the bassinet, handling him with the same confidence he'd once handled a football. "Here, why don't you hold him?" With a sly grin, Cody deposited the fragile bundle into Nathan's hands. "Get in a little practice."

Nathan's stomach dropped to his toes at Cody's reminder of his own impending fatherhood. He stared at the newborn, marveling over his tiny fingers and toes. Would his son or daughter be this perfect? With Emma for a mother, why not?

Cody wrapped his arm around his wife. The look Jaime bestowed on her husband was equal parts pride, contentment and desire. Love. Nathan recognized the expression. But more than love. Completeness. As if together, the two were stronger than either could be on their own.

Would Emma ever look at him that way? Or had he blown his shot at deserving her love a dozen times or more already? Caught up in protecting himself from hurt, he hadn't wanted to admit that he needed her. He'd never let himself trust her the way Cody trusted Jaime.

From the beginning, he'd been the one to reject love and rely on more practical reasons to get married. But what Cody shared with Jaime wasn't just passionate love or friendship. It was deeper, more elemental. Permanent and unshakable.

"You're a natural," Jaime said. "You'll make a great father."

Yes, he would. And he'd make a great husband as well.

"So, what do you think of my son?" Cody asked, smiling down at the sleeping infant.

Nathan had a lump in his throat as he observed his happy friend. "I think you're the luckiest man alive."

* * *

Emma stopped the car in front of her father's house and braced herself for battle. The four-hour drive from Houston to the hospital in Dallas had given her plenty of time to sort through her jumbled emotions. She knew what to do about Nathan.

But first, she wanted to settle things with her father. She'd left the hospital after the briefest of congratulations because she wanted this confrontation behind her.

As she crossed the driveway to the front door, another car drove up. Nathan. What was he doing here? She waited for him at the foot of the steps, her heart bucking wildly as he advanced toward her.

"I don't want to fight with you," he said, drawing close enough to touch her.

She took a half step back, afraid if he took her in his arms, she would dissolve. "I don't want to fight with you, either." Side by side they climbed to the front door. "What are you doing here?"

Nathan opened the door so she could enter. "I know your father didn't give you back your trust fund."

"Cody." She shook her head as they crossed the grand hall, their footsteps echoing in the cavernous space. "Just once I wish my family would let me take care of things my way."

"Like telling me about the baby as soon as you knew you were pregnant?"

Grinding her teeth had become an all-too-frequent habit since Nathan had come back into her life. "Okay, I should have come to you sooner."

"You're damn right."

She cocked her head and regarded his stern expression and the uncompromising glint in his gray eyes. "But I had things I needed to think over."

"Such as reconsidering your refusal to marry me?"

"Can we have this discussion after I've gotten my father to agree to give me back my trust fund?"

"Let me help you with that."

"I can take care of it myself." They neared the hallway outside her father's study. She whirled on Nathan and put her hand on his chest. "You stay here. This is between my father and me. I need to do it alone." She emphasized the last word and hoped Nathan would stay put.

He captured her fingers and brought them to his lips for a quick kiss. Releasing her, he leaned his back against the wall and crossed his arms. "I'll be right here if you need me."

Heart tripping unsteadily, Emma gave a satisfied nod and walked on. The speech she'd prepared for her father vanished from her mind as she neared his study. The door stood open so she stepped in.

"Hello, Daddy."

Her father looked up from the papers on his desk. "Hello, Emma." He came to her, took her hands, and kissed her cheek. "How are you?"

"I'm fine." The words slipped out automatically. "I was at the hospital visiting your first grandchild. He's beautiful."

"I'm heading over in a few minutes," her father said, surveying her with a slight frown. "Are you sure you're all right?"

"I'm fine."

"Cody told me about the baby."

She was going to kill her brother.

"I hope you're here to tell me you're going to marry Nathan."

"I came by today to talk to you about our wager. I won. I want my trust fund back."

Silas frowned. "I don't want my grandchild growing up illegitimate."

"That's for Nathan and me to decide, not you." She met

her father's gaze, letting him see her determination. "I had the money by the deadline."

"But it wasn't in your account. So you forfeit. Now, what have you and Nathan decided about getting married?"

"That it's none of your business."

"But it *is* my business. I'm your father and I say you need someone to take care of you and the baby."

Emma kept her voice level. "I don't. I am perfectly capable of taking care of myself but you're too stubborn to see that."

"You think so? And how do you think you're going to do that without money?"

"I have money."

"Bah. The hundred thousand I gave you? How long do you think that's going to last?"

Emma shook her head. Stubborn old man. "Quite a long time, I imagine, since I'm not planning to live off it."

"No? Then how do you plan to support yourself?"

Emma braced herself against a wave of frustration and pulled the newspaper article about the Baton Rouge show out of her purse. She slapped it on the desk in front of him.

"This is about my jewelry. The article calls me 'brilliant' and describes my work as some of the finest around. I've worked hard for this recognition, and you've never given me any credit." She ran out of breath. With her heart pounding fiercely, she inhaled and spoke with deliberate force. "I'm good."

"You can't seriously expect to live on what you make from it."

Resentment injected steel into her voice. "I can. And I'm going to." She clenched her hands into fists so he wouldn't see how hard she was shaking. "You can keep my money. I don't need it. I'm going to make a go of my jewelry business. I'm going to take care of myself and my baby."

"Our baby." Nathan spoke the words softly from the

doorway behind her, but there was no denying the determination in his tone. "The baby is as much mine as it is yours, and you are going to marry me and let me take care of both of you."

Emma turned from her father and confronted Nathan. Everything inside her cried out to stop fighting him and let him take care of her. He held her heart in his hands. And now, with his child inside her body, she'd gone way past the point of trying to forget him and move on.

"We'll talk about that later."

"Putting me off isn't going to change my mind. I'm not letting you go. We belong together." He caught her by the arms. "Marry me," he whispered urgently. "Not because of the baby or a business deal, but because I can't live without you."

Joy seared her, sharp and unexpected, stealing her breath. She blinked away tears. Those words might be as close to a declaration of love as she would ever get from Nathan.

And it was enough. Nathan couldn't live without her. And she couldn't live without him. She'd been a stubborn fool to believe otherwise.

She cradled Nathan's cheek in her palm. "That's definitely something I want to discuss with you later. But first I need to settle things with my father."

Turmoil swirled in his gray eyes at her request. He wasn't the sort of man who backed down when he set his mind to something. But she was equally determined.

"But let me help you with this," he murmured.

It was a precarious tightrope that stretched between accepting help and standing on her own two feet. Could she trust herself and Nathan enough to achieve the right balance?

With her heart pounding dangerously fast, she wavered. She'd been fighting to stand on her own for so long that it was hard to stop. But for all her assertion that she could take care of herself, she liked having him to rely on.

Emma put her hand against Nathan's cheek as her sleepless night took its toll. Let him take care of you, her mind whispered. And at last she was ready.

"You can help," she said. "But just this once."

Teeth flashing in a mischievous grin, Nathan turned to her father. "She had the money on the fourteenth. I can attest to that. She refused to marry me because of it. And if you don't give her what she deserves for all her hard work, she will continue to refuse me out of a sheer stubborn need to prove that she doesn't need anyone to take care of her. Which, by the way, she's been doing really well for a long time, only none of us have given her credit for it."

Strengthened by Nathan's support, she confronted her father. "I want my money signed over to me as soon as possible. I have a nursery to decorate."

"And a wedding to plan," Nathan prompted, demonstrating that he wasn't kidding about persisting until she agreed to marry him.

"And if I don't?" Her father hadn't made his billions by being a poor negotiator.

"Then it will always be between us. I need you to look at me and see that I am a grown woman, capable of supporting herself. I deserve your respect because I earned it through hard work and determination."

Her father scowled, but Emma stood her ground until grudging approval transformed her father's expression.

"I only want the best for you," he said at last, his tone gruff, but gentle.

"I know you do." Emma gave him a weak smile. "And what's best for me is to know that you believe in me and in my ability to take care of myself."

"Very well. I'll give you your trust fund back. You did earn it, after all."

Emma mastered her shock before it showed on her face. Her knees weakened with relief. She pulled her spine straight.

"And no more interfering," she continued, capitalizing on her victory. "Meddling in my love life is wrong in so many ways." She pinned her father with a fierce scowl and waited until he nodded. Then, she turned to Nathan. "Daddy is going to visit his new grandson. I don't think he'll mind if we use his study while he's gone. You and I have a couple things to sort out."

Her father looked nonplussed at being ejected from his domain, but went without protest. As he passed Nathan, he paused and stuck out his hand. "Welcome to the family. I always liked you."

"Daddy!"

Once her father had exited the room and closed the door, Emma leaned against his desk and regarded Nathan.

"I'm sorry about the way I handled things earlier," he said. "I never should have let you walk away from me like that."

"I overreacted, too."

"You had cause. I've been acting like a stubborn fool."

"At last we agree on something." She took the sting out of her words with a smile and pushed off the desk. "Thank you for helping me out with my father."

He stood in place, his features like granite, but his eyes alive and wary as she advanced toward him one slow step at a time. "I'll always be there for you."

"I know that," she said, putting her hand on his chest and backing him toward the study door.

It no longer scared her that he might never love her the way she loved him. Nathan was the perfect man for her. He would honor their marriage vows and be a great father to their children. And when it came right down to it, she had enough love in her heart for both of them.

When his back met the door, Nathan stared into her eyes but made no attempt to touch her. "You should also know that the only merger that's going to happen between our families is you and me."

His announcement startled her. "After everything we've been through, you're not doing the deal with my father?"

"I don't want it to come between us," he said. "Plus, my brothers aren't ready for the sort of risk it involves and I've decided to stop fighting them on it."

"I don't understand." Her hand dropped away. "I thought you wanted to take over the company."

"I thought that's what I wanted, too. When my dad asked me to come back and help out Max and Sebastian, all I wanted to do was get back at them for the way they've always excluded me. But lately, I've realized that what I really want is to be accepted as part of the family."

Seeing the way his mouth curved downward, she leaned her body into his and framed his face with her hands. "How about becoming part of my family?"

At first, Nathan's expression reflected disbelief and hope. Then, his teeth flashed in a broad grin and his hands settled on her hips. "I think I've wanted that since the day you strutted past me in high heels and those ridiculous short shorts."

"I was sixteen." She regarded him in disbelief. "You turned me down flat, and I didn't see you again for ten years."

"I was way too old for you. I had to get out and stay gone. You scared the hell out of me." Lightning danced in his eyes. "You still do."

She was only half-ready for the arms that locked around her and pulled her up onto her toes. Her breath caught as his mouth claimed hers. Her body came immediately to life. She threaded her fingers through his hair and met the thrust of his tongue with matching passion while urgent encouragement issued from her throat.

She wanted him more than ever and wasn't afraid to let him know.

Nathan broke off the kiss and swept his lips toward her ear. "Sweet, sweet woman. I adore you."

His confession sparked a tremor inside her. She pushed

him to arm's length. "Say that again," she demanded, thinking she'd misheard him.

"I love you," he said, his smile softer than she'd ever seen it. "I'm sorry I didn't realize it sooner than I did."

She'd grown accustomed to his imposing will and powerful personality. But it was the tender expression on his face at that moment that made hope surge in her.

He loved her.

"But you said you didn't believe in love." The devilish quirk that weakened her knees returned.

"I believe in it. I just didn't want it in my life. With the exception of your brother and Jaime, everyone I've ever known has cheated on their spouse or been cheated on. After I moved in with my father's family, I watched my stepmother's love for him destroy her a little more each year. I was afraid to let that happen to me."

Emma recalled her own worries about how loving Nathan and keeping it to herself would eat at her. "What changed your mind?"

"You did. I couldn't understand how you could put such faith in love when you'd seen how miserable it made your parents. Then, yesterday, after finding out that you were pregnant, after you walked away, and today, seeing Cody and Jaime with Evan, I realized that having you in my life, in my bed, wasn't going to be enough unless I was in your heart and you were in mine. I love you."

"You do love me." Her voice trembled with awe.

"More than I ever thought it was possible."

He swept his lips across her eyes and down her nose. His hands slid over her curves, gentle, measuring caresses that awakened her to the quiet house and the lock on the study door. Desire rushed through her, sweeter than ever now that she knew Nathan loved her.

She eased her hands down the front of his shirt, loosening buttons as she went. Two weeks without him had been too long. She couldn't wait to get him naked and reacquaint herself with all those lovely rippling muscles.

"You know," she said, "I think my father is right after all. I do need someone to take care of me."

Nathan waited until she'd tugged the shirt down his arms and tossed it aside before he asked, "Got anyone in mind?"

"There was this really hot guy I met when I was a teenager." Enjoying the way her touch disturbed the cadence of his breath, she trailed her fingers down his chest and abdomen until she ran out of naked skin. "I wonder what ever happened to him."

When Emma started to unfasten his belt, Nathan caught her fingers and lifted them to his lips. "I think he finally figured out what's been missing in his life."

Soaking up the love and sincerity she saw in his eyes, Emma knew she'd found her happily-ever-after at last.

"And what's that?" she whispered.

Nathan's lips dipped toward hers. "You."

* * * * *

HOW TO SEDUCE A BILLIONAIRE

BY
KATE CARLISLE

New York Times bestselling author **Kate Carlisle** was born and raised by the beach in Southern California. After more than twenty years in television production, Kate turned to writing the types of mysteries and romance novels she always loved to read. She still lives by the beach in Southern California with her husband, and when they're not taking long walks in the sand or cooking or reading or painting or taking bookbinding classes or trying to learn a new language, they're traveling the world, visiting family and friends in the strangest places. Kate loves to hear from readers. Visit her website at www.katecarlisle.com.

Champagne, chocolate and many thanks go to my
brilliant editor, Stacy Boyd, for helping me give
Brandon and Kelly's romance a truly happy ending.

One

"Memo to self: Cancel all employee vacations," Brandon Duke muttered as he reached for his coffee cup and realized it was empty. Yet another reminder that his invaluable assistant, Kelly Meredith, was still away on vacation. She'd been gone for the past two weeks, and that was fourteen days too long as far as he was concerned.

It wasn't like Brandon couldn't get his own cup of coffee. He wasn't that lame. It was just that Kelly always beat him to it, showing up with a piping hot refill at the right time, every time. She was a dynamo in every other way, too. Clients loved her. Spreadsheets didn't intimidate her. And she was an excellent judge of character, something he'd recognized early on. That was a quality worth its weight in gold and he'd taken advantage of it from the start by having Kelly accompany him to various business meetings all over the country.

Brandon's own instincts were spot on when it came

to judging a potential business partner or the motives of a competitor, but Kelly was a strong backup. Even his brothers had gotten into the habit of having Kelly vet new hires and solve problems in other departments. They called her the miracle worker, for good reason. If there was a thankless job that needed handling, Kelly grabbed it with both hands and worked her magic. Everything ran more smoothly because of her.

Taking advantage of the early morning quiet in the still empty office suite, Brandon grabbed a legal pad and began to scribble notes for a meeting with his brothers later today. Now that the Mansion at Silverado Trail, the Dukes' newest resort in Napa Valley and the jewel in the crown of the Duke hotel empire, was about to celebrate its grand opening, it was time to focus his energies on new properties and new challenges.

Reading what he'd written, he was reminded of another reason he needed his assistant to come back from vacation: she could decipher his handwriting.

In the middle of bullet-pointing several options for a takeover bid on a small chain of luxury hotels along the picturesque Oregon coast, Brandon checked his calendar. Every hour of the day was filled with appointments, conference calls and deadlines, many of them connected to the grand opening celebration. Good thing his assistant would be back today, and about damn time. The temp replacement had been competent, but Kelly was the only one who could handle the myriad pressures and scheduling conflicts involved in the upcoming festivities.

And speaking of pressures, his brother's wife was about to pop out a baby soon. This would be Mom's first grandkid, and you would've thought no other child had ever been born. Talk about a major celebration. But what in the world was Brandon supposed to buy the kid? Season tickets on the 49ers' fifty-yard line he could swing, but otherwise, he was clueless. Didn't matter. Kelly would know the perfect gift to buy and she'd probably wrap it, too.

Brandon heard rustling and the sound of drawers opening just outside his partly opened door.

"Good morning, Brandon," a cheery voice called out.

"About time you got back, Kelly," he said with relief. "Come see me after you've had a chance to settle in."

"You bet. I'll just make a pot of coffee first."

Brandon checked his watch. Sure enough, she was fifteen minutes early, one more indication that she was an ideal employee who deserved all the perks the job offered. But he still planned to outlaw vacations from now on.

"Ah, it's good to be back," Kelly murmured as she powered up her computer. Hard to believe, but she'd actually missed Brandon Duke while she was gone. The sound of his deep voice gave her a little thrill she attributed to the fact that she loved her job.

She stashed her tote bag and purse in the credenza behind her desk and quickly made coffee. Her hand shook as she filled the pot with water at the small kitchen kiosk across from her office and she forced herself to relax. She really was happy to be back at the job she loved, so why was she so nervous?

Okay, she'd made a few changes while on vacation, but nobody would notice, right? Nobody ever noticed anything about her except for her savvy business sense and can-do attitude, and that was just the way she wanted it. So if she happened to be wearing a dress today instead of one of her usual pantsuits, who would care? The fact that she'd never worn a dress to the office before wouldn't stand out to anyone here. Even if today's dress was a beautiful dark gray knit that buttoned up the front and clung subtly to her curves. And that was just fine and dandy.

And if she'd finally changed over to contact lenses, so what? She'd been wearing the same boring eyeglasses for the past five years. Change was a good thing.

"Kelly," Brandon called from his office. "Bring the Dream Coast file with you when you come in, will you?"

"Be right there."

The familiar sound of Brandon Duke's voice made Kelly smile. He should've intimidated her from day one. At six feet four inches tall, he towered over her, and she knew for a fact that he was rock-solid muscle underneath his designer suits. She knew, because she'd run into him more than once at the hotel gym and seen him in shorts and a T-shirt. A former NFL quarterback bench-pressing ridiculously heavy barbells was quite a sight. Sometimes, while watching him, she found it hard to breathe steadily, but she chalked up those moments to spending too much time on the treadmill.

She chuckled at the thought of some of her girlfriends, who'd told her they would kill for a chance to see the stunningly handsome Brandon Duke working out in gym shorts. Luckily for Kelly, she'd never been tempted by her boss.

Yes, he was gorgeous, almost unbelievably so, but to Kelly, having a great job meant a lot more than having a brief, meaningless affair with some superstar athlete. And yes, an affair with Brandon Duke would never be anything but brief and meaningless. She'd seen firsthand the women who lined up to date him, and she'd seen them flicked off without a backward glance within a couple of weeks. It wasn't pretty, and she never wanted to find herself in that line. Not that she would qualify to stand in that line, but—

"What are you thinking?" she whispered to herself.

She'd never thought of her boss in those terms before and she wouldn't start now. Shaking her head in disgust, she had to wonder if maybe she'd taken too many days off.

As the coffeepot filled, Kelly took a moment to glance out the wide bay window and felt both proud and lucky to be here in this job. Who wouldn't want to work on a hilltop in the heart of Napa Valley, overlooking lush fields of grapevines as far as the eye could see?

Brandon and his small corporate staff had been working on-site at the Mansion at Silverado Trail for the past four months. They would stay here another month or so, until the resort was up and running and the grape harvest was over. Then they would all relocate back to Duke headquarters in Dunsmuir Bay.

By then, Kelly's plan would be complete, and her life would settle down to normal. But until then, she would simply have to remind herself to relax and breathe.

"Do you hear me, self? Just relax," she murmured as she ran her hands over her dress to smooth away any wrinkles, then filled two large mugs with hot coffee. "Breathe."

She stopped at her desk to drop off her own mug and pick up a short stack of mail, then pushed her boss's door fully open.

"Good morning, Brandon," she said breezily, and placed the mail on his desk.

"Morning, Kelly," he said, as he wrote rapidly on a legal pad. "Great to have you back."

"Thank you, it's nice to be back." She placed his mug on his blotter. "Coffee for you."

"Thanks," he said absently, still writing. After a moment, he reached for his coffee and looked up. His eyes widened as he cautiously put the cup down. "Kelly?"

"Yes?" She gazed at him, then blinked. "Oh, sorry. You wanted the Dream Coast file. I'll be right back with it."

"Kelly?" His voice sounded strained.

She stopped and turned. "Yes, Brandon?"

He was staring at her in…disbelief? Shock? Horror? Oh, dear. Not a good sign. And the longer he stared, the more nervous she became.

"Oh, come on," she said. "I don't look bad enough to have stunned you into speechlessness." She fiddled with her dress collar as she felt heat moving up her neck and settling into her cheeks. No need to be embarrassed, she scolded herself.

"But, what did you do to…" His voice trailed off as he continued to stare at her face.

"Oh, you mean the contact lenses? Yeah. It was time for a change. Be right back with the file."

"Kelly." His tone was demanding.

She turned again. He was still staring, this time at her hair. With a sigh, she brushed a strand back from her cheek. "I had it lightened and shaped. No big deal." Then she waved him off and rushed to find the file.

Great. If Brandon was any example, people would be staring at her as if she were an alien. How was she supposed to relax and breathe and put her plan into action under those circumstances, darn it?

As she anxiously rifled through the file drawer, she heard the distinctive sound of Brandon's leather executive chair rolling back from his desk. Seconds later, he was standing in the doorway. Still staring.

"Kelly?" he said again.

She stared up at him from the files. "Why do you keep saying my name?"

"Just making sure it's you."

"Well, it is, so cut it out," she told him, then found what she was looking for. "Ah, here's that file."

"What did you do?"

"You asked me that already."

"And I'm still waiting for an answer."

Her shoulders drooped for a split second, then she straightened. There was no reason to feel self-conscious, especially not with Brandon. He'd given her glowing reviews and generous raises. He respected and admired her ability to work hard and solve problems. He was her employer, not her overlord, for goodness sake. "I got a little makeover."

"Little?"

She raised one shoulder in a casual shrug. "That's right. I lost a few pounds, got a haircut, some contact lenses. No big deal."

"It is from where I'm standing. You don't even look like you."

"Of course I look like me." She wasn't about to mention the week spent at the pricey spa or the private etiquette and speech lessons. He would think she'd gone insane. Maybe she had. She'd always been levelheaded, and rational to the point of being called a nerd back in college. Now she wasn't sure what they would call her.

"But you're wearing a dress," he said accusingly.

She looked down, then back at him. "Why, yes, I am. Is that a problem?"

It was his turn to look discomfited as he took a step back. "No. God, no. No problem at all. You look great. It's just that…" Scrubbing his jaw with his knuckles, he searched for the words. "You don't wear dresses."

He'd noticed? Color her surprised. With a resolute smile, she said, "I do now."

"I guess so," he said, searching her face, still looking doubtful. "Well, like I said, you look great. Really great."

"Thank you," she said, still smiling. "I feel great."

"Yeah. That's great." He nodded, then gritted his teeth and exhaled heavily.

If everything was *great,* why was he scowling?

"Oh!" she said, feeling ridiculous as she thrust the thick manila folder at him. "Here's the Dream Coast file."

His hand grazed hers as the file passed between them and she felt a buzz of awareness all the way up her arm.

Brandon's frown lines deepened. "Thanks."

"Sure thing."

He walked back into his office, then turned. "It's great to have you back."

And that was how many *greats* so far? she wondered.

"Thank you," she said. "And I'll have the month-end sales figures calculated for you in twenty minutes."

He closed the door and she sagged down into her chair. Grabbing her own cup of coffee, she took a big gulp. "Oh yeah, it's *great* to be back."

Brandon tossed the Dream Coast file onto his desk and continued walking across the plush office until he reached the floor-to-ceiling window that lined one long wall. He and his team were working out of the owner's suite on the penthouse level of the Mansion at Silverado Trail, and he never grew tired of the view. Normally, when he gazed out at the gently sloping hills of chardonnay grapevines, he relished the pride he felt when he saw such visible symbols of his family's success.

A hot air balloon drifted silently in the sky overhead and birds skittered from tree to tree across the hills. But he ignored all of it as he caught the barest whiff of flowers and spice drifting in the air. He wasn't used to his assistant wearing perfume, or maybe he'd never noticed that she did, but for the first time ever, the arresting scent conjured up visions of a cool hotel room and a hot blonde. Naked. Wrapped in sheets. Under him.

Kelly. He could still smell her. Damn it.

He'd made a fool of himself just now, gaping at her as though she were a juicy steak and he were a starved puppy. Hell, he hadn't even been able to speak. He'd sounded like a damn parrot, repeating her name over and over. But he would lay the blame for that solely at her feet. She'd succeeded in shocking the hell out of him and that never happened to Brandon Duke.

A makeover? He shook his head as he paced the length of the wall of glass. Who could fathom a woman's mind? Kelly didn't need a makeover. She'd been fine the way she was. All business, completely professional, smart, discreet. Never a distraction.

Brandon didn't like distractions in the workplace. In his office, it was all business, all the time. After ten years in the spotlight of the NFL, he was all too aware that distractions ruined your game. You took your eye off the ball and the next thing you knew, you were buried in a pile of tough, ugly defensive ends who would just as soon see you dead.

Brandon splayed one hand on the plate glass window. Talk about a distraction. Who knew his competent assistant had those amazing curves and world-class legs hidden beneath the boxy pantsuits she'd worn every day? And those eyes, so big and blue a man could get lost in them?

Most disturbing of all, she seemed to be wearing some kind of new, glossy lipstick. It had to be new, otherwise he would've noticed her incredibly sexy, bee-stung lips long before today. But he was noticing now. He'd almost spilled his coffee noticing.

Her new dress clung to every curve of her lush body. Curves he'd never known existed before. Even though he saw her in the hotel gym regularly, she always exercised in a big T-shirt and sweatpants. Who knew she'd been hiding a body like that under all those layers of sweaty workout clothes? She'd clearly been working here under false pretenses all this time.

"Now you just sound ridiculous," he groused. But who could blame him? His sedate, hard-working assistant was simply gorgeous. It was such a betrayal.

And what the hell had happened a minute ago when her hand touched his? He thought he'd felt something sizzling inside him. It had to be his imagination, but recalling that sensation of skin against skin caused his groin to leap to attention. He smacked the wall in disgust.

"Change is good," he grumbled sarcastically and he sat back down at his desk. No, change *wasn't* good. Not when he was used to Kelly's nondescript hair and the way she'd always worn it pulled back in a sensible ponytail or bun. Now it was the color of rich honey tumbling across her shoulders and down her back. It was the sort of color and style that begged a man to run his hands through the lustrous strands as he eased her down to feast on those luscious lips.

His body continued to stir to life and he squelched the feeling by slapping the file folder open and riffling through the papers to find the document he needed. It was useless.

"This is unacceptable." He refused to lose the careful sense of order and decorum he had always maintained in the workplace. The job was too demanding and Kelly was too important a part of his staff to allow her to suddenly become a distraction. Or more aptly, an *attraction*.

It was time to nip this in the bud. He reached across his desk and pressed the intercom button on his phone. "Kelly, please come in here."

"Be right there," she said briskly. Seven seconds later, she walked into his office carrying a notepad.

"Sit down," he said, standing up to pace some more. He didn't quite trust himself with taking another glance at her legs. Damn it, this just was not going to work. "We need to talk."

"What's wrong?" she asked in alarm.

"Look, we've always been honest with each other, haven't we?"

"Yes," she said carefully.

"I trust you completely, as you well know."

"I know, and I feel the same, Brandon."

"Good," he said, unsure of his next move. "Good."

Now what? He'd never been at a loss for words before. He glanced at her, then had to look away. How and when had she become so beautiful? He knew women. He loved women. And they loved him. Some might even say he had a sixth sense when it came to women. So why hadn't he known Kelly was this attractive? Was he blind?

"Brandon," she said slowly. "Are you unhappy with my work?"

"What? No."

"Did Jane do an okay job while I was gone?"

"Yeah, she was fine. That's not the problem."

"Oh good, because I would hate to—"

"Look, Kelly," he interrupted, tired of this cat and mouse game. "Did something happen to you on your vacation?"

She was taken aback. "No, why would you think—"

"Then what's with this makeover thing?" he blurted out. "Why'd you do it?"

"That's what you called me in here for?"

"Yeah." And he wouldn't go into how ridiculous he felt

for bringing it up, but he had to know. "Why do you think you have to get all dolled up to—"

Her eyes narrowed. "All dolled up?"

"Well, yeah. You know, all made up and...hell."

"There's something wrong in trying to look my best?"

"That's not what I said."

"Did I overdo it somehow? I mean, the makeup counter woman showed me what to do, but I'm new at this. I'm still practicing." She lifted her face to gaze at him and her lips seemed to glisten as they caught the light. "Tell the truth. Is my makeup too much?"

"God, no, it's just right." *Too damn right*, he thought, but didn't say.

"Now you're being nice, but I don't believe you. The way you looked at me when I came in this morning..."

"What? No." *Oh, crap,* he thought. She wasn't going to cry, was she? She'd never cried before.

"I thought I could do it. Other women do it, for heaven's sake, why shouldn't I?" She jumped up from the chair. It was her turn to pace as she pounded her fist into her palm. "I thought I was being subtle. Do I look like a fool?"

"No, you—"

"You can be honest."

"I'm being—"

"This was a crazy idea to begin with," she muttered and leaned back against the wall with a sigh. "I can figure out complex mathematical calculations in my head, but I don't know the first thing about seduction."

Seduction? Something hit him low in the solar plexus and he wasn't sure of his next move.

"This is so embarrassing," she moaned.

"No, it's not," he said, silently hoping he'd come up with something profound to say. He had nothing.

"What am I supposed to do now? I've only got a week

left to…oh, God." She covered her eyes for a moment, then stared up at the ceiling. Finally, she folded her arms across her chest and tapped one toe of her shiny new heels against the carpet. "How could I be so stupid?"

He walked up to her and grabbed her by the shoulders. "Stop that. You're one of the smartest people I know."

She glared up at him, her plump lips pouty now. "Maybe in business, but never in romance."

Okay, romance and seduction were definitely on her mind. And now he realized they were on his mind, too. The question was, why? In all the years he'd known Kelly, Brandon had never once heard her mention a name connected to any romantic interest. And now, all of a sudden, she was making herself over to attract some guy? Just who was she thinking of seducing? Did Brandon know the guy? Was he good enough for Kelly?

Brandon paused to carefully word his next question. "Who are you trying to seduce?"

Frowning now, she stared at her fingernails. "Roger. My old boyfriend. But I should've known it wouldn't work."

Roger? Who the hell was Roger? Brandon had to admit that the part of him that should have been relieved to hear she wasn't out to seduce *him* was surprisingly disappointed. Not that he would ever allow anything to happen between them. But still, who the hell was she talking about?

"Who's Roger?" he asked aloud.

"I just told you, he's my old boyfriend. His name is Roger Hempstead." She stepped away from Brandon's grip and moved back to her chair. "We broke up a few years ago and I haven't seen him since."

"How long ago did you break up?"

"It's been almost five years."

He made a quick calculation. "But that's about how long you've been working here."

"That's right." She leaned one elbow on the armrest and looked up at him with a valiant smile. "After Roger and I broke up, I couldn't stand living in the same small town where everyone I knew could dissect my every word and movement. I decided to relocate as far away from home as possible, so I looked for jobs in California and found this one."

"I'm glad you did, but it must've been quite a breakup."

"It wasn't fun," she said carefully, "but I've moved on."

"Have you?"

"Yes, of course." She nodded her head resolutely. "But then, last month I found out that Roger's company booked their corporate retreat here at the Mansion. He'll be here next week." She took a deep breath and exhaled. "And I wanted to knock his socks off."

"Ah, I see." And he did, sort of. Resting his hip on the edge of his desk, he said, "If it's any consolation, I can pretty much guarantee you'll knock his socks off."

She gazed at him skeptically. "You're just saying that to be nice."

"I'm not that nice. Trust me."

Her lips twisted into a frown. "I do. Usually."

"I never lie, remember?"

"True, you don't typically lie. To me, anyway," she allowed.

He chuckled. "So it's been about five years since you broke up with this Roger character, and now you want to make an impression."

She nodded with determination. "I really, really do."

"You will. I promise."

"Thanks." Her brief smile faded. "But I don't know what I'm doing. I'm fine at business, but the world of romance is beyond me."

"Tell me what I can do to help."

Kelly regarded him with interest. "You mean it?"

"Sure." He was willing to do almost anything to get things back on track. If Kelly felt secure, she'd be able to do her work and stop worrying about this clown Roger. Then, once Roger was gone, she'd go back to behaving like the Kelly he was comfortable with. His universe would once more be in alignment.

"That would be wonderful," she said with enthusiasm. "I could really use advice from someone like you."

"Someone like me?"

She smiled and he was struck again by how beautiful she was. Damn, how blind had he been all these years?

"It's just that the two of you are so much alike," she said. "You and Roger, I mean. It would really help to get your perspective on things."

"What do you mean, we're alike?"

"I mean, both of you are strong and handsome and arrogant and ruthless and, you know, type A all the way."

Huh. That was accurate enough, although he'd always thought he was fairly laid-back compared to his two brothers. He did appreciate the strong and handsome part of her description, though.

Kelly had stopped to ponder what she'd just said, then added softly, "Wow, no wonder Roger didn't think I was enough for him."

Brandon bristled. "*Enough* for him?"

She sighed. "You know what I mean. I wasn't attractive enough for him."

"What makes you say that?"

"He told me so when he broke up with me."

For some reason, Brandon felt an irresistible urge to pulverize something. Like Roger's face. "You're kidding."

"No," she said wryly. "I'm really not. But you saw what I looked like before the makeover, Brandon. Plain, wholesome, unremarkable. Not exactly supermodel material."

A twinge of guilt pinged inside him as he realized that was exactly how he'd always felt about her. But he'd considered that a good thing. Now he was just glad he'd never mentioned it out loud.

"But I understood where Roger was coming from," she continued. "He is very special, after all."

"Special? He sounds like a jackass."

She tried to stifle a giggle but didn't quite succeed. "Oh, he is, but he can't help it. His family has a very strong influence on him. His mother's ancestors came over on the *Mayflower,* you know."

"Members of the crew, were they?" Shaking his head, he said, "Listen, Kelly, do you want me to have him killed? Because I know someone who knows someone who could—"

Kelly laughed. "That's a sweet offer, but no. I just want to make him regret what he said when he broke things off, that's all."

He studied her for several moments. "He hurt you."

She shook her head. "No, no, he told me the truth and I have to be grateful for that."

"Grateful? Why?"

She smiled tightly. "Because he helped me see things more clearly."

"What kinds of things?" Brandon asked warily.

"My own shortcomings."

Once again, his fists were itching to punch something. Roger's stomach, maybe, since he'd already mentally broken the jerk's nose.

She smiled brightly. "So that's why I've decided to get him back."

"What? Get him back?" Why in the world would she

want that scumbag back? Hell, Brandon didn't even know Roger and he already hated him.

"Yes." She spread her arms out. "And that explains the makeover."

And with that, she made a show of checking her watch, effectively ending the conversation. Probably a good idea.

"So," she said, changing the subject, "do you want me to order lunch from catering?"

He wasn't finished talking about this, but clearly Kelly needed a time out. So he'd let it go. For now.

"Yeah, that would be great. I'll have the steak sandwich."

"Sounds good. I'll call it in."

He leaned forward in his chair. "Listen, Kelly, if you need any help or advice, anything at all, you'll come to me. Promise?"

"Really? You mean it?"

"Absolutely."

She studied his face as if she were weighing the depth of his sincerity. "You're sure?"

"I wouldn't have offered if I wasn't."

She seemed to carry on a short debate with herself, then said, "Okay, there is one tiny thing you could help me with. If you wouldn't mind."

"You name it," he said, reaching for his coffee mug.

"I'll be right back." She rushed out to her desk and was back in less than twenty seconds, holding a shopping bag from a well-known and expensive lingerie shop. Taking a deep, fortifying breath, she pulled some wispy scraps of sheer material from the bag and dangled them for him to see.

"Which do you like better, the black thong or the red panties?"

Two

He choked on his coffee.

Dismayed, Kelly ran around and pounded his back. "Are you okay?"

"Fine," he managed to say. "I'm fine." He'd be even better once she backed off and her curvaceous breasts were no longer rubbing against his arm. He was only human, for God's sake. And hard as granite.

He'd been tackled by some of the biggest linebackers in football history, but nothing had ever rendered him apoplectic before now. As he took a deep breath and let it out, the thought entered his mind that maybe she was trying to kill him. Could Roger have treated her so badly that she was going to take it out on every man she knew?

It wasn't enough that she'd changed the playing field with her hot new look, but now she was shoving her panties at him. Didn't she know that those little scraps of silk would be forever imprinted on his fragile male psyche?

Now he would be forced to spend the next millennium imagining her in that black thong. Was she really that clueless?

"I didn't mean to shock you," she said. "But you said you would help."

"Didn't shock me," he insisted, his voice sounding as if a frog had taken up residence in his throat. "Coffee went down wrong. Just…give me a minute."

She finally moved back to her side of the desk and quickly shoved the bits of lace into the shopping bag.

"They'll work just fine," he said softly, not trusting his voice yet.

Her eyes glittered with hope. "Really?"

"Believe it," he said with a nod. "Any normal guy would be grateful to see you in either pair."

"You mean it?" Her eyes cleared and she smiled. "Thank you, Brandon. Oh, and I apologize again for springing them on you."

"No problem."

"To make this work, I really need to know what guys consider sexy." She frowned, then admitted, "Roger never thought I was."

"Never thought you were what?"

"Sexy."

Brandon sat forward in his chair. "Does Roger have some kind of learning disability or something?"

She laughed. "Thanks for that. I'll go order lunch now."

"Good idea," he said, thankful his voice had returned to full volume. "Oh, and Kelly?"

She stopped at the door. "Yes?"

"Go with the black thong."

Later that afternoon, Brandon hung up the phone from a two-hour teleconference with his brothers and their lawyer.

"That guy never stops talking," he said, shaking his head at the sheer immensity of the lawyer's convoluted vocabulary.

"I was thinking you must pay him by the word," Kelly said, flexing her fingers. She had taken notes during the entire meeting and now she stood and stretched her arms. The movement caused the knit fabric of her dress to stretch so tightly across her perfect round breasts that Brandon had to look the other way to stifle the first stages of another rock-hard erection.

"I'm getting more coffee," she said. "Would you like some?"

"No, thanks. Will you have a chance to type up your notes and analysis this afternoon?"

"Definitely. I'll get right on them."

"I appreciate it."

She closed the door and Brandon gritted his teeth. He needed Kelly to rethink this new wardrobe situation if he was going to survive the week. Hell, even her ankles were causing him palpitations. There was something about those high heels she was wearing that did awesome things to every inch of her legs.

An hour later, after the rest of his team had gone home, he walked out to Kelly's area to find a property file and caught her pouting at herself in her compact mirror.

"Oh." She blinked in surprise and quickly slapped the mirror closed and threw it in her drawer.

He rested one hand on the doorjamb. "I know I'm going to be sorry I asked, but what were you doing?"

"Nothing. What do you need? A file? Which one? I'll get it." She jumped up and pulled the top file drawer open.

"See, now you're just raising my curiosity level," he said, "so you might as well tell me."

She clenched her teeth together irately. "Fine. Roger

complained about the way I kissed, so I was practicing in the mirror. There. Are you happy?"

He shook his head. "Roger is a complete idiot. Why do you care what he thinks?"

She glared at him. "I told you, I want to get him back."

"Yeah, that's what I don't get." Disgusted with the subject of Roger, he moved to the file drawer and began to sift through the folders himself. "Where's the new Montclair Pavilion file?"

"I've got it right here." She picked up a thin folder and handed it to him. She looked so dejected, he couldn't help but feel sorry for teasing her.

"Look, I'm sure you kiss like a goddess," he said. "So stop worrying about what Roger thinks."

"I just wish I could practice on something besides a mirror," she said gloomily.

"Yeah," he agreed absently as he thumbed through the file. "It usually works better to go with a real-life target who'll actually kiss you back."

She shot him a hopeful look. "I don't suppose you'd be willing to help me out with that."

He glowered at her. "Get real, Kelly."

"What do you mean?" Realization dawned slowly. "Oh! No, no! I didn't mean for *you* to kiss—oh, dear. I would never want *you* to…well, this isn't going to come out right, no matter how I say it."

"So just say it."

"Okay. I wasn't talking about *you* kissing me." She sat on the edge of her desk. "But the thing is, I've made a list of potential, um…participants. So I was thinking maybe you could help by looking it over and making some suggestions?"

"You have a list?" Why was he surprised? Kelly made

lists for everything. It was just one of the ways she stayed so organized.

"Of course I have a list." She jumped up, ran around the desk and pulled a pad and pen out of her drawer. "I'm good at making lists."

"Let me get this straight," he said, absently slapping the file folder against his pants leg. "You've made a list of men you're thinking of approaching to ask for help with— what? Kissing lessons?"

She flipped a page over and studied it. "That's right."

"But I'm not on the list?" he asked warily.

"What? No, absolutely not." She shook her head as she held up her hand in a pledge. "Of course you're not on the list. You're my boss."

"Good. As long as we've got that settled." He should've felt nothing but relief. So why was he getting more annoyed by the minute? She considered him good enough to judge her damn panties but not good enough to kiss?

Okay, that might be the most ridiculous thought he'd had all day. This entire situation was getting out of hand. With a heavy exhalation of breath, he shoved away his own ludicrous reactions and tried to empathize with Kelly's bizarre quandary.

"So who's on the list?" he asked, almost afraid to hear her answers.

She glanced up. "What do you think about Jean Pierre?"

"The hotel chef?" She couldn't be serious.

"He's French," she explained. "They invented the sport, right?"

"No way in hell. Not Jean Pierre. You'd probably start an international incident. Absolutely not."

"Okay, okay." She crossed Jean Pierre's name off her list. "What about Jeremy?"

"The guy who mows the lawns?"

"He's a landscape designer," she said pointedly. "Practically an artist. He might know a thing or two about the art of *l'amour*."

"He's gay."

"Really? Why don't I know these things?" She blew out a frustrated breath as she drew a line through Jeremy's name. "Nicholas the winemaker? He's German, right? He might be—"

"Let me see that list." He snatched the pad from her and gazed at the names. "Paulo, the cabana boy?"

"He's cute," she insisted, a little too desperately.

"Forget it. Who's Rocco?"

"One of the limo drivers."

"Which one?"

"The big guy with the—"

"Never mind." He shook his head. "No."

"But—"

"No," he said, handing the list back. "Throw that away. I don't want you going around kissing the staff, for God's sake."

"Fine." Glaring at Brandon, she ripped the page out, crumpled it up and tossed it in the waste bin. "I suppose you're right. It might send the wrong message."

"You think?" he said, his voice tinged with sarcasm.

She folded her arms tightly across her chest, which only served to emphasize her world-class breasts, damn it.

"So who can I ask for help?" she wondered, leaning her hip against her desk. "I've got a full week before Roger gets here. I could do a lot of practicing in that time. Do you have any friends you could recommend?"

"No."

"Too bad." She pursed her lips in thought. "Maybe there's someone in town who—"

"Not a good idea," he said in a tone that cut off all

discussion. *Not a good idea?* Talk about an understatement. Hell, it was one of the worst ideas Brandon had ever heard. He didn't want her kissing the staff *or* any poor, unsuspecting Napa Valley residents. All he needed was to have the locals talking about the crazy kissing woman from the Mansion on Silverado Trail.

But he could tell by the tension building along Kelly's soft jawline that she was determined to carry out this cockeyed plan of hers. And if she went behind his back and enlisted one of the pool attendants...

Brandon stared at those pouty, glossy lips and realized the only man who could help her improve her kissing technique was him. Mainly because he suddenly couldn't stand the thought of her kissing anyone else.

"Fine," he said brusquely. "I'll help you."

She pushed away from the desk. "But you're not on the list."

"Doesn't matter. I'm going to help you myself because I don't want you scaring away the staff."

She placed her hands on her hips and tilted her head at him. "I know you meant that in the nicest way."

"Sorry. Yes." He shook his head as if to erase the comment. "Of course I did."

She continued staring at him. "I don't think it's a good idea."

"It's the only way I'll know for sure that you're not getting into trouble around here."

"I won't get into trouble."

"I know, because I'll be the one helping you."

Inhaling a deep breath, Kelly let it out slowly, then seemed to brace herself for impact. "Okay. I appreciate this, Brandon." She took a hesitant step toward him, but he held up his hand to stop her.

"Wait. We need to set some ground rules first."

"Ground rules? Why?"

"Because there's no way I'm having you fall for me."

"Fall for you?" She blinked, then began to laugh. "Are you kidding?"

"Something funny?" he asked, insulted.

"Yes," she said, giggling like a schoolgirl. "The idea that I would ever be dumb enough to fall for you is pretty funny."

"*Dumb* enough?"

"Yes, dumb enough. Let me count the ways." She held up one hand and began ticking off fingers. "You're a grouch in the morning. You leave newspapers lying around everywhere. You date a woman once and then never call back. You're a big baby when you're sick."

"Wait a minute," he protested.

But she was on a roll now and seemed to be enjoying herself. "And all your weird superstitions left over from when you played in the NFL? My gosh, wearing the same socks for every game was bad enough, but I also heard that you ate only sardines and blueberries the night before every game. Do you still do that before big negotiations? Who does that?"

Brandon had heard enough. He placed the file on the chair in front of her desk and stalked closer. "The socks were washed between games."

"Oh, really?"

"Yeah, really." He brushed against her, then slipped his hand around her nape and urged her closer. "And sardines and blueberries are both excellent sources of omega-three fatty acids."

"Fascinating," she whispered, as she stared wide-eyed at him.

"Helps the brain function better," he added as he caressed her cheek.

"G-good to know." She sounded wary now, probably smart of her.

He bent to kiss her neck, then murmured in her ear, "The quarterback's the brains of the team, did you know that?"

She moaned. "What are you doing?"

"What do you think I'm doing?"

"I'm not sure."

"I am." And he kissed her. She tasted as sweet and hot as he somehow knew she would. Even more so. He had to work to keep the contact light and simple, because it wouldn't do to get carried away. But that didn't stop him from wishing he could lay her down on the desk, run his hands up her thighs, spread her legs and bury himself inside her.

He had to stop. This was wrong in too many ways to count. If he stepped away from her right now, they could both forget this kiss ever happened.

Then she groaned in surrender and he knew she wanted the same things he did. And he was helpless to stop. He used his tongue to gently pry her lips open, plunging inside her sexy mouth. Her tongue met his in a sensual play of thrust and parry.

He wanted to cup her breasts and flick his thumbs across her peaked nipples, but that was a sure road to madness. So with every ounce of will inside him, he forced himself to end the kiss, reluctantly pulling himself away from her warmth.

"Oh," she whispered, licking her lips as she slowly opened her eyes.

Brandon's insides clenched at the sight of her pink tongue tasting him on her mouth.

"Oh, that was good," she said with a note of surprise. "That was really good."

"Yeah," he said, brooding. "It was."

"I liked it a lot."

So did he, but he remained silent. Otherwise, he might've been tempted to follow through on his desire to have her naked under him. But that would never happen and right now, he needed to regain some degree of control over whatever strange emotions were still churning inside him.

"Roger never kissed like that," she said, watching him thoughtfully.

"Did I mention the guy was an idiot?" he muttered.

"No wonder he didn't think I was sexy," she reasoned. "It's because he didn't make me *feel* sexy."

"I rest my case."

"But *you* did," she declared and smiled up at him. "And now…wow. You know, I really think Roger was the problem, not me. But I can't be sure."

"Yeah, you can," he said gruffly. "Roger was the problem. End of story."

She touched his arm. "Thank you, Brandon."

"You're welcome." He started to head for his office, still trying to steady his breathing.

"Wait," she said.

He turned and looked at her. A slight line of concern marred the smooth surface of her forehead. Her lips were pink and tender and about the sexiest thing he'd ever seen. The fact that he wanted more than anything to kiss her again, made him forge ahead into his office.

"I think I could get really good at this and blow Roger's mind, but I need to practice," she said, following him. She had her notepad in hand again, probably hoping she could make another damn list of all the different ways they could kiss each other. If she only knew.

"Not a good idea," he said, sliding the Montclair file into his briefcase.

"But you said that before and it turned out to be a really good idea."

He pierced her with a look. "No more practicing. Ground rules, remember?"

"I remember, don't worry." After scrutinizing him for a moment, she nodded her agreement. "Okay, I guess you're right."

"I know I'm right," he said, and snapped his briefcase closed.

"Thank you for your help," she said. "It was wonderful. On a purely educational level, I mean."

"You're welcome," he said and led the way out of his office. "Now let's call it a night."

"Oh, I'm going to stay for a while," she said, flipping to a clean page, all business now. "I need to make some notes while everything is still fresh in my mind. I'll need to remember everything later."

"You're going to make notes on that kiss?"

"Yes, for future reference." She'd already begun scribbling what looked like mathematical calculations. "If I write everything down—what you did and what I felt, I'll be able to recall each sensation the next time, and I'll know I'm doing it right."

"The next time," he echoed hazily.

"Yes. I tend to remember tactile experiences more clearly if I make a record of it immediately. Then later, I'll study my notes in anticipation of the next occurrence." She beamed at him. "I'm quite confident I can achieve an exponential jump in my skill level and understanding."

"Really?"

"It makes perfect sense on paper."

"On paper. Good."

Tapping her pen against the pad, she murmured, half to herself, "Of course, an actual kiss would give me a lot more insight.…"

She looked up and studied Brandon closely. He wasn't liking the look in her eyes. "Don't even think about it."

"Think about what?" she asked, her eyelashes fluttering innocently. If she were any other woman, Brandon would know she was playing a dangerous game of seduction. But this was Kelly, who didn't seem to have a clue about feminine wiles and whose every emotion was evident on her face.

That made it Brandon's responsibility to set her straight.

"Forget it, Kelly. I am not going to kiss you again."

"Oh, I know," she murmured, her moist, glimmering lips pursed in thought.

He lost all memory of what they were talking about. He only knew that right now, his throbbing body parts wanted to put those lips of hers to the best use possible. Maybe after that, he would be able to carry on an intelligent conversation with her.

In the meantime, however, it appeared that he had created a monster.

Three

"*I am not going to kiss you again.*"

Every time Kelly played the words over in her head, she could feel her cheeks heat up in embarrassment. And since she was incapable of putting a halt to the mental words and images, she wouldn't be surprised if, any minute now, her head spontaneously combusted.

"So stop thinking about it," she demanded aloud as she popped a frozen dinner in the microwave oven and slammed the door shut. Now she had four minutes with nothing to do but wait. And think. And remember. She glanced around her comfortable mini-suite with its corner kitchen nook and figured she could use the time to straighten up, but there was nothing out of place. Her room was pristine, as usual.

The Mansion had a world-class housekeeping service and even though Kelly was part of the corporate staff, the housekeepers kindly insisted on stopping by every day to clean and straighten up and make sure everything was perfectly comfortable for her.

So, lucky her, she had plenty of time to dwell on all those damning thoughts that wouldn't stop circling through her mind.

"The fact that you practically begged your boss to kiss you," she berated herself, "in the office, in broad daylight, wasn't bad enough. No, you also had to dangle your panties in his face. So classy. And why couldn't you keep that silly list of kissing candidates to yourself?"

A small sigh escaped as she slid miserably onto the stool at her kitchen counter. Reaching for the bottle of sparkling water she'd opened, she filled her glass and took a sip. And pondered her next move.

There were a few ways she could remedy the situation. One was to go in tomorrow morning and simply apologize to Brandon. She could explain, somewhat truthfully, that she'd ingested nothing but spa cuisine for ten days straight and it had left her brain incapable of clear thought.

He probably wouldn't believe that story since everyone in the entire company knew that Kelly's mind was a steel trap. She could recall the minor details of a telephone conference from three years ago or the specifications of a particular construction job from months back. She had the dates of every birthday, anniversary and important occasion in Brandon's life memorized, along with phone numbers, credit card accounts and travel preferences for him and every member of his family.

There was no way he'd believe she'd suddenly lost the ability to think straight. So her only other solution was to simply move away, somewhere remote, like Duluth, leaving no forwarding address. She was fairly certain Brandon's memory of the outlandish panty-dangling incident would fade within months, a year at the most.

"Oh, God." She leaned her elbows on the counter and buried her face in her hands. The fact that Brandon had obligingly recommended the black thong really didn't help matters right now.

The microwave buzzed and she removed her small dinner. She was proud of herself for continuing to eat lighter portions since leaving the spa, but she could feel a serious ice cream binge coming on.

It was because of the kiss.

She'd vowed not to think about it and had been semisuccessful, deliberately switching tracks whenever her train of thought veered too close to the memory of Brandon's touch, the feel of his mouth on hers. But now, just for a moment or two, she let herself go and thought about it.

She'd never experienced anything like it. It was just one kiss, but she'd felt more passion and excitement in those few seconds than she'd known in the entire two years and seven months she'd dated Roger.

Now, she closed her eyes and gave in to temptation, reliving the exquisite pressure of Brandon's hands, the warm smoothness of his mouth…

After a moment, her eyes flashed open and she stared down at her rapidly cooling dinner. She'd completely lost her appetite. For dinner, anyway.

"You need to snap out of it, right now," she reprimanded herself. Brandon Duke was her employer. Her job was important to her. She couldn't afford to get dreamy-eyed and moony about the man who signed her paychecks. Especially not *that* man.

Once upon a time, Kelly had envisioned a fairy-tale romance and a happily-ever-after with Roger. He had been her handsome prince and she'd considered herself the luckiest girl in the world. But her prince had turned out to be a frog, and not very charming at all. He'd made promises he never intended to keep and had busted her dream of love and marriage flat. The breakup had not been pretty and Kelly had to admit she hadn't handled it well.

Before she met Roger, she had been upbeat and open to every possibility. She knew she was smart and reasonably attractive, knew she wanted to fall in love, get married and have children some day. But after Roger dumped her so cruelly, she'd felt broken, cynical, awkward and unsure of herself, especially around men. She had lost her confidence and she couldn't think about dating for a long time after the breakup.

Ironically, working in the office with Brandon had been the best antidote for her fears and insecurities. He'd made it clear early on that he considered her an indispensible member of his team. He relied on her intelligence and organizational skills to help him run his projects.

Her self-confidence blossomed and grew until she finally decided she was ready to start dating again. She still wanted to fall in love, get married and raise a family some day. And the only way to achieve that goal was to find the right man.

Being her organized self, she began by calling on her friends and coworkers. Then she'd compiled a list of online dating services as well as a number of local organizations she could join and activities in which she could participate in hopes of meeting eligible men.

She was convinced that she was ready to hit the dating scene—until the day she saw Roger's name on the hotel's upcoming conference list. Her throat tightened and her stomach churned. She couldn't catch her breath. The old insecurities rushed back with a vengeance. That's when she realized she would never be able to love another man until she came to terms with Roger and the damage she'd allowed him to inflict on her life.

If that meant confrontation, then so be it. The only problem with confronting Roger was that his ego was so overblown, he might get defensive and lash out at her. She wasn't sure she could endure another unpleasant war of words with him. But how else could she get around his ego? she wondered. And in that moment, Kelly had devised her life-saving plan.

If she could somehow lure Roger back, then reject him, it would help her recapture some of her old optimism and enjoyment of life. She would be free to move forward and love again. In other words, she would get her mojo back.

She also knew for a fact that Roger wouldn't be hurt by her rejection. Thank goodness, because Kelly could never hurt him on purpose, no matter how unkind he'd been to her. No, the fact was, Roger's ego was much too healthy to allow himself to be wounded by a woman. He would brush off the insult as easily as he would a speck of lint on one of his impeccably tailored suits.

As far as Kelly was concerned, Roger could make up any story he wanted to about why she'd refused him. The point was, *she* would be healed and ready to live again, to open her heart to the possibility of finding love and happiness. Right now, that was all that mattered.

The makeover would certainly help her cause. Kissing lessons couldn't hurt, either, especially from a master of the art. And that brought her back to her current predicament.

"Brandon," she said aloud, moving her fork around on her plate.

The problem was, she wasn't sure she had the experience to lure Roger in after just one kiss from Brandon, even though it had been a potent one, for sure. That's why, on the one hand, she wished she could continue learning the secrets of kissing from Brandon. On the other hand, she knew better. He was her boss! How many times did she have to remind herself? And worse than that—if anything could be worse—was that Brandon could jeopardize her plans for Roger's payback. After all, if Brandon continued to help her with her kissing, it might lead to something more. Kissing often did.

It was useless to deny that she was susceptible. All she had to do was think back to a few hours earlier when Brandon had kissed her. If he'd wanted to take things further, she would've gone right along with him. That's how good his kiss had been.

"Okay, fine, the man can kiss." She tossed her fork on the plate and stood, too antsy to eat.

Even if he kissed her again and it led to something more, she would never be so stupid as to fall for Brandon Duke.

She strode around the room, picking up her jacket and hanging it in the small closet, then sorting through her clothes for tomorrow's outfit.

Yes, she'd laughed at his ground rules earlier that day, but now that she'd kissed him, was she still willing to guarantee that she could remain resistant to his charms?

"Yes," she said firmly, and shoved the closet door shut. She wasn't a complete dummy. She knew Brandon's reputation with women, knew his habit of dating one woman for a brief period of time, then moving on to the next. It would be insane for any woman to expect Brandon Duke to reciprocate her tender feelings. So why would Kelly ever fall for him? She simply wouldn't.

Brandon wasn't the "settle down and get married" kind of guy Kelly wanted to meet and fall in love with. He didn't fit in with her life plan at all.

"And that makes him perfect for *this* plan," she said, as comprehension dawned. Since she would never fall for him, Brandon Duke was the perfect man to teach her how to kiss!

Now, if she could just convince him to continue helping her. After all, look how much she'd learned with just one try. Her eyes were now opened to the fact that Roger had been the problem all along. It was obvious now. He had never kissed her the way Brandon had kissed her. She would've remembered.

"Oh yes," she said with another sigh as she forced herself to take another bite of her dinner. She would've remembered a kiss like that.

So how could she convince her boss to let her practice her kissing with him some more? Roger would be here next week so it wasn't as if he would be forced to keep kissing her forever. It would only be for a few days. She needed to make it clear that lessons in romance and seduction would be all she needed. The more skilled she became at romance and seduction, the better her chances would be of putting Roger in his place.

Brandon could appreciate that, right?

Still, it was a dilemma. Brandon was her boss. If she was smart—and she *was*—she'd just forget about Brandon and use her own best instincts to attract Roger.

What instincts? she wondered, and grimaced. When it came to romance, she had none!

As she took another bite of chicken and rice, she realized there had to be a website somewhere with instructions she could follow. There was a website for everything else, so why not seduction?

Oh, but it would be so much better to learn from a real live expert. And Brandon was indeed an expert. She couldn't help thinking that if mere kissing had given her this much perspective into her problems with Roger, then having sex with Brandon would be absolutely revelatory.

"What?" She jumped off her chair and wrapped her arms around herself. Where had that thought come from?

"You stop thinking about that right now," she admonished herself as she grabbed her plate and glass and carried them to the sink. "You'll just embarrass yourself." *Again.*

But now that she'd thought it, she couldn't get the image out of her mind. What in the world would happen if she and Brandon ever had sex?

"Oh, no," she said, gasping. What if they had sex and she found out she really *was* bad at it? How could she face Brandon at work? She would have to quit.

But wait. What if she was really *good* at it? Would he think she'd been lying about her lack of experience? Would he assume she'd been having sex all along, with every guy in town? How could she face him at work? She would have to quit.

And oh, dear Lord. What if Brandon was no good at sex? Would she have to lie and tell him it was wonderful? He was her boss, after all. She couldn't exactly tell him he was a loser in bed. She would have to quit.

She moaned and took another sip of water.

"Okay, that's it," she said, as she tapped her fingers on the counter anxiously. "Just forget the whole thing."

This whole kissing thing was too much to think about. She had to figure out some other way to deal with Roger. She would explain to Brandon tomorrow that she'd been wrong. He would have to forgive her. And she was certain that he would. After all, before today, she'd never done anything to cause her employer the least bit of consternation. Tomorrow, after she explained to Brandon that her brief lapse into lunacy was over, everything would be fine. They'd go back to normal. She would assure Brandon that he would never have to worry about inappropriate behavior from her again.

And a year from now, she would look back and be able to laugh over this momentary ripple in her otherwise unblemished record.

The doorbell chimed and she jumped.

Checking her wristwatch, she wondered if it might be Housekeeping at the door. She'd asked them not to stop by with those yummy evening chocolates anymore. But tonight, maybe she'd take one. Anything to provide a diversion from her disconcerting thoughts. She ran to open the door and her resolutions of a moment ago flitted away.

"Brandon," she whispered.

"We need to talk."

Brandon stared at Kelly and could no longer remember why he'd thought it would be a good idea to come by her room.

After a long run around the hotel grounds after work, then another brief conference call with his brothers to finalize arrangements for their family's arrival to attend the resort's grand opening, followed by a quick taste of the chef's latest creations for the harvest festival menu, Brandon had retired to his suite to watch Dallas eviscerate Denver on TV. But he hadn't been able to concentrate on the football game, and that was a first.

He blamed it on Kelly.

The fact was, he couldn't get her out of his mind. Not in a sexual way, he hastened to tell himself, despite the vivid memory of her warm mouth and sweet tongue and an explicit picture of exactly what he'd like to do with… but he wasn't going to go there. No way. Not with Kelly. Not in this lifetime.

In the first place, she worked for him. How big a fool would he be if he jeopardized his working relationship with the best assistant he'd ever had? And even if he was willing to overlook that little fact, Kelly just wasn't his type. She wasn't sophisticated and worldly like the women he usually dated. She wasn't the kind of woman Brandon would ever think of calling on the spur of the moment for a night on the town, followed by a rousing round of sex, followed by no commitment to call again.

No, Kelly was more like the girl next door, the one who was meant to find a nice guy and get married. As far as Brandon was concerned, she might as well have worn a banner that said Hands Off. And he would be wise to heed that invisible warning.

He'd had some pretty awful role models early in his childhood, before Sally Duke adopted him. He'd seen all the ways people could hurt each other in the name of love and marriage, so he wasn't about to go that route. With that in mind, he had decided not to touch Kelly again.

But she'd looked so pensive and uncertain when he'd left the office earlier this evening. He'd never seen Kelly less than one hundred percent confident in herself and her abilities, so this change in attitude worried him.

And then there was that kiss. Which he wasn't going to think about again, damn it.

So why was he standing here at her door, holding a bottle of wine? Oh, yeah.

"We need to talk," he repeated. He'd used the same stupid line in the office much earlier today. It sounded somehow lamer now, even if it was the truth. When she stepped aside, he strolled into her mini-suite. "I hope I'm not interrupting your dinner."

"No, I'm finished," she said, and rushed to dispose of the remnants.

He held out the bottle of wine, a Duke Vineyards pinot noir. "Will you have a glass of this if I open it?"

She stared at the bottle, then up at him. "Sure. I'll find an opener."

He could tell she was nervous as she rattled around in one of the kitchen drawers. And why shouldn't she be? It wasn't every day a woman kissed her employer. And it wasn't every night that said employer showed up at her hotel room carrying a bottle of wine. He just hoped she wouldn't get the wrong idea. All he wanted to do was clear the air so their working relationship could go back to being as exceptional as it had been before the kiss. It was a simple problem and it wouldn't take him long to explain his feelings, but he had to admit that a quick glass of wine would probably help them both relax.

"Here you go," she said, and handed him a corkscrew. "Glasses?"

"Oh." She swallowed anxiously. "Right."

As he worked to remove the cork, he took a moment to study his longtime assistant—and wondered how he'd ever thought he'd be able to relax in her hotel room.

She wore cutoff shorts and a T-shirt, an outfit that a jury of his peers would consider thoroughly appropriate for spending a balmy night alone in her room. But as she reached for the wineglasses on the second shelf of the cupboard, he watched her T-shirt inch up to reveal the leanness of her stomach. On her tiptoes now, her shorts stretched just enough to show the soft, pale skin above her tan line where the curve of her bottom met her perfectly toned thighs.

"Here you go," she said, placing two glasses on the counter.

Brandon let go of the breath he hadn't realized he was

holding. "Thanks." He took his time pouring wine into the glasses and handed her one. "Kelly, I—"

"Look, Brandon—"

"Sorry. What were you going to say?"

She blinked, then said in a rush, "No, you go first."

"Fine. I just think—"

"Okay, I'll go first." She glanced briefly toward the ceiling as if she were looking for guidance from above. Brandon watched her chest move up and down as she inhaled, then exhaled. She was clearly edgy. She picked up her wineglass and took a gulp, paced a few steps back and forth across the small kitchen, then stopped and met his gaze, her face a mask of regret.

"I want to apologize for the way I behaved today," she said. "I don't know what got into me. I've been going crazy ever since I learned that Roger would be coming here and I guess I…I lost my head. I'm mortified about what happened. I just hope you'll accept my apology and trust that it'll never happen again."

She looked exhausted when she finished and he felt a twinge of sympathy for her.

"Why don't we sit down?" he said, and he led the way to the cozy sitting area of the mini-suite. They each sat at one end of the small couch, leaving barely two feet of space between them.

He should've been relieved that she'd apologized, but for some unfathomable reason, it didn't sit well with him. "So what, exactly, will never happen again?"

She opened her mouth, then closed it. Frowning, she placed her wineglass down on the end table and shifted against the plush sofa cushions until she was facing him more directly. "You know what I'm talking about."

"Tell me."

"Fine." She exhaled heavily and Brandon was once

again mesmerized by the movement of her breasts. "I backed you into a corner. I practically propositioned you." With a groan of disgust, she lifted her arms and waved them for emphasis. "I threw myself at you." She shot him a quick glance. "Figuratively speaking, of course."

"Of course," he said cautiously.

"I left you no choice but to kiss me, Brandon. It was horrible of me." She grabbed her wineglass. "Don't get me wrong, I appreciate what you did. It was wonderful, really. It was so…well, anyway, you helped me confirm a few important things I'd been confused about. But it was still wrong of me to ask it of you, and I'm sorry. I took complete advantage of you."

"Did you?" He stifled a grin. She didn't honestly think any woman had ever taken advantage of him, did she?

"Yes." She pressed two fingers against her eyelids as though she were getting a headache. "I practically begged you to kiss me."

"Well, you didn't exactly beg." Now Brandon had to smile. He was starting to enjoy this. "But go on."

"I'll understand if you can't forgive me, but I hope you will. All I can do is promise it will absolutely never happen again."

"Never?"

"Never, I swear. In fact, if you could just wipe the entire experience from your memory that would be very helpful."

"You're saying I should just forget it ever happened."

"Exactly! I would be so grateful. You know I've never been a problem employee, so if you could just take this day off the books, I promise it'll never happen again."

He rubbed his jaw, considering. "You've always been above reproach."

"I like to think so," she said, clearly relieved. "Honestly, it was just some kind of momentary aberration. We can chalk it up to vacation-induced insanity or something."

"Or something," he murmured.

Beaming, she said, "You've been really understanding. Thank you so much." She picked up her wineglass and took another sip. "I'm so glad we had this little talk. I feel so much better."

"That's what I'm here for."

She gazed at him, her smile tentative. "I was afraid you came here tonight to fire me."

The words stopped him. "I would never fire you for what happened today. I only came by to talk to you and assure you everything was fine. I knew you'd be too hard on yourself."

"Well, the fact is, I behaved inappropriately and I'm sorry for that."

"Yeah, I got it." It was exactly what he'd hoped to hear her say, but something was still bugging him. "There's one thing I'm concerned about, Kelly."

"What's that?"

"Why the hell do you want to get this Roger clown back?"

"It's something I have to do. And I will," she added with quiet intent. "But honestly, Brandon, please don't give it another thought. I shouldn't have dragged you into my personal issues in the first place."

"Kelly, stop apologizing. I'm the one who insisted that you tell me what was bothering you. If you want to know the truth, I'm glad I'm the one you confided in."

"You are? Why?"

"Because it tells me you trust me, and I appreciate that. You're very important to me."

Her eyes grew soft. "Thank you, Brandon. It means a lot to hear you say that."

"I guess I don't say it often enough." He frowned again. "But that's why it bugs me that you'd want to get this guy back. He hurt you."

"He won't ever hurt me again."

"Good to hear," Brandon said. But he didn't believe it. Kelly was too naïve to know how guys like this Roger creep operated. And Brandon was very much afraid the man knew exactly how to hurt her again. He sipped his wine and considered his next move. "So when does Roger arrive?"

"Not until Monday."

"But he'll still be here for many of the opening week events."

"Yes."

Brandon scowled. Somehow, the thought of watching Kelly coming on to the guy for a whole damn week, pissed him off all over again. To distract himself, he swirled his glass and studied the rich color of the pinot. "Would you like me to talk to him?"

"No!" She bolted straight up. "Thank you for offering, but no. You wouldn't, would you?"

"Yeah," he said matter-of-factly. "If I thought it would help, I would. But it's pretty obvious you'd rather I didn't, so I'll honor your wishes. But I'm warning you, if he makes one wrong move…"

She held up her hand to stop him. "He won't. I won't let him."

"I'm glad." He went back to staring at his wine. "But you're still planning on kissing him?"

Kelly froze. "Um…"

Brandon leaned forward and casually rested his elbows on his knees. "I don't mean to pry, Kelly, but we've got a full agenda for opening week and I'm going to need your undivided attention. So if you're planning on kissing the guy or, you know, getting involved, that could present a problem."

"Brandon, whatever I do with Roger will have no effect whatsoever on my attention to my job."

"I'm not sure I want to take that chance."

She shifted uneasily. "We're just talking about a kiss or two. No big deal."

"It's a big deal if it's done right."

"Oh." She bit her lower lip, considering. "Of course. But Roger won't…well."

He studied her. "Roger won't do it right. Is that what you were going to say?"

"Yes, but what I meant was…" Jittery now, she jumped up from the couch and folded her arms across her chest. "Everything will turn out fine."

"You think?"

She smiled through clenched teeth. "Yes. Absolutely. I know what I'm doing now."

"Oh, I see," he drawled. "Now that I've kissed you, you think you'll be able to show Roger how it's done."

Her jaw tensed up even more as she met his gaze defiantly. "Maybe."

"He won't be here for almost a week," Brandon said. "You sure you'll remember how to do it?"

"Of course," she said, then licked her lips nervously, almost bringing Brandon to his knees. Good thing he was sitting down. And now that he thought about it, why the hell was he sitting here when she was halfway across the room, looking more beautiful than anything he'd seen in a long time, if ever?

Damn, he wanted her. He didn't care if it was stupid. He knew what he wanted. And he always went after what he wanted.

Giving in to the inevitable, he pushed himself up from

the couch and moved toward her. "You weren't thinking of practicing with someone else, were you?"

Her shoulders sagged as if she'd been caught plotting to do just that. "No, of course not."

"Good." Brandon approached slowly, his gaze never leaving hers. "Because I wouldn't want to hear any rumors of unbridled kissing going on."

"You won't, I promise," she murmured as she inched backward.

"I hope not."

"Nothing unbridled, anyway," she said, biting back a smile.

"You think that's funny?" he asked, inches away now. "There's nothing funny about unbridled kissing."

"I'm sure you're right," she said, nodding slowly.

"Oh, believe me, I am." From this close, he could see a dusting of freckles across her cheeks and nose that he'd never noticed before.

"Brandon?" She chewed on her lower lip, nearly driving him crazy. "What are you…"

"Shh," he said, watching her delectable mouth. When it curved into a smile aimed directly at him, he couldn't see any possible way to resist temptation. So he did what any other man would do in his position. He kissed her.

And wondered if he'd ever feasted on anything half as sweet.

Her taste was even more incredible than he remembered and he wanted all of her. He angled his head and deepened the kiss, feeling an urgent need to touch her, to bury himself in her. Enveloping her in his arms, he breathed in her delicious scent as he planted light kisses along her neck, forcing himself to go slowly.

"Brandon, I know you didn't want—"

"Shh." He pushed aside the neckline of her T-shirt and kissed the skin of her shoulder. "I want."

"Are you sure?" she whispered.

"That's my line, sweetheart," he said with a sideways glance.

"Oh." She stared at him, her bright eyes sparkling in the soft light. "Well, I'm sure. I'm really, really sure."

"That's all I wanted to hear."

"Please," she murmured.

"That, too." He slid his hand up her side until he reached the swell of her breast. With his thumb, he did what he'd wanted to do all day, teasing her nipple through the material until he felt it stiffen.

"Please don't stop," she moaned.

"I wouldn't dream of it." He lowered his head and covered her mouth with his. The pleasure was instant, intense. How had he waited all day to do this?

She was eager and opened her mouth to welcome him into her warmth, wrapping her arms around his neck to bring them closer.

"I want my hands on you, Kelly," he muttered.

"Mmm, I want that, too."

It was all the encouragement he needed. He swept her into his arms in an effortless move and walked toward the bed.

"Oh, I like that," she said, her lips curved in a sweet smile.

"Babe, you ain't seen nothing yet."

She cuddled in his arms and rained little kisses along his neck and shoulder. When they reached the bed, he placed her gently on top of the covers, then knelt and straddled her. Reaching for the hem of her T-shirt, he lifted it up and off in one swift move. With her arms raised languidly above her head and her lustrous hair spread over the pillow, she looked like the stuff of Brandon's dreams. He had to force himself to take it slow and easy as he slid his hand under her back and unclipped her bra in one smooth move.

"You are gorgeous," he whispered reverently.

She smiled as she reached up and caressed his cheek, almost as though she couldn't quite believe he was real, either. Brandon wasn't sure he'd ever felt quite so alive as he did in this moment. He bent his head to her breasts and took first one nipple, then the other into his mouth. She gasped and arched off the bed, pushing herself into him, straining his control. Had there ever been a woman so responsive to his touch?

His hands continued to move over her breasts as his mouth carried on his sensual exploration, moving down her taut stomach, stopping here and there to kiss and taste her soft skin. When he reached her heated feminine core, she writhed in anticipation and he rushed to satisfy her and appease his own desperate need as well. He might've lost track of time, aware only of her soft moans of delight and his own heady satisfaction. Through the haze of pleasure, he heard her utter his name.

"Please, Brandon," she said. "I need you, now."

With those words, Brandon moved. He stood and quickly tore off his clothing, tossing his things on the chair nearby. Then he pulled a condom from his pocket and slipped it on. As he made his way back to her, Kelly licked her lips in expectation and Brandon's knees nearly buckled. In that moment, he wanted her more than any woman he'd ever known. The thought meant nothing, he assured himself. It was all the heat of the moment.

Joining her, stretched out beside her, he urged her onto him, gripping her lush bottom with both hands as he guided her sweet center toward his rigid length. As his mouth devoured hers, he plunged himself into her heat and filled her completely.

Their bodies moved in perfect rhythm, as though both had been created for just this moment. The passion was explosive. Brandon had never felt more powerful, more driven by one singular need: her ultimate pleasure.

Her body strained to get closer to his, so close that he could feel her heart pounding against his chest. Her lips found his and molded themselves tenderly to his mouth in a gesture so sweet, it caused a shudder to spread through his body. With a desperation he'd never known, he again thrust himself into her, then again and again. She cried out his name and trembled uncontrollably. He tightened his hold on her, pushing himself to the limit until he answered her with his own deep cry and followed her over the edge.

Four

"So that's what all the fuss is about," Kelly said finally, her soft voice full of wonder.

It had taken a while, but Brandon's head had eventually stopped spinning and his breathing had returned to normal. Now he turned onto his side and, despite being more shaken than he'd like to admit, he flashed a confident smile at her. "Yeah, that's what it's all about. Why do you sound so surprised? I know you've done this before."

"Not like that," she murmured, then quickly looked away and fiddled with the pillow beneath her head.

He reached over and placed his fingers under her chin, urging her to meet his gaze. "Are you telling me your dumb-ass ex-boyfriend never satisfied you?"

She met his gaze warily. "Roger told me I wasn't very good in bed."

Maybe his ears were still ringing from the exertion of a

few minutes ago, because he couldn't have heard her right. So he leaned in close and said, "What did you say?"

"The actual term he used was 'lousy,'" she admitted softly. "According to him, I was *lousy* in bed." She sighed. "When he broke up with me, I made the mistake of asking him why, and that's what he told me."

Brandon wondered if Kelly could see the smoke coming out of his ears because right now he was so angry, he was ready to kill that jackass Roger at the earliest opportunity. This wasn't the time to rant about that, but soon. Very soon. He went up on one elbow and peered at her intently. "He's dead wrong, sweetheart. You know that, right?"

"I do now. Back then, I wasn't so sure."

He shook his head, unwilling to think about that dumbass anymore tonight. "Well, that was then and this is now. And I'm sure."

"Really?"

Her smile was tenuous and it almost broke his heart. He touched her soft shoulder with his fingers and said, "Damn it, Kelly, can't you see how tempting you are? Forget what that fool told you. He obviously blamed you for his own inadequacies."

Brandon sat up and leaned against the headboard and pulled her into his arms. "He was wrong, do you hear me? You're amazing. You're hot. I've never..." He stopped and took a deep breath. "Let's just say my brains are still bouncing around my head from your hotness."

She smiled brightly and he was suddenly mesmerized all over again by her mouth.

"Okay," she said, nodding slowly. "I believe you."

"Good," he growled. "You should also believe me when I say that guy needs to be taught a serious lesson."

Her smile dimmed. "That's exactly what I plan to do."

She touched his chest and gazed up at him. "Would you do me a favor?"

"Another one?" he said, and chuckled when she smacked his chest lightly. He grabbed her hand before she pulled it back and held it pressed against his skin where it seemed to belong. "Of course I'll do you a favor, sweetheart. What is it?"

"I don't want to hear any words of remorse or blame or embarrassment tomorrow," she said. "Please, Brandon. This was wonderful and I'm so happy. I don't want a shadow to fall on what happened tonight."

He stared at her for a moment, then nodded. "It's a deal. No shadows."

"Thank you." Her smile was sexy as she added, "And by 'thank you,' I mean it in every possible way."

He smoothed a strand of lustrous hair off her cheek. "Now it's your turn to do me a favor. I don't want to hear any more words of thanks. No more undying gratitude from you, do you hear me?"

"But—"

"No." He pressed his finger to her lips. "I didn't do you any favors, believe me. We both made the decision to do what we did, we both had a good time, and that's all there is to it."

She nodded. "You're right. Okay, fine, no more thank yous."

"Thank you." They both laughed and he leaned in to kiss her.

"I really like the way you kiss," Kelly confessed. She moved closer and touched her lips to his and he felt himself spring to life against her.

"In case you couldn't tell, I think it's pretty clear that I really like everything about you." And he proceeded to show her just how much.

* * *

Much later that night, after the second time they'd made love—or was it the third?—Brandon pulled Kelly into his arms and fitted her warm backside against his body.

"Mmm," she said. "That's nice."

"Yeah, it is," he agreed. But part of him questioned what he was doing. Everything felt way too good. That could be a problem. Maybe he should leave now and go to his own room. It had to be after midnight. He could still get a decent night's sleep.

Kelly chose that moment to stretch her muscles, pushing herself even closer against him. On a soft moan, she said, "Oh, I feel so good."

Brandon's head reeled. Was he really thinking of leaving her now? Was he out of his mind?

Not yet. But he would be if he walked out while she was pressed up against him like this.

But if he was going to stay any longer, he knew they needed to talk. So he wrapped his arm around her waist and with his last ounce of brainpower, he murmured, "Hey, you're not falling for me, are you?"

"What?" She managed to twist and roll around until she was facing him and he was glad to see her smiling lightheartedly. "I should ask you the same question."

"Am I falling for you?" he asked, grinning.

She pressed her finger against his chest. "Well, are you?"

He chuckled. "Hey, I know the rules."

"Good," she said in mock seriousness, "because I'm a busy woman and I don't want to have to deal with you mooning all over me in the office."

Smirking, he said, "I'll try to contain myself."

She laughed softly. "I certainly hope so." Her smile

faded as she added, "But since we're talking about it, we should probably decide on a few things."

"Like what?"

"Like the fact that I really don't want the staff discussing our private affair."

"I don't want that, either," he said. "So we'll be discreet."

"Okay, good." Then she grimaced. "Oh dear, what about your family? They'll be here in a few days and I would rather they didn't find out that I'm sleeping with my boss."

Brandon touched her cheek. "I understand." And he did, because even though he had the utmost respect for her, he realized that others might consider their intimate relationship inappropriate.

"So once your family arrives," she said, "we should stop seeing each other."

"Much as I hate to admit it, that's probably a good idea," he said grudgingly, then he ran his hand down her side and stroked her thigh. "But until then…"

Her eyes lit up as she smiled and moved closer. "Mmm, yes. Until then, maybe you could show me again what all the fuss is about."

"Where did you disappear to last night?" Cameron Duke asked when Brandon answered his office phone the next morning. "I tried to call you a few times and finally gave up."

Brandon thought fast for a way to respond to his brother. "I might've been out on a run. What time did you call?"

"First call was around seven, then I tried twice more until about eight."

"Sorry, bro. I guess I plugged my phone in to recharge and forgot all about it. What did you need?"

"Mom was bugging me to call you and confirm the reservations for everything. I finally decided I'd rather talk to Kelly than you, so I gave her a call, but she didn't answer her phone either."

"Huh. Maybe she went into town for dinner."

"Without her phone? Not our Kelly."

"That's weird all right." Brandon rolled his eyes. He hated lying to his brothers but there was no way he could tell them he was sleeping with his assistant. He didn't need the grief they would give him. The fact was, he and Kelly were wrapped up in each other almost from the time they left the office until early this morning. And thinking about it now, he wished he was back in bed with her still, holding her. Inside her. Her soft, naked skin against his.

"So we'll have the use of two golf carts for the wine and vineyard tour?"

"What?" Brandon shook his head to clear his mind of the erotic images he'd conjured up. Damn. "Uh, yeah."

"You okay, bro? Sounds like you've got something else on your mind."

"Yeah, you know how it is. I've got a whole list of stuff." He scratched his jaw, wondering what the hell was going on with his brain. He'd never been distracted by a woman during business hours. Especially when things were so busy. He really needed to shape up and concentrate on the business at hand.

"I definitely know how it is," Cameron said. "I just hope you're ready for the onslaught."

Brandon dragged a hand through his hair and forced himself to swipe another picture of a gorgeous, naked Kelly from his mind. Hell, it wasn't like him to be preoccupied once he was in the office working.

Like his brothers, Brandon left nothing about the business up to chance. He'd held countless management meetings with his hotel and restaurant managers and had brought the entire staff on full-time in the past few weeks before the official opening. Every day, managers would assign different staff members to play guest while those serving meals or cleaning rooms or arranging sightseeing tours or serving wines on the patio could practice their job skills with the same professionalism they would show any true, paying guest. The management team reviewed any problems or difficulties they encountered, then they repeated the process the next day. It was the tried and true way of working out any kinks before they went "live."

The head chef and kitchen staff in the restaurant had worked out the new menu and Brandon knew the reviews would be fantastic. The Mansion on Silverado Trail would soon be the hottest new wine country destination on the map.

His brothers and their wives would arrive on Thursday for a final pre-opening meeting. Then Mom and her friends would arrive Friday morning. Was he ready?

"I'm as ready as I'll ever be," Brandon said, chuckling at the picture of his mom and her girlfriends living it up at the Mansion.

"Glad to hear it," Cameron said, then took a moment to entertain him with the latest stories about baby Jake before they finished the call. As Brandon hung up the phone, he thought about his family and how much they'd all changed over the past year. Who would've guessed how quickly Sally Duke's sons would go from being sworn bachelors to happy family men? Well, two out of three sons, anyway. Cameron and Adam had both succumbed to the charms of two beautiful women, but Brandon wasn't about to follow in their footsteps. No how, no way.

He flashed a determined grin as he vowed, once again, never to fall victim to his mother's matchmaking skills. Sally had denied up and down that she'd had anything to do with Cameron and Adam meeting and falling in love with their respective spouses, but none of the men believed her. Brandon and his brothers still didn't know how she'd managed it, but there was no doubt in their minds that their mother had had something to do with their eventual fall into matrimony.

But not Brandon. It wasn't going to happen to him. Hey, she was welcome to take her best shot. And he had no doubt she would continue to try. Now that he thought about it, he realized he would have to be extra vigilant this weekend.

It wasn't that he didn't love Sally Duke like crazy. On the contrary, he owed her his very life. From the day she'd rescued him from an imminent sentence to juvenile hall, he'd been indebted to her. Brandon had been the worst kind of bad risk, but that hadn't deterred Sally from taking a chance on him.

Sally was a young, wealthy and generous widow whose beloved husband, William, had been a foster kid, too. She'd wanted to give back to the system that had produced such a wonderful guy as William, so she'd adopted three boys all around the same age: Brandon, Adam and Cameron.

Once the three eight-year-olds had learned to trust each other, they'd sworn an oath of allegiance to themselves and Sally. They were blood brothers and nothing would ever split them apart. As part of their pact, they'd vowed never to marry or bring children into this world because they knew that married people hurt each other, and parents— except for Sally—hurt their kids.

Sally had raised them well and they'd grown up to be good, strong, smart men. Well, smart most of the time, Brandon thought. He'd warned his brothers that Sally was out to get them all married, but did they listen? No. Adam met Trish and fell in love. Months later, Cameron reunited with his old flame Julia and discovered he had a son with her, little Jake. Both couples had married recently and were ridiculously happy. Adam and Trish were expecting a little one any day now.

So Adam and Cameron had both fallen flat on the brotherly pledge, but that was okay. Brandon had already explained to them both that he understood they were weak, so he'd sworn to uphold their blood pact all on his own. They'd laughed and given him a hard time. But the fact was, Brandon had been determined long before he met his new brothers, that he would never marry and have kids. Not if it meant carrying on his own son-of-a-bitch father's legacy. And in case he forgot, he just had to recall the hundreds of brutal beatings delivered by his old man after his drug-addicted mother hit the road. He would never forget the lessons those poundings had taught him.

It's not that he begrudged his brothers any happiness. Hell, he was half in love with Trish and Julia himself. But Brandon had seen the worst kind of human behavior and he didn't want his parents' weaknesses rubbing off on any children he might've ever dreamed of having.

For that reason, he kept his relationships with women on a strictly superficial level. He never stayed in a relationship longer than a few weeks, a month or two at the most. Another thing Brandon rarely allowed himself to do was spend the entire night with a woman. He didn't believe in leading them on, giving them hope that an affair with him would be anything more than a momentary fling.

That practice had fallen by the wayside last night with Kelly. He'd planned to leave her room and sleep in his own bed, but he hadn't been able to tear himself away from her sweetness. He'd awakened several times during the night with an urgent need to be inside her. And this morning, they'd showered together and made love again.

The thought of Kelly and the way she'd looked, with her

body glistening in the soap-scented water, almost made him groan out loud.

It stunned him to think that he'd actually had sex with Kelly. She was a fascinating woman and he'd known that for years, but now he'd seen a completely different side of her. And he wanted more. She'd been so uninhibited and sweet, so unlike any other woman he'd been involved with in the past.

It was a good thing they'd reaffirmed their ground rules last night. The absolute last thing he wanted was to hurt Kelly, so he was glad they'd talked things over. It was good to see her smile as she reassured him that it wouldn't be a problem for her if they kept seeing each other. She insisted they were just having a good time and she was happy to be learning so much about the art of seduction. But, she'd said, there was no way in the world she would ever be dumb enough to fall in love with him.

His mind deep in thought, he didn't notice when Kelly walked into his office until she placed a hot cup of coffee on his desk blotter.

Looking up at her, he murmured "Hey there, stranger," and was about to grab her hand and pull her into his lap when she cut him off brusquely with a sharp look of warning.

"Good morning, Brandon." She said it loudly and followed it with an overly obvious nudge of her chin, just as their concierge manager rushed in behind her. "Serge has a matter of some urgency he'd like to discuss with you."

Serge paced in front of his desk. "Do you have a moment, Brandon? A problem has arisen with the new tour company."

"Sure." He gave Kelly a brief but meaningful nod, then turned to Serge. "What can I do for you?"

* * *

Kelly poured water into the coffeepot and stifled a yawn. It was no wonder she was tired. Besides attending to all the general preparations and last-minute emergencies that went with the grand opening of the hotel, she'd also spent the entire night making love with Brandon. That meant she had gotten almost no sleep and now her body ached in all sorts of places she never even knew she had. Not that she was complaining. No way. And she refused to feel guilty. In fact, she felt wonderful.

She still couldn't quite believe that Brandon had simply appeared at her hotel room door. She was even more incredulous over the fact that she'd spent hours after that having spectacular sex with him. It was so much more fun when you did it right, she thought.

But then this morning as she got dressed, she began to worry about how Brandon would react to seeing her in the office. Even though they'd made a pact that neither of them would feel remorseful or embarrassed, she couldn't be sure. Maybe she'd made a huge mistake by sleeping with him.

Or maybe not. After all, it was sex, nothing more. There were no emotions involved. She was just having a little affair with a man millions of other women would kill for. No pressure.

By the time she walked into the office, she'd worked herself into a state of anxiety, wondering over and over again what in the world she'd been thinking the night before. Had she lost her mind? Why had she slept with him?

But then she'd walked into Brandon's office and he'd smiled broadly and reached for her. And she knew why.

It had been wonderful and totally worth it.

She should've known Brandon would do it right. Besides

being tall, gorgeous, utterly captivating and totally sexy, he'd lived a charmed life ever since he'd been adopted by Sally Duke at the age of eight.

Sally had once given Kelly a thumbnail sketch of Brandon's life, starting with him being a high school honors student and an All-American football player in college. He was drafted into the NFL where he played quarterback for many years before becoming a sports commentator for the premier sports news station in the country. But he'd grown weary of the limelight and had joined his brothers' hotel and real estate development team a few years ago.

Sally had also confided that the man attracted women like flies. Kelly was already well aware of that. For the past four years, she'd been charged with the job of keeper of the keys to the inner sanctum. In other words, she screened every woman who called or came by to speak with Brandon. Depending on his instructions, she would either put them through or put them off.

Never in her wildest dreams did she think she would end up as one of those women. The thought didn't appeal to her as she sat down at her desk and powered up her computer.

"I'm not one of those women," she argued with herself, recalling their conversation late last night. "We've got an arrangement. This is a temporary situation only."

But now she could see why all those women had had such stars in their eyes. Brandon's touch had put a twinkle in her eye, too. The thought made her smile as she gathered the mail and began to open each envelope, sorting the enclosed documents and letters into several different piles, depending on priority. When she caught herself humming off key, she giggled. Then she froze.

"What in the world was that?"

Kelly never giggled. What was wrong with her? Was she coming down with something? She held her hand against her forehead to check her temperature, but her skin was perfectly cool and dry. She was pretty sure there was only one answer to the question. She was…happy?

Okay, happy was a good word to describe how she felt. She couldn't believe her good luck and even though Brandon had warned her not to say the words out loud, she couldn't help but be grateful. She wished she could thank him for his…what? His *assistance?* No, that made it sound like he was helping her bake a cake. Grateful for his *special friendship?* Kelly shivered. No, that sounded vaguely icky.

"For his expertise," she said aloud, and nodded at the description. "I'm in training." She smiled again. It sounded much better, more subtle, than the other choices. After all, she often went for training on new computer systems and software programs, so why not sexual expertise? It made perfect sense and besides, it was true. She really was in training to improve her sexual proficiency. She was the student and Brandon was the master.

She could only imagine the syllabus.

She giggled again. Okay, maybe she was getting a little carried away.

"Kelly, do you have the Redmond file?"

"It's right here, Brandon." She managed to refrain from calling him *Obi-Wan,* then stifled another giggle.

"What's the smile for?" Brandon asked genially.

"I'm just in a good mood," she said. "Coffee'll be ready in a few minutes."

"Thanks," he said, and strolled into his office, closing the door behind him.

She knew Brandon had a conference call starting momentarily that would last an hour or more. She planned to use that time to check on Roger's conference agenda. He and the employees of his small, high-powered hedge-fund company would arrive on Monday. They had reserved two mid-sized conference rooms each day as well as one of the small banquet rooms each evening for dinners and a special event or two. But Kelly remembered that the schedule showed that Thursday night was a free night, during which the attendees could dine at their choice of any one of Napa's world-class restaurants or go off to sample wines at any number of local wineries.

Kelly planned to lure Roger to her room Thursday night, get him all hot and bothered, then kick him out. That would teach him a thing or two. And Kelly looked forward to being the one to teach him. In fact, she was eager for the chance to show her ex-boyfriend a few of the incredible moves Brandon had showed her. She already felt more sure of herself and more sure of her sensuality and attractiveness, thanks to Brandon. Ever since yesterday morning when he got all tongue-tied while gawking at her and her new look, she'd felt her confidence soar. She really appreciated that his gawking turned out to be good in all the right ways.

The telephone rang, startling her. She grabbed the receiver quickly so the ringing wouldn't disturb Brandon's conference call. "Mr. Duke's office, Kelly Meredith speaking."

"It's Bianca Stephens," a breathless voice said. "Let me speak with Brandon immediately."

"I'm sorry, Ms. Stephens, Brandon is on a conference call and can't be disturbed."

The woman gasped. "What? Well, interrupt him. Tell him I'm waiting. I know he'll want to talk to me."

"I'm sure you're right," Kelly said, trying not to roll her eyes, "but he's on a long-distance call with several business clients and his partners. I'll have to take a message and have him get back to you."

"Kathy, do you know who I am?"

"Yes, I do, Ms. Stephens, and it's Kelly."

"Whatever," she said. "Look, just slip a note under his nose. I know he'll take my call."

"Except he gave me instructions not to interrupt him, and since he signs my paycheck, I generally do as he asks. I'm terribly sorry, but I will give him your message."

"What did you say your name was?"

"Kelly," she said distinctly. "Kelly Meredith."

"Well, Kelly," Bianca said with a tone that implied that she was talking down to a particularly stupid first grader. "I'll be sure to tell Brandon how uncooperative you have been."

"Yes, ma'am. And I'll be sure to give him your message."

"You'd better," she said imperiously. "He won't be happy to find out he missed my call."

"I'm sure that's true," Kelly said. "I—"

But the line was already dead.

Shaken, Kelly stared at the phone. "Gosh, I hope I don't forget to give him that message."

After hanging up the phone, she had to get up and walk around the office. She stretched her arms and rolled her neck around, just to get rid of some of the anger she was feeling. Of course she knew who Bianca Stephens was. She was the daughter of a former secretary of defense who hosted a national morning talk show. She was model-thin and Playmate gorgeous, and she was probably really smart, too. Damn her.

Walking into the kitchenette to pour a soda, Kelly gave herself a stern lecture. She understood that there had always been women like Bianca Stephens in Brandon's life and there always would be. They were supermodels, heiresses, actresses and designers. Some were nice and some were awful, like Bianca Stephens. It didn't matter to Brandon. He dated them because they looked good on his arm and probably in his bed, although she didn't want to dwell too closely on that possibility. The plain fact was that Kelly was disappointed by the fact that Brandon would ever want to be with anyone as rude as Bianca Stephens.

Kelly took a moment to thank her lucky stars that she wasn't so emotionally involved with Brandon that she cared one way or the other, but she had to admit it was upsetting to be treated as though she were nothing but the hired help.

That thought stopped Kelly in her tracks. She took a few deep breaths, shook her hair back, did some more shoulder rolls, then headed for her desk feeling cranky and restless.

"Not to put too fine a point on it," she muttered as she sat in her chair. "But *hired help* is exactly what you are."

Fine. Didn't mean she had to dwell on it. She grabbed her knifelike letter opener and pulled out another short stack of mail. Being the hired help wasn't the issue, she insisted to herself. It was having to deal with rude people like Bianca who looked down her nose at someone like Kelly just because she was hired to answer the phone. The fact was, Bianca thought she was better than everyone else, not just Kelly.

But that wasn't the real problem, Kelly realized as she slashed open another letter. She'd fielded these sorts of phone calls from petulant women in the past and she'd always let them roll off her back. So what was different about Bianca's call?

"You wouldn't care so much if you hadn't slept with him," she whispered aloud as she tossed several letters into a file for Brandon's review. With a frown, she ripped open a small parcel and tried to deny the words.

Was that why she was so upset? Did she suddenly care too much for Brandon? She didn't think so. She *cared* for him, of course, but she certainly didn't, well, *love* him, God forbid. There was no way she would ever let that happen. Not only had they talked about it and she'd assured him that she'd never fall for him, but also, she knew better!

But, thinking about it now, she was willing to admit to feeling a little sensitive. After all, they had spent last night doing the most intimate things a man and a woman could do together. So of course she was a bit distressed. Who wouldn't be? But she'd snap out of it, quick. Because if she didn't, she'd wind up with black and blue marks from kicking herself in the behind. No way would she ever allow herself to be that much of a twit.

The telephone rang and she jumped. "Now what?"

Hoping it wasn't Bianca calling back, she grabbed it and answered in her most officious voice.

"Hello, Kelly dear. It's Sally Duke."

"Oh, Mrs. Duke, hello," Kelly said, and relaxed. Brandon's mother was always so lovely and kind. "How are you?"

"Fine, sweetie. I'm looking forward to seeing you this weekend."

"I'm looking forward to seeing you, too." She opened one of the folders on her desk. "I've got your itinerary right here and I see you'll be arriving around two o'clock Friday afternoon. The limousine will be waiting for you at the airport. Did Brandon make dinner reservations for you?"

"I hope so. Would you mind checking for me?"

"Not at all. I don't see anything noted in the file, but I'll ask Brandon as soon as he's off his conference call. We'll make sure you're taken care of."

"I know you will and I must admit I'm excited," Sally

said. "There are hundreds of fabulous restaurants in Napa I'd love to try."

"Oh, me, too."

Sally paused, then said, "Kelly, dear, is something wrong? You don't sound like yourself."

It was not a good thing when the boss's mother could tell you were in a blue mood.

"No, I'm fine," Kelly insisted. "Or I will be. I just had to deal with something unpleasant."

"Something or someone?"

Kelly sighed, knowing she'd already said too much. "Really, it's nothing I can't handle."

"Ah," Sally said. "Some*one*."

Kelly laughed ruefully. "You're good at that."

"I raised three boys. I've learned to read nuance."

Kelly laughed again as her mind raced to change the subject. It wouldn't do to involve Mrs. Duke in her problems. "I see Brandon's taking you and your friends on a private tour of the winery on Saturday. That'll be fun."

"Oh, we'll have a ball," Sally said jovially. "Now Kelly, we're having a family dinner Saturday night at the hotel restaurant. Adam and Cameron and their wives will be there and it would be wonderful if you could join us. That is, if you're free. You always do so much for all of us. We feel like you're a member of the family."

Sudden tears sprang to her eyes and Kelly quickly brushed them away. Her own mother had died when she was twelve and she still missed her every day. Her father was very much alive, but he lived back in Vermont near her two sisters and their families. She missed them, too, but she could always pick up the phone and say hello. She couldn't do that with her mom.

"As far as I know, I'm free," she said. "And I would love to join you, Mrs. Duke. Thank you so much for asking me." She had the sudden thought that Brandon might bring a date to the dinner, but told herself it didn't matter. The invitation had come from his mother.

"Wonderful," Sally exclaimed. "Oh, by the way, how was your trip to the spa? Did they do everything they promised?"

"It was amazing," Kelly said. "Thank you so much for recommending it."

"I had a fabulous time when I was there last year," Sally said. "So when you mentioned you wanted a bit of a makeover, I thought it would be the perfect place for you."

"It was."

"I'm so glad. I can't wait to see all the fun changes in you."

They hung up from the call, and Kelly spent the rest of the morning answering emails and scheduling conference calls for future projects. She almost wished she wasn't so organized because she could've used a few more hours concentrating on something other than her thoughts. Anything would be preferable to being completely distracted by memories of Brandon and everything they'd done together the night before and early this morning. It was impossible to think straight when she remembered the way he'd touched her, the way his body had quickened inside her, the way his breath had lingered hot on her skin. She thought of the words he'd used, the pleasure he'd shown her, the urgency of their needs, and almost moaned out loud.

"Oh, God." She gulped in air and grabbed her soda to soothe her parched throat. She needed to concentrate on her job, but it wasn't working. She continued to daydream about the way he made her feel, the places he'd touched her, the words he'd whispered in her ear, the heights he'd driven her to.

She stared at the red light on the phone. Thank goodness Brandon was still on the conference call because if he were to walk out and take one look at her, he would know what she'd been thinking. And if he knew she was obsessing over their lovemaking, he would probably accuse her of falling for him. But nothing could be further from the truth. There was no way she would ever fall for Brandon Duke. She'd never been that big of a fool.

Forcing herself to concentrate on work, she got a lot done in the next hour. Still, every few minutes or so, she caught herself imagining his arms around her. The man had a gift, that was for sure.

She spent part of her lunch hour at her desk, eating a sandwich and paying some bills. Brandon left for a meeting outside of the office, so after lunch, Kelly placed all his messages—including Bianca's—on his desk and took the opportunity to go for a short walk along the brick path that skirted the vineyards. It was a beautiful fall day and the leaves on the vines were every shade of orange, red and burnt sienna. She waved to a few of the winery staff who stood a few rows away, testing the vines for ripeness.

She glanced up at the six floors of terraced balcony suites that graced the hillside, with their French doors and elegant patio furniture, then looked over at the many sophisticated, private two-bedroom *maisons* that swept across the length of the hill. She couldn't help but feel a glow of pride whenever she thought of the small but important role she'd played in the development of the luxurious Mansion at Silverado Trail.

With its ivy-covered stucco walls and Mediterranean style, the resort was a first-class mix of old-world charm and modern elegance. The restaurant had already earned a rare three stars from an international travel guide. No wonder she was so justifiably proud of the company she worked for.

In three days, the first guests would arrive, anxious to take part in the grand opening weekend that included full participation in the grape harvest and autumn festival that followed. There would be lovely dinners and wine tastings and a gala celebration Saturday night.

Kelly had worked on the opening events for months. She considered the project her baby. She had sweated out every last detail, down to the color of the ribbon for the cutting ceremony in the lobby that would take place Friday afternoon when the first guests checked in.

But since the project had started, several major changes had occurred in her life. She needed to be at the top of her game in order to focus her energies on the week ahead. First, she hadn't counted on ever having to see Roger again. Now, within days, he would be here and her plan would swing into action.

But a more important change was her involvement with Brandon. Never in her wildest dreams had she imagined she'd be caught up in a lovely affair with Brandon Duke. It was a major distraction and she knew she would require every last ounce of brainpower, discretion and good judgment in her arsenal to make it through the week working so closely with him. Not only that, but she would have to be especially careful that the hotel staff and Brandon's family never suspected a thing.

She was certain it wouldn't be a problem. They'd already decided to end their affair once Brandon's family arrived. And, then she'd have Roger to deal with.

But for the moment, she just breathed in the crisp air and looked around at the welcome signs of autumn. Growing up in Vermont, she'd always been able to recognize the telltale signs of each new season. But here in California, where the hillsides seemed a permanent shade of green and the weather was distressingly mild even in winter, the hints were much more subtle: the dappled hue of the falling leaves, a trace of mesquite in the air, the delicate play of shadows and light on the mountains at sunset.

She loved it here in Napa, but she had to admit she'd be happy to return home to Dunsmuir Bay in a few weeks. She had a charming duplex apartment with a view of the bay and a number of good friends she would be glad to see again. And of course she loved her job and her spacious office at Duke headquarters.

Once she was home, she would be long finished with the Roger Project. She planned to start dating again as soon as possible and would have no reason to ever sleep with Brandon again. Especially since she had no intention of jeopardizing her position at Duke Development, it was absolutely imperative that she go back to being the practical, professional, well-organized assistant Brandon deserved.

And that meant no more sex with Brandon, ever again.

She would use those words as a mantra because within a few days, they would become reality. *No more sex with Brandon,* she repeated and emphasized the words with a firm nod of her head as she turned and walked back to the office.

Five

The lunch meeting took longer than Brandon had expected and now he wasn't looking forward to playing catch-up. He stalked down the hall toward his suite of offices and braced himself for the onslaught of urgent messages he knew Kelly would hand him as soon as he walked in. He had half a mind to toss every last message in the trash, grab Kelly and go for a drive into the hills where they could hide out for the rest of the day.

He chuckled, figuring he was lucky he still had that half of his mind left, considering the things he and Kelly had done the night before. An erotic image of her gorgeous, naked body spread across the bed flashed in his mind and he gritted his teeth to keep from embarrassing himself in the middle of the hotel. Damn. If that wasn't enough to make him crazed, the fact that he planned to stay with her again tonight was almost enough to drive him the rest of the way to madness. But what a way to go.

Back in his office, he sorted through his message slips, crumpling one from Bianca, a woman he dated once in a while, and tossing it into the trash can. One thing he didn't need right now was another distraction.

He forced himself to concentrate on work, but stimulating thoughts of Kelly kept circling his mind whenever his vigilance slipped. He needed to keep his mind on business. And there was plenty of business to think about.

His brothers would arrive Thursday, two days from now, and things would really start cooking. No doubt, there would be several last-minute meetings, emergency conference calls, inspections and tests of various departments before the festivities began Friday. His mother and her friends would be arriving then, along with the first official guests of the Mansion.

The guest list included numerous wealthy wine lovers, a reviewer from a prestigious travel magazine, several old friends of the Duke brothers and a well-heeled state official they'd done business with. And, lest he forgot, Kelly's idiot ex-boyfriend. Roger and company wouldn't arrive until Monday, but that was still too soon as far as he was concerned.

Part of him still couldn't believe he'd succumbed to Kelly's pleas for help in luring the jerk back. Not that he minded helping her, he thought, his blood pumping faster as he once again pictured her beneath him. No, he didn't mind that at all. But if she truly had the intention of taking Roger to bed, Brandon wouldn't hesitate to obstruct her at every turn.

Hell. Brandon knew if he was smart, he would cancel his plans for Kelly tonight and call last night's passionate activities a one-time-only deal. He knew they were playing with fire and shouldn't continue sleeping with each other.

And he knew he should be the one to call it quits, right now, before they got involved any further. Kelly would understand. They'd already had that discussion.

But every time he thought about cutting her loose, he changed his mind. He couldn't bring himself to do it. He just wanted her too damn much. He also knew those feelings would subside. They always did. He made sure of it. And when that happened, Kelly and he would go back to being companionable working partners and bring the sexual side of their relationship to a civil, friendly end. No mess, no fuss.

Their affair was a strictly temporary arrangement and they were both consenting adults. Once this whole ugly Roger situation passed, Brandon and Kelly would settle down and get back to work and everything would be fine. Fine as wine. No problem.

The following evening, Brandon coaxed Kelly to come to dinner with him at a charming trattoria in downtown Napa. They dressed casually, both glad to escape from the hotel for a few hours. They spent the meal having a good time, chatting about business and family matters. Kelly told Brandon about her sisters and their families and Brandon mentioned his mother's new project to track down her deceased husband's brother.

"Sally's husband, William Duke, had a brother, Tom," Brandon explained as they shared an antipasto platter. "When their parents died, the boys were sent to an orphanage in San Francisco."

Kelly nodded as she filled her small plate with a delicious mixture of baby artichokes, roasted peppers and grilled zucchini. "Sally told me her husband was the reason she wanted to adopt you three boys."

"That's right. Bill's dream was to symbolically give

back to other kids he'd met in the system by adopting children of his own, but he passed away before he could do it."

"It was good of Sally to carry out his dream."

Brandon grinned as he sipped his wine. "I thank my lucky stars every day that she did."

"Has she had any luck finding Bill's brother?"

"Not yet. Apparently the orphanage was a pretty grim place and the boys ran away a few times. Bill told Sally that he was finally adopted, but his brother was still stuck there. Years later, when he was old enough to conduct a search, he found that the orphanage had burned to the ground and all the records were destroyed."

"Oh, that's terrible. Does Sally know if Bill's brother survived?"

"Yeah, Tom would've turned eighteen by the time the fire happened, so he'd be out on his own. But Bill tried to track him down and couldn't find him. His best hope was that Tom was adopted and his adoptive parents changed his name."

"I hope so," Kelly said. "That place sounds awful."

"Yeah. Anyway, Sally's got her work cut out for her."

Kelly reached for an olive. "Please tell her I'll be glad to help if she needs someone to do research. You know I love a challenge."

He smiled at her. "Thanks, Kelly, I appreciate that. I'll let her know."

"That was fun," Kelly said as they strolled back to her hotel room. "And the pasta was delicious. I'm so full."

"Yeah, me too," Brandon said. "I'm glad we could get away for a while. We won't have much of a chance to leave from here on out."

"I know." Kelly stared up at the cloudless night sky.

Countless stars stretched from one horizon to the other and the full moon lit the way along the terrace path.

"It's a beautiful evening," she said.

"Still warm out," Brandon remarked. "It's a perfect night for a swim."

She raised her eyebrows. "I'm not sure it's that warm."

"It is for what I have in mind," he said, grabbing hold of her hand. "Come with me."

Puzzled but willing, Kelly allowed him to change direction and he led her to the owner's *maison* where he was staying. The sleekly comfortable bungalow had been built into the hillside beyond the main building. It was large, with two bedrooms and a vaulted ceiling and a fireplace in the living room. Shuttered French doors opened on to a cozy patio.

Brandon led her through the doors to a lovely space surrounded by a wall of shrubs and flowers and weeping olive trees. A rustic flagstone patio encircled a small hot tub built for two.

Kelly glanced around, intrigued. The thick, lush vegetation grew high around the patio and assured her that they had complete privacy out here.

"It's beautiful," she said, gazing at Brandon.

"I think so." He pressed a button on the wall by the doorway and Kelly watched, smiling, as bubbles began to rise in the water.

Then Brandon reached for Kelly's jacket, slipped it off, folded it and laid it on the chaise. Kelly did the same for him, and together they made quick work of removing their clothes before stepping into the warm bubbling water.

"Oh, it's heaven," she said, and slid down until the water covered her shoulders.

Brandon followed her into the spa and sat on the step, then pulled her onto his lap, facing him.

"Yes, this is definitely heaven." Touching her cheeks with both hands, he leaned forward and kissed her. As his lips touched hers, Kelly's mind emptied of all thought and everything within her focused on this one man and his thrilling touch.

He took his time with her, working his magic, kissing her, touching her, his tongue gently stroking hers. She floated on a sea of pleasure, weightless in his arms.

He cupped her breasts in his hands and bent his head to taste one, then the other. "You're so beautiful."

"Brandon," she whispered.

"I want to make love with you."

"Yes," she said.

He stood up in the water with her in his arms and she wrapped her legs around his waist. He eased her down onto his length and she drew him in so deeply, so fully, she wondered if she would ever feel this complete again. Then he grabbed hold of her bottom and squeezed gently, causing a jolt of rapture to rush through her. She cried out her pleasure as he moved inside her, stroking her faster and harder, plunging deeper, then deeper still. She moved with him as pure sensation pulsated and radiated from her center outward, stirring every part of her body and soul.

She ran her hands over the taut, rippling muscles of his back, relishing his strength as his powerful hips thrust into her, urging her toward completion. She felt her body melt into his and with a guttural groan of release, he let himself join her, flying headlong into an abyss of pure ecstasy.

The next day, Kelly finally began to see that there were flaws in her Roger Plan. As the days had passed and the weekend loomed, her original plot to seek revenge against Roger was becoming less and less important to her. That was fine, of course; she really needed to get over Roger once and for all.

But now she couldn't quite recall the hurt and emptiness anymore. The truth was, in the last few days, whenever she searched her mind, heart and soul for traces of the sadness she'd felt since Roger broke up with her, she couldn't find any painful remnants. That was truly amazing, and she knew she had Brandon to thank for her new acceptance. He'd helped her see that Roger had been wrong; she was perfectly capable of attracting a man. She wasn't lousy in bed. On the contrary, she thought with a happy smile, she was pretty darn good in bed. And she was a good kisser, too. Brandon didn't seem to have any complaints, and he would know, wouldn't he?

But now, since Brandon was in her bed every night, he was also beginning to show up in her daydreams during office hours. If she wasn't ruthlessly diligent, she would find herself sighing like a teenager whenever he walked by her desk.

She'd managed to cover up her reaction the few times it had happened, going so far as to fake a coughing fit one time, then making a quick reference to a missing invoice another time. She needed to get a grip. Not just for Brandon, but for herself.

For goodness sake, where was that practical-minded girl who wouldn't be caught dead giggling or mooning over anyone, *especially* her boss? The last thing she wanted was for him to see her pining over him!

She would drive herself crazy if she didn't nip these feelings in the bud right now. They had ground rules, had she forgotten? She was absolutely forbidden to fall for Brandon Duke. Not only would it never work out, but she'd wind up losing the job she loved.

Any time she caught herself wondering, hoping, or

wishing that she and Brandon could be together for real, all she had to do was log on to his personal address list and count the number of women he'd so nicely dumped over the past year or two, with nothing but a lovely parting gift to remember him by. Kelly should know; she'd been the one to purchase and send out most of those lovely gifts on his behalf.

It didn't help her cause that Brandon had come to her room every night this week and stayed until morning. He would always leave well before Housekeeping came on duty, knowing it wouldn't be appropriate for the rest of the staff to know they were sleeping together. He was an amazing lover, and every night they laughed and talked and…played. And recently, during the day, he had taken to piercing her with long, intense looks that could easily drive her to sin.

What was a girl to do?

She gave herself a mental shake and told herself to get back to work. There was plenty to get done today and it was about time she concentrated on earning her paycheck.

"It is dreck!" head chef Jean Pierre exclaimed, his lips curved in revulsion.

"Are you insane? It's the finest Montepulciano produced in Tuscany in fifty years," Antonio Stellini, the wine steward, countered.

"Italian," Jean Pierre muttered in disdain. "It figures, no?"

"What's that supposed to mean, you French fruitcake?"

Jean Pierre turned on Brandon. "*Qu'est-ce que c'est* fruitcake?"

It was Thursday morning and Brandon had spent the last hour running interference between his autocratic head chef, Jean Pierre, and Antonio, the brilliant sommelier he'd recently hired. The two were in a power struggle over the choice of wine pairings for Saturday night's special tasting menu. Brandon walked out of the meeting feeling a special kinship to King Solomon for effectively negotiating a reasonable solution to an impossible problem. Of course, they'd now added three new premium wines to the elaborate menu, that would have to be reprinted immediately.

Later that afternoon, Cameron and Adam and their wives arrived. Brandon had arranged for each couple to stay in their own private *maison* complete with fireplace, private spa patio and stunning views of the valley. Trish and Julia were able to indulge in soothing massages and facials while he and his brothers held meetings with their key managers.

That night, Brandon hosted dinner for his brothers and their wives in the hotel dining room. He'd tried to convince Kelly to join them, but she'd demurred, saying she had some personal matters to attend to. He couldn't tell if she was telling the truth, but he'd finally let it go. Then, throughout the superb meal, he struggled to avoid thinking about her and the fact that he missed her.

As the main dishes were cleared away and dessert orders were taken, Adam's wife, Trish, turned to Brandon. "I wish Kelly could've joined us. You're not making her work late, are you?"

"No way," Brandon said. "I invited her, but she said she had some personal stuff to take care of."

Cameron shrugged. "Can't blame her. After all, who really wants to have dinner with their boss?"

Brandon said nothing as he made a point of keeping a vigilant watch on the wait staff.

"She looks wonderful," Julia said after finishing the last sip of her wine. "What did she do to herself?"

Baffled, Brandon shook his head. "Some kind of makeover. Not sure why. Who can figure these things out?"

Trish laughed. "Women love to get themselves made over. It's fun."

Brandon shot her a skeptical look. "If you say so. I've got to tell you, though. I love women, but I'll never understand what makes them tick."

Adam chuckled. "Whereas, we men are an open book."

"Exactly," Brandon said, jabbing the air with his finger. "No games. No subterfuge. No *makeovers*." He used air quotes to emphasize the last word.

With a laugh, Julia turned to Trish. "Kelly went to Orchids, didn't she?"

"That's right," Trish said. "It's supposed to be fabulous. Didn't Sally go there last year? I think I remember her raving about the seaweed massage one day when we were sitting around her pool."

"Wait, Mom went to a spa?" Brandon asked, incredulous.

"Yes," Trish said easily. "Just last summer, with Bea and Marjorie."

Brandon felt a chill cross his shoulders. "To the same place Kelly went to?"

"I think so. You should ask her."

Brandon watched as Adam's wife rubbed her ever-expanding stomach. He thought of the eight-month-old baby waiting inside there, all set to emerge and be spoiled silly by its aunts and uncles and one doting grandmother.

"God," Trish said, "I would love to spend an entire weekend getting pampered and rubbed and polished and primped."

"Sounds like heaven," Julia agreed with a happy sigh.

Brandon had worked in hotels and resorts long enough to recognize the allure of an elegant spa for female guests.

And hell, after having spent ten years in the NFL, he could readily admit to the restorative benefits of being pummeled by a physical therapist. He even enjoyed relaxing in a hot tub once in a while. But that had little to do with therapy, he thought, as the vivid memory of a naked Kelly in his own spa almost made him double over.

He gritted his teeth and continued to listen to his sisters-in-law wax poetic over this fabulous spa his mother had recommended to Kelly. They made it sound like some magical realm where dreams came true. His eyes narrowed. "What was the big deal about that place?"

"Oh, there's every type of wonderful massage, of course," Julia said. "You feature several of them here, along with your mud baths and yoga classes. But this place Sally found is designed for women only, and even though they offer more rigorous activities like hiking and horseback riding, they also concentrate on every aspect of a woman's body and mind. You're pampered from the minute you walk into the lobby. But that's not the best part."

Brandon exchanged glances with his brothers, who both looked clueless. "Go on."

"It offers total makeovers," Trish explained. "They do hairstyling and give makeup tips and even offer clothing advice, with suggestions for colors and shapes that will better suit one's body type and season palette."

"Season palette?" Brandon said. It was like they were speaking in a foreign language.

"Oh, and don't forget the meals," Julia added. "They serve these artfully designed portions that look beautiful on the plate but contain maybe fifty calories total."

"That's why I wouldn't last more than one weekend," Trish said, laughing.

"You and me both," Julia said.

Brandon had heard enough. Why hadn't he known that his own mother had been giving Kelly advice on this makeover nonsense? Of course, now that he was aware of the reality of the situation, he had to admit he shouldn't have been completely surprised that his mother had taken Kelly on as her latest matchmaking project.

Didn't it just figure? Sally had made no secret of the fact that she wanted all three of her sons married with children, and she'd accomplished two-thirds of her goal. Now there was just Brandon left to fall.

He knew his mother, knew how sneaky she could be, so he'd been hypervigilant for months now. But Kelly had no idea about Sally's nefarious plotting and had innocently played along with her to such an extent that she'd actually taken two weeks of vacation to the very place his mother had recommended.

Kelly had returned from her holiday a completely new woman. And, lo and behold, her return to the office had signaled the beginning of an affair that he—against his better judgment—didn't want to end.

Brandon scowled. If his mother thought Kelly could lure him to the altar with a change of hairstyle and a few wardrobe modifications, she was sadly mistaken.

And how much did Kelly really know about his mother's desire to marry him off? Frankly, he hesitated to lay any blame at Kelly's feet. This situation had Sally's fingerprints all over it. And, yes, Kelly had told him that the makeover was all about getting Roger back. But had she been telling him the truth?

"I don't like that look at all," Adam said, studying him carefully.

Brandon picked up his wineglass and swirled it thoughtfully. "Tough."

"What's going on in that bizarre head of yours?"

Cameron said. "You look like you're about ready to chew on some nails."

"I'm about ready to chew on something," he muttered.

There was a knock on her door and Kelly's stomach tingled. She couldn't help it. She'd spent a quiet evening catching up on reading and watching television, secure in the knowledge that now that his family was on the scene, Brandon would no longer be spending his nights with her. She'd accepted it and insisted to herself that the only emotion she felt was gratitude. She would be grateful for the rest of her life for the past few wonderful nights with Brandon.

But now he was here and she was bubbling with happiness. That was absurd. Okay, yes, she liked him and all, but she really needed to calm down. It wouldn't do to behave like a giddy schoolgirl every time she saw him. Besides, he probably just wanted to assure her once and for all that they would no longer be spending their nights together. She was okay with that.

She took a few quick, deep breaths and forced herself to walk calmly to the door instead of racing like the wind to greet him.

"Brandon," she said. "I didn't think I'd see you tonight."

"I need to ask you something," he said as he walked in, immediately filling the room with his masculine presence and his faint but intoxicating scent of leather and spice.

"Of course, anything," she said. "Did you enjoy your dinner?"

"What? Oh, yeah. Dinner was fantastic. Jean Pierre outdid himself."

"I'm so glad. It was nice to see Trish and Julia again. They both look so beautiful, and your brothers look so happy."

"Yeah. Nice. Beautiful. Happy."

"Is something wrong?"

He stared at her and frowned. "You're beautiful, too."

"Thank you, I think."

"No, you are," he assured her, studying her features. "You always were, but I guess I didn't realize it before. But you are beautiful, Kelly."

"Brandon, what's wrong? What happened tonight?"

"Nothing." He paced a few steps, then returned to stand directly in front of her. "Let me ask you something. Did my mother suggest that you get a makeover?"

"Your mother? Heavens, no."

"She didn't give you the idea?"

"No." It was Kelly's turn to frown. "Why?"

"Didn't you go to the same place where she went a year or so ago?"

"Well, yes, I did." She led him over to the kitchen area and grabbed her water glass. After taking a long sip, she said, "Your mother only recommended Orchids after I told her I was interested in finding a spa where I could…" She stopped and glanced up at Brandon's expression. "Brandon, what's this all about?"

He stared at her for a moment before looking away. He stalked slowly in one direction, then another, like a caged animal, then stopped and met her gaze again. "You're sure my mother didn't suggest that you needed to get a makeover?"

Kelly blinked. "My goodness, Brandon. Your mother is the sweetest woman in the world. She would never say anything like that to me."

"You're sure?"

"Of course I'm sure. She simply recommended a place after I asked her for suggestions."

His eyes continued to focus on her, then he nodded briefly. "Okay, good."

"I'm surprised you would think so poorly of your mother."

"Whoa." He held up his hand to stop her. "Believe me, I love my mother and don't think poorly of her at all. It's just that she's been known to manipulate a situation or two, and I was just concerned that she might've given you some unsolicited advice."

"Well, please don't be concerned on my account. I simply mentioned my interest in, you know, making a few changes to my hair and…well, other things, and your mother gave me the name of the spa she'd visited. I took it from there."

He seemed satisfied with her explanation. "Okay, I'm glad to hear it."

She shook her head, realizing he was in a mood and she wouldn't get much more of an explanation from him. "Would you like a glass of wine or something?"

"Yeah, something. Come here." With that, he reached out to her with both hands, pulled her against him and wrapped his arms tightly around her. He stroked her back slowly, spreading tendrils of heat up and down her spine.

She rested her cheek against his shoulder. "But we weren't going to do this anymore, remember?"

"Yeah, I thought so, too," he muttered, glancing down at her. "But I changed my mind. Just this once. That okay with you?"

"Oh, yes, more than okay," she murmured, feeling at home in his well-muscled, broad-shouldered embrace. "This is nice."

"Yeah, it is," he said. After a moment, he added, "I missed you at dinner."

"Oh, Brandon," she said, blinking rapidly so he wouldn't

notice the sudden sheen of tears in her eyes brought on by his sweet words. "I didn't want to interfere in the time spent with your family."

"You wouldn't be interfering." He touched her chin and angled her face so that he was gazing into her eyes. "My family's great, but it would've been more fun if you'd been there."

Feeling ridiculously pleased, she smiled up at him. "Well, we're together now, so let's make the best of it."

"Babe," he said with a grin as he led her toward the king-size bed. "I thought you'd never ask."

Early the following morning, both Brandon and Kelly hit the ground running. The first guests began arriving at noon, excited to be a part of the highly anticipated grand opening.

The official ceremony was performed and executed with precision, flair and happy celebration. Brandon's knowledgeable sommelier stood by to pour champagne for everyone as they checked in. Wine tasting tours were recommended, hot air balloon reservations were taken and guests were whisked away to their rooms without a snag. As Brandon watched things unfold, he felt a whole new sense of pride in his employees, each of whom was in outstanding form today. So outstanding that Brandon was beginning to feel almost redundant. Strangely enough, it was a great feeling.

What added to the good vibe was the news his reservations manager had shared with him. The resort was already completely booked for the entire season. Brandon knew the Mansion would soon be recognized as the hottest destination spot in Napa Valley. And he was confident that he'd be able to walk away in a few weeks, leaving the duties of running the small, luxurious hotel to the experienced service experts he'd hired.

It was early afternoon when his mother and her two girlfriends finally arrived. Brandon met their limousine outside in the elegant *porte cochère* and ushered them into the lobby.

"Oh, it's beautiful, Brandon," Sally said as she and her friends gazed around in awe. They were all dressed in light, casual clothing and looked ready to vacation in style.

"I love the colors," Marjorie said.

He'd known his mother's two best friends, Beatrice and Marjorie, for well over twenty years. They were like favorite aunts, and Marjorie was also one of his employees. She'd headed Duke Development's human resources department for years. Now as the women strolled around the well-designed lobby, Brandon tried to see the spacious room through their eyes and concluded, not for the first time, that he was justifiably proud of what he'd accomplished here.

Brandon had been in charge of the Mansion on Silverado Trail project from day one and every decision had been his, including the design and overall concept of the place. All the rooms featured the best of California style blended, as their sales brochure stated, "with Tuscan flourishes and Provençal sensibilities."

The guest rooms were light and warm with rounded, Old World-style fireplaces and cozy hearths, terra-cotta tile floors, elegantly rustic furnishings and bold tapestries on the pale stucco walls. At one end of the wide lobby, French doors opened on to a wide terrace where colorful umbrellas shaded teak patio furniture and plush cushions. A stunning view of the vast acres of vineyards and olive groves that spread across the valley completed the picture.

"I can't wait to take the 'vine to barrel' tour," Beatrice exclaimed. "Do we get to taste the grapes as we pick them?"

"Wouldn't you rather taste the final product?" Sally asked her.

Beatrice grinned. "That, too."

"You can do it all," Brandon said. "Let's get you and your luggage settled and then you can take your pick of afternoon activities."

"I'm definitely up for wine tasting," Sally said.

"Oh, me, too," Marjorie agreed and Beatrice nodded enthusiastically.

Brandon grinned. "Then I'll show you to your suite so you can get started."

"I want to stay here forever," Marjorie cried as she turned in a circle to take in every inch of the cleverly designed and furnished two-bedroom *maison*. "All this and champagne on ice? Brandon, it's so beautiful. I'm so proud of you, and you must be proud of yourself, too."

"I'm feeling pretty good," he admitted with a chuckle. "It's nice, isn't it?"

"Nice?" Beatrice said as she opened the glass doors that led out to their private balcony. "It's glorious."

"I'm glad you think so." After showing them the button that would automatically light up the fireplace, then pointing out the secluded walkway that led to the spa facilities, Brandon headed for the door. "I'll leave you to unpack and relax. If you need anything, including me, just dial the front desk and ask."

Sally rushed over and wrapped her arms around him in a hug. "Thank you, Brandon. This is wonderful."

"You're welcome, Mom. I just want you all to relax,

pour yourselves a glass of champagne and have a great time."

His mother laughed. "Believe me, sweetie, that's exactly what we had in mind."

Two hours later, Brandon had finished up a short meeting with his brothers and the restaurant staff. Adam was on his way back to his room to check on Trish, who'd been taking a nap, while Cameron and Julia had decided to pour themselves glasses of wine and stroll through the vineyards to enjoy the sunset.

Brandon headed back to his office, but as he crossed the lobby, he spied Marjorie and Bea in the gift shop located next to the wine bar on the opposite side of the lobby from the front desk. Marjorie clutched a box of expensive chocolates and Bea held a bottle of good red wine and they were deep in conversation with the clerk. He grinned as he imagined them discussing the best wine to drink with chocolate. Glancing around, he looked for his mother, but she wasn't in the shop. A movement caught his eye and he glanced out at the terrace where Sally stood talking animatedly with Kelly.

For a brief moment, he stopped and simply enjoyed the sight of Kelly's short skirt wafting in the soft breeze and let his mind wander to what she might be wearing underneath. Another thong, he hoped, allowing himself to imagine the feel of featherlight lace against her silky—

He snapped back to reality. That was *his mother* talking to Kelly. And knowing his mother and what she was capable of in the name of matchmaking, Brandon's mood shifted immediately into suspicion. His mother and Kelly chatting? This couldn't be a good thing, so he strolled outside to put a stop to whatever mischief Sally Duke was up to.

"Hello, Mother," he said.

Sally whipped around. "Oh! Brandon, dear, you snuck up on me."

That was exactly what he'd meant to do, but he wasn't about to say so. "What were you two talking about?"

"I was just telling Kelly how marvelous she looks," Sally said. "Don't you agree?"

"Yeah, she looks great," Brandon said warily. "So what?"

Sally gave him a perplexed look. "Are you feeling all right, sweetie?"

"He's probably wondering what I'm doing away from the office," Kelly said lightly. "Which means I'd better get going. It was lovely to see you again, Mrs. Duke."

"You, too, Kelly." Sally gave her a quick hug. "I'll see you tomorrow night, if not sooner."

"I'm looking forward to it," Kelly said, then rushed through the lobby toward their offices.

"What's tomorrow night?" Brandon asked cautiously.

"Kelly's joining us for dinner."

His eyes narrowed. "Mom, what are you doing?"

"I'm not sure what you mean," she said, straightening her shoulders and meeting his gaze head-on. "Kelly does so much for all of us, I thought it would be a nice gesture to include her. My goodness, I haven't booked my own travel in over a year, thanks to her, and she helped me track down that fabulous imported baby gym for little Jake's birthday. And that's just the tip of the iceberg. She works wonders, but all that is beside the point. Kelly is simply a delightful woman and I've come to think of her as a member of our extended family. So I invited her to dinner. Frankly, I'm surprised you didn't invite her yourself."

If she only knew, Brandon thought. "Look, Mom,

Kelly's great, but that doesn't mean I want you playing matchmaker between me and her."

"Matchmaker?" She looked truly mystified, but Brandon knew for a fact that his mother was an excellent actress when she wanted to be.

He rolled his eyes at her attempt to play dumb. "You can deny it all you want, but I know you've been trying to get all of us guys married off." He folded his arms across his chest to show her he meant business. "You might've succeeded with Adam and Cameron, but you won't with me. There's no way you'll ever get me to propose to Kelly, so you might as well give up right now."

"Propose?" She blinked. "To Kelly?" She stared at him in shock for a few more seconds, then began to laugh. And she kept laughing until she was doubled over. Finally, she thumped her chest as she tried to catch her breath. "Oh, my goodness, I haven't laughed like that in years."

"And I'm sure you were laughing *with* me."

She choked on another laugh. "Of course."

"What's so damn funny, Mom?"

"Oh, honey, come on. You? Marry Kelly? That's ridiculous."

"Oh, yeah?" he said, his tone challenging as he loomed over her.

She laughed again. "Brandon sweetie, I love you dearly, but I would never do that to Kelly!"

"To *Kelly?*" Now it was Brandon's turn to be surprised. "What about me?"

"You'll survive," she said dryly, and patted his arm. "My point is, you and Kelly would be a horrible match."

"No, we wouldn't," he said, outraged, then shook his head. Damn, she was deliberately trying to trap him. "I mean, yeah, we would. I mean…what are you talking about?"

She smiled at him patiently. "Kelly is a darling girl and I would be thrilled and honored to have her as a daughter-in-law, but it's never going to happen. You two would never work out. She's too much of a romantic at heart."

"I'm not sure I agree," he said carefully. Sally had already tricked him once so he was watching every word he said.

"Yes, darling, she is," Sally said softly. "Kelly's been hurt and her heart is still tender. But that doesn't mean she's given up on love. She's still looking for a man who will truly love her. She wants the dream, Brandon. She wants to live happily ever after."

"Most women want that, I guess," he allowed, with a philosophical shrug.

"Yes, and you've made it abundantly clear that you are completely unwilling to provide any woman with that blissful scenario."

"True," he said with a rueful grin.

"So why in the world would I want to match Kelly up with you?"

His eyes narrowed. "I don't know. Why would you?"

"Exactly, I wouldn't!" she said triumphantly, effectively ending the conversation. She grabbed him in another hug, patting his back as though he were a clever four-year-old. "Now, the girls and I are going to Tra Vigne for an early dinner, so we'll catch up with you in the morning."

He watched her scurry off, wondering how in the world she'd managed to win that conversation.

Six

The grape harvest began the next morning. Guests were invited to join in as part of the complete "vine to barrel" experience, despite the fact that the Dukes employed plenty of workers to get the job done. It was a tradition for many people who vacationed in Napa Valley to take part in the harvest ritual. There was something essential and gratifying in the physical act of picking the grapes that would some day become the wine served at one's table.

"How do you know when the grapes are ready to pick?" one of the guests asked.

Brandon turned and recognized Mrs. Kingsley, who'd been one of the first to reserve a room for the harvest. This was her and her husband's first trip to Napa. Brandon stepped forward to say something, but hesitated when Kelly spoke up.

"Different winemakers have various ways of judging the readiness of the grapes," she said, reaching for a cluster of plump grapes and severing it from the vine with her shears. She plucked a few grapes off and handed one each to Mr. and Mrs. Kingsley, then popped one into her own mouth. "You can't usually taste the flavor of the finished wine in the fruit."

The elderly woman chewed her grape. "It's very sweet."

"Yes," Kelly said. "All I can taste is the sugar. But an expert will also taste some tannin and acidity in the skin."

Mrs. Kingsley chewed another moment, then nodded slowly. "I see what you mean."

"There are all sorts of instruments and analyses used to gauge the readiness of the grapes," Kelly continued. "But I also think there's quite a lot of art mixed in with the science. And luck, as well. After all, who knows what the weather will bring from one season to the next?"

"So true, my dear," Mr. Kingsley said, patting his wife on the back.

Kelly had impressed Brandon many times in the past with both her business acumen and her social skills, and today was no different. He watched her walking from row to row, greeting guests, passing out bottles of water and offering advice on everything from how to pick the fruit—grab the large clumps of grapes rather than the individual grapes—to counseling on the dangers of sunburn under the warm October sun. For that problem, she would reach into her backpack and hand out individual tubes of suntan lotion provided by the hotel spa, as well as bright burgundy baseball caps with the Mansion's logo emblazoned on the front. One by one, as the guests got a look at the classy, fun caps, everyone wanted one, and Kelly cheerfully obliged them.

Brandon was both impressed and amused by her resourcefulness. And apparently, so was the well-known hotel reviewer from the national trade magazine, if his exuberant announcement offering vineyard photo opportunities was any indication. The man pulled a small but expensive digital camera from his pocket and began shooting photographs of willing and enthusiastic guests in various stages of grape picking.

The wine-colored baseball caps had been designed to be a part of the marketing team's grand opening promotional giveaway package, but nobody had thought about using them in the vineyards to shield guests from the bright sun. Kelly deserved a bonus for that PR coup.

He made a mental note to make sure the signature caps would always be available to any guests who wanted to work or simply wander through the vineyard fields.

"She's really something," a voice said from behind Brandon.

He turned and saw his brother Adam standing nearby, also watching Kelly. "Yeah, she is."

"Maybe we should talk about promoting her to marketing or public relations."

"No way," Brandon groused. "I'm keeping her."

Intrigued, Adam lifted one eyebrow. "Keeping her?"

Brandon waved away his previous comment. "You know what I mean. Keeping her as my assistant."

"Yeah, your assistant." Adam smirked. "Right."

"What's that supposed to mean?"

"It means I don't blame you," he said, watching Kelly with new interest. "If I had someone that special working for me, I wouldn't let her go either."

"No kidding," Brandon said, knowing Trish had been hired as Adam's temporary assistant. They'd fallen in love and had married each other last year. "But we've all accepted the fact that you're a weak man."

Adam threw back his head and laughed. "Weak, huh?" Glancing around, he spied his beautiful pregnant wife sitting under the umbrella of a patio table the crew had set up earlier for guests, drinking from her water bottle. With a satisfied nod, he turned back and gave Brandon a look fraught with meaning. "It takes a strong man to recognize his own weakness."

"Whatever that means."

"I think you know what that means," he said, turning to take another look at Kelly before glancing back at Brandon.

"Nice try, bro," Brandon said, "but you're barking up the wrong tree. It's not going to happen."

"I hope you're convincing yourself because you're not convincing me."

Brandon shrugged. "I'm only convinced that you don't know what the hell you're talking about."

With a grin, Adam whacked Brandon on the back, then walked away to check on Trish, leaving Brandon to gaze over at Kelly who was still laughing and smiling and working her magic with the guests.

He scowled again as he played Adam's words over in his mind. Great. So Adam thought Brandon was falling for Kelly, while his mother had warned him that falling for Kelly was the worst thing he could do.

What was wrong with everyone in his family?

Just because he wanted Kelly as much as he wanted to take another breath, didn't mean he'd be stupid enough to propose marriage to her. Their affair was all about sex. Not marriage. Brandon didn't *do* marriage. Not now, not ever.

He shook off the serious subject matter and accepted that it was no longer just his mother he had to worry about; it was his brothers, too. Now that they were both married, they probably couldn't stand the fact that Brandon was still footloose and having a good time. In other words, he was a bachelor, unattached, single, happy. And he intended to stay that way permanently, so they would all just have to suck it up.

Meanwhile, he couldn't take his eyes off Kelly. He noticed she was wearing that glossy, berry-flavored stuff on her lips again. She'd been wearing it last night when Brandon arrived at her door after dinner. The memory of what she'd done with those sexy lips of hers made him grit his teeth with the effort it took to keep from turning rock-hard and embarrassing himself in front of his guests.

It didn't help that she wore a flimsy, feminine knit shirt that clung to her curves, along with long, dark blue jeans that showed off her world-class bottom to perfection. She'd pulled her thick, shiny hair into a flirtatious ponytail that swung back and forth, teasing him with every move she made.

If things were different, if he and Kelly were a real couple, he wouldn't hesitate to walk right over there right now and kiss her. But they weren't a real couple, and the longer he hung around staring at her, wanting her, the dumber he felt. He had plenty of work to do in his office and if he was smart, he'd leave right now and get something done. But just then, Kelly laughed, and the sweet, lighthearted sound touched and warmed some part deep within his chest, and he knew he wasn't going anywhere.

"Thanks for all your help, Kelly," Mr. Kingsley said, tipping the brim of his baseball cap toward her. "See you at the wine tasting."

"You bet, Mr. Kingsley," Kelly said, waving to the last guest and his wife as they headed out of the vineyard and back to the hotel. They both looked so cute in their matching caps as they walked away holding hands.

Kelly hadn't realized how much she would enjoy

mingling with the hotel guests. She'd never considered herself shy, but she had to admit she'd never been quite as outgoing as she'd been today. She attributed it to the newfound confidence and self-assurance she'd gained in the past week since she and Brandon had started sleeping together. And that reminded her of something else that was different about her today. She should've been utterly exhausted and ready to take a nap, but instead, she felt energized, exhilarated. How weird was that?

"Don't question it," she advised herself. "Just enjoy the feeling for as long as it lasts."

"What did you say?" Brandon said, coming up behind her.

Kelly sucked in a breath and turned around slowly to gaze up at him. He seemed taller and broader somehow, but maybe that was because she'd worn low-heeled boots today instead of high heels. Or maybe it was because he looked so gorgeous and larger than life in his rugged denim shirt and blue jeans instead of a suit and tie. Whatever the reason, she had to stop staring like a fool and answer the simple question he'd asked her.

"I was just talking to myself," she muttered, then forced herself to smile casually. "Wasn't this a fun day? I think everyone enjoyed themselves."

"Thanks to you," he said with a teasing grin. "My brothers want to give you a bonus and promote you to head of marketing for coming up with the idea to pass out suntan lotion and baseball caps to the guests."

"Oh, that was just a spur of the moment thing," she insisted, but her smile broadened at the compliment. "When I saw the weather report and realized how warm it was going to be, I grabbed a few caps on the way out, just in case. Then when everyone seemed to want one, I ran back and got more. Same goes for the suntan lotion."

"Well, thank you for thinking ahead," he said, slinging a friendly arm around her as they walked. "It really paid off."

The praise, together with his touch, made her feel as warm and cozy as a happy cat. She had the strongest urge to wrap herself around his legs and purr contentedly, but she managed to control herself.

"I understand you're joining us for dinner," Brandon said as they left the vineyard and walked along the flower-lined brick path back to the hotel.

She glanced at him sideways. "I hope that's okay with you."

"Of course it's okay. My mother considers you a part of the family. We'll have a good time. Even though we'll have to keep our hands off each other."

"I guess we can manage that for an hour or two," she said, laughing softly. "I really like your mom."

"That makes two of us," he said, squeezing her shoulder companionably.

Purr, she thought to herself, and snuggled against him, wanting to be wrapped up in his warmth for as long as it lasted.

"A toast to the Mansion at Silverado Trail," Adam said, raising his wineglass.

The rest of the Duke family, along with Beatrice and Marjorie and Kelly, raised their glasses to meet his.

"To the Mansion," Cameron echoed.

"Long may it reign as the supreme destination among all the Duke properties," Brandon said with a grin.

Adam chuckled. "In Napa Valley anyway."

"Yeah," Cameron said. "Can't compete with Monarch Dunes."

"Or Fantasy Mountain," Adam added.

"They're all fabulous properties," Marjorie said. "You men have done an incredible job. I'm so proud of you."

"Thanks, Marjorie," Adam said. "But it's partly your fault for making sure we hire only the best people."

"Like Kelly and Trish, for instance," Cameron said, grinning as he raised his glass to both women.

"Ah, yes," Marjorie said, winking at Trish. "I'm glad you've finally recognized the true genius behind Duke Development."

"Since you were the one who hired Kelly and Trish, I would have to agree," Brandon said, his gaze sweeping over Kelly.

Kelly felt her cheeks heating and rushed to change the subject. Turning to Julia, she asked, "Did you enjoy your massage today?"

"Oh, it was heavenly." She looked across the table at Brandon. "I hope you're paying Ingrid, the masseuse, a lot of money. She's worth her weight in gold."

"That's what I like to hear," Brandon said with a firm nod.

Trish pursed her lips in thought. "A massage every day is so civilized, don't you agree."

Kelly laughed. "I really do."

"Absolutely," Beatrice chimed in.

Since there were nine of them, Brandon had reserved the small but elegant private room next to the wine cellar for their dinner. When they first arrived, he'd pulled Kelly's chair out for her and as she'd begun to sit down, he'd let his hand glide from the small of her back up to her neck. Shivers ran through her and she almost gasped from the provocative touch. He'd flashed her a very private, very wicked grin as he took his seat.

They'd all chosen to dine off the tasting menu, that meant a different wine with each course. The food was delicious and the pairings were perfect. Kelly savored each delicate bite and every sip of the outstanding wines. Everyone agreed that the kitchen staff had outdone themselves.

She found the conversations that circled the table to be fascinating and enjoyable. Sally and Marjorie teased Beatrice about some of the men she'd met through her online dating service, urging Beatrice to describe a few of her funnier moments.

Julia talked about the trials and tribulations of turning her massive family estate into an art museum and learning center for children, complete with vegetable garden and petting zoo. She regaled them with stories about the monkey that entertained the kids by riding the goat, and the new zookeeper she'd hired who wanted to give falconry lessons.

As Julia spoke, Cameron reached for her hand and tucked it into his. Kelly found herself both captivated and wistful, looking at the way he gazed at Julia. Both of Brandon's brothers were deeply in love with their wives and weren't afraid to let their feelings show. Was it too much for Kelly to hope that, some day, a man would look at her that way?

A few minutes later, as their first course dishes were cleared, she happened to glance at Brandon who was laughing at something his brother Adam had said. As if he sensed her looking his way, Brandon turned his head and his gaze locked on to hers. The heat was instant, powerful and profound. Her breath caught in her throat and her heart fluttered. Her vision fogged, then narrowed to a point where only Kelly and Brandon existed together in the room. Sounds and voices ceased to be anything more than a mild buzzing in her ears.

Seconds later, she blinked, and just as quickly, Brandon

turned away as though he hadn't experienced the same lightning bolt moment. As though nothing monumental had just occurred between the two of them. So why was her heart still beating too fast? Why had her appetite suddenly vanished?

Kelly would've sworn in that moment that Brandon had looked at her with the same level of intensity and love she'd seen in his brothers' eyes when they gazed at their wives. Had she imagined it? Was she going crazy?

She glanced around to see if anyone else had noticed her sudden discomfiture, but everyone, including Brandon, was talking and laughing, carrying on conversations, sipping their wine and reaching for bread as they'd been doing since the meal began.

She'd clearly misconstrued his look, and the realization made her feel like a lovesick idiot. It had just been wishful thinking, probably because only minutes before, she'd been mooning over the soulful way Cameron had been gazing at Julia.

She reached for her water glass and took a long sip. Then she ordered herself to breathe evenly and resolved to forget what she thought she'd just seen, brushing it off as an inane figment of her imagination.

"You didn't eat much at dinner tonight," Brandon said later that night after they'd made love. They were stretched out on her bed, facing each other, and his hand rested on her arm.

"My first course was so much more filling than I thought it would be," Kelly said, and cursed herself for lying. "But everything I tasted was wonderful. Jean Pierre has a megahit on his hands."

"I think so, too. And I received a number of compliments about you today, too."

"Me?"

"Yes, you," he said, moving closer as he began to slide his hand up and down her back in slow, sensual strokes. "The guests appreciated the way you helped out in the vineyards today. You were a regular social director out there, making sure everyone had whatever they needed and showing the guests how to harvest the grapes. Where did you learn how to do that?"

She sighed as his hand grazed her shoulder, causing little tingles of excitement to surge through her system. "Sometimes I walk through the vineyards on my lunch hour, so I've gotten to know some of the guys who work there. They showed me how to do it."

"Really?" He reached over and swept a strand of hair off her forehead. "Well, you're obviously a natural. If you ever want a job in the vineyard, you just let me know."

She smiled. "I'm sure the perks are enticing. All the wine I can drink?"

"That's right. As long as you pick the grapes and crush them, you can drink all the wine you want."

"I'm kind of a lightweight drinker," she said, "so I'm not sure all that hard work would be worth it."

"But wait, you'd get to wear that really cool hat."

She laughed. "Now you're talking my language."

"Yeah?" He tugged her closer and rolled until she was straddling him.

Her laughter faded and she splayed her hands against his firm chest. "Brandon, our ground rules have gone out the window again."

"You noticed that, too?"

"I did," she said, smiling to hide the sadness she felt. "I think we need to accept the fact that this will be our last night together."

He covered her hands with his. "Do you think so?"

"We're both getting so busy," she added lamely, "and your family's here now."

"Yeah," he said. "And we can't forget that the clown-who-shall-not-be-named will be here in a day or two."

Kelly sighed. She'd been so anxious to carry out her Roger plan, but now the thought of seeing him was simply depressing.

"Tell you what," Brandon said, tapping her chin so that she looked up and met his gaze. "Tomorrow is hours away yet, so for now, let's forget about the world outside this room."

She moaned in pleasure as he lifted her up and onto his solid length. "Oh, that feels so good."

"Now you're talking *my* language," he murmured, and proceeded to please her in every way possible.

A long while later, as Brandon held her in his arms, Kelly tried to commit to memory every sensual feeling she'd experienced tonight. This would be the last time they ever made love with each other, and she wanted to remember the heat of his skin against hers, the weight of his leg on her thigh, his manly scent, the taste and pressure of his lips when he'd kissed her so thoroughly.

She thought back to the dinner with his family earlier tonight and the lovely feeling of warmth and inclusiveness she'd felt. She remembered that moment when Brandon looked at her with all the intensity of a man in love. Oh, maybe it wasn't real, maybe she'd imagined it, maybe she was a fool. But she would never forget how, for those few sweet moments, she'd felt like a woman who was loved by Brandon Duke.

The following morning, Brandon left her room before dawn. Kelly found it impossible to drift back to sleep and eventually tossed the covers aside and sat up. Today was the day, she thought, and mustered every last ounce of resolve she had within her. It was time to accept the unhappy fact that she and Brandon had just spent their last night together.

Climbing out of bed, she made her way to the shower. Today was Sunday and Brandon would spend the day with his family. He'd rented a limousine to take them all on a champagne tour of the valley. It would be fun for everyone, but it was partly a business excursion as well, because he and his brothers had discussed going into partnership with one of the champagne vintners. Last night, he'd been sweet enough to ask Kelly to join them, but she'd demurred. Since they'd decided to bring their delicious affair to an end, it would be awkward for her to spend more than the minimum amount of time required around Brandon.

Tomorrow, Monday, was the day Roger and others from his hedge fund company would check into the Mansion. They would be here for five long days. So besides having to deal with the countless other demands of her job, Kelly would have to deal with her ex-boyfriend.

But that was exactly the way she wanted it to be. She had no intention of calling off her plan to get even with Roger. This small act of revenge was all she'd thought about and worked toward for the past few months. It would bring her much needed closure and allow her to move forward in her life with confidence and a new sense of assurance that she was a strong woman in charge of her own life. Strong enough to take those first daunting steps into the dating arena where she hoped to find a good, decent man who would cherish her as much as she would cherish him.

But because of what she hoped to accomplish with the Roger Plan, she and Brandon had agreed to put an end to their romantic evenings together. It was bad enough that they'd vowed to end things when his family arrived—only to handily break that vow in their rush to make love again. Breaking their ground rules simply couldn't happen again.

For one thing, it wasn't fair to Brandon to use him the way she had been using him. In the beginning, she'd begged him for help in the area of romance and seduction and he'd agreed. At this point, he had more than lived up to his end of the bargain.

And for another thing, it couldn't be healthy for her to keep pretending that the two of them had any sort of loving, caring relationship beyond the walls of their office. No, outside of the office, all they had between them was a few long nights of mutually satisfying sex.

Satisfying? As she blew her hair dry, Kelly couldn't help but roll her eyes. *Satisfying* was putting it mildly. What they'd had was a firestorm of passionate, hot, wild, electrifying jungle sex. Whew. She was getting hot just thinking about it. She turned off the hair dryer and patted her wrists with a damp towel. As she dried off, she thought about last night, their final evening together. It had been memorable, to say the least.

Despite losing her appetite during dinner, Kelly was glad she'd been able to bounce back after that one odd, surreal moment when she'd thought she'd seen true emotion in Brandon's eyes. She laughed at herself now, recalling that she'd definitely managed to rally when her favorite chocolate soufflé dessert was placed in front of her.

She'd honestly enjoyed herself with Brandon and his family and his mom's friends. They all shared so much love for each other. It was obvious they enjoyed laughing and teasing each other, telling jokes and sharing old family stories with anyone who was new to the group. It was lovely to hear about Sally's latest victories in tracking down her husband's family members.

As they all left the restaurant and walked back to their rooms, Kelly realized she hadn't had that much fun in years.

Brandon's two sisters-in-law, Trish and Julia, were sweet, funny and smart, and they'd generously welcomed her into their small circle. She'd felt an instant camaraderie with both of them.

And she didn't mind admitting that she was already half in love with Sally Duke. There was no one more gracious and friendly than Brandon's mother. She and her girlfriends, Bea and Marjorie, giggled like teenagers and always managed to have the best time together. Kelly had to admire the three women, who'd staunchly maintained such a strong friendship throughout their lives.

Brandon's brothers were officially her employers, but that hadn't kept them from acting like her own big brothers with their good-natured teasing and clever banter.

After she and Brandon returned to her room for the night, their lovemaking had run the gamut of emotions for both of them. By turns he'd been sweet, funny, passionate, tender, erotic and completely breathtaking. Perhaps it was due to the fact that they both knew this would be their last night together, but it seemed as if their lovemaking had reached a new level of passion and heat. The night had been wonderful and she would never forget it. What woman in her right mind wouldn't hold those memories in her heart forever?

On the other hand, what woman in her right mind would look at Brandon Duke's magnificent naked body and tell him their affair was over? Was there a woman in the world who was that strong?

So maybe she was crazy for insisting they end their

affair now. But on the off chance that Brandon showed up at her door tonight, thinking he could break their ground rules once again, she would have no choice but to turn him away. It was the best thing for both of them. This time, she would have to be firm. They had no future together, except in business. Their fleeting love affair was over.

"He won't care," she whispered. Why was she making such a big deal about it? Brandon attracted women like flies to honey. For goodness' sake, the man had his own gravitational pull! He would have some new woman in his bed in the time it took Kelly to say "Bye-bye."

As she brushed her teeth, she forced herself to recall the many women Brandon had dated and broken up with in the past. She thought of the numerous diamond bracelets she'd purchased, just so he could give his date of the month a lovely parting gift before he kissed her goodbye for the last time.

The last thing Kelly wanted was her very own diamond bracelet from Brandon. Dear God, she would die of humiliation if he tried to give her one as he held the door open for her to leave.

That settled it. There was no way she would ever allow herself to remain in a relationship that was guaranteed to end in such a pathetic, clichéd fashion.

No, her long-range plans to fall in love and get married had to be her overriding single focus from now on.

"He'll follow the rules this time," she murmured as she slipped on a pair of yoga pants and a sleeveless T-shirt. After all, Brandon had been reluctant to get involved with her from the beginning. Oh, he'd been more than reluctant; he had absolutely refused to help her. Of course, he'd obviously changed his mind and she had to admit he'd definitely warmed up to the task. *In more ways than one,* she thought, as a sudden image of his clever hands and mouth on her most intimate parts flashed through her mind.

"Oh, God." With a shake of her head, she calculated that she would only have to suffer from these erotic flashbacks for the next few decades or so. Forcing the images away, she quickly tied her sneakers, grabbed her purse and a light jacket and left the room to do her weekly shopping and errands.

Monday morning, Kelly was seated at her desk bright and early, determined to be the proficient and talented assistant Brandon had hired in the first place—and nothing more. She felt fully rested for the first time in a week and as she made a second pot of coffee, she marveled that she'd actually been able to sleep through the night. She'd worried at first that she'd become so used to sleeping curled up next to Brandon's warmth that she would no longer be able to sleep on her own. But as soon as her head hit the pillow, she'd fallen into an exhausted slumber and when she woke up this morning, she was surprised to realize she'd slept straight through the night.

It helped that Brandon had stayed out late with his brothers and a potential new partner the night before. When he called her on his way back to the hotel, just to say good-night, she'd cut the conversation short, claiming to be half asleep.

Another reason she was grateful for a good's night sleep was because today was the day that Roger would arrive. Kelly would need every ounce of her brainpower to concentrate on him. Earlier, in her room, she'd spent way too long on her hair and makeup and wardrobe choices. But she was glad she'd taken the time, glad she'd chosen the elegant blue-and-white swirly wrap dress that accentuated her narrow waist and curves, because when

Brandon walked into the office this morning and saw her, his eyes had lit up and he'd grinned wolfishly. That was exactly the reaction she'd been hoping for, and it made her feel all warm and glowing inside. Brandon's appreciative gaze had infused her with all the confidence she would need to stand up to Roger this afternoon.

The telephone rang and Kelly answered it immediately.

"Let me speak to Brandon," an imperious female voice demanded.

Kelly's lips twisted in a grimace. Bianca Stephens again. She'd grudgingly given Brandon the woman's message last week, but she had no idea if he'd returned the call.

"Just a moment, please," she murmured, and put the woman on hold. Pressing the intercom button, she announced the call to Brandon.

There was a pause, then Brandon said, "Take a message, would you please, Kelly? I don't have time to talk to her right now."

"All right." Kelly stared at the telephone, knowing the woman wouldn't take the news well. She composed herself, then muttered, "Ah well, here goes nothing," and pressed another button. "I'm sorry, Ms. Stephens, but Brandon is unable to take your call right now. May I give him a message?"

"You must be kidding."

"No, ma'am, I'm not. He's unavailable, so I'll have to take a message for him."

"Fine, I have a message for him," she said heatedly. "Tell him he needs to fire his receptionist, or whoever the hell you are, because you are simply incompetent."

Kelly gasped. "I…I beg your pardon?"

"You didn't hear me? So now you're deaf, too?"

"No, I'm not deaf, but—"

"Then put me through to Brandon now."

"I don't think so," Kelly said, and quickly disconnected the call. Shaking, she jumped up from her desk and paced back and forth, pressing her hands to her cheeks as she shook her head in numb disbelief. Had she actually hung up on someone her boss considered a friend? Yes, she had! On the other hand, she couldn't believe Brandon was actually friends with such a horrible person.

Was it too soon to take another vacation? She must be under more pressure than she'd realized if she'd actually hung up on someone.

How would she explain her actions to Brandon? She had to say something. He would hear about it eventually from the rude queen bee herself. With one last shake of her head, she slid back into her chair and tried to dream up a reasonable explanation.

Brandon breathed deeply in relief as he watched the red light on the phone disappear, signaling that the call was disconnected.

Bianca had phoned last week and he'd never returned her call, and now he'd just refused to talk to her again. He'd never been someone who avoided confrontation, and, hell, Bianca had always been good for some laughs. She'd also made herself available to him countless times and was always up for a hearty round of purely casual sex whenever they were in the same part of the country. So why hadn't he taken the call? What was his problem?

He dug his fingers through his hair, trying to figure it out. Bianca rarely made demands on his time, only calling when she was on the West Coast and wanted to get together for the aforementioned casual sex.

But unfortunately, he reasoned, right now wasn't a good time for him to see her. No, right now, it was important that Brandon make himself available for Kelly and help her get through this difficult time with that idiot Roger. So yeah, that's why he couldn't see Bianca. That was his excuse. He was being Mr. Helpful. That was just the kind of guy he was.

His intercom rang and he picked up the phone. "Yes, Kelly?"

She spoke in a rush. "I wanted to let you know that I accidentally dropped Ms. Stephens's call and she might be a bit angry with me. I know you don't have time to speak with her right now, but would you like me to get her back on the line and explain what happened?"

"Don't bother, she'll get over it," he said. "I'll call her next week."

"All right," she said, sounding relieved. "Thank you."

He hung up the phone, sat back in his chair and stared out the window. Maybe he would call Bianca next week and maybe he wouldn't. To be honest, Bianca had never been someone he'd call "fun." Her world revolved around herself, her job, her problems, her triumphs, her own importance. In other words, she talked about herself all the time. Yes, he'd always found her mildly amusing when she bitched about the people who ran her television network, the people she worked with, the people who came on her show. She was always complaining about something or other.

He didn't need that kind of aggravation right now. He had to concentrate his energy on watching—and possibly "helping"—Kelly complete her warped plan to get Roger back.

And he had to focus on keeping his hands to himself. She'd made it clear two nights ago that he wasn't allowed to break their ground rules again. He might have to revisit that decision sometime in the near future, but not while Roger was here. That didn't mean he would leave Kelly alone, though. He wasn't about to let her get hurt implementing her crazy plan.

Today was the day Roger the schmuck would be arriving. Brandon smacked his hands together in anticipation of finally meeting face to face the jerk who'd made Kelly's life so miserable.

Let the games begin.

Seven

"Perhaps you don't understand just who you're dealing with," said a cool blonde woman standing at the registration desk. An elegantly dressed man stood nearby, tapping his well-shod foot impatiently.

Kelly would know that foot tapper anywhere, even with his back to her. It was Roger, of course. Watching him now, she recalled that any small inconvenience often sent him into an emotional tailspin. The first warning sign was the foot tapping.

Gathered around the lobby were the rest of Roger's group, ten or twelve businessmen and several women, all waiting to check in.

Sharon, the front desk clerk, smiled warmly. "We're all well aware of Mr. Hempstead, and we're happy and honored to welcome him and his associates to the Mansion on Silverado Trail. We're so pleased that your company has chosen our resort for your retreat. We've arranged for

Mr. Hempstead to stay in *Sauvignon,* our most deluxe and private *maison* suite. I'm just finishing up with his paperwork and I'll take care of the rest of your people right away."

"I certainly hope so."

Sharon's smile never faded as she slid two plastic suite cards inside a sturdy cardboard case and touched the shiny brass bell on the counter. A clear chime rang out. "One of our bellmen will be here momentarily to accompany Mr. Hempstead to his suite. I can show you where it is on our map."

"Don't bother," the woman said frostily. "Just book me into the room nearest Mr. Hempstead's."

Kelly studied the woman curiously and assumed she was Roger's assistant or an associate of some kind. She was attractive in a cold-blooded sort of way. Her black pinstriped designer suit and gray silk shirt seemed overly businesslike and out of place in the casually elegant lobby, but Kelly had to admit that the look suited the woman. She didn't come across as the casual type.

The thought suddenly occurred to Kelly that this woman and Roger might be sleeping together. That could pose a problem, one Kelly hadn't even considered.

She shifted her gaze back to Roger. He was still very good-looking, naturally, but she noticed that his dark blond hair was beginning to thin on top. He looked unnaturally tan and she wondered if he'd taken to visiting a tanning salon. His brown suit was impeccable, of course, but slightly dated, at least by West Coast standards. His striped tie showed off his beloved burgundy and gold college colors. He looked exactly like what he was: the spoiled, privileged scion of a venerable East Coast family.

At that moment, Sharon glanced around with a mildly anxious expression on her face, and Kelly knew it was time to defuse the situation. But just as she started to approach Roger, Brandon entered the lobby from the opposite doorway. He walked right up to Roger as Kelly watched in fear and horror.

"Hello, Mr. Hempstead," Brandon said spiritedly, grabbing Roger's hand, shaking it with enthusiasm. "It's a pleasure to meet you. We've been looking forward to your visit for quite some time. I'm Brandon Duke. Welcome to the Mansion on Silverado Trail."

"Thanks," Roger said, clearly impressed that the former NFL quarterback and billionaire hotel mogul had singled him out. "We've heard good buzz about the place, but there must've been a mix-up because our rooms…"

"Not a mix-up," Brandon said quickly, shaking his finger for emphasis. "An upgrade."

Kelly frowned. What in the world was he up to?

The differences between the two men were blatantly clear to Kelly now, and she couldn't believe she'd ever told Brandon they were similar. Yes, they were both wealthy, Type A and driven to succeed. But she had also called Brandon arrogant. Yes, he was bossy and wanted to have things his way, but now, as she watched him converse with Roger, she could see that Brandon didn't have one iota of the haughty arrogance that her former boyfriend had.

As the men continued to talk, the cool blonde turned around and eyed Brandon from head to toe as if he were a succulent steak and she a hungry lioness.

She'd seen enough. Kelly straightened her shoulders and shook her hair back, then walked briskly toward the front desk.

"Hello, Roger," she said.

Roger looked at her with mild disinterest, then did a double take and his eyes goggled. "Kelly?"

"Yes, Roger, it's me." She circled around to the other

side of the counter. "Now, let's get you registered and off to your rooms, shall we?"

"You work here?" Roger said, unblinking.

"I certainly do," she said, and accompanied the words with what she hoped was an alluring smile. "Welcome to the Mansion on Silverado Trail. Let me see what I can do to speed up the registration process."

Just then, Michael, the other registration clerk, came rushing over. "Thanks, Kelly. I can take over now." He leaned closer and whispered, "I had to change all their restaurant reservations. They brought two extra people with no notice."

It figured that Roger would do something to botch up the works, Kelly thought, but she said nothing as she rounded the counter.

Brandon stepped up beside her and smiled genially to the crowd. "Ladies and gentlemen, Michael and Sharon will have you settled as quickly as possible. I'd like to extend my wishes for a pleasant stay, and hope you'll all enjoy the complimentary champagne basket our catering staff will be delivering to your rooms within the next half hour."

There were smiles and a chorus of thanks from several in the group, but Roger ignored all of it.

"Kelly?" He took hold of her arm and pulled her aside. "I hardly recognized you. It's been a long time. How have you been?"

"I've been wonderful, Roger. How about you?"

He ignored the question and continued to stare. "You look fantastic. What have you done with yourself?"

"Oh, nothing special," she said nonchalantly as she fluffed her hair. "I cut my hair."

"It's more than that," he said, frowning. "There's something else…"

"Oh, you know, I work out, eat right, drink great wine." She beamed a confident smile at him. "Life is good."

"Well, whatever you're doing, it's working," he said raptly, and leaned in close. "Listen, are you free tonight? We could have dinner."

"Tonight? No, I'm afraid—"

"She's busy," Brandon said abruptly, looming directly behind her. "She has to work late."

Kelly turned and stabbed him with a pointed look that clearly said *buzz off.* Then she turned back to Roger and smiled tightly. "Yes, unfortunately, I'm working tonight, but I'm free Thursday night. Are you?"

"Yes," he said immediately. "We'll have dinner."

"Wait a minute," Brandon muttered.

Kelly elbowed him in the stomach discreetly.

"Oww," he said under his breath.

She ignored him and continued to focus her energy on her ex-boyfriend. "I've got to get back to my office, Roger, but I'm sure I'll run into you around the resort between now and Thursday. I hope you all have a wonderful visit."

Roger raised one eyebrow rakishly. "Oh, I'll definitely see you around."

"So that's Roger," Brandon said as they strolled back to the office together.

Kelly stopped and planted her hands on her hips. "And what did you think you were doing, butting in like that?"

"Hey, I did you a favor."

"You said you wouldn't say anything to him."

"I was being my charming hotelier self. Extending an open hand to one of our *important* guests."

"Open fist, you mean."

He snorted. "Don't tempt me. Guy's a real snake oil salesman, isn't he?"

She shook her head as they continued walking. "He's not that bad."

"Yeah, he is," Brandon countered. "And who's the ice queen?"

"That woman with him?" Kelly frowned. "I just assumed she was his assistant, but she was awfully pushy, wasn't she?"

He glanced at her sideways. "Yeah, kind of like you."

"I'm not pushy," she said in mock outrage.

"Yeah, you are," he said as he led her into their office suite and closed and locked the door.

"Well, I guess I can be pushy once in a while, but I'm nothing like—"

Without warning, he spun her around. She let out a tiny shriek as he urged her back against the wall.

"Just look at the way you push me around," Brandon said. "The way you force me to do this…" He lowered his head and began to nibble her neck. Kelly felt the electric sensation all the way down to her toes.

It had only been two days. But oh, how she had missed him.

"And this…" Brandon used both hands to flip her short jacket off her shoulders, trapping her arms behind her and causing her breasts to be thrust forward.

"But…oh, yes."

"So damn pushy." He quickly unknotted the thin ties that held her dress together and reached for her breasts.

"Brandon," she whispered, then moaned when he swiftly maneuvered her bra out of the way and used his fingers to tease and excite her nipples. But through the thick haze of pleasure, she remembered something important and grabbed his hand. "Brandon, wait. We weren't going to do this anymore. We should stop. We should…"

"We'll stop after this, I swear," he muttered. "But I can't stop. I've got to have you now."

"Yes, please," she said, straining to remove her jacket as he bent to lick her breasts. "Hurry."

"Pushy," he murmured again as he kissed and nibbled his way back and forth between her breasts.

"Oh, shut up and kiss me," she grumbled as she reached up and whipped his jacket off.

His laugh was deep and full. "I do love a pushy woman."

Then his lips covered hers in an openmouthed kiss and his tongue swept inside to tangle with hers. Through the mindless haze of passion, Kelly's hands fumbled with his belt, finally undoing it and pulling it loose. She unbuttoned his pants, then started on his zipper, easing it down over his burgeoning erection.

In the back of her brain, she registered the words he'd said, *I do love a pushy woman,* but knew he didn't mean anything by it. It was just something he'd said in the heat of the moment. She wouldn't make more of him using the word "love" than that. Otherwise, she'd go crazy overthinking every word he'd ever said.

Seconds later, Brandon made her forget to think at all as he took first one nipple, then the other, into his mouth, sucking and licking until she thought she would die of sheer pleasure.

He yanked her dress off her shoulders and watched it fall to the floor, revealing the black thong she wore.

"Whoa."

She boldly kicked the dress away, then leaned back against the wall. "Do you like it?"

He simply stared at her for several long moments, taking in every inch of her, from her hair down to her feet. "I recall telling you it was my personal choice."

"I do recall you mentioning it."

His smile was slow and wicked. "The heels are a nice touch, too."

"Why, thank you."

"Damn, you're incredible," he whispered, skimming his hands down the outside of her thighs as he knelt in front of her.

"Brandon, what…"

"Shh, let me have you," he said, gently moving her legs apart to allow him to kiss the inside skin of her thighs, starting above her knee and moving up, up, until he reached her heated core.

"So beautiful," he murmured.

She was incapable of speech as he cupped his hands around her bottom, angled her toward him and feasted. He took his time, lavishing kisses and strokes of his clever tongue everywhere, touching her, urging her up, closer and closer to the peak of oblivion, only to ease back, teasing her, playing her until she was ready to scream.

"Brandon, please," she cried.

"Soon, love," he promised.

"Now." It had to be now or she would die from need.

He moved then, his mouth trailing kisses across her stomach, then up and over her breasts as he stood once again.

She opened her eyes and looked into his, saw the tender passion reflected there and knew in that moment that he felt the same way she did. It was more than simple need or wanting. She couldn't name it, could only feel it, deep in her bones. It flowed through her bloodstream, filling her with an age-old understanding, warming her down into her soul. He felt it, too. She knew it, saw it in his eyes. That stunning awareness filled her with joy as he kissed her lips and met her need with his own.

With no effort at all, he lifted her up and turned so that

he now leaned against the wall with her in his arms. She wrapped her legs around his waist and moaned as he eased her onto his firm erection, filling her completely.

"Yes," he uttered, kissing her, his mouth taking hold of hers in an explosion of heat and pleasure. Together they pushed each other to the limit, then slowed, unwilling to bring an end to the ecstasy. They moved together in a deliberate, unhurried rhythm, until the passion built again and he pumped into her until she couldn't catch her breath. But she didn't care, it didn't matter. He was all she wanted, all she'd been waiting for. He moved with an urgency that matched her own, bringing them back to that edge where they teetered for an instant, then drove themselves over in a climax so all-consuming, so shattering, she wondered if they would survive the fall.

"What just happened here?" Kelly asked, her voice betraying her dazed and confused state.

Brandon nudged her with his foot. "You forced me to have my way with you, remember?"

She tried to work up the energy to smack his leg, but there was no power behind it and she ended up merely grazing his skin with her fingertips.

"So much for ground rules," she said under her breath as she took in the unbelievable scene. Somehow, they'd staggered over to the office couch where they were now sprawled at either end in various stages of undress. Clothing was scattered across the floor. Kelly had grabbed the colorful shawl that was draped over the back of the couch to cover herself, but it didn't do much good. Brandon was gloriously naked. The sight reminded her of some decadent tableau painting.

"Come here," Brandon said, grabbing her ankle and tugging her closer, then pulling her up to sit on his lap.

Kelly wrapped her arms around his middle and allowed herself a moment to cuddle with him and feel cherished.

"Now what were you saying about ground rules?" he said.

"Oh, nothing."

"Well then," he said, taking her at her word as he combed his fingers lazily through her hair. "How about if we get dressed and go grab some dinner?"

But she knew what she had to do.

It was now or never. Breathing in deeply, filling her lungs with fortifying air, she let it all out slowly as she gathered her wits. Then, before she could change her mind, she blurted, "Brandon, we have to stop doing that."

He leaned his head over to meet her gaze. "Stop doing what? Eating dinner?"

"I'm serious."

"About eating?" he asked, stroking her back. "Me, too. I'm starving."

"Brandon."

She could feel his lips curve in a smile as he kissed the top of her head. Then he said, "Yes, Kelly?"

"You know what I'm talking about." She reached to take hold of his hand for strength. "We have to stop, you know, breaking the rules, having sex."

"Do we?"

"You know we do." She stared solemnly into his eyes as she squeezed his firm hand. "We talked about it before. We were supposed to stop when your family got here."

"That didn't work," he said.

"No kidding."

He chuckled and kissed her shoulder.

"Then we said we'd stop when Roger arrived," Kelly said, stretching her neck to allow his mouth to roam her skin. "And now he's here, and look at us."

"Yes, just look at us," he said, and lifted her hair to run more kisses along her neckline.

She could barely speak, but knew she had to say what was on her mind. "You've been so generous to help me with all of this. We've been together almost every night for a week and it's been wonderful. I'm having the most amazing time of my life." Her eyelashes fluttered and she looked away, not wanting him to see the confusion and pain she knew was so close to the surface. "But now we should stop before we get…"

He tipped her chin up gently to get a better look at her. "Before we get…what, Kelly?"

Before we get involved. Before you get tired of me, she thought, but didn't say aloud. Instead, she ruffled his hair lightly with her hands and said, "Before we get caught by the housekeeping staff."

Brandon knew he should be glad that she was calling him out on breaking the ground rules—again. He knew they had to finally end their affair.

So why was he so eager to change her mind?

She was right, they definitely needed to pull back—to stop. After all, he knew their affair had been temporary to begin with, and the last thing he wanted to do was jeopardize their working relationship.

But gazing at Kelly now, he also knew there was something else happening here that he wasn't ready to give up on. It was hard to explain, but she touched him on a level that he hadn't known existed before. It wasn't just the sex, although sex with Kelly was incendiary, to put it mildly. No, it was more than just sex. He *liked* her, damn it, and he wanted to be with her. When they weren't together, he missed her. The feeling wouldn't last; it never did. He knew that much. But as long as they were having a good time now, why should they call it quits and be miserable when they could keep seeing each other and be happy?

Ultimately, Brandon knew he would never be the man she needed him to be. His mother had been right about that. Kelly was the type of woman who was made for love and marriage. For family. Real family. The kind of family he knew nothing about.

Yes, it was true that Sally had saved him all those years ago, and together with Adam and Cameron, the four of them had formed a strong family bond. But until Sally came along, all Brandon had ever known of family life was misery. And that kind of memory stayed with a man. Haunted him. Reminded him that he would never be able to live up to the ideal man he saw reflected in Kelly's eyes.

But that didn't mean they couldn't enjoy each other for as long as it lasted.

"Look," he said, stroking the hair back from her face and resting his hand on her neck. "Maybe it's crazy, but I don't want to stop seeing you. I'm having a great time. And you're enjoying yourself, too, aren't you?"

She smiled and reached over to touch his cheek. "Yes, of course. You know I am."

"Then for now, that's all that matters." And to settle it, he pulled her close and met her lips with his.

Eight

Kelly poked her head inside Brandon's office the next morning. "I'm running these invoices over to the concierge desk. Do you need anything while I'm out?"

"No, thanks," Brandon mouthed and waved her off as he was still wrapped up in a phone call with the lawyers.

As she strolled along the sun-kissed terrace that led toward the lobby, Kelly thought about the night before. She and Brandon had snuck out of the hotel together and driven into St. Helena for the best cheeseburger and French fries she'd ever tasted in her life. Maybe it was the company, but she couldn't remember ever having a better time. They'd laughed and shared stories as though they were a real couple out on a real date. But it hadn't been a real date and they weren't a real couple. They were just enjoying sex and the occasional dinner out.

"But isn't that what dating is all about?" Kelly murmured aloud. "Sex and dinner?" After all, if someone were watching them, they would've thought she and Brandon were a normal young couple in love.

But they weren't in love. Far from it.

But so what? Last night, Brandon had said he was having a great time with her, so why not keep it going? Where was the harm in that?

"We're having fun," Kelly insisted to herself as she turned onto the flower-lined brick walkway that circled the main building housing the lobby, then added to her own conscience, "So back off."

"Kelly?"

"Oh." She'd been wrapped up in her thoughts, paying no attention to where she was going and suddenly, Roger stood a mere three feet in front of her. "Hello, Roger. What are you up to this morning?"

He pointed in the direction of the spa. "We've taken over the Pavilion for the day to conduct some team-building exercises."

The Pavilion was a large, open-beamed cottage used for special occasions, weddings, dinners and small conferences. Secluded, private, it was situated beyond the spa in the midst of old growth olive trees and towering oaks. It was one of Kelly's favorite secret places on the property.

"Oh, how interesting," she said politely. "I hope it's a successful exercise."

He stepped a few inches closer and took hold of her elbow in an intimate gesture. "Listen, Kelly, I've been thinking about you all night. I've really missed you. Do you think we could—"

"Roger?" a female voice called out. "Are you coming?"

Kelly turned and saw the ice queen approaching. Today she wore a severe black suit with a crisp gray blouse and five-inch, patent-leather black heels. She looked like Della the Dominatrix, minus the leather whip.

"Hello, Ariel," Roger said. He didn't sound thrilled to see her.

"We can't start without you," she said, shielding her eyes from the sunshine.

She was pretty, Kelly thought, except for two unfortunate vertical lines between her eyebrows that dug in deep when she was aggravated, which seemed to be her permanent state. The lines pulled on her eyebrows, causing them to arch almost comically, giving her the look of a demented cartoon witch.

Kelly felt instantly ashamed for thinking such bad thoughts about a woman she didn't even know. After all, if Ariel really was interested in Roger, she deserved nothing but Kelly's sympathy.

"Go ahead and get started," Roger said, dismissing her with a wave of his hand. "I'll be along shortly."

He watched her stomp away, then turned back to Kelly. "Kelly, what I'm trying to say is that I think you and I could really be—"

"There you are," Brandon said pleasantly as he strolled up from the opposite direction. "Morning, Hempstead. Hope you slept well."

Roger didn't take his eyes off Kelly as he said, "I plan to sleep even better tonight."

"Good luck with that," Brandon said, and gave him a fraternal slap on the back. "I recommend a cold beer right before bed. Works wonders. Come on, Kelly, weren't you headed over to the concierge desk?"

With that, he maneuvered himself between Kelly and Roger and extracted her arm from the other man's grip. "See you around, Hempstead."

"Are you insane?" she whispered when they were a discreet distance away.

"Did you hear what he said?" Brandon griped. "The guy's delusional. He's got it in his head that you're going to wind up in his bed tonight."

"Yes, I know. And I don't mind letting him think it will happen."

He stopped and glared at her. "Why?"

"Because it'll feel so good to tell him no," she said, her eyes narrowed with rock-solid purpose.

"No?" he repeated.

She glowered at him. "Do you honestly think I would sleep with that man?"

"No," he said slowly, as though it were just occurring to him. "But he doesn't know that."

"Right, and we'll just keep it that way, won't we?"

Brandon frowned in puzzlement, but Kelly merely smiled and said, "Let's please not talk about Roger anymore. I need to get these invoices delivered."

The following night, Brandon wondered for the hundredth time why he hadn't punched Roger in the face when he'd first met him.

Brandon's lead bartender in the wine bar had called in sick, so one of the restaurant waiters was filling in. The hotel was filled to capacity and Brandon was concerned that everything should continue running smoothly. He'd decided to oversee things in the bar until they closed at ten o'clock. If anyone wanted to continue socializing, the restaurant bar would stay open until midnight.

Naturally, Roger the Jerk had chosen this night to tie one on. It was more than clear that the man was a pompous ass who couldn't hold his liquor, but because he was the boss, there was no one around to tell him no, to call it a night and drag him off to his room. If that wasn't bad enough, the more Roger drank, the more impressed with himself he became. At this point, he must've thought he was a regular Fred Astaire, because he'd just grabbed hold of Sherry, the cocktail waitress, and spun her around. Sherry, a consummate professional, had barely managed to keep her tray of drinks from upending.

Personally, Brandon would've loved to have seen Sherry empty all those drinks onto Roger's head, but Brandon knew that wouldn't be good for business. So, with great reluctance, he stepped between them, grabbed hold of Roger's shoulders and turned him in the other direction. "You've had enough, pal."

"You again," Roger slurred. "Back off, will ya? She wants me."

"I'm sure she does," Brandon said, easing his arm around Roger and walking him in the opposite direction. "But I'm doing this for your own good. She's got a wicked right hook, along with a husband who has no sense of humor. He's a big, mean guy. You don't want to piss him off."

"But I can tell she likes me. And she's hot."

"Yeah, pal, I'm sure they all like you," Brandon muttered, leading him toward the door. "Come on, time to call it a night."

The ice queen suddenly appeared at Roger's other side and slipped her arm around his back. "I can take care of him from here."

"Hey, you," Roger exclaimed, pointing a wobbly finger at her. "I know you."

She patted his chest. "Yes, and I know you, too."

"You sure you're okay here?" Brandon asked, concerned that Roger could overpower this thin woman with one careless swipe of his arm.

"Been here, done that," she said, with a brief nod of her head. "I've got it covered."

Roger threw his arm around her shoulders and stared into her face. "How 'bout you and me go back to my room? I've got a hot tub."

"Sounds irresistible," she said, and walked away with him.

Brandon watched them stumble out the door and shook his head in disgust. The man was truly a jackass, but the woman with him seemed okay with that. Guess it took all types. And watching Roger's antics here in the bar tonight, Brandon had clearly recognized Roger's type. He'd seen it before and he didn't like it.

Roger was the type of man who thought he could do whatever he wanted, with whomever he chose, anytime at all. He could drink to excess and order people around with impunity, simply because he had wealth and power. He'd been born with it, grown up knowing it, and now he wielded it like a club.

Brandon had been around plenty of other men like that when he worked in the NFL. Big men who'd always gotten what they wanted by virtue of their size and salary.

Brandon's father had been like that, too, minus the wealth. He'd been a big hulk of a man and he'd used his strength to make others cower. It had been like a game to him, and Brandon and his mother had been his favorite objects of contempt. He'd shown it with his fists.

His father and guys like Roger had a lot in common. Brandon could just imagine what kind of damage a man like that could inflict on someone as gentle and sweet as Kelly. And it made his fists clench and his jaw tighten to know that Kelly had made a date to have dinner with Roger tomorrow night.

Brandon also knew that she'd been putting Roger off

for the last few days, that had the effect of making the guy want her more than ever. The reason Brandon knew this was because he'd been watching her every move. And when Brandon couldn't be around, he'd had others watch her and report back to him. He didn't like Roger, but more than that, he didn't trust him as far as he could kick him.

And while he'd promised Kelly not to do anything that would interfere with her dinner plans with her ex-boyfriend, Brandon had no intention of leaving her truly alone with the guy for a minute. He would remain close by, waiting, watching, making sure that nothing Roger did could ever hurt Kelly again.

The next evening was Kelly's big night. She dressed for her dinner with Roger in a seductive black dress she'd been saving for the occasion. It fit her like a soft, silky glove, with subtle ruching along the sides that accentuated her best curves. Before her makeover, she hadn't even known what ruching was. But now she knew its power, and she liked it. The sleeves of the dress were barely there and the neckline dipped into a heart-shaped curve, nicely showing off just the right amount of cleavage.

She stared at herself in the mirror as she fastened her faux diamond necklace and matching earrings, pleased by her reflection. She'd come a long way and every step had been worth it.

She had decided to join Roger in his elegant suite instead of having dinner in the hotel restaurant. That way, their discussion would be private. In other words, Brandon wouldn't be able to overhear everything and interrupt them for no good reason.

Even though Kelly had known Roger for years and felt perfectly safe with him, she'd gone ahead and checked with the kitchen, just to make sure he had actually ordered dinner. She didn't want him to think he could simply invite her to his room and try to seduce her on an empty stomach. It was a big relief to find out that Roger had, in fact, ordered a lovely dinner for the two of them.

They were to start the evening off with a nice bottle of champagne and a small platter of hors d'oeuvres, then proceed to the entrée of prime rib for two, with chocolate soufflés for dessert. Kelly approved, especially because back when they were dating, Roger had begun to show a touch of cheapness when they dined out. But tonight, he'd pulled out all the stops. Kelly figured he wanted to impress her, and that was exactly what she'd been hoping for.

Now, if she could only get him to beg her to come back to him, her plan would be a success. She would gently refuse him, of course. And if he asked why, she would tell him. He would probably protest and he might even be reduced to insulting her. He excelled at that. But she didn't care. She just wanted the satisfaction of knowing he still found her attractive and wanted her back. Then she could walk out of his life forever and straight into a rosy future.

She had gone over the plan in her mind and even though a part of her knew the whole thing was somewhat petty, she also knew it was something she needed to carry through to the end. Closure. That was her goal. That was all she wanted tonight.

And maybe it was a tiny bit selfish, but she'd been much too nervous to eat lunch earlier, so if she could just arrange to walk out on him *after* she finished that delectable chocolate soufflé, the evening would be a total success.

She never should've come for dinner. The past three hours were a wasted chunk of time she could never get back.

The good news was, the prime rib was cooked to perfection

and the chocolate soufflé was divine. The bad news was, it all sat in her stomach like a brick.

Roger had greeted her at his door looking handsome and debonair in his Armani jacket with his Brooks Brothers pinstriped shirt collar standing up jauntily. She thought the gold ascot was a bit much, but she had to confess that he'd been a perfect gentleman all evening. He'd complimented her and asked her all about life in California. They chatted about mutual friends back East and he shared confidences with her about the people who worked for him.

She was bored stiff.

They'd sipped champagne, nibbled on appetizers, then enjoyed dinner and dessert. And he hadn't made a move on her. What was wrong with him? There simply *must* be something wrong with him tonight. After all, since he'd first checked into the hotel on Monday, he'd been approaching her, seeking her out at least twice a day with an urgency she'd obviously mistaken for desire. Because tonight, there was nothing coming from him. No attraction, no interest, just politeness. A regular snooze-fest.

Maybe it was just as well. After all, she was well and truly *over* Roger. She knew that now. Finally and completely over him. And she had Brandon to thank for it.

"It was such fun catching up with you, Roger," she said, pushing back from the table and standing. "Dinner was wonderful, but I should be going now."

"Kelly, wait," he said, jumping up abruptly and grabbing hold of her hand. "Don't go. We need to talk. About us."

Taken aback, she glanced down at his hand on hers, then up at him. "We've been talking all night, Roger."

He tightened his grip and moved closer. "I know, I know, but I've been holding off saying what needed to be said. Look, Kelly, I want to apologize."

"You do?"

"Yes. God, you look great." He ran his fingers across her shoulder. She shivered, but not in a good way.

"What's this all about, Roger?"

He gritted his teeth, then frowned. He looked vaguely embarrassed. "I've been trying all night to...well, look, I know I said some things I shouldn't have said back when we were together. I was wrong. I was...stupid. But seeing you this week and remembering what we had together, I miss that. I miss you. I want another chance with you. Come back to me, Kelly."

Kelly just stared at him. Now that he was finally saying everything she'd hoped he would say, she didn't believe a single word of it. "I...Roger, I don't know what to say."

"Say yes. Pack your bags and come home with me."

"Roger, I..."

"Wait, don't say a word yet. Just...feel." He made his move, bending his head to kiss her. Actually, it was more of a smashing of his lips against hers.

Maybe it was wrong, but she let him do it. Then he kissed her again with slightly more finesse and Kelly tried really hard to work up some sort of yearning, something, anything. But there was nothing. And she realized it had always been that way. She'd never felt the slightest attraction to Roger. But she'd always thought it was her problem, not his.

Where were the lightning flashes? Where were the fireworks? The rainbows? Sunbursts? She always felt them when Brandon kissed her.

Roger pulled her close and kissed her neck. "Oh, Kelly, we were so good together."

She frowned at that. "We were?"

"You remember." He breathed in her ear. "Don't you feel it all over again when we touch?"

She leaned away to avoid his heavy breath. "I really don't. I'm sorry, Roger. I don't feel anything."

He grabbed her close again. "Yes, you do. I can tell."

"Roger, please don't."

"Now you're just being difficult," he said, trying to angle his head to kiss her again as she tried to push away from him. "Fine, I suppose I deserve some of this after saying the things I said to you five years ago. But you've had your fun. Just admit that you want to come back, and we'll put the past behind us."

With that, he pressed his mouth against hers again and her stomach roiled in protest. She smacked his arm hard enough that he broke off the kiss, giving her a chance to back away from him.

"Don't touch me again," she said when he started walking toward her. "I told you I don't feel the same way about you anymore. I'm leaving now."

He continued to approach her stealthily. "Come on now, Kelly. You're not going to leave after I've spent over three hundred dollars on dinner, are you? You're just nervous because you still don't know how to make love to a man. But don't worry. This time, I'll teach you."

She held up her hand to stop him. "Oh no, you won't. You're the one who doesn't know what you're doing. I know what a really good kiss feels like, Roger. And I just don't feel it from you."

As she stopped to snatch her clutch off the sideboard, Roger grabbed her again. Just then there was a sudden pounding on the door.

Kelly jumped. "What in the world?"

Roger swore loudly. "What is wrong with this damn place?"

"There's nothing wrong with this place!" Kelly said, more insulted by his affront to the hotel than by his disgusting kisses. "There must be something wrong. An emergency."

Someone shouted, "Open up, Hempstead!"

Her eyes widened in shock and she ran to open the door. "Brandon?"

"Duke?" Roger said, scowling at him. "What the hell do you want?"

Brandon walked in and pulled Kelly into his arms. "Are you all right, sweetheart?"

"Take your hands off her, Duke," Roger said in a threatening tone.

"I don't think so," Brandon said, holding her closer.

She took a brief moment to absorb his presence, his scent, his warmth. Then she eased back and gazed up at him. "Brandon, what are you doing here?"

He held Kelly at arm's length and looked her in the eyes. "I know you wanted to get him back, babe. But trust me, he's not the man for you."

Kelly stared at him in bewilderment. "Don't you think I know that?"

"Wait," Roger said. "You want to get me back? Then why aren't you—"

"No," she said immediately, turning to face him. "I didn't want to *get you back*. I wanted to *get back at you*. Big difference."

"I'll say," Brandon said, as his gaze flipped back and forth from Kelly to Roger.

Roger shook his head. "I'm confused."

"Let's get out of here, Kelly," Brandon said, slipping his arm through hers.

"Wait a minute," Roger demanded. "You're leaving with him?"

"Yes, I am."

He snorted. "You think this guy wants you? You really are a fool."

"That's enough, Hempstead," Brandon said quietly.

"Oh, wait. I get it." Roger's laugh was scornful. "You think you're in love with him, don't you? What a load of crap. He just wants you for sex, Kelly. Though God knows why. I'm sure you're still just as lousy in bed as you ever were."

She cringed, but ignored him and kept walking. But Brandon wasn't about to let that go. He turned and said with deceptive calm, "Don't make me hurt you, Hempstead."

But Roger persisted, his eyes wild and desperate. "You can't seriously believe he actually wants you, Kelly. He dates the most beautiful women in the world. Do you really think you can compete with that? You're nothing to him."

She gripped Brandon's arm and forced him to keep walking.

"I mean it, Kelly," Roger said loudly. "You know you'd be better off with me."

At that, Kelly whirled around and shook her finger at him. "No, I wouldn't. I don't mean to be unkind, but you just don't do it for me, Roger. I feel nothing when you kiss me. No spark. No excitement. Nothing. And you know what? It's not my fault. You just don't know how to kiss a woman."

"Fine! Who needs you? Just go," he shouted. As soon as they were out the door, he slammed it behind them.

The night air was crisp and cool as they walked along the wide brick path in silence.

"Well, that was unpleasant," she said finally.

Brandon stopped and studied her in the moonlight. "Are you okay? Did he hurt you?"

"His words were hurtful, but they're nothing I haven't heard before."

He wrapped his arm around her shoulder and pulled her closer. "You managed to get in a few digs."

She nodded. "But it wasn't as satisfying as I thought it would be."

"I'm sorry, sweetheart," Brandon said, as he leaned in close and touched his forehead to hers. "But he's not worth losing sleep over. Especially since he was totally wrong about everything."

"What do you mean?"

"You're fantastic in bed."

She laughed. "You're right."

As they continued walking, she slipped her arm around his waist. "Well, dinner was great anyway. Jean Pierre came through with flying colors."

He chuckled. "Glad to hear it."

After a few more moments, Kelly said, "Roger was right about one thing."

Brandon frowned at her. "No, he wasn't."

"Yes, he was," she said solemnly, and looked up at him. "You only want me for sex."

"You say that like it's a bad thing."

She laughed lightly.

"Come on," he said, squeezing her closer. "Let's go home."

Brandon knew he should've put her to bed and then left her alone. She'd been through a lot with Roger and he could still see remnants of the pain the guy had caused her. But the last thing he wanted to do was leave her with the slightest worry in her mind that anything that schmuck had said was correct.

Tonight, he simply wanted her to feel cherished. Instead of her room, he led her over to his spacious master suite. Once they were inside and the door was closed and locked, he lifted her into his arms and carried her into the bedroom, then eased her down until she was standing beside the bed.

"You look beautiful tonight," he said.

"Thank you," she whispered, gazing up at him.

"Sexy dress." He reached behind her back, found the zipper and maneuvered it down slowly. "But your skin is even sexier."

He slipped her sleeves off and inched the dress down her body, first revealing her luscious full breasts.

"Beautiful." He bent and took first one nipple, then the other into his mouth, licking, nibbling, sucking until she was moaning with delight and Brandon felt her fingers thread through his hair, holding him in place.

Minutes later, he continued removing her dress, baring her skin inch by soft, gorgeous inch until it dropped to the floor. He held her hand as she stepped out of the dress, leaving her wearing a tiny scrap of red lace and her black heels.

"I can never get enough of you in this wardrobe combination," he said, moving his hands over her skin, then dipping his finger between the elastic band of her panties.

"Brandon…"

"I want to feel you surrender."

She hummed with pleasure. "Yes, please."

In one swift move, he tugged the lace free. Then he touched her heat and felt her body arch into his.

Unable to resist, he took two seconds to rip his own shirt off so he could feel her skin against his, then returned his full attention to her hot, wet core.

As he listened to her sighs and whispers of encouragement, he felt his own body harden and burn with the anticipation of filling her completely. He moved to cover her mouth with his, parting her lips with his tongue and sliding inside to taste her essence.

As her breathy groans grew more frantic, his own body tightened with unbearable need. Then she screamed and collapsed against him. He quickly gathered her in his arms and placed her onto the bed. He stripped completely and joined her, wondering if he might expire from the agony of need that had built up inside him.

Blood roared in his ears and he felt himself tremble as he angled his hips and filled her to the hilt. She gasped and lifted herself to allow him to fill her even more, then wrapped her legs around him. They moved in harmony, as though they'd been lovers for years and not just a couple of weeks. He lost himself inside her, lost control, lost sense of everything except the exquisite joining of their bodies as their heartbeats thundered in unison.

He opened his eyes and looked directly into hers and saw the raw desire reflected back at him. As he plunged and thrust to meet her need with his own, he watched as her mouth rounded and she whispered sweet moans of pleasure. The craving for her was so strong, he couldn't resist the pull and he kissed her, swallowing her cries of joy as he followed her to the peak and emptied himself inside her.

Nine

Roger and his group checked out the next day, and Kelly couldn't have been happier or more relieved to see the last of him. As she strolled back to the office along the pretty, flower-lined path, she thought about the night before. Brandon had been right; Roger really was a jackass and seeing him again made her wonder what she'd ever seen in him in the first place. But that didn't matter anymore.

The only thing that mattered was that before he started insulting her last night, Roger had made it clear that he wanted her back in his life. And Kelly had turned him down flat. Everything had gone according to plan. She had to admit it had been painful to see his true colors, but she finally had closure and that felt really good.

But now she had a much bigger problem to deal with. Brandon. She knew she had to be strong and end things with him, for good. They couldn't continue sleeping together, because even though she'd been teasing him the night before, what she'd said was true. He really did only want her for sex!

Well, of course he also wanted to keep her as his office assistant. He'd told her over and over that she was indispensible to their business. That was nice to hear, and she certainly didn't want to lose that part of her life.

But as far as playing the role of his girlfriend? She couldn't do it anymore.

Facts were facts. Brandon never stayed with one woman longer than a month or so, and he'd already spent almost two weeks with Kelly. Two wonderful weeks. She'd much rather have the happy memories contained in those two weeks than suffer through a painful breakup and be left with nothing but sad memories. And no job.

But above and beyond all of those worries, there was one more thorny issue that Kelly hadn't been willing to face until now.

She was in love with Brandon Duke.

"Oh God," she whispered, and sucked in a breath. How foolish could she get?

She'd finally realized it last night when Brandon came rushing into Roger's room to defend her. He'd been her shining knight, willing to break down doors to protect her, and she'd just about melted at the sight of him. That's when it had dawned on her that she'd lost her heart.

So that was it. She was a fool. She'd broken all the rules and fallen in love.

She would never be able to tell Brandon the truth because she knew it would make him uncomfortable. And if he was uncomfortable, it meant that ultimately, she would have to leave her job and then she would never see him again. So she had already decided to say nothing, to brave it out. She would break up with him, and then get back to doing the job he was paying her to do.

It would have to be strictly business between them from now on. And somehow, some way, she would eventually figure out how to get Brandon Duke out of her heart.

Kelly turned on to the highway and headed south.

Instead of facing Brandon with the truth, Kelly had returned to the office, taken one look at her handsome boss and completely chickened out. She'd claimed exhaustion and begged to take the rest of Friday and all day Monday off. Brandon was gracious enough to give her the time, surmising that she had to be wiped out from her unpleasant run-in with Roger.

She hated lying to Brandon, but she wasn't ready to face the truth and do what she had to do. Now she would use the long weekend to gather her thoughts and figure out the best way to deal with her new reality.

She'd packed a small bag and chosen to drive down the coast and home, to Dunsmuir Bay. Less than four hours later, she pulled her car into the driveway of her marina duplex apartment and turned off the engine. Climbing out of the car, she stretched her limbs and breathed deeply, filling her senses with the pungent scent of cool, salty ocean air. It was good to be home.

She spent what was left of the afternoon dusting the living room and bedroom. Then she poured herself a glass of wine and sat on her terrace, trying to think of nothing at all as she stared at the dark blue water and the movement of boats in the marina.

The next morning, she woke up early and went for a long walk along the waterfront. On her way back, she detoured through the charming block-long section of shops and restaurants known as Old Town Dunsmuir. The intoxicating scent of baked goods lured her into CUPCAKE, Julia Duke's bakery.

She was cheered by the bright blue and white décor and attractive bistro-style tables and chairs that lined the wide, bay windows on either side of the door. She stepped up to the counter and began to drool over the view of so many delicate pastries stacked neatly inside the case.

"Kelly?" someone said.

She glanced over at a small table at the opposite end of the room and saw Julia, Trish and Sally Duke sitting together, enjoying lattes and freshly baked scones.

"Come join us," Sally said.

"Oh, I don't want to intrude on your breakfast."

"You're kidding, right?" Julia teased, and pulled a chair over from a nearby table. "Come sit down. What are you doing here?"

She sat down and smiled gratefully. "I decided to take a few days off and drive down to open up my apartment. We'll be moving back to headquarters in another week or so and I wanted to be prepared."

"Oh, I'll be so glad to have you both back in town," Sally said.

"I'll be glad, too."

Julia stood. "Let me get you a latte."

"Oh, please don't go to any trouble."

"It's no trouble, it's my job," she said with a grin. Just then, Lynnie, the counter girl, came over to take her order and refill Trish's teacup, so Julia sat down again.

"It was great to see you all up in Napa," Kelly said.

"We had a wonderful time," Trish said. "I still dream about Ingrid's magical massages and wake up moaning. I'm sure Adam's getting all sorts of strange ideas."

They all laughed.

"Your husbands are both so wonderful," Kelly said to Trish and Julia. "I probably shouldn't say anything because they're my bosses, after all, but it's so nice to see how much in love they are with both of you."

"It's lovely, isn't it?" Sally said, smiling fondly at her daughters-in-law. "But what about you, Kelly? Wasn't this the week you were going to see a special visitor from your past?"

"Sounds intriguing," Julia said, pulling her chair closer. "Tell us everything."

Kelly laughed. "Oh, it all amounted to a bunch of nothing, really."

"But that's why you wanted the makeover, wasn't it?"

"Yes." Kelly felt herself blush and was glad that Lynnie brought her latte just then. She took a few sips to hide the awkwardness she felt.

"Oh, come on, don't stop now, tell us what happened," Trish said.

Julia patted Kelly's hand. "We promise it won't leave this room, if you're worried that Brandon will find out."

"I'm not worried about that," Kelly said with a frown. "He was right in the middle of it."

"Curiouser and curiouser," Julia said.

They all laughed again, and Kelly went ahead and spilled the story of Roger breaking up with her years ago and her wanting to get back at him.

"He sounds vile," Julia said.

"I'm just happy you got to eat a full dinner," Trish said, rubbing her stomach as the Duke women commiserated with her.

Kelly laughed again. "Yeah, I was happy about that, too." She took another sip of her latte, glad that she'd decided to stop by the bakery. She really liked these women and felt a bond with them, even though she didn't really fit in. Yes, she was sleeping with one of the Duke men, too. But they didn't know about that. And it was over anyway.

That thought was too depressing, so she swept it out of her mind for now.

"This back pain is getting worse," Trish said, arching and twisting to find a more comfortable position. "I hope it doesn't last much longer."

"How long has it been bothering you?" Sally asked.

"All morning."

"Any contractions?"

"Yes, but they don't mean anything. I'm not due for three more days."

Sally and Julia exchanged looks.

"Should we call Adam?" Kelly asked.

"No, no," Trish said, her voice sounding a bit weaker as she stretched her shoulders. "He's at the office today. They've got another big closing this week. I guess you all know that."

"I'll drive you home," Sally offered.

"Or to the hospital," Kelly said.

Trish waved them away. "I'm fine. It'll pass. I'd much rather hear more dirt on Roger. It'll distract me from my aches and pains."

Sally's smile was strained. "Yes, Kelly, and tell us how in the world Brandon got in the middle of this mess."

Kelly willingly explained what happened when Brandon pounded on the door and everyone was impressed by his heroics.

"Uh-oh," Trish said, trying to stand up. "I hate to interrupt the story, but I think my water just broke."

"Don't move," Kelly said, and helped Trish ease back down in the chair. Kelly grabbed her phone and called the office to alert Adam, telling him to meet Trish at the hospital and offering to alert his brothers. That wasn't necessary, since Adam was on a conference call with both men at that moment.

Julia ran into the kitchen and brought back clean dish-cloths.

Sally rubbed Trish's back. "Oh, honey, I'm sorry you're in pain, but I'm so excited. We're going to have a baby!"

At the hospital, Kelly kept trying to leave but Sally wouldn't let her.

"But I'm not part of the family," she protested.

"Yes, you are," Sally insisted. "Besides, you're so cool and calm under pressure, much better than any of us. So if you don't mind, I'd appreciate it if you'd stay."

"Okay, maybe for a little while."

Adam came racing down the hall. "Where is she?"

"She's right inside that room," Sally said, and grabbed Adam's arm. "Take a deep breath first and relax. And fix your hair or you're likely to scare her to death."

"Right." Adam sucked in some air and let it out. His hair looked like he'd been grabbing it to keep from going crazy on the drive from his office to the hospital, so now he smoothed it back with his fingers. Then he grabbed Sally and planted a big kiss on her cheek. "I love you, Mom."

Kelly smiled as happy tears sprang to Sally's eyes.

Cameron jogged down the hall a moment later and greeted Julia with a kiss, then turned to Sally and Kelly. "Brandon's taking the jet down so he should be here in an hour or so."

"Good," Sally said after pulling Cameron close for a hug. "I know Adam will want you all to be here."

Hearing that Brandon would be arriving soon, Kelly touched Sally's arm. "I really should go."

"Please don't," Sally said, then paused and took a long

look at Kelly. "Sweetie, did you want to leave because Brandon is coming?"

"No," she said too quickly, causing Sally's eyebrows to arch.

"Let's have a seat over here," Sally suggested. "I want to ask you something."

Kelly didn't dare refuse or Sally would be even more suspicious, so she followed the older woman over to a quiet corner seating arrangement.

"Now Kelly," Sally began, "I don't mean to pry, but I'm concerned. Do you have feelings for Brandon?"

"Well, of course," she said, trying for a casual tone. "We've worked together for years and he's a great guy. I like him."

Sally folded her arms across her chest. "I think you know what I mean."

Kelly couldn't exactly lie to Brandon's mother so she came clean. "Yes, I know what you mean, and yes, I do like Brandon. A lot. But I also know him really well, and I know that a relationship between us would never work out. He's got women lined up from here all the way to New York City, Mrs. Duke."

"Yes, I know."

"Gorgeous, sophisticated women," she continued with a note of resignation she couldn't disguise. "I can't deal with that kind of competition."

"Oh, I think you can," Sally said.

Kelly shook her head and tried to smile. "Thank you, but I really can't. And even if I could, Brandon just isn't a one-woman man. He goes through them like…well…" She stopped and frowned. It wouldn't be polite to give Sally too many details about her son and all the women in his life.

"Oh, don't bother trying to sugarcoat it, sweetie," Sally

said with a shake of her head. "I know my sons have always been popular with women."

"To say the least," Kelly muttered.

Sally took hold of her hand. "I also know that Brandon is a good, good man, and he's so worthy of love."

"I think so, too," Kelly whispered. "I really do. I just wish, well, I wish I was the one he wanted."

Sally hugged her. "If it means anything at all, I would love it if you were."

Kelly felt tears spring to the surface and she brushed them away. "That's so sweet of you. Thank you."

Sally's eyes narrowed in steely resolve and she murmured something Kelly wasn't sure she heard correctly. But it sounded something like, "We'll just see how sweet I can be."

Brandon walked swiftly down the hospital hall and into the large waiting room. Glancing around, he spied his mother sitting with Julia and Cameron. His brother held a sleepy little Jake against his shoulder.

"What's going on?" Brandon asked.

"Oh sweetie, I'm so glad you're here." Sally jumped up and gave him a hug, then walked with him out into the hall.

Brandon took another visual sweep of the room but didn't see Kelly anywhere. Adam had said that she was the one who had called him earlier to say that Trish was going into labor. So for the last two hours, Brandon had been wondering what the hell Kelly was doing back in Dunsmuir Bay. He'd tried calling her when the plane landed, but she wasn't answering her cell phone. And that rarely happened.

He'd known she was upset about Roger, but now he was

worried that there might be something else bothering her. Otherwise, she would've answered her cell phone.

He glanced up and down the hall. Maybe she'd just gone off to the ladies' room for a minute.

"Are you looking for someone?" his mother asked.

"Yeah, I thought Kelly would be here. Adam said she was on her way to the hospital with all of you."

"She was here for a while, but she left."

"Oh. Is she coming back?"

"I don't know," Sally said, looking a little puzzled. "She seemed to be concerned about not being here when you showed up."

"Not being here?" Now it was Brandon's turn to be puzzled. "Why wouldn't she want to be here when I got here?"

"She said that she wasn't part of the family, so she thought it best if she left."

"What?" he said in disbelief, then muttered, "Well, that's dumb."

"Is it?" she asked.

"Okay, Mom, what are you getting at?"

"We talked about this before, Brandon," she said. "I thought we were in agreement. But now I have to ask you, are you involved with Kelly?"

"Why? What did she say?"

Sally rolled her eyes. "She didn't say a word, but she seemed uncomfortable sticking around. And you didn't answer the question."

"Come on, Mom, let it go."

But his mother gave him "the look," and he capitulated.

"Okay, fine, but it's not like we're really involved. We're just having a good time."

"Oh, sweetie." Sally shook her head. "I don't think Kelly is that kind of girl."

"You've said that before," he said, rubbing his jaw in frustration. "I'm not even sure I know what you mean."

"Yes, you do. She's not as sophisticated as most of the women you date. She doesn't know the rules of the game like those women do. Kelly's sensitive and sweet. She wants to meet a nice guy and fall in love and settle down. And we both know that's not you."

"Hey, I'm a nice guy."

She patted his arm. "Yes, you are, and I know you wouldn't hurt her deliberately. But if you don't stop seeing her, you're going to break her heart."

Trish gave birth to an eight-pound baby boy at two o'clock the following morning. They named the baby Tyler Jackson Duke. Despite the late hour, Adam passed out cigars to his brothers and the whole family celebrated with champagne and apple juice for Trish. Brandon snapped a picture with his phone and sent it along with a text message to Kelly, announcing the birth. A few hours later, he received a two-word message back from her. "Congratulations, Uncle!"

So at least she was communicating with him again, Brandon thought with relief. He decided not to press her any further, knowing he would see her on Tuesday, less than two days from now. By then, she would be long over Roger and back to being her old self. Then she and Brandon could talk about a few things. Meanwhile, as long as he was in Dunsmuir Bay, he'd planned a busy day for himself that centered on finding new and creative ways to spoil his brand-new bouncing baby nephew.

Ten

Tuesday morning, Brandon walked across the wide terrace toward his office, amused to find he had a spring in his step. He knew where it had come from.

Kelly would be back in the office today and he was really looking forward to seeing her again.

But when he walked into the office, she wasn't at her desk, and he felt a trickle of panic seep down his spine. He ruthlessly shoved the feeling away. It was no big deal. In fact, it was still early. She would be here any minute.

He walked into his inner office, took off his jacket and hung it on the back of his door. Sitting at his desk, he pulled up his calendar to study what was in store for the week. Meetings, conference calls and the start of organizing the move back to headquarters in Dunsmuir Bay. The brief visit home over the weekend had reminded him just how much he missed his family and all the amazing advantages there were to living on the California coast.

It was a full ten minutes later when he finally heard Kelly walk in. A part of him he hadn't even realized was tense began to relax.

"Morning, Kelly," he called. "Come on in when you're settled."

"Okay."

A few minutes later, after starting the coffee and powering up her computer, she walked in.

Brandon looked up and started to grin, then felt his mouth drop open. She was dressed in an old, dull gray pantsuit with a black turtleneck underneath. Her hair was pulled back in a ponytail and she wore the thick horned-rim glasses he thought she'd destroyed.

"What happened to you?" he asked before he could stop himself, then quickly shook his head. "I mean, did you lose your contact lenses?"

"No, the glasses are just easier," she explained. "Now that Roger's gone, I thought I'd go back to wearing some of my more comfortable outfits. This looks okay, doesn't it?"

"Yeah, sure," he said, stymied by her decision.

"Good." She hesitated, then sat down in the chair in front of his desk. "We need to talk, Brandon."

"Okay, let's talk," he said, and watched her take her glasses off and fiddle with them nervously.

Studying her, he realized she looked even better than ever, without any makeup on. True, those pants she wore were too damned baggy and the color did nothing to complement her complexion, but Brandon knew that underneath all that material was a stunning pair of world-class legs. The sudden image of her naked thighs caused his groin to stiffen instantly. With a silent groan, he wheeled his chair closer to his desk to mask the problem.

She took a deep breath and finally started talking. "Don't be angry, but I have to thank you."

He scowled at her. "I thought we'd agreed you wouldn't do that."

"I'm sorry, but I can't help it," she said. "Just let me get through this, okay?"

"Of course. Go ahead."

"Okay." After another deep breath, she said, "First, I have to thank you for helping me prepare for Roger's visit. I think you know what I mean by that. And second, thank you for coming to his hotel room door when you did. Your timing was perfect and it was nice to know that you had my back while I was in there sparring with Roger."

He grinned. "Right. You're welcome."

"Good," she said with a nod of her head. "I'm happy to say that I've kept my original bargain not to fall for you, and now I'm ready to go back to life as we knew it before my ex-boyfriend's name was ever mentioned in this office."

"And what does that mean, exactly, Kelly?"

She refused to meet his gaze as she clutched her hands together in her lap. "It means, you know, we'll no longer be sleeping together."

"Sleeping together."

"Oh, you know." She looked up and her smile was shaky. "Not that I didn't enjoy every moment, I really did. You know I did. But…I'm sorry, Brandon, it's time to end things, once and for all. It was wonderful, but I'm…so sorry." With that, she bolted out of the chair and walked briskly out of his office, closing the door behind her.

As he watched her go, he pondered her words. Part of him was highly dissatisfied with her decision not to continue with their sexual arrangement.

On second thought, *all* of him was dissatisfied. Hell, he

wanted her right now. Even in that ugly suit of hers, she was hotter than any woman he'd known in a long time.

Leaning his elbows on the desk, he thought about his next move. Maybe he would let her stew for a few hours, then ask her to have dinner with him tonight. A great meal, a few glasses of wine, and he was confident they'd end up back in his bed again.

His mother's words suddenly echoed in his brain. Damn, that was the problem with having a conscience. He knew Sally was right. Kelly was sweet and sensitive and deserved to find love some day. If Brandon had his way and their affair continued, Kelly would wind up being hurt eventually. If he wasn't careful, he might just break her heart.

But what about Brandon's heart?

He sat back in his chair and rubbed his chest thoughtfully. Maybe he'd pulled a muscle because for some strange reason, he felt an aching twinge that felt almost like grief.

Brandon asked her out to dinner that night and she politely refused.

The next day, he asked her to join him for lunch and she said she had other plans.

Finally, he asked her if she'd like to come to his room later that evening.

"You know I can't do that, Brandon," she said and tried to smile.

"I figured it was worth a shot," he said.

"I'm sorry," she said, staring up at him from her desk chair. "This whole situation is my fault."

"How's that?"

"It was completely unprofessional of me to drag you into my problems in the first place. But now I'm just anxious for everything to return to business as usual. I hope you can help me do that."

"Right. Okay. Sure." He nodded and walked back into his office, and Kelly had to take great gulping breaths to keep from bursting into tears.

She wasn't sure she could continue working in the same office with him every day. But the alternative was to never see him again and there's no way she could go through that.

She simply had to stop thinking about kissing him and touching him. She had to stop thinking about the way he had touched her and made her laugh. She just had to stop thinking! And she would.

It might take another thirty or forty years, but she was absolutely positive she would get over him.

"It's your mother on line two," Kelly announced over the intercom line.

"Thanks, Kelly," he said, and pressed the button. "Hi, Mom."

"Hi, sweetie, I haven't heard from you all week so I'm calling to make sure you're all right."

"I'm fine. How are you doing?"

"Oh, everything is wonderful. The baby is so beautiful." She went on for five minutes about the joy of baby Tyler. When she finally exhausted that subject, she said, "How's Kelly?"

"She's fine," he said. "Why do you ask?"

"You sound a little irritated. Is everything all right?"

"Sure, why wouldn't it be?" Brandon snapped. "Kelly seems to have forgotten that we ever had sex with each other in the first place, so things are just dandy."

"Ah," she said.

What the hell? Did he really just say that out loud?

Great. Now if only he could kick himself in the ass, everything would be fan-freaking-tastic. "Sorry, Mom, I'm just a little busy right now."

But she wasn't buying that line. "Brandon, are you in love with Kelly?"

"What?" he shouted.

"No need to yell," she said softly. "Sweetie, why else would you be so upset that she doesn't want to sleep with you?"

"Who said I was upset?"

She started laughing, which just annoyed him more.

"Look, Mom, I really don't have time for—"

"Now you listen to me, Brandon Duke. It's as clear as the nose on your face that you're in love with that girl, and I expect you to marry her."

"Mom, what've you been smoking?"

"Very funny, Brandon," she said drily. "You can deny it all you want but I know you better than you know yourself."

He sighed. "I really have to go. I love you, Mom."

"I love you too, son. Call me later and tell me how it went. Bye-bye."

He hung up the phone and rubbed his neck. Damn, between his mother's wild assumptions and Kelly's stiff-shirted business competence, he was likely to go insane.

For the past three days, he'd managed to put up with Kelly's firm need to work professionally and reliably in his office. She was the ultimate assistant, always answering his phones, making his coffee, transcribing his calls, typing his letters, being polite and businesslike at all times.

It was enough to make him spit nails.

He'd made it clear when she returned from Dunsmuir Bay that he would be more than happy to continue their sexual relationship. But Kelly had refused him. He might've asked her again once or twice, maybe three times more during the week. Okay, maybe four times, max.

All of a sudden, she'd turned on him and accused him of being attracted to her only because she'd gotten her makeover!

He'd attempted to deny it, but she'd seen right through him. She'd asked him point-blank, how could she trust his feelings for her now if that was the only reason he'd originally been interested in her?

It seemed an unfair question given his almost constant state of arousal these past few days. Because the irony was, even though she'd gone back to wearing her drab and dowdy pantsuits, he was still getting turned on whenever she walked into the room. But now that he could safely admit that her getting a makeover had nothing to do with his attraction to her, she didn't want to hear him out.

And ever since she'd asked the question, Brandon had seriously wondered why he'd never realized how sexy she was before. Because now it was so damned obvious.

She was a beautiful woman in every way and he couldn't keep his eyes off her whenever she walked into a room. And if he didn't see her right away, he would catch a whiff of her scent, and it drove him wild with desire. But when he accused her of wearing too much perfume, she had the audacity to claim that she never wore perfume.

So maybe he really was going crazy. Maybe he needed a vacation. But where would he go? He already lived in a beautiful part of California and that was pretty close to paradise. He didn't know where to go or what to do and he didn't care. All he knew was that he couldn't keep seeing Kelly every hour of every day and not hold her in his arms again.

"I'll be back in a while," he said to her and rushed out of the office. He headed for his room and once he was there, he decided to go for a run. It would be good to work off some of this insanity. Maybe he'd eaten some bad mushrooms and his brain was filled with toxins. It could happen. Exercise was the answer.

As he ran, he contemplated the situation objectively. He had to admit that breaking up with Kelly had been the best for both of them. She was his employee, after all, and he shouldn't have taken advantage of her in the first place. Of course, that wasn't really fair because, after all, the whole affair had been her idea.

He smiled at the thought, then chuckled. Okay, he was willing to admit that maybe he'd nudged her in the right direction. But nothing changed the fact that it was still best if they didn't sleep together again. But damn, he missed her, and not just in bed. She had a savvy business mind and it was fun to bounce ideas back and forth with her. She made him laugh. How many women had ever made him laugh?

But that didn't matter, because his mother was right about one thing, much as he hated to admit it. Kelly had "white picket fence" practically tattooed across her forehead. She deserved a good man who would love her and treat her right, give her a couple of kids, plus a dog, a couple of hamsters and a fish bowl.

The fact that he hated to picture another man in her bed was something he didn't dwell on too deeply.

Somewhere during his fifth mile, as his breath wheezed out and he had to sweep the sweat from his eyes, Brandon figured out the solution to his problem. It was so simple. He just needed to get laid.

Tonight he would make a few calls to some women he knew, arrange a date or two for the weekend, and participate in some mind-blowing sex. And maybe then this out-of-control desire for Kelly would disappear.

* * *

Kelly adjusted her glasses and continued typing the letter Brandon had dictated. She hated these old eyeglasses but she knew it was better to wear them and look drab, if only to keep Brandon at a distance.

Today, she wore the dark purple pantsuit she'd owned forever. It was so old, it still had lumpy shoulder pads sewn into the jacket. With her sensible brown shoes and her hair pulled back, she looked like someone's maiden aunt. But she could live with that.

It helped to stare at herself in the mirror each morning after she was dressed and ready to go and realize she truly had no business falling in love with her handsome boss. *You are a total cliché,* she would repeat to herself daily. But no matter how many times she had scolded herself, she still hadn't been able to keep from rushing right toward that cliff.

Every time she saw him, she had to fight to ignore her feelings. After all, it wasn't as if he would ever ask her to marry him, for God's sake. So who was she trying to fool? He would never settle down, certainly not with her. A woman would have to be a blithering idiot to think that he would, and Kelly had never been an idiot. Well, not until recently, anyway.

The door swung open and an absolutely beautiful woman walked into the office. She was tall and willowy, with long flowing blond hair and the bluest eyes Kelly had ever seen. Were those contact lenses? No, they had to be real. She was too perfect, too ethereal, not to be completely real.

Kelly shook her head in defeat as she recognized the woman. This was Bianca Stephens, the beautiful wicked witch of her nightmares. Live and in person. And she was the most stunning woman Kelly had ever seen.

"You must be Karen," she said haughtily. "I'm here to see Brandon. He's expecting me."

Kelly didn't have the strength or interest to correct her name again, nor did she care to have the unpleasant woman standing around glaring at her while she checked with Brandon.

"Go right in," Kelly said, and swept her hand toward Brandon's closed door.

"I certainly will."

Bianca closed the door behind her and Kelly felt as though the wind had been knocked out of her. She slumped forward and laid her head on her desk. This was the last straw. She couldn't take it anymore.

When she realized she was crying, she knew she had to act immediately. She couldn't continue living like this. She was hopelessly in love with the big jerk in the next room and she could no longer sit by and watch him play his games with other women.

She was finished making romantic dinner reservations for him and his flavor of the week. She was finished buying diamond tennis bracelets for his civilized breakups.

She was finished.

With all the energy she could muster, she sat up and wiped the tears away, then quickly typed a letter of resignation and emailed it to him. Pulling her purse from the bottom drawer, she stood up and walked out of the office.

"Hello, Brandon darling," Bianca said, closing the door behind her.

"Bianca," he said, unable to disguise his shock.

"Aren't you happy to see me?"

"Uh, yeah, sure," he said, pushing away from his desk and standing to greet her. "But what are you doing here?"

"It was just so good to hear from you the other night," she said, kissing his cheek, then using her little finger to smooth her lipstick. It was a move meant to entice and he'd seen her do it a dozen times before. He watched as she strolled over to the floor-to-ceiling window and gazed nonchalantly at the view. "I didn't feel like waiting for the weekend, so I had Gregory drive me out here to you."

"I see."

She spread her arms in invitation. "And here I am. Are you happy to see me?"

"Happy? Yeah, sure." He looked beyond Bianca over to the closed door. "Did you see my assistant out there?"

"Yes, and honestly, Brandon, I can't believe you still have that rude woman working for you."

"Rude? Kelly?"

"I shouldn't criticize," she said, staring at her fingernails, "but she was very unpleasant to me on the phone the other day."

"Kelly?" Distracted now, Brandon checked his telephone. There was no red light to indicate that his trusted assistant was on the phone. So why hadn't she buzzed him to warn him about Bianca? Where the hell was she? "I'm a little busy today, Bianca."

"Too busy for me?" she said, pouting.

Okay, that might've come across a little harsh. "Uh, no, of course not. It's nice to see you."

"I certainly hope so," she said. "I've come all this way."

He stared at her for a moment. He'd forgotten how beautiful she was, and how self-centered. "Yeah. What a surprise. I just need to handle a few things…"

"You're going to keep working?"

"Just for a minute," he said, folding up the files that were spread on his desk. "Then I guess we can go have a drink or something."

"Sounds yummy." She sat in his visitor's chair and pulled out her smartphone. "I'll just sit here and check my messages until you're ready."

"Fine."

A soft ding came from his computer and he rushed to check his email. It was from Kelly. Good. Maybe she was going to explain exactly how in the hell Bianca had gotten in here.

He opened the message, skimmed the words, but couldn't believe them. *Two weeks' notice...Resignation... Thank you for the opportunity...*

"What?" He stood up. "No, no, no."

"No?" Bianca said.

He stared at her again, wondering why she was here. But he knew why. He was the one who'd called her and told her he wanted to see her. What the hell was wrong with him? He shook his head and muttered, "I'm an idiot."

"Brandon?" Bianca said. "Are you ill?"

He'd made a huge mistake.

"Sorry, Bianca," he said, pulling her gently from the chair and walking her to the door. "You'll have to tell Gregory to drive you back to the city. Something's come up."

He raced out the door.

Kelly had just pulled her suitcase out of the closet when the pounding began. She sighed as she walked across the room to answer the door.

Brandon stood there, looking so handsome, so tall and rugged. And so concerned. "You can't just leave me."

"I'm not just leaving you," she said, leading him into her room. "I'm giving you two weeks' notice."

"But why? Did Bianca say something to make you angry? Is that what this is about?"

"No, of course not." She opened a drawer, grabbed a neatly stacked pile of shirts and put them in her suitcase.

"She did. She said something. I knew it." He paced across the floor. "I've sent her away. I didn't ask her to come to the office, Kelly. She's gone and you'll never see her again. You can't quit."

"Yes, I can. And it's not about Bianca." Kelly shook her head, still a little horrified that Brandon could enjoy spending time with someone as awful as Bianca. But that was none of her business. Not anymore.

"Then why are you leaving? We work really well together."

"We do. Or we did." She smiled sadly at him as she stacked a few pairs of jeans into her suitcase. "But then I broke the rules."

"What rules?" he asked as he walked back and forth behind her. "What are you talking about?"

"The ground rules, remember?" She took a deep breath and turned to gaze up at him. "I fell in love with you, Brandon."

He was stunned into silence.

"I know," she said lightly, reaching for her lingerie and tossing it all onto the bed. "It was a shock to me, too."

"What?" He grabbed her and whipped her around to face him. "No. No, you didn't. I'm a jerk, remember? A big baby when I'm sick. I'm…I'm superstitious. You'd be crazy to fall for me, remember? That's what you said. And you promised you wouldn't…"

"I know what I promised," she said. "And I'm really sorry, but it looks like I wasn't able to keep my word."

"I don't believe it."

"It's true." She patted his arm and stepped back. "I'm sorry."

He blew out a heavy breath, then said slowly, "It had to

be Bianca's fault. When she walked in, you got mad and left."

"I'm not mad," she insisted, shaking her head.

"Then why did you leave? She's gone. I don't want her around. I realized that as soon as I saw her. Was she rude to you? She can be a little abrasive."

"Oh, Brandon." Kelly smiled sadly. "Don't you see? If it's not Bianca, it'll be someone else. My point is, there will always be other women in your life."

"But I want *you* in my life."

"I want you, too, but not in the way you're talking about. Look, I know you're not in love with me. And that's okay. You're not the sort of man to settle down with one woman and I've always known that. This isn't your fault. I'm the one who broke the rules."

"I forgive you."

She laughed. "Thank you. But today I realized that I can't sit outside your office and watch women come and go. Call me a weakling, but I can no longer go shopping for gifts for the women you're sleeping with. I'm sorry."

He grabbed her hands. "This is all my fault."

"How do you figure?" she asked, forcing herself to look into his deep blue eyes.

"We were just too good together. But that's not love, Kelly," he hastened to explain. "That's just good sex."

She laughed again, then realized she'd begun to cry and ruthlessly swiped away the tears. "Yes, the sex was good, really good. But I know my own heart, Brandon. I know that what I feel for you is love, and I know you don't feel the same. I'm okay with that."

"Well, maybe I'm not."

"I'm sorry. But you must understand, I can't work for you anymore."

"Damn, Kelly." He raked his fingers through his hair in frustration. "I don't know what to do to make this right."

"There's nothing you can do to make it right. I'll stay on for two weeks and hire my replacement. Then I'll leave."

The two weeks went by too quickly, and before Brandon was ready to deal with the change, Kelly was gone. Her replacement was Sarah, an older woman so amazingly well organized that she scared Brandon a little. Kelly had trained the woman so well that in no time at all, she could do almost everything as well as her predecessor had.

But she wasn't Kelly.

Sarah organized the major office move back to Dunsmuir Bay, and it went flawlessly from start to finish. Brandon was back in his office without a wrinkle in his schedule. Sarah was an organizational genius.

But she wasn't Kelly.

Brandon knew he would snap out of this funk any day now. After all, it wasn't like he was in love with Kelly. He wasn't in love with anyone. He didn't *do* love. It was just that he missed her. And why not? They'd worked together for over four years. That was all. They'd gotten to know each other well and it was weird that she wasn't around. That was all it was.

And he'd get over it. As usual, he knew exactly what he needed to do to wipe her out of his mind. He would have to make some more phone calls. He had to find another woman to take her place. Not Bianca of course, remembering her visit. Why had he ever wanted to spend time with that vacuous, vain woman? There were plenty of other women out there.

But frankly, he couldn't quite imagine himself having a romantic conversation with another woman. He couldn't picture himself sitting across a dinner table, asking another woman about herself, sharing a bottle of wine, spending an entire evening with her, whoever she might be. He tried to picture the sort of woman he'd dated in the past, tried to remember what he'd talked about with them. But he couldn't remember. They had all faded into the fog and now all he could recall were the fun times with Kelly, when they'd talked and laughed and shared secrets for hours. Whenever he tried to imagine spending time with someone else, he found himself bored to death.

So he buried himself in work, knowing he would snap out of it any day now.

The following Saturday, Adam and Trish invited everyone over to see the baby. Brandon pulled up in front of their sprawling Craftsman home and parked his car, then sat with his hands on the wheel and contemplated whether he should even go inside the house. It had been an effort to get out of bed that morning and he wondered if he'd caught some kind of flu. He didn't want to be around the baby if he was sick.

But his head and sinuses were perfectly clear and he wasn't coughing or anything. His stomach was fine, although he hadn't given a lot of thought to fine dining lately. And he was feeling kind of run-down. He chalked it up to the big move back home and climbed out of the car.

Cameron stood on the front porch. "Hey, did you forget the beer?"

"Nope, got it right here," he said, and jogged back around to the trunk of his car. He shook his head as he grabbed the case of beer he'd bought ten minutes ago on the way over to Adam's house. Where was his brain today?

He found himself asking that same question all afternoon. Whenever his mother or brothers asked him a question, he'd realize halfway through his answer that he'd wandered off on some tangent or another.

They were gathered around the wide bar that separated the kitchen from the family room when his mother finally reached up and pressed the back of her hand to his forehead. "Are you feeling all right, sweetie?"

"Yeah, I'm fine," he said, and grabbed a tortilla chip. "Just a little distracted."

"I hope you're not coming down with something."

"Nope, just working too hard. I might need a vacation."

"Oh, speaking of vacation, I ran into Kelly yesterday," Julia said as she crossed the kitchen with a bowl of salsa. "She just got back from visiting her family. She looks wonderful."

Brandon's ears perked up. "She was back east?"

"That's right," Sally said, dragging a chip through the fresh salsa. "You know her family lives in Vermont."

"Yeah." He studied his beer bottle.

Julia sipped her lemonade. "Roger lives in her hometown, doesn't he?"

"Roger?" Brandon felt the sudden, bitter taste of bile in his throat. "She saw Roger when she went home?"

Trish shut the refrigerator door and turned. "Well, they're both in the same town."

There was no way Kelly had gone back east to see Roger. Brandon knew that in his gut. She wouldn't waste a minute of her time with him. But if Roger was from her hometown, maybe he knew her family. Maybe Kelly's father knew Roger's father. Had her family wanted her to marry Roger? Hell. Brandon knew all about family pressure.

"Sweetie, you do look pale," Sally said, clutching his arm.

Brandon swallowed the last of his beer. "I just need a damn vacation."

He decided to spend a few days back at the Napa resort, but he didn't go there as the boss. Instead, he brought along his oldest boots, his rattiest blue jeans, some tattered shirts, and put himself to work in the vineyards.

As teenagers, Brandon and his brothers had spent a few summers on construction sites around Dunsmuir Bay, so he knew what hard labor was good for. It was basic and tough and real. Sweat and hard work helped a man think about his life, what was authentic and what was fantasy, what was important and what was crap. At the end of a long day, a man could look around and see what he'd accomplished.

As Brandon walked across the fields past the newly weeded and raked rows of grapevines, whose leaves were dry and brittle in the autumn twilight, he looked around and saw what he'd accomplished.

And he knew exactly what was missing.

Kelly had been back from Vermont for over a week now and knew it was time to start compiling her list of social organizations. She'd been putting the task off for long enough. She had a goal, remember? It was time to dive into the dating pool before she grew too old to swim.

There was a knock on her door and Kelly's heart fluttered in her chest.

"Oh, stop it," she scolded herself as she glanced up at the wall clock. It had to be the mailman, that was all. Brandon didn't even know where she lived! What earthly reason would he have for being here? Would she always flip out every time the doorbell chimed or the telephone rang? She put the last dish away in the cabinet and hung up the damp dish towel, then walked over to open the front door.

And forgot how to breathe.

"B-Brandon?"

"Hey, Kelly," he said. "Listen, I need some help."

She blinked, not quite believing her eyes. He stood leaning against her doorjamb looking better than she remembered, and she remembered him looking pretty darn good.

"You gonna let me come in?" he asked.

"Oh, sure." She swung the door open wider for him. "Did Sarah quit?"

"No." He walked into her home, filling the space. "Sarah's fine. She does good work."

"Oh. Okay." She closed the door and stared at him. It had been four long weeks since she'd last seen him and she'd spent all that time trying to stay busy, trying not to think about him, trying to get on with her life. She'd traveled back east for a week to see her father and sisters and their families. It had been a lovely visit, but the trip had cemented in her the understanding that Dunsmuir Bay was truly her home. Now she just had to put the pieces of her life back together. She'd started her list of dating possibilities. And she'd spent all day yesterday on her computer, searching the various employment sites, looking for a new job. She had a list of promising prospects and she planned to send résumés tomorrow.

But now, seeing Brandon, she couldn't remember exactly what any of those job prospects were.

"This is a nice place," he said, glancing around, then walking over to the wide picture window. "Great view."

"Thank you." Was he even taller than she remembered?

Maybe it was seeing him in her house for the first time that made her think so. She licked her lips nervously. "You said you needed my help with something?"

"Yeah." He seemed to consider something for a moment, then walked up close and took hold of her hand. Kelly tried not to focus on the fact that her hand fit so perfectly in his.

He gazed down, then back at her. "You know, this is a little embarrassing. I wonder if maybe we could sit and talk for a few minutes."

"Okay." She led the way to her comfortable sofa and he sat down way too close to her. "What is it, Brandon?"

"The thing is, Kelly, I need some help with my kissing. I'm not sure if I'm doing it right anymore."

She tried to swallow around her suddenly dry throat. "You're kidding, right?"

"Nope. I'm desperate."

She shook her head. "Brandon, you're the last man on earth who needs help with his kissing."

"See, that's where you're wrong," he said, clutching her hand more tightly.

"Okay, fine. But you could get any woman in the world to help you out. Why are you here?"

"Well, that's the thing." He touched her cheek, then ran his fingers through her hair. "I found out it only works right when I'm kissing the person I love."

"Oh Brandon," she said on a sigh.

"I'm in love with you, Kelly."

"No," she whispered.

"I don't blame you for questioning me, because I've been an idiot. I convinced myself that there was no way you could really love me."

"But that's—"

She stopped when he pressed his finger to her lips. "Just

let me get this out because it's not easy for me to admit some things."

With a nod, she said, "Okay."

He clenched his jaw, then began. "My parents were really bad people, really bad. They taught me some hard lessons early on. I'd rather not get into the specifics, but one of the luckiest days of my life was when Sally took me in. But even though she's a fantastic mother and I owe her everything, those first ugly memories lingered."

She put her hand on his knee for her own comfort as well as his, but didn't say anything.

"Because of those old memories," he continued, "I decided a long time ago that I would never really matter to anyone, you know? So I just made up my mind that I would never fall in love. That way, nobody could ever get close enough to hurt me."

"Oh, Brandon."

"It took your leaving for me to realize just how much I wanted to matter to you," he said. "I was blown away when you told me you were in love with me. At first, I couldn't make myself believe it. It was too...*important,* you know?"

"Yes, I know."

He covered her hand with his. "To be honest, it scared the hell out of me. But I want to be important to you, Kelly. I want you to love me, because I'm so in love with you. My heart is empty when you're not around. I can't really live without you in my life."

A tear fell from her eye and Brandon ran his thumb along her cheek to catch the next one. "Please, Kelly. Please put me out of my misery and tell me you still love me."

"Of course I still love you, Brandon," she said. "I love you with all my heart."

"Marry me?" he asked, as he touched her face with both

of his hands. "I want to spend the rest of my life showing you how much I love you."

"Yes, I'll marry you."

"I love you so much."

"Then will you kiss me, please?"

Holding back a smile, he said, "I'm not sure I remember how. Maybe you'd better show me."

She laughed and wrapped her arms around him. "Practice makes perfect."

His laughter joined hers. "Then we'd better get started."

Joy swept through her as he enfolded her in his arms and kissed her with all the love that was overflowing in his heart for her alone. And it was perfect.

Epilogue

Two years later

Midsummer along the central California coast meant warm days and balmy nights and Brandon Duke couldn't think of a better reason to throw a party. Unless it was also a surprise party celebrating his mother's birthday.

As he walked the perimeter of the backyard where family and friends were gathered, Brandon soaked up the sights and sounds of the party. He couldn't help smiling as he realized just how different his and his brothers' lives were now than they had been just a few short years ago.

Back then, this would've been a stylish cocktail party with subdued conversations. Instead, there were sudden bursts of laughter and splashing around the pool. He grinned as he caught a flash of his mom's shocking pink Capri pants that made her look like a teenager. The scents of an ocean breeze and suntan lotion blended with barbecued chicken and ice-cold lemonade.

At that moment, from across the patio, he caught Kelly's eye and felt the fierce punch of joy he always experienced when he gazed upon his beautiful wife. He watched with pride and love as she stroked her stomach where their unborn child, a baby boy, waited patiently to be born. Kelly had changed everything in his life for the better and was just days away from making him a father. Brandon knew without a doubt that with Kelly by his side, he could face any obstacle, conquer any fear. Their future was rosy indeed.

And even though his mother had denied it a thousand times, Brandon was positive she'd had something to do with bringing the two of them together. He would have to thank her some day.

Cameron came up behind him and slapped Brandon on the shoulder. "Great party, man. I think Mom was really surprised."

"For a minute there, I thought she stopped breathing," Brandon admitted, shaking his head.

"Yeah, then she burst into tears." Cameron laughed. "It was perfect."

They both glanced over and Cameron grinned as his son Jake loudly explained to his baby sister Samantha how to race a dump truck on the brick path surrounding the house. In the pool, their little cousin T.J. bobbed confidently in his proud father Adam's arms. Adam continued to insist to whoever would listen that his boy would be competing as an Olympic swimmer any day now.

"Hey, thanks for the invite, Brandon."

Brandon whirled around and saw his cousin, Aidan, popping open a bottle of beer.

"Glad you could make it," Brandon said. "It's about time

we all finally met. And it was a perfect way to surprise Mom on her birthday."

Aidan's identical twin brother, Logan, grabbed his own bottle and the two men joined Brandon and Cameron to survey the activity.

"You have a terrific family," Logan said, smiling his approval.

"Thanks," Cameron said jovially. "We're happy you guys are a part of it."

"It's all because of your mom," Aidan said, chuckling. "She shocked the hell out of Dad when she first called him. He'd been trying to track down his brother Bill for years, but when their orphanage burned down, the records were lost and he finally gave up trying."

Brandon shook his head as he thought of that fateful fire. Sally's husband Bill and his brother Tom were adopted by different families and lost touch with each other. If not for Sally Duke and her stubborn refusal to give up, the Duke brothers might never have met their cousins.

"It almost broke Sally's heart when she heard about the fire," Cameron said. "But Mom is nothing if not tenacious. Once she got the hang of Google and started searching through every bit of information she could find, it was inevitable that she would track you guys down."

"We're thankful that she did," Logan said. "Dad was over the moon about finally getting to meet all of you."

The four cousins stared across the covered patio at Sally and the tall, good-looking older man standing next to her. This was Tom, her deceased husband Bill's brother.

Brandon peered more closely and couldn't help but notice the goofy grin on Tom's face as he gazed down at Sally. He turned and frowned at Logan. "Your father's a widower, right?"

"Yeah, and your mom is a widow," Logan said with a speculative look. "What the hell?"

Adam wrapped a towel around his waist and walked over to grab a bottle of beer before joining his brothers and cousins. After taking a healthy sip of his drink, he jutted his chin in the direction of Sally and Tom, then looked at Brandon and Cameron. "They seem to be enjoying themselves."

"Yeah, we were just noticing that," Aidan said.

Cameron scratched at his beard thoughtfully. "Not sure what to think yet."

Brandon took a long, reflective pull of his beer. "Maybe this family isn't quite finished with matchmaking after all."

* * * * *